# Daughter of the Bone Forest

# Daughter of the Bone Forest

### JASMINE SKYE

FEIWEL AND FRIENDS
NEW YORK

A Feiwel and Friends Book
An imprint of Macmillan Publishing Group, LLC
120 Broadway, New York, NY 10271 • fiercereads.com

Our books may be purchased in bulk for promotional, educational, or business use. Please contact your local bookseller or the Macmillan Corporate and Premium Sales Department at (800) 221-7945 ext. 5442 or by email at MacmillanSpecialMarkets@macmillan.com.

Library of Congress Cataloging-in-Publication Data is available.

First edition 2024
Book design by Maria W. Jenson
Feiwel and Friends logo designed by Filomena Tuosto
Printed in the United States of America

ISBN 978-1-250-87245-6
10  9  8  7  6  5  4  3  2  1

To my various grandparents,
the living and the lost,
in no particular order:
Grandma Laurel, Carl,
Grandma Nancy, Alvin,
Grandma Alice, Grandad, Catherine,
Nana, Pappy, Bill, and Susan.

With all my love, this book is for you.

# Chapter 1

## ROSY

THE BONE FOREST CALLED MY NAME THROUGH WHISTLING pine needles and groaning branches. *Rosy*, it sang. *Rosy. Rosy.*

"I'm here," I said, crossing the stark border where groves of silent red cedar became clumps of creaking bone pines. "Can it wait? Got a lot to do today."

The Forest ignored me, tugging at my hair and skirt like a needy child. I rubbed the sleep from my eyes. It wasn't yet dawn and I had a basket of warm breakfast hanging from one arm. I considered brushing the Forest aside so I could deliver the food to Gran first.

The bone pines shook and shuffled, blocking the usual path to Gran's cottage. Whatever it wanted to show me, it didn't want to wait.

I gave up and held the basket to the nearest tree. "Keep it safe for me?"

A branch drifted down, slow enough that the unobservant might think it moved by the wind. Of course, they'd have to be unobservant *and* ignorant not to know that the Bone Forest was alive. Or as alive as anything teeming with bone magic could be.

I let the branch take the basket. Breakfast safely stored, I reached into my heart. Most of the voices waiting there were still groggy with sleep. Few animals were awake at this predawn time. It wasn't dark enough for the prey to feel safe nor light enough to wake for the day. But I had one voice who was always ready to join with me, and it was that one who rose to meet my call now.

I shifted. My knees and elbows elongated, ankles and wrists lengthening into legs. Hands and feet became paws, nails sharpened into claws. Thin brassy hair shortened to ash-gray fur while more sprouted across the rest of my body. Along the base of my tail and up my entire right front leg, exposed bone rose to the surface of my skin and jutted out above my fur like grotesque pieces of armor.

As a bone wolf, I stood just above four feet tall—only a foot shorter than my human height. I was so used to the shift that it took barely a second to adjust to the change of perspective. The Bone Forest opened a path and I loped down it.

The sky had lightened to a soft bronze by the time the Forest deposited me at the foot of a small mountain-fed river. The sun would crest the horizon soon, though sunrises in the Bone Forest were always more muted than the ones outside it. I'd left early this morning, intending to be back at the ranch before sunrise really began. I loved the Forest, I really did, but it only ever wanted my attention when I had other plans. Moments like these were too common to be anything but aggravating.

Except—just visible, a family of bone otters floated down a large creek. I shifted back to human and put a hand on the nearest pine. I leaned into it, close enough to smell the faint tinge of vanilla that clung to the pine needles. The Forest whistled my name again, softer this time.

"Thank you," I whispered, sorry for my earlier grumbling.

I'd been wanting a shift that could traverse the water as well as the land. Bone animals were always land mammals, just as ice animals were avian, glass animals reptilian, and flower animals aquatic. As a bone familiar, those bone mammals were the only creatures I could shift into. I didn't normally mind that, even when my cousin took wing and I was left stuck on the ground. But Forest's Edge had flooded horribly last spring and ever since I'd wished for a shift that was more capable in the water.

It was months too late, but the Forest hadn't forgotten my wish. Now I just had to make room in my heart to claim it.

I watched the otters drift together. I'd always thought of otters as playful, but they weren't playing now. They were holding hands, little paws linked tight as though they couldn't bear to be parted. I could work with that.

In order for a familiar to gain a new shift, they need to learn the voice—the essence—of that animal. Need to learn it, understand it, and make a place for it inside their own sense of self.

I let the longing well up inside me, the love for my family, the hopeless desire that we might one day be whole again. That Gran might be allowed to leave her prison and return to the ranch, to hold hands with us and never let go.

An otter nestled in my heart alongside the other voices. I waited a single heartbeat to let it settle, then I shifted.

The other bone otters welcomed me with happy chirps. I bumped my nose on the places where exposed bone stood out starkly against their dark brown fur. Two of the pups pulled me into a game of splashing and diving along the creek bed. We played, happy and carefree, as the dawn rose around us.

Then, just as quickly as the otters had accepted me among them, they scattered. The pups gave chirps of fear and the eldest warning hisses even as the group fled down the creek.

I splashed about for a second as I tried to figure out what had scared my new friends away. The otter I'd become wanted to follow, to stay safe in numbers, but I had a human's mind and there were few things in the Forest that scared me. I swam in circles until I caught sight of the threat.

There, in the shadows of a huge pine, was a silver bone wolf. Its fur was too pale to make out the exposed bone, but no normal wolf was that big. Its golden eyes gleamed like miniature versions of the rising sun behind it.

I scampered out of the creek. Fallen pine needles clung to my wet paws as I bounded toward the wolf. It waited for me, silent and still, until I got close enough to touch noses with it. Only then did the wolf move. With a weary sigh, it nuzzled into my dripping fur.

I shifted, a bit sheepish to have been caught fooling around. My clothes stuck to patches of wet skin and my hair had become a damp, knotted ball. I flung it over a shoulder, trying to hide the mess. "Sorry, Gran. The Forest was insistent."

The wolf rose to her forelegs, then shifted into an old woman with hair as silver as the wolf's fur and pale skin marked by wrinkles and age spots. She clicked her tongue at me. "You keep letting these trees pull you this way and that, girl, and one day they'll pull you where you don't want to go."

"Yes, Gran," I said, though I didn't take her words to heart.

To most, the Bone Forest was treacherous, untamed wilderness. But to me, the Forest was home. Ever since I'd first shifted among these pines some six years ago, the Forest had sheltered me. Just as it sheltered Gran, though she didn't see it that way. She must have once. We were both wolf familiars, after all. The wolf was Gran's only shift and, even though I had many more, the wolf was my first. That made it special. That made *us* special. Bone wolves were anchor animals for the Forest, and that gave us an important connection to it, and to bone magic.

But Gran ignored her connection with the magic and the land. The Forest was her prison and she didn't forgive it for keeping her caged, no matter that it wasn't actually the Forest's fault. For years, I'd tried to repair the bridge between them, but each time Gran's weariness only grew more visible.

The otter was close enough to the surface of my heart that I couldn't resist reaching out to hold Gran's hand. She squeezed my fingers, already forgiving me for following the Forest instead of coming straight to her. We'd done this dance too many times.

A nearby tree bent down, basket hanging from its lower branches. Gran let go of my hand to grab it.

"Uncle Inge made mini-pies this morning," I explained. "He said they were your recipe."

"That boy always did get underfoot in the kitchen," Gran grumbled, but there was a sweet bitterness to her smile as she lifted the cloth to peer inside the basket. "Eating with me, girl?"

"Can't, Gran, sorry. Mama asked me to do the market run this morning. I've got to saddle up Tempest." I hesitated, then forged on. "Can I get you anything?"

Like I'd feared, Gran scoffed at my question. "I have everything I need."

We both knew it was a lie, but I didn't dare push Gran on it. There was already enough pain hiding behind her scowl.

"I'll be back later, with lunch."

Gran waved me away. I didn't want to leave. I never wanted to leave, even when I simultaneously wanted to go home. But I had to get to the market before Farmer Iktus sold all his best produce.

A few branches reached down to stroke my head as I turned

toward my family's ranch, trying to comfort me. I thanked the Forest one more time, taking solace in the new voice settling inside my heart, chirping alongside all the rest.

A COMMOTION GREW ALONG THE road leading out of the village as I stood at Farmer Iktus's stall, counting peppers. Drums beat, disturbing the soft murmurs of market haggling. Forest's Edge was not a loud place. Whoever was arriving seemed to think they needed to announce themselves as they would entering a city. I winced, ears ringing. I had excellent hearing because of my shifts and it felt like a curse now. At my side, Tempest lifted his head up from the lush summer grass he'd been grazing on, ears flicking toward the far end of the village square.

"Is the jarl here already?" I asked Iktus as I quickly stuffed the peppers into Tempest's saddlebag.

Our ruling jarl visited rarely, spending most of his time at his manor outside the bustling town of Woodside. We all preferred it that way. Jarl Snass's visits were a nerve-racking whirlwind of all the families in Forest's Edge trying to convince him that yes, we really did need all our land and no, we really couldn't afford to pay more in tithes and taxes.

If the jarl was visiting, I needed to rush home to warn Mama and Papa. After Gran had been arrested, our family's standing had suffered. Every year, my parents argued themselves hoarse so we could keep our ranch. It had only been nine months since the last time—we weren't ready. A surprise inspection was the last thing we needed.

Before Iktus could answer, the riders came into view. Metal horseshoes clattered across cobblestone as the first of the riders trotted into sight. Our jarl traveled with a small guard, but these soldiers didn't bear the Snass family crest. Instead, sewn across the right breast of their military jackets was a distinctive three-eyed raven.

The royal crest.

Half a dozen soldiers rode horseback and another half dozen marched on foot. Two at the front carried drums, which they beat incessantly as the procession filled our village square. All were dressed in dark brown military uniforms, and all bore the royal crest. All except the four figures at the center of the procession, dressed in black despite the unbearable heat.

My stomach flipped. I knew what this was. Toketie had talked about nothing else since coming home from school last week.

"Witches!" Iktus exclaimed. "What are they doing here?"

His surprise was understandable. Forest's Edge was too small to have a resident witch. Too small to have a permanent military posting, either, though the jarl's soldiers patrolled the road between us and Woodside.

I hadn't believed Toketie when she'd said the princess's procession would include a stop at Forest's Edge. We sat near the southern border of the kingdom, half surrounded by the densest acres of the Bone Forest. The Forest didn't tolerate many travelers, so to get to the southern nations, you had to go west and travel through the Waiming Territories. There was no strategic reason for the army to be stationed here and, given how small our population was, not many potential recruits.

But a royal platoon escorted four witches to the center of our village anyway.

A soldier on horseback trotted to the front of the procession. He wore the bright red sash of a thane—an officer—and he lifted his chin imperiously before bellowing, "All bow for Princess Shaw Colchuck, daughter of the Witch King, heir to the Cursed Throne!"

It was easy to tell which of the four witches was the princess. She was the only one who rode a bone horse, a beautiful black-and-white piebald mare with exposed bone that peeked out from underneath her mane and ran down until it disappeared below the princess's glossy saddle.

Shaw was nearly as striking as her horse. Her hair was dark brown and moved like silk, the ends just barely meeting her shoulders. She had pale sepia skin and high cheekbones that accentuated an otherwise squarish face. She sat upright in the saddle, regal in the way she kept her shoulders back, reins clutched in slender fingers. She looked pristine, like something pure and untouchable—but I knew that was an illusion.

I bowed, if only so I wouldn't stand out from the crowd. Princess Shaw was the future of the Cursed Kingdom, the only living descendant of the witch who cursed this land and made this kingdom a safe haven for magic. But the future Shaw promised was a bleak one.

I didn't want to be here, fawning over the girl people called Death's Heir.

Tempest tried to pull his reins out of my hand as I bowed. I held tight, until the leather bit into my palm, and shook hard at his reins to chide him. Bone horses were more aggressive than their nonmagical cousins and, as a stallion, Tempest was particularly stubborn. It didn't matter that I'd trained him since he was a colt, he would seize any chance to take advantage of my distraction.

The procession began to circle around the square, prancing

about like a few dozen villagers shopping in the morning market were worthy of a full royal parade. The whole thing was an ostentatious show and I didn't understand why Toketie had been so excited to see it.

According to my cousin, the princess had spent every break this last year touring different areas of the kingdom to drum up support for the military. As if the Cursed Kingdom's army needed more support. The Witch King had dangled the threat of the prophesied war over everyone's heads long enough that I figured half the adults in the kingdom were either actively serving or registered military reserve.

I hated it. The army gave false promises and discarded the ones those promises snared when they weren't useful anymore. It was all I could do to keep my disgust from showing on my face. Military recruiters preached shared responsibility and squads becoming like family, but that hadn't saved Pops six years ago. Hadn't saved Gran when they'd stripped her rank and imprisoned her for her grief over Pops's death. Just seeing those mud-brown uniforms was enough to make me want to run back to the Forest, back to Gran, and hold her tight.

The first of the soldiers marched past me and I pulled Tempest back. He pinned his ears and curled his top lip to expose his teeth.

"Don't you dare make a scene," I warned Tempest under my breath.

I empathized with his attitude, but I couldn't let him act out. I didn't need that kind of attention, not with the soldiers observing the crowd. I didn't know if I could hold my temper through a recruitment pitch. The wolf in my heart growled. I pressed my free hand to my chest, willing myself to calm down. I hadn't shifted accidentally in years and it would be a disaster if I did so now. The army would do anything to conscript another wolf familiar into their ranks. Gran had made me promise six years ago to hide my wolf, to save myself from the same fate she'd been trapped into and then vilified for.

Princess Shaw and the witches of her entourage approached my section of the square. I knew from Toketie's stories that they were all my age, but they held themselves like they were already ruling the kingdom. Shaw's gaze breezed over the stalls of freshly picked produce and her nose wrinkled.

"It is quaint," she said to her companions, as if continuing an earlier conversation.

Indignation rose in my chest and the wolf in my heart growled louder.

"I think it has a certain charm," the witch riding next to her replied, almost airily. "Like a candle in the darkness. A streak of sunlight after a thunderstorm."

The witch looked at me and held my gaze. He? She? This close, I could tell that they had the kind of features only nobility bred, with a wide forehead and skin like rich river clay. Their blue-black hair was done in two thick braids and their eyes were so dark they were almost black. I couldn't tell the witch's preferred gender— nothing on their black robes or in their hairstyle indicated boy or girl. It had to be deliberate. *They* it was.

"A single rose among a thousand thorns," the witch finished, voice sharpening as if they'd just figured something out.

I spun around so my back was to the procession, blood rushing through my ears. Why had I caught the witch's attention? Hunching over, I pretended to be interested in Iktus's radishes.

"Was that a vision?" a deep voice murmured.

"No, that was just Aklemin's usual horseshit," someone else responded.

"You were the one who wanted to come here, Aklemin," Shaw said. "What could a backwater village like this offer that's worth adding an extra day to our tour?"

I glared down at a lumpy radish, not daring to turn around. Whatever this Aklemin had thought, it sounded like the rest of the witches were dismissing it. I should have been grateful, but a part of me seethed. Forest's Edge was small, but we deserved more than the princess's condescension.

"I wonder," Aklemin began, but just then Tempest yanked his reins hard enough that I had to let go or risk losing a finger.

"Tempest!" I snapped, spinning back around.

I was too late. The bone stallion reared up, glittering white hooves flashing through the air. He came crashing down into the procession. The witches scattered out of the way. One of the mounted soldiers fell off his horse with a scream.

So much for staying unnoticed. Soldiers began to draw their swords, reacting to the perceived threat. The thane shouted for Princess Shaw to get back.

"Stop, don't hurt him!" I cried, rushing after my wayward horse. Tempest was my family's only breeding stallion. Our whole livelihood relied upon him. "Tempest, calm!"

I knew Tempest was scary to those who weren't used to bone horses. Like all animals born out of the magic of the Forest, he had patches of exposed bone growing on top of his skin. His were particularly visible against his dark gray coat, white bone protruding along his right shoulder, back legs, and the entire left half of his face.

Even more terrifying than that, magical animals grew significantly larger than their nonmagical counterparts. Tempest was nearly twenty-two hands at the shoulder—more than seven and a half feet tall. There were few creatures larger in the entire Cursed Kingdom. Shaw's three companions visibly struggled as their horses tried to bolt away from the scene.

The princess had the opposite problem. Shaw's mare looked to be closer to nineteen hands, on the smaller side for a bone horse, but she planted her hooves and snorted at Tempest without fear. Tempest gave a high-pitched whinny in reply. He'd been the sole stallion among several dozen bone mares since his sire had retired. He wasn't used to being challenged.

I wasn't an ice witch, able to see the future, but I knew what would happen if I let Tempest charge at the princess's bone horse. I leaped in front of the stallion and held my arms out wide.

"Tempest, stand down," I said firmly. My neck prickled at putting my back to the other bone horse. I had to hope the princess could control her mount.

Tempest pawed the ground. For a second, I thought he would charge right through me. Bone horses were stronger, hardier, and more loyal than nonmagical horses, but bone rage was scary enough to deter most casual riders from owning one.

But I knew how to deal with bone rage. Bone horses had nothing on a feral bone wolf.

As Tempest lifted his hoof to paw a second time, I reached up and grabbed the dangling end of his reins. With a hard yank, I brought his head to my level. "Stand. Down."

Tempest lunged for my nose, but I just pulled my head back and glared at him. Moving my hands farther up the reins, I held tight just below his chin. We stared each other down.

Slowly, Tempest's ears perked back up, showing he'd snapped out of his rage. I wasn't going to take any chances. I looped his reins over his neck and used a nearby crate of potatoes to vault onto his back. His shoulders bunched, as if he were considering taking off. I sat down hard in the saddle and he settled again.

Only then did I realize how everyone stared at us.

"That's a magnificent bone horse," Shaw said. "You haven't gelded him?" Her tone made it clear that she was judging my inability to control the stallion.

I wanted to snap something back about the nature of bone horses, but Shaw held her mare's reins in a loose grip. Surprisingly, her bone horse stood still, one ear turned forward and the other back as if awaiting orders. It was almost enough to make me forget my anger. I would never have expected the princess to be such a good rider, but she'd obviously earned the trust of her mare.

Tempest stomped the cobblestones and I snapped my eyes back up to Shaw's face. At this distance, I could see that her eyes were the same dark brown as her hair. For some reason, they reminded me of the Bone Forest. Of the darkness at the inside of pinecones, of mushrooms growing out of mulch, of shadows dancing along the Forest floor.

I tore my gaze away. "No, we haven't," I said shortly. "Excuse me, I've got to take him home before the commotion sets him off again." I looked deliberately to the drummers, then back to the princess, making it clear I blamed her for Tempest's behavior.

Before Shaw could respond, I wheeled Tempest around. Like all horses, he knew what direction home was and happily stepped into a heavy trot. It was only then that I realized I shouldn't have been so brusque. Was Princess Shaw the type to react harshly, or would she brush me off as an ignorant peasant and forget the whole thing by tomorrow?

"That's the Holts' breeding stallion," I heard Iktus say behind me, a touch defensive. "You know General Holt? May he rest in peace. His family raises the best bone horses in the kingdom, if you don't mind me saying so, Princess. Their stallion's a handful, just like his sire, but their line's well worth it."

If Shaw replied, I was too far away to hear it.

# Chapter 2

I untacked Tempest in my family's small stable and set the saddlebags of produce down in the barn aisle for Uncle Inge to grab. It hadn't been a long ride, so I didn't bother brushing the stallion down. Instead, I buckled a halter over his face and led him to the pasture where his herd had been rotated that morning.

Tempest aimed a parting kick in my direction as I let him loose beyond the gate. I just sidestepped and rolled my eyes.

A loud trumpetlike call pierced the air. Looking up, I spotted an ice swan circling overhead. Sunlight glinted off frosted wings and a crown of ice feathers splayed out over its long neck.

The call came again. I grinned, knowing a challenge when I heard one. I shifted.

No one except Gran knew about my first shift. I'd kept the wolf and most of the other voices in my heart hidden from my own family at Gran's request—all to keep me safe from the heavy shadow of the Witch King and Princess Shaw's future war.

I might have even kept the fact that I was a bone familiar at all secret from my family, if it weren't for my second shift. It had come on a few days shy of my twelfth birthday. Back then, I'd been inexperienced enough that when the voice sparked in my heart while

I helped Mama train Tempest, I hadn't been able to resist shifting into it.

Gran had been terrified, but the village didn't seem to think much about the daughter of a horse rancher shifting into a horse. Everyone knew Gran and Pops were bone familiars, so my being one too was no stretch.

Besides, bone horses might be fierce, but no one had suggested I should join the army the way they would if they knew about the wolf. So long as I kept my first shift secret and so long as no one else knew how easy it was for me to collect new voices, I'd be okay.

The ice swan made another call as I found my footing on four hooves. I neighed back, then launched into a run.

We raced, ice swan and bone horse, across the pasture. The swan drifted low enough that its webbed feet nearly touched my ears. I threw my head up, white mane whipping through the air, and the swan veered away with a laughing honk.

The race intensified as we circled back around to the gate. I lowered my head and pushed for more speed. The swan flew higher, trying to catch a wind current.

The gate appeared ahead, still open from letting Tempest inside. I barreled toward it.

Just ahead of me, the swan landed outside the gate and trumpeted in triumph.

I shifted, already laughing even before I had human lips. When I opened human eyes, the swan was gone too. Replacing it was a girl my age with waist-length black hair and umber skin—flawless except for a huge, jagged scar that ran from the base of her chin to her shoulder, and along her right forearm. Brown eyes framed by thick eyelashes glinted in my direction.

My cousin smiled smugly at me. "I think you've gotten slower, Rosy."

"No one races with me when you're gone, Tokey," I complained.

Toketie and I were born within days of each other. Destined to be best friends, Pops used to say as we ran past him. Then Toketie had panic-shifted into an ice swan just after her fourteenth birthday and left for Witch Hall without a backward glance. She only returned home for a week each season, during the school's holiday breaks.

"You're the one who wanted to stay," Toketie replied, rolling her eyes.

"I won't abandon our family."

"Is that what I did? Abandon them?"

I grimaced and tried again. "Mama needs me to help with the ranch."

"The last thing our family needs is another bone familiar at risk for going feral," Toketie snapped back.

It was a long-standing argument. Toketie thought that, without training, I would become like Gran. No matter how much I tried to explain that Gran *was* training me. Sometimes I wanted so badly to tell my cousin about the wolf. To show her that I was Gran's pack and Gran was mine. I couldn't leave her.

My gaze dropped to Toketie's scar. Even without Gran's many warnings, I knew I couldn't tell Toketie about my first shift. Not after Gran had attacked her in a feral rage and I'd stood by, too shocked to help. What would Toketie think of me if she knew I had a wolf inside me too?

"I miss you when you're gone," I said instead of continuing the argument.

Toketie lowered her shoulders, letting her guard down just as fast as it had come up. She reached out to hug me. "I miss you too."

"It'll be so nice to have you back next year," I continued into her shoulder. Toketie smelled like winter, like the sharp bite of frost in the air. Against the heat of early August, it was comforting.

Toketie made a little noise and pulled back. I looked up at her.

Toketie was in her final year at Witch Hall. I only had to go through a few more school terms before she'd be home for good. Usually mention of it would start Toketie rambling on about her big plans to use all her new knowledge to revitalize the local school here in Forest's Edge. The one Papa had started to give my two cousins and me a chance to learn to read and write and do more complex mathematics than simple counting.

"Iktus's granddaughter already started reading, you know," I said, trying to coax the excitement out of her. "By the time you settle back home, she'll be old enough to be your first student."

Toketie smiled, but it didn't look quite right. "That's nice."

I let the silence sit for a few seconds, then I nudged her. "Tokey?"

Toketie turned away. "I'm hungry. Come on, let's see if Dad is done with lunch."

UNCLE INGE WAS JUST STARTING to set the table when we walked into the ranch house. Toketie and I helped him with the dishes, then Uncle Inge called the rest of our family to lunch with the large bell hanging above the kitchen window.

Papa and Toketie's older brother walked in together from the family room, talking finances for the ranch. Just hearing it made my head hurt. I was glad to leave the specifics of tithes and taxes to Papa and Solemie. Personally, I liked to work directly with the horses, like Mama.

Uncle Chetwoot walked in next and he gave Uncle Inge a long kiss in the kitchen. Solemie rolled his eyes, but Toketie and I shared a smile. Our childhood had been spent giggling about courtship and finding love as sweet as Uncle Chetwoot and Uncle Inge's. Mama and Papa loved each other, I knew that, but they kept their affection private. As for Gran and Pops, well, Pops had died when we were both too young to really notice how they'd acted around each other. All we knew now was the heavy grief Gran carried in his absence.

Mama was last to arrive. She sat at the head of the table and looked at me. "Find everything at the market, Rosy?"

"It didn't seem like it," Uncle Inge said before I could. "Did Iktus not have a good harvest? Those saddlebags were half empty."

"The day after Lammas? That seems unlikely," Papa said. "Is something wrong with the farm?"

"No, it looked like a big harvest. Sorry, Mama, Uncle Inge. Tempest was acting up and I had to get him home. He yanked the reins out of my hand when I was at Iktus's stall."

"Let me see," Uncle Chetwoot said, reaching across the table.

I showed him my palm, though all that was left from Tempest's tantrum were a couple red lines. Uncle Chetwoot wouldn't be satisfied until he saw for himself. He was the medicinal expert of the family. He'd even helped deliver me *and* my two cousins. According to Gran, both of Uncle Inge's pregnancies had been difficult, and not just because he'd never been comfortable in the body he was born with. But Uncle Chetwoot had apprenticed under a doctor in

Woodside before he'd married Uncle Inge. Since Forest's Edge was too small for a flower witch, Uncle Chetwoot had stepped into the role of village doctor and he was unbearably fussy about it.

"Did something set him off? He seemed calm this morning. As calm as he ever is, anyway," Mama said, while Uncle Chetwoot rubbed salve over my palm.

I grimaced. I hadn't wanted to bring up the procession, but I couldn't lie about it now. "The princess arrived and he didn't like the parade."

"What!" Toketie sat bolt upright. "She's here already? Rosy! Why didn't you say so sooner?"

"Come on, Tokey, it's not like you haven't seen her before," Solemie said, smirking like he always did when he made fun of his sister. "Doesn't she go to school with you?"

"They're in the same year, even," Papa added. "Witch Hall isn't too large, you must have had a conversation with her."

"The princess and her entourage don't interact much with the rest of us," Toketie muttered. "I only knew she was coming to Forest's Edge because I heard Aklemin Alki mention it to a couple ice witches in one of our classes."

"Aklemin? Isn't that the witch you like?" Uncle Inge said.

Toketie's cheeks flamed bright red. "Dad! It's not like that! They're just . . . I mean, the princess chose them to be the ice witch of her entourage, so they'll represent all the ice witches and familiars for the kingdom one day. Of course I pay attention to them, that's all."

A hard lump settled in the pit of my stomach. Toketie gave a good excuse, but we were her family and we knew what that blush on her cheeks meant. She *was* interested in more than just this Aklemin Alki's political power.

As an ice familiar, it made sense that Toketie would be attracted to ice witches. Witches and familiars rarely married like non-magical people, not when the witch-familiar bond gave so many more advantages. But I'd always assumed that, if Toketie bonded to an ice witch, she'd bring them home to live at the ranch with the rest of us. Like Mama had done with Papa and Uncle Inge with Uncle Chetwoot. Like Solemie was going to do with his fiancée once they married next winter.

Except, if Toketie bonded with a strong ice witch, she'd be the one following them. What powerful witch would voluntarily come to live in Forest's Edge? At best, the couple might move to Woodside, where Uncle Chetwoot's ice witch sister made a living reading crop fortunes for the farmers and game fortunes for the hunters. Or maybe they'd move to Gravestown, which was the largest town bordering the Bone Forest.

Toketie moving to Gravestown wouldn't be terrible, I reassured myself. At least we'd get to visit a couple times a year when my family brought our horses to sell at the biannual market. I'd always thought, since there was no one I liked in Forest's Edge or Woodside, that I'd meet my own future spouse at one of those markets. Someone who understood horses like I did. Maybe we'd both try to sell our horses to the same buyer and we wouldn't like each other at first, but we'd respect each other. Then we'd keep running into each other season after season, sale after sale, until I invited them to come see the ranch and they'd fall in love with it. We'd court each other with tack and training techniques. When we finally married, they'd move in with me and become part of the Holt family.

If Toketie lived in Gravestown, like my future spouse's family, we could go visit more often. Make a trip out once a season, so our children would know each other. But if Toketie bonded with Aklemin Alki, she wouldn't settle down nearby. She'd become part of Princess Shaw's entourage, one-eighth of the future ruling council. She'd live up on the Frozen Mountain, inaccessible to her own family.

My mind flashed to Toketie's sudden stillness when I mentioned her coming home for good and my chest felt heavy. The wolf in my heart howled, loud enough that I almost thought my family would be able to hear it.

I stood abruptly and began gathering some food into my cloth napkin. "Got to take Gran lunch," I muttered as my family stared.

"Rosy, finish eating," Mama scolded. "Ma can wait."

Just then, someone pounded frantically at our door.

Papa went to open it and returned with Iktus's youngest son. He was panting hard, as if he'd just been running. "The princess and her entourage are coming to your ranch," he said between gulps of air. "They're just down the road."

"What? Why?" Uncle Inge asked, already standing. "They can't come in—the house is a complete mess!"

"She said something about wanting to pay respects to General Holt's grave," Iktus's son said. "That's all I heard before Dad sent me to warn you."

"I can take the princess and her entourage," Toketie volunteered immediately.

My anger burned so loudly, I couldn't even hear the voices in my heart. I tied the napkin tight, pulling hard enough that the knot squished the food under it.

My chair crashed to the ground as I stepped away from the table with Gran's lunch held tight in both hands. I held it up like an offering. "I'm taking this to Gran."

"Rosamund Holt, you sit back down this instant!" Mama snapped.

"But Mama!"

"Ylva will survive another half hour, you don't need to rush out the door," Uncle Chetwoot added, a touch gentler.

I opened my mouth to try again, but this time Papa cut me off. "Why don't you help Toketie escort the princess to the graveyard?" he said, as if that were any compromise at all. "Then while she's paying her respects, you can slip away to the Forest."

I wanted to say no, but I knew from the looks on my parents' faces that nothing I could say would be enough to sway them. They thought I was being rude, but rudeness was the last thing on my mind.

"She's here," Solemie said, peering out the front door with Iktus's son.

"Quickly now," Mama said. "Invite her in for tea, after. We'll get the house cleaned up while you're at the graves."

Toketie grabbed my wrist and pulled me toward the door.

Outside, Shaw and her entourage handed their horses off to a few guards. Most of the procession was absent, likely back in the market giving their recruitment pitch. Shaw turned toward me and Toketie as we approached, her eyes lingering where Toketie gripped my wrist. I wrenched my arm away.

"Miss Holt, Miss Holt," Shaw said.

"Princess," Toketie replied with a little curtsy. "This is my cousin, Rosamund Holt. We'll take you to the family graves, if you'd like to follow us."

I trailed behind as Toketie led the group away. At least Shaw gestured for the guards to stay behind, leaving only herself and the other three witches of her entourage.

Every royal had a retinue, a group of advisors from among their peers. Shaw's was an eclectic group. The princess walked in the rear, silent as a predator on the hunt. In the center, the ice witch Aklemin was having a spirited discussion about the weather with the smallest witch of the entourage—a girl with straight black hair tied in a low bun. The final member of the entourage was a tall, blond-haired boy. I couldn't help noticing his shockingly deep voice as he asked Toketie about Pops and his military accolades.

The family cemetery was tucked along the edge of the Bone Forest, down the road from my family's ancestral home. The oldest of the graves were so covered in moss and vines that the names were no longer visible, but it was the most recent grave that the princess wanted to see.

Shaw took a knee in front of Pops's headstone. The other three witches of her entourage knelt behind her. I wanted to slip away like Papa had suggested, but Toketie tugged me to my knees too and I fell to the ground with a small *oof*.

"Blessings to you, General Holt," Shaw said. "My grandmother counted you a dear friend. I'm sorry I was too young to know you myself. The Cursed Kingdom thanks you for your years of service."

Hidden in my lap, I curled my hands into fists. The insult of Shaw's words sat heavy on the back of my tongue, like day-old bile. Pretty words could not make up for Pops's death. Pretty words could not hide the fact that the military had failed him. Pops was once the Witch Queen's favored military advisor, the general who led her Royal Company. But when she'd passed, and the Witch King—Shaw's father—rose to power, Pops had been cast aside.

"Is he here?" asked the tall witch.

I lifted my head. Shaw was a bone witch. As a bone familiar,

I was sensitive to the energy of the dead, but it was bone witches who could commune with them.

Disappointment crushed my budding hope as Shaw shook her head. "There's a faint presence, but no way to tell if it's him or an older spirit."

"We shall take a moment of silence, then, so that your words have time to reach him beyond the veil," the tall witch declared.

I dropped my gaze back to my lap. Gran's lunch sack was tied to my belt. Every minute spent here only made the food inside grow colder. I wished I could slip away without the witches noticing, but I'd lost my chance. The moment of silence stretched on.

The prey in my heart began to squeak. I pressed a hand to my chest, wondering what had set them off. I raised my head to look around and saw that Shaw had done the same.

"The Forest is restless," Shaw murmured, glancing beyond the graves to the dense, unnaturally shadowed tree line.

The prey in my heart got louder and I knew Shaw was right. Branches scratched against one another and their needles bristled as if the Forest were an unruly cat awoken from slumber. We weren't within the boundary of the Forest, but several trees reached out to catch my attention anyway.

Something big moved in the corner of my vision. I scrambled to my feet to look.

Like a distorted memory, I saw a bone wolf in the deep shadows at the edge of the Forest. But where Gran had been sitting, patiently watching me play with the otters this morning, now she crouched like the predator she was. Her wolf shift had chunks of bone protruding along its jawline and rib cage, making it look hungrier. Her teeth were bared in a silent snarl.

"Shaw!" the princess's entourage shouted as one, noticing what I had.

But not quickly enough. The bone wolf lunged forward—fangs aimed to tear out Shaw's unguarded throat.

"Gran, stop!" I screamed.

# Chapter 3

My cry was too late. The wolf slammed against an invisible barrier and collapsed ungracefully to the ground.

I rushed over to Gran, heart in my throat. She didn't move from where she'd fallen. I skidded to the ground beside her.

"Are you hurt?" I asked as I ran my hands over Gran's legs, trying to feel if she'd broken something. Bone wolf or not, she wasn't as sturdy as she used to be.

I got a brief warning growl before the wolf snapped at my nearest hand. I pulled it out of reach just in time. "Gran, calm down, it's just me. It's Rosy."

But the wolf wasn't listening. It rose to its feet, a touch shaky, and lunged again to reach Shaw. Once more, it was stopped by an unseen force. The cuff on its leg glowed as the runes activated again to keep Gran from leaving the Forest. The wolf stumbled back with a yelp.

"Gran, you'll hurt yourself," I pleaded. I'd seen Gran lost in the wolf's mind plenty of times before, but rarely like this. So single-minded that she'd injure herself to get at her perceived prey.

The wolf crouched to try again. I grabbed the scruff on the back of its neck and held on as tight as I could. "Come back to yourself. There's no danger here. Come on, Gran."

"Gran?" the smallest witch from Shaw's entourage asked. "That's not Ylva the Red Wolf, is it?"

"Yes, that's our grandmother," Toketie said. "She's crazy, as you can see."

"She's not crazy," I yelled, struck by bitterness at Toketie's callous words. "She's just confused."

The wolf twisted around to snarl at me. I flashed my dull human teeth at it. The wolf turned back toward Shaw.

"She's feral," Shaw said, eyes narrowed as if in thought. She didn't seem concerned about the bone wolf trying to lunge at her only a few feet away. "Yuyan, can you—?"

The smallest witch shook her head. "Shantie's been working on a cure, but I have nothing that can help right now. She just needs to snap out of it."

I knew what normally worked, but I couldn't do it in front of the witches. Especially not *these* witches. The entire reason I'd avoided going to Witch Hall with Toketie was to stay unnoticed.

Gran had proven the kind of damage a bone wolf could do in war. She'd warned me long ago that if the military found out about my shift, I wouldn't get to choose whether to fight. I would be nothing more than a weapon to the Cursed Kingdom. A bloody tool to discard when they didn't need me anymore. Like Gran was.

But Gran wasn't stopping. Trapped in the wolf's mindset, she wouldn't stop until the wolf was either satisfied or forced to submit. I had to do something.

I leaned down close to the wolf's ear.

"Rosy!" Toketie cried.

I knew what she feared. Like this, it would be easy for the wolf to tear into my face or neck. Toketie's deep scar was proof that the wolf would attack its own family in the middle of a feral rage.

But Toketie was an ice familiar, not bone. Gran's wolf didn't have the same kind of instincts toward her that it did toward me.

I summoned the wolf in my heart, growled low into Gran's ear, and prayed that Shaw was too far away to hear it.

For several long seconds, we stayed like that. My heart pounded in my ears. I wondered if I should risk growling again.

Before I could decide, Gran shifted. Claws became nails, fangs became teeth. Silver fur receded into dirty clothes and wrinkled skin.

I fell back on my butt, relieved. My arms shook now that I wasn't gripping the wolf's scruff. I'd never before been grateful for the binding cuff on Gran's right ankle, the one enchanted to trap her in the Forest.

But if she'd managed to hurt the Witch King's only child, Gran would have been executed. No amount of pleading would have saved someone the kingdom already saw as a criminal.

"Are you recovered, madam?" Shaw asked, tone mild. As if the whole event had merely been a minor inconvenience.

"You dare?" Gran said. There was still an echo of the wolf's growl in her voice.

The prey in my heart overwhelmed the wolf's huffing, signaling danger. I moved closer to Gran, worried that she was about to fall back into that feral bone rage.

"Madam?" Shaw asked, raising an eyebrow.

"You dare?" Gran said, louder. "You, Death's Heir. You dare come here to my family's resting place and stand on his grave? You mock us!"

"Madam, I'm not sure—"

"You killed him, Shaw Colchuck! You killed my husband and I would see you pay for it! I would see you burn for it."

Toketie gasped. I grabbed Gran's arm, horrified. The Cursed Kingdom was one of the few places in the world where witches and familiars were supposed to be safe from the threat of fire. Shaw's own father had fled to avoid being burned at the stake. He'd only been nine years old when he was forced to travel across the entire continent to seek sanctuary in this kingdom. I didn't like Shaw or the Witch King, but I didn't want them to burn.

The huge blond witch stepped forward, breaking the terrible silence that followed Gran's shout. "Shaw," he said quietly. "Perhaps we should go."

"No. I'd like to hear what she has to say," Shaw said.

There was something dangerous about the princess's tone. Something that made the hair on the back of my neck bristle and the prey in my heart freeze.

I stepped forward, too, physically putting myself between the princess and Gran. "She needs rest. Tokey can escort you back when you're done here."

"Let me go, girl," Gran said.

But I didn't listen to her. Gran had once been a fierce soldier, and as a wolf she was still fearsome, but as a human she was frail with age. I was seventeen years old and I'd been raised mucking stalls and lugging around bales of hay. It wasn't hard to yank her farther into the Bone Forest.

The Forest helped, like it always did when I really needed it. Even as Gran tried to turn back to Shaw, still muttering insults, the trees moved to block our view of the graveyard. In front of us, a path widened. Branches shifted out of our way and the bone pines tilted as if bowing us on.

*Thank you,* I told the Forest silently as I pulled Gran away from the witches.

Gran knew there was no point in fighting when the Forest got involved. It had never once listened to her over me. She finally stopped struggling against my hold. I let go and she stalked ahead without a word.

My family's ancestral home had been swallowed by the Bone Forest decades ago. The cottage was one bad storm away from falling apart. There were huge holes in the roof thatching and the wooden walls were visibly rotting. The place had been old even fifty years ago, when Pops and Gran were gifted land in commemoration of their military service during the last war. They'd built the ranch house I'd grown up in and pastured off the rest of the land for the horses. They'd only returned to this cottage in the woods when they wanted time away from their three energetic grandchildren.

At least until Pops's death six years ago. Until Gran had attacked the commanding thane of our region and been imprisoned in this ramshackle house like the animal they'd accused her of being.

Gran led the way inside. It was worse than the outside. A single wooden chair sat at a crooked dining table. The fireplace was full of cobwebs from years of disuse. Instead of a bed, Gran had a pile of blankets in the corner of the room where she slept in her wolf shift.

Without looking at me, Gran went to the single small window. She gripped the splintering frame so tightly that the bones of her knuckles were clearly visible even from across the room.

"How could you let Death's Heir intrude upon your grandfather's grave?" she demanded, still refusing to look my way.

I knew this behavior, knew that Gran feared going feral again. It had been so long since I'd made her angry enough that the wolf inside her demanded my blood like it demanded everyone else's.

"I'm sorry, Gran," I whispered, not sure what else I could say.

Pops's death had been an accident. An avalanche on the way home from a meeting with the king's council up on the Frozen Mountain. He'd always taken the shortest path up and down the mountainside whenever he was called to advise the Witch King on military matters, eager to fulfill his duties and even more eager to return home.

The Frozen Mountain was like the Bone Forest—treacherous to those who didn't know its ways. No one questioned how he'd died. No one except Gran.

According to Gran, Pops had taken that same shortcut for decades without incident. He'd been one of the former Witch Queen's best friends and the Frozen Mountain had liked his visits. Gran hadn't believed an avalanche could kill him. She'd believed it even less when she'd learned that no one else in his military escort had been caught in it.

I'd only been eleven and still trying to control my first shift. All I really remembered was that one day Gran had gone feral and attacked the thane who'd been in charge of escorting Pops home. She'd been subdued before she could rip the man's throat out, but she'd tried.

"They murdered him!" she'd screamed during her trial. "Those bastards killed him!"

Only Gran's former military service had saved her from hanging. She'd been a war hero and now she was mad with grief. She was sentenced to life imprisonment in my family's ancestral home, with a magical cuff that prevented her from leaving the boundaries of the Bone Forest.

And every year on the anniversary of Pops's death, she stood just outside our family cemetery, unable to get close enough to lay flowers at her husband's grave.

I hadn't hated the military as a child. I'd been proud of Pops's and Gran's service. I'd thought of joining myself, when I was old enough. But though the soldiers Pops had traveled with hadn't outright murdered him, they also hadn't rescued him when the avalanche came down. And they hadn't done anything to try to help Gran. Pops's death had broken whatever control she'd had over her wolf, and her feral episodes were a result. Instead of trying to save the woman they'd called a war hero, they'd imprisoned her and left her to rot.

For Gran's sake, I despised them with every clamoring voice in my heart.

But for all that Shaw represented the military, and for all that the current state of the military was because of Shaw, she was no older than I was. A child when Pops had died. The soldiers hadn't cared enough to risk their own lives to save an old officer the Witch King had been trying to retire. Their disregard had killed Pops, yes, but attacking Shaw would only make the Witch King even less willing to release Gran from her imprisonment. To let her return home.

I walked over to the small table and placed the napkin with Gran's lunch down. "Here, you'll feel better after some food."

It took me several tries to undo the knot. The food didn't look appetizing when I finally got the cloth open. It had gone cold and the tussle with Gran's wolf had smashed the quiche. Bits of egg and potato spilled out from the edge of the cloth onto the dirty table.

Gran didn't even look at the food. "I need to hunt," she said.

I should have expected that. With the wolf so angry, Gran needed to do something to calm it or she'd go feral again. Hunting was her only outlet these days.

"I'll go with you," I said, worried about letting Gran out of my sight.

Gran nodded. She knew, like I did, that hunting as a pack would keep her wolf calmer.

Hopefully I'd be able to convince her to bring whatever we caught back to the cottage to cook, instead of eating it raw in our animal forms. It was a toss-up with Gran, whether the wolf's instinct took over. The toss-up had favored the wolf more and more in the past couple years.

Gran shifted back into her wolf and trotted out of the cottage. I could feel my wolf's eagerness to join her, but I didn't dare shift into it. Not with Shaw and her military escort in town. Gran would have warned me against it herself if she were in her right mind.

Luckily, I had a few other voices happy to take an opportunity to hunt alongside Gran. The raccoon chittered the loudest and I accepted the shift.

Gran headed off as I was still finding my footing on the raccoon's nimble paws. I scampered after her.

The Bone Forest was denser than a pine forest ought to be and always colder than the outer woods or the far foothills. In this heat, I welcomed the cold and dank forest floor. The canopy of pine needles created an unnatural darkness as the trees bent down to watch us pass, but neither raccoon nor wolf cared.

I ran across the discarded needles, ignoring the little pinpricks as the ends stabbed at my paws. Each pinecone was an obstacle to swerve around or jump over. As a kid, I had made a game of it. Now, I focused on keeping up with Gran's long strides.

Gran caught scent of something and stopped moving abruptly. She flicked her ears to the right. I understood the silent message. Leaping, I grabbed hold of the coarse bark of the nearest pine tree, then scurried halfway up the trunk. The branch moved so that I could see the prey in the next clearing. It was a rabbit. A foothills rabbit, lost in the Bone Forest. Bone rabbits were more aware of their surroundings, but this nonmagical rabbit was unconcerned about the raccoon above its head as it snuffled about for food among the pine needles and ivy roots.

For a second, I felt bad for the poor thing. But that was the prey voices inside me talking and they quieted down after a second. They knew the circle of life. The rabbit had a chance like any other prey, and Gran needed this.

I leaped from my trunk to the next, then dropped to the ground just beyond where the rabbit stood. The rabbit bolted, startled by my sudden appearance. I chased after it, steering it toward where Gran waited. The Forest made a clear path, blocking off the other escape routes.

This rabbit wasn't entirely dumb though. It caught sight of Gran crouched beyond the next tree and veered right through a small gap. The bone pines pulled apart to give Gran room to chase after it. I scampered back up the nearest tree. There were only a few low-hanging branches, but I never worried about missing a jump. The Forest wouldn't let me fall.

Another voice overwhelmed me and between one jump and the next, I shifted into something lighter and more balanced. Squirrel. Perfect.

I picked up speed, darting from one tree to the next. The rabbit was faster than Gran, but it wouldn't be able to maintain that speed forever. As long as I kept it in my sights, Gran would have dinner tonight. My squirrel body was nimble. I flung myself from branch to trunk to branch again.

The wind picked up and I could feel the Forest's impatience as it urged me to go faster. The Forest's warning came too late. The rabbit burst into an already occupied clearing.

A huge bone moose, with two massive antlers, reared up as the rabbit, then Gran, came charging into its clearing. Gran skidded out of the way just before those massive hooves would have come crashing down on top of her. The rabbit was less lucky. The moose's left hoof clipped it over the head and it went flying to the other side of the clearing. It hit the trunk of a thin bone pine and collapsed onto the ground.

I called the raccoon back. My body rippled. I hated the expansions the most. Becoming something smaller was like being squeezed—it was only uncomfortable for a second. Becoming something larger was akin to being stretched, and it made my skin crawl for a good minute afterward. But I was used to working past the sensation by now, even if I could never quite ignore it.

I climbed down the tree and grabbed the dead rabbit by the back of its neck. If it were a bone rabbit, it would have been too heavy, but a foothills rabbit was easy prey for a bone raccoon. I pushed myself back up the tree and out of the way of the enraged bull moose. Gran turned back in the direction we'd come and ran for it. The moose bellowed after her.

I lost sight of them both, slowed down by carrying the rabbit. The branch I was on gently lowered me to the ground and I walked where the pines led.

I found Gran waiting by the creek I'd played in that morning. I dropped the rabbit at her feet and took several large gulps of water. Gran waited until I was done drinking before picking the rabbit up. It didn't seem like she was overwhelmed by the wolf. Good, maybe I would be able to convince her to make rabbit stew. It would last longer, and I wouldn't have to worry about bringing her food from the ranch for a couple meals.

We made our way back toward Gran's cottage together, trotting at a decent pace to recover the distance we'd traveled. The path was wide open before us, bone pines leading us home.

Except, I realized after a few minutes of walking, they weren't leading us back to Gran's cottage. I stopped walking, confused. The Forest was a maze to many, but I'd always been able to tell which way was which. Gran's cottage was behind us. Where was the Forest leading us instead?

Distracted as I was trying to figure out what the Forest was doing, I almost missed the sound of human voices. Gran didn't. She growled around the rabbit's body.

I shifted into my human skin and put one hand on Gran's back. One voice chattered along, and with my human ears I recognized it easily.

"The wild bone horse herds migrate throughout the entire Forest," Toketie said. "They usually end up in this area in late autumn and into the winter. That's when we make observations and set traps for the healthiest so we can bring them back to the ranch to breed. We release most of them afterward. Wild bone horses are near-untamable, but it's a good way to diversify our breeding stock."

"What sort of traps do you use?" someone asked, and I recognized the deep voice as that of the tall witch from Shaw's entourage.

I let go of Gran and carefully crept forward. Around the trunk of a massive bone pine, I saw the group. There was Toketie, standing with her back to me. The four witches—Shaw and her entourage—faced her. Shaw kept her eyes on Toketie, waiting for her answer, but her companions seemed less at ease. They had to know that the Bone Forest was deadly to the unwary. Or perhaps they feared that Gran would come again to attack the princess.

As they should. They were within the bounds of the Forest and Gran's enchanted cuff wouldn't save them if she had another feral episode.

I was furious that Toketie had brought them here. What was she thinking? I knew my cousin didn't care about our grandmother the same way I did. She didn't *get* Gran's wolf like I did. But the disrespect was infuriating. The Bone Forest was Gran's territory. The military had forced that. Death's Heir had no right to be here, and Toketie had no right to let her.

The bone pine I hid behind pushed back against my hand, as if trying to console me. Quickly, I ducked behind the tree and turned back to Gran. She wasn't feral yet—hunting had calmed the wolf. But if she caught sight of the princess, I wasn't sure she'd stay that way. She wasn't unaware, she had heard the talking like I did, but in her right mind Gran didn't *want* to hurt anyone and that was what mattered most.

"Go, Gran," I whispered, so soft that nothing but a wolf's ears would be able to pick it up. "Please."

Gran began to creep away, but when I didn't follow, she stopped and looked back, expectant.

"I'm going to watch until they leave," I whispered. I'd feel better once I saw the witches heading back to the ranch.

Gran pinned me with one long stare. I stood my ground. Gran growled again. I knew what she was thinking—that the witches were dangerous. Shaw would be at the center of the next war, every ice witch in the kingdom had prophesied that. If I wanted to avoid military service, I had to avoid catching Shaw's attention.

"I won't let them see me," I said, then to prove my point I shifted into the squirrel and leaped up into the nearest tree. Gran relented and loped away with the dead rabbit still hanging from her mouth. I resigned myself to the fact that she'd have already eaten it raw by the time I returned to the cottage. It didn't matter, not so long as Gran stayed far away until the witches were gone.

Luckily, it seemed like Toketie's little tour was wrapping up. "We can head back to the ranch," Toketie said. "They're probably done cleaning up, if you'd like that tea Aunt Ida offered."

Shaw nodded. "After you, Miss Holt," she said.

Before Toketie could lead the witches away, a bellow echoed across the clearing.

"What was that?" the smallest witch asked.

"Sounds like—" Toketie was cut off by another bellow.

"Shaw, let's go," the large witch said, grabbing the princess by the shoulder.

The Bone Forest had different plans. The trees moved and, with a distinct crack of branches and a smattering of falling pines, the clearing closed off completely.

I clung to the trunk I was on, now trapped on the inside of the clearing with my cousin and the witches.

*What's going on?* I tried to ask the Forest, but it didn't answer.

The bellow came again. I recognized the call. The bull moose from earlier, it had to be. Had it followed Gran and me? It was still obviously stuck in bone rage. Had the Forest closed off the clearing to protect us?

Shaw frowned, staring at the far end of the clearing. I followed her gaze and my stomach dropped. The clearing wasn't completely shut. A single path was open. At the other end of it, its head lowered to show off gleaming bone antlers, was the bull moose.

*Danger,* I mentally shouted. *Help!*

The path the moose charged down widened. The Bone Forest wasn't trying to save us. Just the opposite. It had trapped us so we couldn't run away from the enraged bull moose again.

# Chapter 4

"DID YOU DREAM OF THIS, AKLEMIN?" SHAW ASKED, once again managing to sound bored even in the face of life-threatening danger.

The other witches turned around. Toketie let out a startled scream. The moose had halved the distance along the path and it wasn't slowing down.

"Perhaps," Aklemin said in that same slow, lazy tone they'd used when talking to Shaw during the parade. "A glint of ice, a splash of red, some delicious lumpy biscuits."

"Oh, food, we should have known," the smallest witch said. "Is this like that time you dragged us into Lake Bloom to catch that fish that tastes like apple cider?"

"If you had but listened to me, Yuyan, we would have caught it and it would have become your new favorite food."

"Oh no, how ever will I live with myself?"

Why weren't they panicking? The moose was almost at the entrance of the clearing now, and none of the witches were moving. Toketie watched it, pale and shaking. I mentally urged her to climb the nearest tree, to get as far away as she could.

But instead, I saw my cousin straighten her shoulders and step between the group of witches and the encroaching bull moose.

*Tokey, no! Forest, please—*

It was too late. The bull moose crashed into the clearing and Toketie shifted in a flurry of sprouting feathers. The moose snorted and stumbled sideways a few steps, trying to get its bearings. Toketie's ice swan shift was large enough to startle the moose back. I hoped it would be enough to break it out of its rage.

Beyond the moose, I could see that the Forest hadn't closed up the path the moose had come down. It had left an escape route. I didn't understand what game the Forest was playing. It had never done anything like this with me before, but there was no time to question it.

I shifted. None of the witches noticed, too focused on the moose. "Run!" I yelled at them even as I slid down the rough bark of the pine. "Look, there's an opening there. Get out of here!"

But they did not run, instead turning to look at me with a mixture of shocked eyebrows and frowns, as if wondering where I'd come from. Toketie stayed where she was, standing between the witches and the bull moose with her frosted wings raised high.

The moose didn't startle at my entrance like it had done with Toketie's shift. It grunted like an angry bear, lowering its head. I knew that if it charged Toketie, neither her size nor the ice coating her feathers would save her from the blunt-force trauma.

For a second, my mind was overtaken with the memory of Gran attacking Toketie. Of sharp claws tearing through her chin and shoulder, my cousin's thin arm crunching under dripping fangs. Of all the nightmares that had put me in Gran's place, hot blood gushing into my mouth. I'd been so useless then, unable to move until Toketie had panic-shifted into an ice swan for the first time.

I couldn't let my cousin be hurt again. I had to do something.

The wolf in my heart howled, pushing to get out, to protect our pack.

With a desperate mental scramble, I called upon the bone horse instead. My horse wasn't as big as Tempest, but compared to Shaw's dainty bone mare, I was sturdy. Exposed bone wrapped around my chest and up my shoulders like a breastplate. The bull moose might still be larger, but I had better odds than Toketie's swan.

The witches fled out of my way as I reared, trying to scare the moose. It charged instead, just barely missing trampling Toketie as it responded to my challenge.

I met its charge head-on, striking out with my front hooves. One hoof hit exposed bone along the moose's left shoulder. The moose skidded away, then came charging back. I dodged away this time and the moose rammed into the bone pine just behind me.

The witches all huddled to my right, staring. Toketie still stood in front of them, as if a single swan could guard against an enraged bull moose. *Get out of here*, I urged, but familiars couldn't talk while shifted and witches couldn't read minds.

The moose shook its massive antlers. It eyed me. I planted my hooves and snorted at it. Bull moose were obnoxiously large, especially those born of bone magic. But bone horses were more agile. The clearing was too small for the moose to get a good charge going, so I had a small advantage.

Throwing its head back, the moose grunted at me. The bone rage had subsided, but the moose wasn't backing off. It didn't want me in its territory. I eyed those six-foot antlers, then slowly began to back up toward the witches. Maybe I could nudge them down the opening. Toketie would follow if the witches left.

An ice-cold hand touched my withers. I startled, lunging forward. The moose bellowed at the perceived challenge. I pranced left, toward the other end of the clearing. The moose lowered its head again. I bumped up against a cluster of pines. The moose charged.

The pine trees around me shifted, giving me room as I shied away from the bull moose's attack. I pushed through, thanking the Forest for opening the clearing.

And then the gap between the trees closed around me. I tried to lunge backward and found myself trapped between the encroaching bone pines. What was the Forest doing?

*Let me out!* I silently screamed at it, but the trees only pushed closer.

The bull moose rammed its antlers into the pines just left of me. I pushed sideways, desperate. The bone along my shoulders caught against the encroaching trunks.

The moose pulled back, preparing to strike out again.

Bark scraped against my neck as branches folded over me. I neighed, suddenly panicked. The horse was too big. I couldn't make it through the gap. I prayed for the Bone Forest to hear my panic, for the trees to move away, but they just kept squeezing me tighter.

The antlers came down. I felt the air change the second before the moose hit me. Between how tightly I was wedged and the force of its attack, I was certain I'd snap in half.

I couldn't stay as the horse. I was too big. But I couldn't shift back into a human either. The moose was too close, it would impale me. I called up one of my smallest shifts instead. Skin shrank, bones cracked, everything compressed impossibly smaller and smaller.

I fell to the ground now so far below. Hitting dirt rattled every bone in my little body, but there was no time to squeal. I skidded across pine needles as long as I was. My slender tail whipped out as I tried to stabilize myself. Above me, the moose crashed into the trees. Chunks of wood sprayed from the impact.

I scampered away as a mouse. A shadow fell over me. The bull moose was stepping back, its hoof more than triple the size of me. I swerved away, heartbeat so loud it overwhelmed my hearing entirely.

Distantly, I was aware that I'd cleared the pines. I should shift back into the horse. I was vulnerable like this. But knowledge of my vulnerability just made that logic harder to cling to. My mind was completely overwhelmed by the mouse's panic.

"That's enough."

That was Shaw's voice, as if all she needed to give was a royal command and everything would stop. The mouse didn't care. Shaw's voice had scared it. All it could think about was finding a place to hide. The mouse swerved away from Shaw and the witches, just as frightened of them as it had been of the moose. Even as I tugged at it, trying to regain control, the mouse scurried mindlessly in the other direction. Back toward the bull moose.

The moose shook its massive antlers, stuck between the same pines that had trapped me. Fragments of bone pine fell to the ground like shooting stars all around me.

I looked up just in time to see the sharp edge of one shattered piece of wood overhead. Then it speared me above my right ear and the world went black.

I WOKE UP IN MY bed. The smallest witch from Shaw's entourage, the one she'd called Yuyan, hovered over me. She lifted a hand to my forehead just as I opened my eyes. I flinched back in surprise as the smell of mint and willow bark invaded my nose.

"Steady," Yuyan said. "I'm not done healing you."

"Tokey?" I asked, my voice a croak. "The moose—"

"She's okay," Yuyan assured me. "Everyone's fine, thanks to you."

I closed my eyes, dizzy with both worry and pain. Flashes of the fight came back to me. Of the panic, the mouse taking over.

"I think . . . I was feral," I said. "As the mouse. I was so scared—"

Yuyan shushed me. "You're not bonded, right? It's normal to go feral in that kind of situation," she assured me.

"But I couldn't— I had no control—"

"At least you just have prey shifts. All you'll ever do is flee. Give it time and you'll regain your mind and be able to shift back."

"Horses can do a lot of damage in bone rage," I argued.

Being feral just meant a familiar's human mind was overwhelmed by the animal's, usually when their instincts were especially strong. Fear was one thing, and even scared bone horses reacted to it by fleeing, but bone rage could affect any bone animal. A mouse in bone rage couldn't do much damage, but a horse? Tempest's tantrum at the market had been the easy end of the spectrum. It took Mama and me working together to calm the stallion out of his worst bone rages, and last time Uncle Chetwoot had been forced to use some of his rare healing potions—bought for more than we could afford from a flower witch in Gravestown—to treat both of us.

It wasn't really my horse shift I was worried about though. I'd never gone feral before, but I wouldn't forget the feeling of it anytime soon. How out of control I'd been. Like I was a passenger, watching in horror as a stranger directed my body.

I didn't know how Gran could stand it, knowing how much

damage her wolf could do while feral. I didn't know how *I* would be able to stand it, fearing what my own wolf might do.

Was it possible for the entire Bone Forest to fall into bone rage? Was that why it had acted so strangely? Tunneling the moose toward us. Squeezing me between its pines. It was a wild thought, but I had no other explanation.

"There." Yuyan brushed her thumb over my temple, then leaned back. "You'll be more tired than usual the next few days, but it was a fairly shallow cut. Head wounds bleed a lot, but they aren't difficult to heal, all things told." She paused, staring down at me. "Going feral isn't hereditary, don't worry so much."

I scowled back at her. Going feral might not be hereditary, but stressful situations could turn any familiar feral. For Yuyan to be so blasé about it just proved my belief that those in power didn't care what happened to familiars once they got their use out of them.

But then Yuyan sighed and something about her expression softened. "If it makes you feel better, I have a friend working on a cure."

"A friend? Another flower witch?" Because that was what Yuyan had to be. I reached up, trying to feel how bad the cut she'd been tending was. It might have only been a small shard of wood that knocked me out, but injuries scaled to size, and I remembered how bad it had hurt the mouse.

All I could feel was a small raised line, as if the wound had already scarred. I wouldn't have believed it if I didn't have the evidence beneath my fingertips. Only very powerful flower witches could heal an injury completely—most had to rely on potions and medicinal herbs. But then, Yuyan was a member of the princess's entourage. I shouldn't have been so surprised.

"Yes. It's her senior project," Yuyan said. "Has your cousin told you about those? The project every witch and familiar at Witch Hall needs to complete before graduating?"

"Tokey's already halfway done with hers," I said, because she'd said as much the first night she'd arrived home for break.

Even though Toketie had been a late bloomer—entering Witch Hall several years after most witches and familiars—she'd now more than caught up with her classmates. I hated her being gone, but I was proud of what she'd achieved. I'd been prouder when I'd thought she was going to bring all she'd learned back to Forest's Edge, instead of disappearing with some ice witch to the far reaches of the kingdom.

Yuyan looked pensive for a second. "Yes, she's reorganizing the school's storage system, isn't she? Witch Hall certainly needed it. I don't think they've updated their inventory system since the school was founded."

I nodded, then regretted it as the world spun. Yuyan carefully helped me sit up.

"You need something to eat. Forcing your body to heal so quickly took a lot of energy."

"Water?" I asked. My throat hurt and my mouth was drier than I'd thought possible.

"That too," Yuyan said. "Come on, up you get."

Yuyan hovered close by as I stumbled out of the room and to my family's dining table. Papa stood as we approached.

"There you are, Rosy," he said, and helped me to a chair. "Feeling better?"

I nodded again, then winced. I had to stop doing that.

Uncle Inge came bustling in from the kitchen just as I got seated. He lowered a tray of tea and biscuits to the center of the table.

With shaking hands, he poured tea into one of our best cups—the one Papa had bought Mama as a birthday present last year, with a horse painted on the glazed side—and passed it to Shaw with an awkward bow. I couldn't help noticing how out of place the princess looked among my family's mismatched chairs and cluttered shelves.

Shaw didn't even say thank you as she accepted the cup, but Uncle Inge didn't seem to notice as he quickly poured tea for the other three witches in the entourage. At least Yuyan and the blond witch murmured thanks. Aklemin just held up a lumpy biscuit and smiled.

My family settled around the table. We didn't have enough seats with Shaw and her entourage taking up four, but Uncle Inge kept rushing back to the kitchen and my parents didn't seem to mind hovering over my shoulder. Finally, Uncle Inge poured me a cup and I thanked him loudly.

Shaw wrapped both hands around her cup, though I noticed that she didn't try to take a sip of the tea. "I owe you my thanks," she said to me.

I swallowed my tea too quickly and burned the back of my tongue. Had she taken my tone to mean I expected thanks for the bull moose situation? "I didn't do much," I said.

"No, you put yourself in danger to save us. You deserve our gratitude."

Shaw's eyes were fixed on my face and it made me anxious. "You should have fled when Tokey distracted the moose," I muttered. The prey in my heart grew nervous again. Their squeaks and squeals reminded me of the mouse's panic and that only made me feel worse.

Shaw inclined her head, acknowledging my point, but then

she said, "And you should have been studying at Witch Hall. Two shifts. That's more than most familiars achieve in their lifetimes."

I crossed my arms, hoping it didn't look as defensive as it felt. "The mouse is new," I lied. "Didn't even know I could do it, but I was stuck between the pines. It was a panic shift."

My eyes drifted to Toketie as I said it. I didn't know if it was possible to panic-shift when you were already a familiar, but I had to hope the princess would accept my excuse.

"Well, regardless of how it came, it's here now," Shaw said. "You need training."

I dug my fingers into my arms, mind racing. I'd been able to convince my family that Gran could train me, but Gran only had the one shift. They'd take the princess's word over my own. "Witch Hall is expensive," I said. "We're already paying for Tokey—"

"Rosy," Mama snapped.

I flinched. Papa put a hand on my shoulder. "We can make it work," he said, speaking to the princess more than to me. "If Rosy needs training, then we'll see to it that she's afforded the same opportunity for success Toketie was."

Shaw inclined her head again. "Your daughter saved my life. I will personally fund her tuition, for however long it takes for her to graduate."

My parents scrambled over each other to thank the princess. I said nothing, staring down at my tea. I couldn't get out of this, not with Shaw offering to pay. I was trapped as surely as Gran, except worse, because I knew to fear what was coming.

"Here, eat."

Yuyan shoved a biscuit in my face. I took it, then looked at her. The fog in my mind suddenly cleared, as if the Forest of my own thoughts had decided to show me the path forward.

Yuyan's friend, that other flower witch, was developing a cure for feralness. If I went to Witch Hall, I could get the cure. I could bring it home to Gran.

It was more than that, I realized suddenly. Graduates of Witch Hall were allowed to petition the jarls' council anytime they wished. I could argue against Gran's sentence. If she was cured of her feral rages, surely they'd agree she'd served her time. She hadn't actually hurt that thane six years ago, just attempted to.

If I could petition them directly, with all the weight of Witch Hall behind me, they'd have to let her come home. Maybe then our jarl would remember that our land had been gifted in honor of Gran's service as much as Pops's and stop trying to take it from us.

A horrible, squeezing hope clung to my throat, making it hard to breathe. I thought of Gran's white-knuckled grip on the windowsill of that dilapidated cottage. Of Mama and Uncle Inge's sorrow every time their ma was brought up in conversation. Of Papa and Solemie, worrying over the ranch's finances again and again. Of Toketie's scar.

"I'll go," I said, cutting into whatever Shaw was telling my parents. "To Witch Hall."

Shaw stared at me and I looked back as calmly as I could. I knew Gran wouldn't approve. She'd tell me how dangerous it was. How risky it would be. If anyone learned about the wolf, or my other shifts, they'd press me into service like Gran had been. They'd expect me to throw away my own life to fight in Shaw's future war.

But all they knew about was the horse and the mouse. Once we were at Witch Hall, there would be no reason for the princess to pay me any more attention.

I wanted nothing to do with Shaw's war. The thought of going feral again was terrifying. I wouldn't let the princess think she could make a weapon out of another Holt familiar. But I also couldn't resist following the path before me.

I would do anything to save Gran and make my family whole again.

# Chapter 5

## SHAW

IF THERE WAS ONE THING SHAW KNEW, IT WAS THAT people were predictable. A single offer and the Holts scrambled to get the two familiars ready to travel with her escort to Witch Hall. The stiffness in the thane's shoulders when Shaw told him of the additions to the party meant he wanted to refuse, until Shaw mentioned that one was a bone familiar. No one dared get in between Shaw and a potential bond, regardless of how unlikely such a bond would be.

Rosamund Holt was not predictable. Predictable would have meant her parents sending her to Witch Hall the instant her first shift settled. Even if finances were the issue, Toketie Holt had been a late bloomer. Rosamund should have been well-established at school before her cousin was revealed as an ice familiar.

Predictable would have meant Rosamund and Toketie being given a pair of mares to ride to school. Instead, once their trunks were loaded into the cart, Rosamund shifted into a horse and let her cousin saddle her.

Predictable would have meant Rosamund walking close to where Shaw and her entourage rode. Whether to eavesdrop, or to give her cousin a chance to talk with Aklemin. Toketie Holt *was* predictable, after all. But Rosamund trailed behind instead, ears rotated back to listen to Toketie's long-winded explanation about how classes worked at Witch Hall.

Shaw didn't understand Rosamund Holt and she despised it. She'd always known what to expect—from people, from events, from her own future. Rosamund's unpredictability made her irrationally angry.

She turned to Aklemin riding beside her. "Tell me, is this another game?"

Aklemin smiled but didn't reply. The two had known each other all their lives and yet Shaw could count on one hand the times the ice witch had been serious about anything. She should have said no when they'd requested to add another village to the tour schedule. She was in no mood for their idea of fun.

Shaw twisted in her saddle just enough to see the Holts. Another surprise—how a girl as plain as Rosamund Holt turned into a horse as beautiful as that. Hay-colored hair had paled into a white mane and tail, the same color as the exposed bone along her chest and shoulders. Sunburnt skin was now covered by a dark gray coat with lighter gray speckling. As a human, Rosamund was short, with visible biceps and thick calves. Working-class proportions, at odds with the soft beauty of the upper class or the lean muscles of the military. But what made her less appealing as a human made her sturdy as a horse, giving the impression that she could carry her cousin a thousand miles before tiring.

"Careful," Aklemin said quietly. "Stare too much and she'll shy away."

"She's not a wild animal," Shaw said.

"You'll have better luck if you treat her like she is."

Shaw wrenched her eyes away from Rosamund to observe

Aklemin's expression. They were her closest confidant—the only witch her age on the Frozen Mountain and thus her childhood companion. She'd chosen Yuyan and Einar for her entourage and one day they'd both be comfortable enough to fulfill their duty as her advisors. But she expected Aklemin would always be the quickest to do so, even when their advice was unsolicited.

"Yuyan doesn't like it when I compare commoners to beasts," Shaw said.

Aklemin rolled their eyes, even though she'd been joking. "Definitely don't let Miss Rosy hear you say that."

"You act as though I'm going to court her."

Aklemin just clicked their tongue, pushing their horse into a trot. Shaw stayed behind and watched as they caught up to where Yuyan was riding. She was too far away to hear what Aklemin said, but by Yuyan's sharp gestures, it had started yet another bickering argument between the two.

So that was Aklemin's game. Shaw had taken too long in choosing her future familiar so they'd thrown a wild card on the table.

Foolish. However interesting Rosamund Holt was, Shaw was expected to bond with a familiar of a certain station. She could get away with courting a commoner if they were like Einar—from a wealthy family with some amount of political capital in their hometown. Or like Yuyan, who had no status in the Cursed Kingdom but was the daughter of one of the leaders of the Waiming Territories. When Yuyan had moved to the Cursed Kingdom as a young flower witch, it had fostered a new era of trade agreements with Waiming.

Rosamund Holt though? Her grandparents were war heroes, but that was no hereditary power. What could a rancher's daughter from a tiny backwater village offer the Cursed Kingdom? She would have to be an extraordinarily strong familiar for Shaw to justify it to the jarls' council, not to mention her father.

Einar broke away from the soldier he'd been chatting with and took the spot Aklemin had vacated. He rode a massive draft, since he was tall enough and broad enough that most normal horses would struggle under his weight for extended distances. Shaw put a hand on her horse's neck to remind her to be good. Cow's ears flicked back for a second, a silent complaint that Shaw wouldn't let her bite Einar's draft. Shaw liked that about her. The runt of her herd, and yet the strongest personality of all the horses she'd looked at the day she chose her. It was a shame she'd let Aklemin nickname the mare, but now Cow responded to nothing else.

"What's wrong?" Einar asked in that endearingly genuine way of his.

"Aklemin is scheming again," Shaw said.

"About what?"

About what indeed. What was it about Rosamund that had caught Aklemin's attention? Shaw frowned down at her hands.

Einar leaned closer, encouraging her to speak. For all that Aklemin was her closest friend, and for all that she trusted Yuyan, Einar was the only one she knew would never, even accidentally, give away her secrets.

She lowered her voice so she could be sure that no one would be able to eavesdrop on their conversation and said, "In the Forest, with the bull moose, did you see where Rosamund came from?"

"Before she shouted for us to run?" Einar shook his head. "No."

Neither had Shaw. But the Forest had enclosed their clearing completely. She would have noticed Rosamund. The most logical explanation was that she had already shifted into a smaller animal that they'd overlooked. Something like the mouse. Which meant that her story about panic-shifting was a lie.

Shaw met Einar's steady gaze. "When the moose charged her, when she shifted from horse to mouse, did you see her become human in the middle?"

Einar frowned, and then he leaned back in his saddle as if physically shocked. "Didn't she? No, there was no time. But can familiars with multiple forms panic-shift that way?"

Shaw shook her head. She wasn't an expert on familiar theory, but as heir to the throne she'd been taught more than most witches. "Even for familiars who learn a second shift, switching directly between them is an advanced skill," she explained. "Panic can force a shift, but as far as I've heard, only from human to animal. From animal to animal? Even for a familiar with two documented shifts, I've seen no record of that happening."

"Which means she's done it before," Einar said.

"Yes." Shaw resisted the urge to turn to look back at the Holt familiars again. Horse and mouse were an unusual combination. Both prey, yes, but as far from each other as two prey animals could be. It made Shaw wonder, were they truly Rosamund Holt's only shifts?

The tour schedule ended in Gravestown. Shaw was ready to return to school. Witch Hall had a comforting structure that she never found on the road and she missed her daily routine.

It took three days to travel from Gravestown to the northern border at Wimahl River. The Cursed Kingdom was centered around the tall peak of the Frozen Mountain, and its foothills and gorges made for winding roads. They skirted west around the Mountain instead of east—Shaw had no desire to get close to the Obsidian Desert in the middle of the summer—and from there it was a straight shot north to Multah. On the final day, Shaw's party picked their way out of an old glacial valley and climbed up the basaltic cliffs that cupped Wimahl River from either side.

They finally settled down for lunch at a guard tower that sat at the crest of a clifftop overlooking the river. The soldiers who had traveled with Shaw's party greeted the guards on duty as old friends. The thane looked relieved to be back to his typical post. Shaw had requested him as her escort that summer precisely because of his distaste for traveling. It amused her, the way his service grew strained over the fortnight they'd been together, how his respectful manner became snappish and curt.

Still, Shaw believed in rewarding good service in the face of hardship. Even, or maybe especially, hardship of her own making. She'd write to the jarl of Multah about giving him a commendation.

The sun was high in the sky by the time Shaw and her entourage finished eating. It cast a yellow glow over Wimahl River, like the water was reflecting fire. The opposite bank, and its small fishing villages that belonged to the empire of Vinland, were encased in shadow. From this vantage point, Shaw could just make out the sprawling city of Multah to the west. Multah was the largest city in the kingdom, contained to the north by the river docks, where trading ships and fishing boats ported by the hundreds, and to the south by the untamed waters of Lake Bloom. Its twin port of Vingate, Vinland's counterpart on the other bank of the river, was too far to see.

Thinking of Vinland and all its recent troubles gave Shaw a headache, so she made quick work of checking Cow's girth and mounting. Einar tacked his draft to the supply cart that held all their chests, then settled into the driver's seat. Rosamund had long ago shifted back into her horse form, and her cousin quickly clambered atop her.

Shaw led the group down the narrow path that wound from the clifftop to the bank of the river. They passed half a dozen waterfalls that exposed chunks of black basalt and patches of bright green moss. Ferns grew out of the cracks in the rock. The waterfalls ended in streams that flowed lazily toward the great river. Most were shallow enough that the horses, and more important, the cart, had no issue crossing through them.

They reached the base of the cliff. A sign marked the crossroads. To the west, it said Multah was some two hours' ride. To the east, only a half hour away, was Witch Hall. FORBIDDEN TO ALL BUT WITCHES AND FAMILIARS, the sign declared.

Shaw steered the group right. Lush grass surrounded either side of the path. Several more signs warned that the area was forbidden to nonmagical visitors. As they grew closer, Shaw picked out the half-hidden runes and ward stones that provided enchantments to keep the school campus safe from intruders.

The school soon came into view. She couldn't help glancing toward Rosamund. She wished the familiar weren't a horse, so she could more easily see her reaction.

Witch Hall was a bit of a misnomer. There was no single hall. Three massive longhouses stood at the center of campus, surrounded by a dozen smaller buildings. A distant creek marked the eastern border of campus, where it ran from a massive waterfall, taller than any they'd passed thus far. The only true entrance was the road they walked now, coming in from the west. The entrance itself was marked by four massive columns, each from a different type of tree, each representing a different type of magic. Shaw looked, as she always did, to the one made of pine. Carved into it were bone animals of all shapes and sizes. Mice and voles, squirrels and rabbits, deer and moose, and at the top, overlooking them all, the head of a massive bone wolf.

She nudged Cow into a faster walk, passing the open iron gate that spanned those four columns and entering into the boundaries of Witch Hall. Immediately to the left of the entrance was a large stable with several attached corrals and a pasture that stretched all the way down to the river. Cow headed toward it without Shaw having to shift the reins. Like Shaw, she considered Witch Hall more a home than anywhere else in the kingdom.

Shaw dismounted Cow as the rest of her entourage joined her at the front of the stable. She handed Cow's reins to Aklemin with a reminder to be good.

"Me or the horse?" Aklemin asked.

"If you have to ask, then it's for both of you," she responded.

Rosamund had shifted back by the time Shaw turned around. She was upset to have missed it. She would have liked to try to time the speed of Rosamund's shifting. It had seemed fast in the Forest, but was that because of the danger of the situation or was she always capable of quick shifts?

Shaw reminded herself that there'd be plenty of time to observe the bone familiar later. First, she needed to get her enrolled. "Follow me," she told Rosamund.

She wasn't surprised to see Rosamund's cousin join as she led the familiar across campus to a cluster of houses nestled near the base of the waterfall. This close, the air held a touch of mist from the crashing water. Shaw lifted her face higher, enjoying the coolness against the summer heat.

"These are the teachers' cottages," Toketie explained to Rosamund softly as they approached. "They're color-coded, see? White for the bone teachers, black for glass, the pink there is for flower, and the pale blue is ice."

Shaw knocked on the blue door once, to warn the teachers inside that a student was about to enter, then walked in. Rosamund and Toketie stayed outside, which suited her just fine.

Madam Kawak sat around the communal fire in the lounge of the house, saving Shaw the time of having someone fetch her.

"Welcome back, Princess," she said.

"Thank you, Headmistress."

Tikha Kawak had been the ice witch of her grandmother's entourage, but when the Witch Queen had died, Madam Kawak had retreated down the Mountain to take over running Witch Hall. She'd never given Shaw special treatment as a student, but outside of schoolwork she'd always listened to Shaw's requests. Shaw had no reason to believe this time would be an exception.

Before she could say anything, though, Madam Kawak pierced Shaw with a heavy stare. "The stars warned me of your arrival. Venus was particularly bright a week ago, and then last night the North Star flickered. You bring with you an uncertain future."

Shaw frowned. "Uncertain?" Ice witches had never struggled to see her future, not once since she was born.

"Let's see who this herald of change is," Madam Kawak said, as if Shaw hadn't spoken. She stood and left the house. Shaw quickly followed and watched as the headmistress stared at Rosamund.

"Well," the headmistress continued after what felt like the

longest pause in history. "I am Madam Kawak, head witch of this establishment. I see that you will be joining us, Miss . . ."

"Rosamund, ma'am. Rosamund Holt."

Madam Kawak nodded. "You've made things difficult, arriving so close to the beginning of term, and as such a latecomer, but we'll do our best to place you. As for your tuition fees—"

"I will pay for her," Shaw said.

"Hmm," Madam Kawak said, but like Shaw had expected, the headmistress didn't turn it down. "Are you an ice familiar like your sister, Miss Holt?"

"We're cousins, Headmistress," Toketie said. "And Rosy's a bone familiar. She has two shifts."

"Two?"

"Horse and mouse," Rosamund said quietly. "The mouse is new."

The lie sounded better the second time. Shaw wondered if she'd rehearsed it. She wondered why Rosamund would need to.

Madam Kawak nodded. "Fetch Mister Voll if you please, Princess."

Mister Voll? The librarian? Shaw frowned but said nothing. Mister Voll was on duty at the fire when she entered the bone teachers' cottage. She said the headmistress needed to see him about a new student and he jumped to follow.

Mister Voll held out his hand for Rosamund as Madam Kawak introduced them. He was a small man with long blue-black hair kept out of his eyes by a half braid. Far less intimidating than Madam Kawak, and Shaw saw that Rosamund relaxed slightly as she shook his hand.

"Mister Voll will give you a placement exam to determine what grade level you will join," Madam Kawak said.

Shaw wanted to shake herself for not foreseeing this. Of course

Rosamund might be put in a different grade, no matter her age. The chance of observing her in classes diminished greatly if she was placed a few grades below.

But Shaw needed to see Rosamund in action again. She needed to figure her out. If Shaw could only predict what she'd do, how she'd act, she'd be able to return to her own affairs without worrying over this new distraction.

The horseshoe charm at the end of Mister Voll's courtship necklace caught the light as he talked with Rosamund. Shaw let her eyes trace the charm up to the braided white leather it hung from. It was a simple design for a bonded pair, but then, Mister Voll's witch had simple tastes.

Thinking of Mister Voll's witch gave her an idea. She might not get any classes with Rosamund, but every student at Witch Hall was assigned a daily duty. There were no servants to clean or cook, so it was the students who did so under the supervision of the staff. Most new students got assigned cleaning, but that would be a waste of Rosamund's talents.

"Let me show you around," Mister Voll was saying. "Miss Toketie, will you get a couple sets of the school uniform for your cousin? We'll meet you at the stable at the end of our tour. I assume your trunk is there?"

"It is, Mister Voll," Toketie said. "I'll be right back, Rosy."

Mister Voll turned to Shaw then. "Are you joining us, Princess?"

She was tempted, if only to see Rosamund's first impression of campus, but she needed to speak to the stable master before Rosamund was settled into cleaning duty. She declined the offer. Rosamund looked relieved. Did Shaw intimidate her? Some of the other common-born students could barely speak in her presence, but Rosamund hadn't seemed shy before.

She walked back to the stable. Einar had stored their cart near the other wagons under the western stable awning. She checked, but someone in her entourage must have taken her things to her room. Only Rosamund's and Toketie's chests remained. She thanked Einar for guarding them and told him he could go.

She left the cart and headed into the stable building. Mister Jostein was in one of the first stalls, brushing down Einar's draft. She grabbed one of the brushes from the tack room and headed to the stall where Cow had been put.

"That you, Colchuck?" Mister Jostein asked.

"Yes." She began to rub large circles along Cow's saddle line, scrubbing extra hard along the edges of exposed bone. "Have you selected someone to replace Erik, Mister Jostein?"

"You know I haven't," Mister Jostein grumbled.

Erik had graduated last spring, leaving only Oluk Blackwell to help Mister Jostein with the daily horse chores. Mister Jostein had spent the entirety of the summer term burning through replacements, but his standards were high and he'd sent everyone back to their former duties within the week.

"May I suggest a candidate?"

Mister Jostein left the draft's stall to peer over at Shaw. Cow stomped a foot. The mare wasn't a fan of Mister Jostein, but then she wasn't a fan of anyone except Shaw—and even that had taken years to foster.

"None of your entourage have your talent with horses, Colchuck," Mister Jostein said.

"Not my entourage. A new student. Your familiar is giving her a tour right now."

Mister Jostein raised an eyebrow. "Bone witch?"

Shaw looked away, pretending to work at a particularly dirty spot along Cow's withers. "A familiar," she said as casually as she could. "Daughter of a bone horse rancher. I assume she'll be easier to train than Blackwell was."

"Headmistress said no bone familiars can be assigned the same duty as you, Colchuck, you know that."

"I asked her to make that rule and now I'm asking you to grant an exception."

"Princess."

She turned back to the stable master. It was never a good sign when Mister Jostein reverted to formality. "It won't become a problem, sir. I promise."

Mister Jostein scowled. "I don't like this."

"Give her a chance. I witnessed her calm a rampaging bone stallion with a few words and a tug of the reins. Blackwell still flinches when he has to feed the bone horses. You need her."

Mister Jostein said nothing, which was better than an immediate no. Shaw finished brushing down Cow and checking her hooves. There was a murmur of voices as someone approached the outside of the stable. Mister Jostein followed Shaw as she put the brush away and strolled through the stable doors. Mister Voll and Rosamund stood just outside. She leaned against the stable doors, waiting.

"Tupso," Mister Jostein said. He brushed past Shaw to get to the two bone familiars and gave Mister Voll a casual kiss.

"Stop it, Stein, not in front of the students," Mister Voll said, slapping his chest lightly. "Rosamund, this is Jostein Voll. My witch, and the stable master here. Stein, this is Rosamund Holt, a new bone familiar."

"I hear you're from a horse ranch," Mister Jostein said, glancing back at Shaw. She met his gaze evenly.

"I am, sir," Rosamund said.

Mister Voll looked from his witch to Shaw, then back at his witch. "I already told Rosamund that we won't be able to give her stable duty," he said quickly.

Shaw crossed her arms, wondering if she needed to go to the headmistress to get the rule revoked. She wasn't willing to let this go. Rosamund Holt was a puzzle she was determined to solve, one way or another.

Mister Jostein snorted, as if he could hear Shaw's thoughts. "Colchuck pointed out that it'd be foolish of us to pass up the opportunity to play to Holt's strengths," he said. "But I'm never convinced by words alone. You want stable duty, we'll have tryouts tomorrow. See how you do with the horses. Be here soon as lunch ends."

Shaw smiled, successful. Rosamund looked over at her and she could tell the familiar wanted to ask what had happened, but before she could her cousin arrived with a bundle of clothes in her arms. Froya Falk walked next to her, in all her pale, icy glory. Sharp blue eyes missed nothing as she looked from Shaw to the Volls, then to Rosamund.

"Here, Rosy!" Toketie said. "Two white dresses. White is for familiars, black for witches, you know how it is. And this belt here shows your type. Also white, since that's the color representing bone magic. Yes, I know. Bone familiars and glass witches get the short end of the stick with that white on white and black on black. But it's all enchanted not to get dirty easily so you should be okay."

"You're allowed to wear your own clothes on the weekends, but school uniforms are required during class hours," Mister Voll said. "You'll need to repair small tears yourself. Anything larger, ask about getting a replacement. Is that all clear?"

Rosamund nodded, looking overwhelmed.

"Excellent. Now, let's get your trunk and settle you into your new room."

"Let me get mine first," Toketie said. "Froya's going to help me bring it to our suite."

"Will we share a room?" Rosamund asked.

"I'm afraid not, Miss Rosamund," Mister Voll said before Toketie could. "The suites are assigned by grade and classification. You'll get your own room, but you'll share a suite with the senior bone familiars for now. If you end up in a lower grade, we'll see about moving you."

"The rooms are tiny," Toketie said. She grunted as she pulled her trunk to the edge of the cart. Froya grabbed one end and they lifted it out together. "But at least it's private. I know where the bone familiars' suite is, so I'll come visit you later, okay?"

Rosamund looked a bit lost as her cousin left her. Shaw stepped forward, unwilling to let this chance slip away. "I'll take Miss Rosamund to her new room."

Froya glanced back, visibly startled. She was the highest-ranked familiar currently at Witch Hall, socially speaking, and she controlled the gossip like only a Falk could. Shaw could guess what rumors would be flying around school about Rosamund by tomorrow.

Shaw wanted to know what Rosamund would do with the attention of the rest of the school. She hoped it would give her insight into why the familiar had avoided Witch Hall for so long.

If Rosamund Holt was unpredictable, that just meant Shaw needed more chances to observe her in action. Her father always said the truest way to test someone was to throw them into fire.

Time would tell if Rosamund was the type to flee, fight, or sit still and burn.

# Chapter 6

## ROSY

I COULDN'T HELP THINKING I WAS WALKING INTO A TRAP when I headed to stable tryouts Sunday morning. Mister Voll had explained the duties all students got and I knew working in the stable would be better than cleaning the bathrooms, but it bothered me that Shaw had been the one to suggest it. I felt like I was missing something.

The main barn doors were open when I arrived. I headed inside, then stopped and stared. I'd only seen the outside of the barn yesterday, and while it was a large building, barns were rarely impressive from a distance. The inside was a different story. My family's stable only had a few stalls and a couple storerooms. This building, in comparison, was designed to house several dozen horses. I inched forward and saw that every stall had a back opening that led to a small individual corral, connected to one another by a long trough. Through the wide opening in the back of the barn, I could easily see a large pasture where a good twenty more horses grazed.

"Good, you're here," Mister Jostein said from the huge hayloft to the left. "We've got a bit of time still. Let me show you the important bits."

Mister Jostein took me through the rooms on the right. The

first was a massive tack room with an entire wall of cubicles large enough to hold saddles and horse blankets. A peg hung above each cubicle for bridles. Many of the pegs had names written in chalk next to them. The horses' names, judging by some of the more ridiculous ones. I breathed in deeply, enjoying the stark scent of well-oiled leather. Whoever maintained the tack did a good job—even the oldest saddles gleamed with polish.

The next was a storeroom with different types of grain in labeled barrels with buckets and feed bags stacked high next to them. There was a chalkboard on the wall by the door that listed the feeding details for each of the horses. Next to it was the pasture rotation schedule.

Mister Jostein scowled at the boards. "I'll need to update those once the term starts. Students never think to warn me if they decide to bring a new horse, so the beginning of term is always chaos around here."

He turned on his heel and stalked out of the storeroom back to the hayloft. It looked as though he'd been separating out the flakes of a few barrels of hay. I stepped up to help as Mister Jostein explained that we needed to get a good dozen piles of hay ready to put in the stalls.

"Any minute now, the glass witches and familiars will be returning from their trip—" Mister Jostein began, only to be interrupted as someone ran into the barn.

"Mister Jostein! Are you in here?"

"What?" Mister Jostein shouted back.

A boy about my age came into the hayloft, panting for breath. "Mister Jostein! I heard you were having tryouts for stable duty."

Mister Jostein scowled. "It's not open to everyone."

"But you know how much I want to work in the stable."

"Holt's spent her life around horses."

"So have I."

"Taking joyrides on your mother's prize mare isn't the same as working the stable. I've told you this before."

"Please, Mister Jostein, I can prove it to you. Just let me try out with . . ." He trailed off, looking at me.

"Rosamund Holt," I said. I vaguely recognized him as one of the other bone familiars in my suite, but I'd gone to bed early last night, too overwhelmed with everything that had happened to want to socialize with my new suitemates.

"Charles Almstedt," he returned, far more curtly than he'd been talking with Mister Jostein.

Charles was taller than me by a good foot and he wore a beautifully embroidered shirt that I was afraid would get horribly damaged if the bone horses here were anything like the ones back home. His hair was an eye-catching red, brighter than any I'd seen, and kept back in a short braid. His skin was smooth, unblemished by sun or dirt. He would be handsome, if not for the way he stared down his nose at me. I was short, yes, but I knew the difference between being looked down at and being looked down on.

Mister Jostein grumbled a few words under his breath, but then waved his hand for Charles to come closer. "As I was explaining to Holt, we've got a dozen exhausted horses set to arrive this afternoon. They've been out in the Desert for most of the break, so I want to get all of them in stalls. That means we need to move the horses that are currently in the stalls out to the pasture. Clear?"

"Yes, sir," Charles said. I nodded.

"Good. Do the bone horses last or they'll cause a fuss as you bring the others in. Get to it."

Charles was hot on my heels as I went back to the tack room and grabbed a halter and a lead rope. I started with the horses closest to the back of the barn. It was simple work to open up a stall, notch a halter over the horse's face, clip the lead rope to the bottom, and take the horse to the pasture.

It took me and Charles barely ten minutes to get most of the horses to the pasture and turn them free to join the herd. And then we were down to the two stabled bone horses.

I stopped in front of one of the stalls. The mare stuck her head out toward me and I patted her on the nose.

"That's the princess's horse," Charles said.

It was. I recognized the piebald bone mare from that awkward week I spent traveling with Shaw and her entourage. Without the saddle, it was easy to see her exposed spine and the top of her ribs. She was deceptively small for a bone horse and had been surprisingly well-behaved during our travels. I would have thought her exposed bones sewn on, if not for the moment she'd challenged Tempest in the market square.

"You want to take her?" I asked, trying to be nice as I moved over to where the other bone horse was stabled.

Charles didn't answer, but it wasn't like I expected him to thank me. I concentrated on getting the other bone horse haltered. This one was a massive mare that looked more draft than racehorse. She pinned her ears back as I came into the stall and threw her head every time I got close with the halter.

"Don't you want room to stretch your legs, girl?" I asked, trying to soothe her. "That's a nice big field out there."

It took a while, but eventually I was able to fit the halter around the mare's head. I didn't turn my back to her like I'd done with the other horses. It was never a good idea to turn your back on a bone

71

animal. Instead, I kept the lead rope taut as I walked backward out of the stall and down the barn aisle.

The bone horse dug her heels into the ground once, but I coaxed her along with little clicks of my tongue, and eventually the mare realized where we were going. Her ears popped up and then I had the opposite problem of trying to stop her from running me over as she trotted to the pasture.

"Almstedt, control her!" Mister Jostein yelled at Charles.

I finally got my bone horse released and turned back in time to see Shaw's horse bite Charles in the arm. He jerked back with a yelp and, as he did, the mare yanked her lead rope out of his hands.

The bone horse panted, the whites of her eyes showing the telltale signs of bone rage. It was shocking to see, after how calm she'd been all week. What had Charles done to make her snap now?

The bone mare reared up and turned on a single back hoof so gracefully it took my breath away. But then she faced me. She came down on all fours, then bunched up on both back legs. I recognized that look.

She was fully in bone rage now, and I had become her next target.

The mare lunged. My instincts kicked in. I stepped left, then forward. The mare was fast. She pivoted midlunge and snapped at me. Her teeth caught my sleeve. I let myself be pulled with it and got both hands around the mare's mouth, holding it closed. The mare reared and I jumped with her, using my weight to pull the bone horse off balance.

The mare stumbled. I tucked my legs out of the way, then, before the horse could right herself, I swung myself bodily over top of her.

She bucked, back legs kicking high enough that I was thrown

forward. I used the momentum to my advantage, reaching down and snagging the dangling end of the lead rope. I pulled as hard as I could to the right, trying to circle her. The mare took an uncertain step and tried to throw her head. I held tight, keeping her face twisted back toward her shoulder. Slowly, the mare stopped moving, the rage leaving as quickly as it had come.

I looked back at the other end of the aisle where Charles was watching with his mouth gaping open and Mister Jostein with his arms crossed. He tilted his head in my direction, then turned to Charles.

"Almstedt, get the gate for Holt."

Charles stomped forward until he was in reach of the horse. "You did that on purpose to make me look bad. Everyone knows Cow only listens to the princess."

Cow? What a horrible name. I could see it in the pattern of her coat, but it seemed so inelegant for such a beautiful bone horse.

I patted Cow's neck, still miffed at Charles for setting her off. "She's listening to me just fine."

Charles opened his mouth, but then Cow turned toward him with her lips pulled back in warning and he snapped it shut. He skirted the walls of the stalls to keep away from her. I wanted to tell him not to act so scared. Even regular horses would take advantage of that, but bone horses were worse. No wonder she'd acted out if that was how he'd been when taking her from the stall.

Charles opened the gate and I rode Cow through. I was a bit worried about her taking off on me, but I knew better than to show it in my body language. I had no saddle and no reins—only a lead rope to keep control of her head.

But Cow gave me no trouble as I walked her a few feet into the pasture, then dismounted. She did try to bite my arm just like she'd bit Charles when I went to pull her halter off her face, but I pushed her nose away.

"Go on, I've got work to do," I told her.

Cow cantered off to join the herd. I followed her path until my gaze landed on a figure leaning against the other side of the pasture fence.

It was Shaw.

I walked up without fully thinking through my actions. My heart still raced from the tussle with Cow. "What are you trying to do?" I demanded.

"Pardon?" Shaw asked. She sounded surprised, but something in me thought she was putting on an act.

I stalked closer to her, the wolf in my heart urging me to confront this threat before the trap sprang. "Why did you ask the stable master to make an exception for me?"

Shaw looked from me to the herd grazing along the other fence line, then back to me. "Why shouldn't the daughter of a horse rancher be assigned to work the stable?"

I stared, but I could find no hint of duplicity on Shaw's face. I had no proof, but something about the way Charles stormed into the stable made me think that she'd tipped him off about the tryouts. Why? To test him? Or to test me?

This wasn't good. Shaw wasn't supposed to be giving me any attention. She'd paid me back for saving her life and that was supposed to be it. I needed to keep my head down until I got the feralness cure and graduated. I couldn't do that if the Witch King's daughter kept seeking me out.

"Why did Mister Voll say bone familiars weren't allowed to work the stable?" I asked.

Shaw shrugged. It was a surprisingly plebeian gesture.

Before I could figure out what else to say, Mister Jostein yelled for me. "Holt, hurry it up! The group has arrived!"

I turned my back to Shaw, though it felt as dangerous as turning my back to a raging bone animal, and ran back into the barn.

Mister Jostein led Charles and me out the front of the stable in time to see a huge party coming in from the main road. Two staff members rode in front of the group. Trailing behind them was a caravan of four large carts. Older students held the reins to the cart horses while, on either side, younger students walked in small groups. Another adult rode a horse to bring up the rear of the caravan.

"We're back!" yelled the closest staff member. She waved her arm wildly, nearly falling off her white gelding.

"I do believe they're aware," said the staff member riding next to her, tone exasperated. This one rode a beautiful black gelding, which matched her glossy black belt. Everyone in the group, adult and student, had a black belt. It took me a second to remember what Toketie had told me about the color system, but it came to me eventually. Glass magic. These were all glass witches and familiars.

"Welcome back, Madam Bai, Madam Xu," Mister Jostein said. He gave the two women a brusque nod, then strode to the back of the party to help the man bringing up the rear.

"I'll get Madam Xu's horse. You get Madam Bai's," Charles said.

Charles walked up to the woman on the black gelding without delay. Behind the two women, the older students steered the carts next to the stable and stopped the horses there. The rest began unloading the carts, jostling one another to collect their belongings.

I assumed the energetic woman on the white gelding was Madam Bai and went to her. She was even stranger up close. She wore a mismatched combination of pink and yellow. Her hair was cut shorter than I'd ever seen on a woman and it stuck up like she'd just rolled out of bed. Her black belt was the only tame thing about her.

"Hello there," Madam Bai greeted me, volume too loud for how close I stood. "You're tall for a new student."

I'd never been called tall before. Did she really think I was eleven or twelve? Or was she joking? I just smiled, not sure what to say, then focused on dealing with her horse.

After stabling Madam Bai's mare, I went to help with the draft horses attached to the carts. The glass students swarmed around me, taking their trunks and heading to their suites. A few gave me curious looks. Apparently Witch Hall was small enough that new students stood out. I did my best to ignore the attention.

Once all the horses were stabled and the carts stowed away, I headed into the tack room. The saddle from Madam Xu's horse, the one Charles was supposed to care for, had been dumped uncere-moniously in an unlabeled stall. One of the flaps was folded the wrong way. I wrinkled my nose at the potential damage to the leather.

"Mister Jostein?" I called. "What's the name of Madam Xu's horse?"

"Banye. Top left."

I put Banye's tack away, making sure to store it properly, then I grabbed a curry comb from one of the tables and headed out to Banye's stall to brush the gelding down.

One of the students wandered in through the barn doors. Judging by his black belt, he'd come in with all the glass students who had just arrived.

"Do you need more help?" he asked.

Before I could answer, Mister Jostein popped his head out from the hayloft. "Where's Almstedt?"

"He's outside, talking to Madam Xu," the student said. "Telling her that he won't be working the kitchens this term. Did you really agree to put him on stable duty, Mister Jostein?"

"I haven't agreed to horseshit," Mister Jostein said. "He barged his way into Holt's tryout and now he's skiving off? Does he think I'm just going to ignore that?" Mister Jostein turned to me. "Give me your honest opinion, Holt. Would you give Almstedt stable duty after what you saw today?"

I lowered the curry brush, uncomfortable. "He did fine?"

"That a question or a statement?"

I looked at the other student. He made a funny face, then shrugged.

"I wouldn't put him in charge of bone horses," I said finally. "But it looks like there's only a few of those compared to, what, three dozen nonmagical horses? So that's probably okay?" I hesitated, remembering Banye's saddle. "He did seem a bit rushed sometimes."

"And if I had to choose between you and him? Who would do a better job?"

This time, I didn't hesitate. At the end of the day, no matter Shaw's reasoning for getting me this chance, I would prefer stable duty to anything else. "I have more experience than him, sir, and I enjoy the work. I'm not sure why he wants stable duty, but it didn't seem like that was his reason."

"No, it most certainly isn't," Mister Jostein said dryly. "I've decided. Blackwell, walk Holt here through our typical check-in procedure with the horses. I'm going to have a chat with Almstedt."

"Yes, sir," the student said. "Nice to meet you," he added to me as Mister Jostein stalked away. "I'm Oluk."

My head was starting to hurt from the number of new people I'd met. At least Oluk seemed friendlier than Charles. He was cute too. The tips of his brown hair were sun-kissed blond. His eyes were a beautiful brown, the color of pine bark, and he had freckles covering his face. He was only a few inches taller than me, but there was enough bulk to his arms that I guessed he was used to the kind of labor that horse care required.

"Rosamund," I returned. "Do you have stable duty, then?"

"Sure do. For a couple terms now. Was one of the cleaners before that, but I prefer mucking stalls to scrubbing walls, personally."

I smiled at that, because I'd been thinking the same thing. I was still uncertain about being at Witch Hall, but working the stable was a little slice of home away from home.

"Come on, I'll show you around," Oluk said.

Oluk Blackwell was a chatterer. He talked his way through brushing down the horses, then checking their hooves and the lines of their girth straps and saddles. I really didn't need much help knowing what to do in the stable, so Oluk talked about other things. He explained how he and the other glass students had been out at a large Lammas celebration in the Desert. Each of the seasonal holidays were associated with one of the magical types and Lammas was the time when glass magic was strongest, just like Samhain was for bone magic, Candlemas for ice magic, and Beltane for flower magic.

Lammas always included extravagant feasts and fun competitive games for people of all ages to play. I knew the festival was a much bigger deal in the Obsidian Desert than it was in the towns at the edge of the Bone Forest, but hearing Oluk speak about it made the event sound even more magical.

I said little, happy to listen as Oluk jumped from topic to topic. He'd been at Witch Hall since he was twelve. He was a glass familiar in his final year. His first shift was a garter snake, but he'd just gotten his second—a rattlesnake—that summer. He'd grown up on the outskirts of the Desert, but he spent most of his breaks at Witch Hall.

"My parents are obsidian miners and we don't have much," he said, a touch of embarrassment in his tone. "I'm a scholarship student, actually, but that only pays for tuition, not travel home. The only time I can see them is over summer break, since us glass students all caravan to the Desert for the Lammas ritual."

"Can't you write them letters?" I asked. Toketie usually sent a few each term.

"I could," Oluk said slowly. "But my parents don't really know how to read."

He looked horribly ashamed to have to admit it, and I felt bad for asking. "My family's not rich either," I said, to try to make up for it. "We're horse ranchers. My cousin's only able to visit home over break because she hitches a ride with a student a few years younger than us who lives in Woodside. That's the next town over from ours."

"Your cousin?"

"Toketie Holt. She's an ice familiar."

Oluk made a funny face. "Oh, yeah, I know her." He refilled the grain bucket, silent for a second. "I hope you don't mind if I ask . . . you're kind of old to be a new student?"

"My family needed help with the ranch. Witch Hall is expensive and I didn't know about the scholarships." That wasn't even a lie. It would have helped my family a lot if Toketie had been able to get her tuition funded. It was too late now—Papa had already paid for Toketie's senior year. Then again, maybe there was only one scholarship per year. It sounded like Oluk's family needed it more than mine did.

Shaking my head, I continued, "It's okay though. My gran's a bone familiar, so she trained me. But the princess came to visit our village and she offered to pay for me."

I paused. Maybe that was what Oluk meant by scholarship. Maybe the royal family paid for all poor students who showed potential? Had I been overthinking it too much?

But Oluk had stopped in the middle of pouring some grain into Banye's feeder, as if my words had shocked him. "The princess is paying for you?"

"Yeah," I said, then nothing else.

"Is that why Mister Jostein made an exception for you?"

I glanced sharply at Oluk. "Do you know why bone familiars aren't usually allowed on stable duty?"

Oluk bit his lip and looked down the aisle, as if checking that Mister Jostein wasn't listening in. "Because the princess works here. And she doesn't have a familiar. Before stable duty, she worked at the library, and a ton of bone familiars requested that duty to get closer to her. Or they'd pretend to study in the library just for a chance to talk to her. So when she transferred to the stable, Mister Jostein put his foot down and said he didn't want any distractions. Charles has been trying to change his mind for years."

I slowly put the pieces together in my mind. "Because Charles wants to bond with her?"

"I mean, who wouldn't? Whichever bone familiar bonds with the princess will help rule the kingdom one day."

"Why doesn't he just ask her, then? Or any of the bone familiars? Why go through all the trouble of switching duties?"

"You mean, why doesn't Charles ask to court her?" Oluk shook his head wildly. "That's not how courtship works! You can't ask someone of higher status than you. And Shaw and her entourage have the highest status in school."

"Oh." Courtship rules weren't nearly so strict back home, but the idea of higher status was a lot less clear too.

Oluk followed me into the feed room to put the leftover grain away, his eyebrows furrowed in thought. I clanged the bucket lid and looked at him pointedly.

"Oh, sorry," he said, and quickly poured his own grain back in. "It's just, none of the princess's entourage have courted anyone yet. Most of us think they're waiting for her to choose her familiar first. Because Shaw's familiar is supposed to lead them. The other familiars of the entourage, I mean. That's why Charles is so popular. Because he's the strongest bone familiar in school and everyone thinks the princess will choose him eventually."

"So, Charles wanted to work at the stable to get closer to Shaw so she'll decide to court him," I summarized. "Why hasn't she done it yet? Courted him?"

Oluk shrugged. "I've heard him say that she doesn't want to bond too quickly or it might hurt the other bone familiars' feelings, so that's why she's put off asking him." Oluk leaned forward and lowered his voice even more. "But it's her final year and if she hasn't asked to court Charles yet, she never will."

"She should just court another familiar, then. Make it clear so he'll move on."

"She's never shown interest in anyone." He paused and I could guess what he was thinking. That Shaw had personally paid for me to come to Witch Hall. That she'd told Mister Jostein to make an exception and let me have stable duty.

In truth, I figured her interest had more to do with Gran, with how Gran had gone feral and accused Shaw of murdering Pops. I couldn't let Shaw figure out what my plan was. She'd seen the worst of Gran—she'd probably tell the jarls' council to reject my proposal if she knew what I was going to do.

The trap I felt hanging over my head creaked in warning.

"We're done for the day," Mister Jostein said from the doorway of the feed room. "If you haven't figured it out yet, Holt, you passed. I'll tell the headmistress to put you on stable duty. Be here the hour before breakfast. Blackwell, make sure she understands the routine tomorrow morning. I have a staff meeting, but I'll double-check your work after."

"Yes, sir," Oluk said.

"Good. Dinner's probably started. Get out of here."

Oluk led me out of the stable and toward the western long-house. "Sounds like you'll have the same schedule as me," he said. "I help with feeding and mucking twice a day. And with pasture rotation, but that's only on the weekends."

"What about Shaw?" I asked. If she was on the same schedule, it would be hard to avoid her.

Oluk gave me a long look. "I don't see her much. Her duty's more about exercising the horses and maintaining the tack."

I relaxed. Perhaps Shaw had been hoping I'd be assigned the same, since I had the experience for it, but I was glad Mister Jostein had paired me up with Oluk instead.

I just had to figure out how to keep my head down to starve any rumors that started about Shaw wanting to court me. No matter how ridiculous the thought, I knew how gossip spread. I did not want that kind of attention.

# Chapter 7

I'd been sitting with Toketie at meals and unfortunately that also meant sitting with her suitemates. The ice familiars were loud and talked over one another like, well, like a flock of birds. There was never a moment of silence at their table. It made me long for quiet mornings in the Bone Forest, eating breakfast with Gran as sunlight began to trickle through the dense canopy.

The ice familiars were particularly chatty at breakfast on Monday, going over their class schedules for the term.

I nudged Toketie when she took a break to fork up some food. "You said classes were assigned based on year and magical type? Like the suites?"

"That's right," Toketie said, holding a hand up to cover her lips even as she talked with her mouth full. At home, Mama would have scolded her, but I'd noticed all the ice familiars doing the same thing, as if they didn't dare stay silent long enough to chew and swallow.

"Everyone has three classes a day and one free period," one of Toketie's friends told me. I hadn't bothered remembering any of their names, except Froya Falk. And I only remembered Froya's because of how often everyone in the group said it. Froya, it seemed, was the undisputed leader of the senior ice familiars.

"Except on Fridays," another ice familiar said, speaking over the first. "There are only two classes on Friday. Double-length."

"Those are the specialty workshops," Toketie said, cutting in. "Monday through Thursday, everyone in the same grade and magical type will have the same schedule. Most classes are mixed with at least one of the other types. As ice familiars, we share a lot of classes with the ice witches in our grade. But here"—she showed me her schedule—"we have this class with the senior flower familiars. And this one is with all senior familiars."

"The Friday workshops can be mixed though," the first familiar added. "Depending on your workshop, you may be with much younger students or witches from other types or whatever."

"What grade have you been placed in?" Froya asked.

There was a second's pause as I realized she was addressing me. No one spoke while they waited. None of the ice familiars ever interrupted Froya.

"Uh, not sure yet," I said. "I have my placement exams with Mister Voll today."

"You'll be starting classes a day late," Toketie said, frowning.

I shrugged. "I'll catch up. It's just a day. Hopefully I'll be in that class with you. The one with all the senior familiars."

"You think you'll be placed as a senior?" Froya asked.

I didn't like her tone. I looked to Toketie, hoping she'd say something about how I was always Papa's best student in our village school, but she'd turned to talk with another familiar and wasn't paying attention anymore.

"Guess we'll see," I mumbled, and quickly finished eating.

84

I HEADED TO THE LIBRARY after breakfast. Mister Voll had pointed it out during our tour, but now that I had to find it on my own, I was a bit lost.

I knew the library wasn't in any of the three main halls. Two of them had all the classrooms, while the one in the center had the kitchens and the massive dining room. The four buildings by the waterfall were for the teachers. The bone familiars' dormitory was a building near the stable. The two buildings at the bank of Wimahl River, just left of the school's small boat dock, were bathhouses.

I headed for one of the smaller buildings south of the stable, but as I got close I saw that it had multiple entrances. I knew from my own dormitory building that each entrance led to a different suite. I didn't know whose building it was—the bone witches or the glass familiars or any of the other possibilities—but it clearly wasn't the library.

I turned right and headed across campus. Students ranging in age from about ten to eighteen moved around me, heading to their first class of the term. Several stared at me as I passed. I thought about asking for directions, but I didn't want to look like even more of an outsider.

The third building I came upon had a single entrance. I opened the heavy door and peeked in.

*Yes*, I'd found it. I pulled the door open the rest of the way and stepped inside.

The library was cluttered in the best way. There were books everywhere. Stacks as tall as me teetered on the floor. Smaller stacks covered several tables. Even the bookshelves that lined each of the walls had jumbled messes of books and scrolls facing in every possible direction.

A large firepit sat in the center of the room, directly under the circular opening in the roof. It was unlit—no need for heat in the middle of the summer—but I imagined how nice it would be in the winter to study at one of the dozen or so low tables scattered about the room while a roaring fire provided warmth and light.

A bone squirrel chittered from the top of one of the bookcases. It had a scroll tucked under its arm and as I watched, it climbed down to the middle shelf and placed the scroll between two leaning tomes. Task done, the squirrel jumped from the bookcase and turned into a human midair.

Mister Voll landed on his feet and smiled at me. "There you are, Miss Rosamund. Ready for your test?"

"Yes, sir."

Mister Voll led me to one of the low tables. It was too short for chairs, but plump cushions circled it. A few sheets of paper already lay at one of the spots, alongside a graphite stick to write with.

I sat down and picked up the stick. I knew I had to do well on this test. I didn't want to be placed a few grades back. I needed to graduate with Toketie this spring, so I could go to the jarls' council and petition Gran's release.

Besides, I didn't want to stay at Witch Hall any longer than I had to.

The exam wasn't terrible. There were questions on the history of the Cursed Kingdom and its surrounding nations, most of which I knew from lessons with Papa. The writing section made my hand cramp from how quickly I answered it. I had to write the draft of a formal document giving land to a military veteran. Little did Mister Voll know, I'd read over that exact type of document so many times—the one the former Witch Queen had written to gift our land to Gran and Pops. I'd spent many hours pulling sections from it in order to help my family prepare for the next time the jarl came to town. It was easy to re-create it for the test, though I had to change the signature to the Witch King.

The math problems were simple too. I didn't enjoy math, but Papa was something of an expert. He'd been apprenticed to the financial advisor of Gravetown's jarl when Mama courted him. He'd forced me to do a fair share of mathematical calculations growing up.

The hardest part was the section on magical theory. I discovered quickly that I knew very little about the hows and whys of witch magic or familiar shifting. I wrote my best guesses, but I had to hide my nerves as I handed the completed test back to Mister Voll.

Mister Voll said he would grade my test before lunch and gave me the rest of the morning to explore the campus and familiarize myself with Witch Hall. I did so, not wanting to get lost again like I had that morning. Luckily the campus was small—only an acre or so larger than my family's ranch. It wasn't long before I'd made a mental map of all the buildings, even if I couldn't tell which dormitory was which.

I returned after lunch for my practical exam.

"You did very well," Mister Voll told me. "Tested out of all the basics, at least. You'll need to catch up on magical theory, but your comprehension scores were high enough."

"Does that mean I can be a senior?"

Mister Voll hesitated. "Let's see how well you do on your practical exam."

As we walked outside, I tried to figure out how I could do well enough to get Mister Voll to place me as a senior, without doing *so* well that he got suspicious about my shifting abilities.

We arrived at a small clearing at the edge of the waterfall's creek. Mister Voll stepped back, giving me space to shift.

"Start with your first shift," he said, holding up a handheld clock. "I'll time the seconds."

I wanted to downplay my abilities, but the threat of being put in a lower grade was too high. So long as I only showed off the horse and the mouse, I'd be okay.

Mister Voll nodded for me to begin, and I shifted into the horse.

"Excellent!" Mister Voll said, jotting down a time in his journal. "Now to human."

I shifted. Then again. And again. Mister Voll timed me from human to horse to human a dozen times, before calling for a break.

"You are remarkably consistent," Mister Voll said. "Not the fastest I've seen, but steady. Now, the headmistress mentioned that you have a second form? A new one?"

"Yes, sir."

"Shift into it, if you please."

I shifted into the mouse. Far above me, Mister Voll muttered, "Just a touch slower," then he called for me to shift back.

I had to show off the mouse a few more times, then Mister Voll announced the next test. "You'll shift into horse or mouse as I call for it. I'll try not to fall into a pattern, so listen closely. We'll see if you can be consistent with the mouse, or if you'll fall back onto the more familiar horse shift."

He called for the mouse first, then the horse. I breathed through the pain as my skin expanded and my bones stretched up and up and up, finishing with my tiny mouse ears elongating into the horse's fuzzier ones.

Mister Voll opened his mouth, closed it, and opened it again.

Only then did I realize my mistake. I should have shifted into a human between the mouse and horse. I'd only figured out how to quick shift between my forms a few years ago. It wasn't a skill a beginner would have.

I stomped a foot, angry at myself. It snapped Mister Voll out of his stunned silence. He cleared his throat.

"Apologies. I do believe we can safely place you above the basics, Miss Rosamund. Now, let's keep going. Mouse. Yes. Human now. Mouse. Human. Horse. Human. Mouse. Horse. Look at you, Miss Rosamund! Very impressive."

The test finally ended and I shifted back into my human skin. Both the horse and the mouse were a bit miffed to have been called and sent back so many times, but I soothed their voices with a hand over my heart and a promise to spend a longer stretch of time exploring Witch Hall in both forms later.

Mister Voll led me back to the library. "Well, you've certainly earned a spot in the Advanced Shapeshifting workshop," he said. "It's the highest level we have, only for familiars with two or more consistent shifts."

"What about the other workshop?" I asked.

"Ah, that one will depend on your grade. All seniors are in the same workshop this term. Let's do your final test and then we'll see."

We arrived back at the library and Mister Voll held the door for me. He gestured for me to sit, then bustled around pulling out small jars. Only once they were all in front of me did he explain.

The final test was about my sensitivity to the dead. As a bone familiar, I had an innate amount of it, but apparently with training I could learn to increase it. I spent fifteen minutes having to point out which of the identical jars once held a trapped phantom. I got it right only a third of the time.

"Don't feel discouraged," Mister Voll told me. "That's very normal for unbonded familiars. We may be connected to death, but familiars are more sensitive to active magic, while witches can feel traces of magic. It helps them with rituals and the like. For us, the ability to sense the dead is more about natural instincts to protect our witches."

"Does that mean I should be able to sense if a ghost is nearby?" I asked, thinking about my family's graveyard. Gran had never taught me much outside of shifting. I wondered if she knew any of this herself. If I could learn how to sense when Pops's ghost was nearby, and could teach that to Gran, would that help her with her grief?

"With training, yes, though the quickest way to increase your sensitivity is to bond," Mister Voll said. "But there are tricks to improving even without the bond. Don't worry, you're not behind on this. The senior bone students actually have a class this fall about learning to distinguish between the different types of dead, and then I believe there's a course in the spring that covers communing with the dead more directly."

Mister Voll put the jars away in the corner of the library, then grabbed a blank piece of paper, writing my name at the top.

"Now, you did pass the minimum requirements to slot in with the seniors," he said. "But I want to encourage you to start one grade back. Since you missed the first term of the year, you won't be allowed to fail a single course if you want to graduate in the spring. Students are only allowed to fail five courses a year in order to move on to the next grade, or in the case of seniors, to graduate."

I understood what he was saying. "And since each term has five courses, that means I've basically already failed them. Since I wasn't here for them."

"Yes, exactly. Now if you start a grade back, you'll get more of a chance to settle into the learning environment of Witch Hall with classes that will be slightly easier to adjust to."

"I want to be a senior."

Mister Voll frowned at me.

"I can do it," I insisted. "Please, Mister Voll."

"Yes, well, it's your choice." He began to write out a schedule for me. "Now, there is one other thing you'll need to do in order to graduate this year," he said as he inked over his own writing so the schedule wouldn't smudge. "Your senior project."

"I know about that. Tokey, I mean, Toketie told me about hers."

"Has she? Wonderful. You'll need to decide on a topic and choose a faculty advisor. One of the teachers who you think has the most experience with your topic. You're at a deficit on this too. You must get an advisor to approve your project idea before the end of the term, understood?"

"I will. Thank you, Mister Voll."

"My pleasure, Miss Rosamund." He handed me my schedule.

I looked over it eagerly.


Rosamund Holt
BONE FAMILIAR—SENIOR

MONDAY—THURSDAY
    DUTY BLOCK—STABLEHAND
        Jostein Voll—Stable
    BREAKFAST
    BLOCK 1—THE DEAD AND UNDEAD
        Moll Dyer—RM 4
    BLOCK 2—SURVIVAL SKILLS
        Xiaoqing Bai—GR 2

LUNCH

BLOCK 3—FREE PERIOD

BLOCK 4—COURT ETIQUETTE

    Gudmund Sorensen—GR 1

DUTY BLOCK—STABLEHAND

    Jostein Voll—Stable

DINNER

<u>FRIDAY</u>

DUTY BLOCK—STABLEHAND

    Jostein Voll—Stable

BREAKFAST

MORNING BLOCK—ADVANCED SHAPESHIFTING

    Suzhen Xu—GR 2

LUNCH

AFTERNOON BLOCK—FAMILIAR COMBAT

    Suzhen Xu & Xiaoqing Bai—GR 3

DUTY BLOCK—STABLEHAND

    Jostein Voll—Stable

DINNER

I recognized Court Etiquette, as that was the class on Toketie's schedule she'd said all senior familiars were taking. That and the second workshop. My gut twisted at the title of it. Familiar Combat.

"I thought you said all seniors were taking a workshop together? Why does this say it's for familiars?"

"Ah, all seniors take Combat, but it's split into two sections. You'll be learning with the other familiars except for a few combined classes," Mister Voll explained.

I shouldn't have been surprised that Combat was a required

class. Witch Hall was at the service of the Witch King and the Witch King's army. Shaw's future army. I didn't want to learn how to fight, but I'd have to do well enough to pass.

For Gran, I reminded myself. I was doing this for Gran.

I thanked Mister Voll, schedule held tight in one hand.

Before I could leave, Mister Voll called out to me again, "Miss Rosamund?"

"Yes, sir?"

"Feel free to come to the library any time you need help. It's what I'm here for."

I nodded and left. I was determined to do well. I would graduate on time like my cousin and Froya Falk and Charles Almstedt. I would show everyone that Papa's schooling had prepared me just fine for the rigor of Witch Hall.

I WAS ANNOYED TO SEE that Shaw was in my very first class—The Dead and Undead, taught by Madam Dyer. Mister Voll had told me this class was for all senior bone students, but I hadn't thought through what that meant until walking into the classroom. It was almost enough to make me wish I'd taken Mister Voll's offer to drop down a grade. I still didn't know what game Shaw was playing, but I couldn't let it distract me from my goals: find the flower witch with the cure for Gran, pass all my classes to graduate, and petition the jarls' council.

Shaw sat in the very first row with Charles on her right, angled in his chair as he talked to her about something. There were about two dozen senior bone witches and familiars, judging by the size of this class. I was looking around for an open seat when a middle-aged woman with dark auburn hair breezed passed me on her way to the front of the room.

"Take a seat, Miss Rosamund," the woman I assumed was Madam Dyer said. "I don't tolerate tardiness or absences in my class. You will study what you missed yesterday on your own time and do not come to me if you fall behind on your work. Is that understood?"

"Yes, ma'am."

"Why are you still standing there?"

I spied an open desk in the middle of the room and hurried over to it. Several of the bone students snickered. I felt my face redden and hated that my pale skin would make it obvious to everyone. Shaw, I noticed, didn't turn back to look at me and I was begrudgingly grateful for it. Maybe she'd moved on from her dangerous interest in me. I could only hope.

The Dead and Undead could have been an interesting class, but Madam Dyer spent as much time expounding on the virtues of the Witch King as she did actually talking about the differences between ghosts and phantoms. If Madam Dyer was to be believed, before the Witch King took over, the Cursed Kingdom was a lawless land covered in roaming monsters and vengeful spirits.

Still, I stayed after class to talk to her. I'd spent yesterday evening coming up with ideas for my senior project. I wanted to see if it would be possible for unbonded bone familiars to commune with the dead like witches could. It seemed like Madam Dyer would be the best advisor for that kind of project.

"Miss Rosamund Holt," Madam Dyer said, with a particular emphasis on my last name. "What do you need?"

"I wanted to talk to you about maybe advising my senior project." Under her unforgiving stare, I explained my idea. "But I don't really know the best place to start. If you could just give me an idea of where to begin—"

Madam Dyer sniffed. "I don't know what Tupso was thinking, putting you with the seniors. You are untrained and underqualified for Witch Hall."

"I'm not," I said, too angry to stop myself. "My grandmother is a bone familiar and she trained me."

"Your grandmother is a traitor. I wouldn't trust a word of her so-called training."

I bristled and the voices in my heart all woke up to grumble their displeasure, but Madam Dyer continued before I could say anything.

"In case you're too ignorant to take a hint, I will not be your advisor. I don't expect you to pass this term, so why would I waste my time helping you with a senior project?" Madam Dyer turned her back on me and began to erase what she'd written on the chalkboard.

I took several deep breaths. I couldn't afford to yell. Madam Dyer might not believe in me, but I *would* pass my classes, and that included hers. I turned on my heel and stormed out.

"Rosamund."

Shaw, it seemed, had been waiting for me outside the classroom. A good half of our class was still milling about in the hall, shooting sideways looks between the princess and me. Charles outright glared as I marched up to Shaw, still fuming over Madam Dyer's dismissal.

"Yes?" I asked, still struggling to control my temper. I didn't need this right now. I had to find my next class, wherever it was.

A few murmurs started up among the eavesdropping bone students. Should I have been more polite? Greeted Shaw with a curtsy and a "How can I help you, Princess?" No, thank you, I wasn't interested in being courteous to Death's Heir.

"I would like to offer you a chance to look over my notes," Shaw said. "Since you missed our first class yesterday. Madam Dyer covered specters."

"One of my suitemates can help me," I said curtly. "Excuse me, I have to get to my next class."

I left before Shaw could insist and did my best to ignore the prickle of dozens of eyes at my back.

# Chapter 8

APPARENTLY, THE GR ON MY SCHEDULE STOOD FOR grounds, meaning those classes were in one of the clearings designated as outdoor classrooms. I was several minutes late by the time I found my Survival Skills class.

For a second, I thought I'd gotten the location wrong after all. Despite the wooden signpost saying GR 2, there was no one in the clearing.

Then I heard a hiss near my feet. I froze, knowing better than to move if a snake was nearby. Except it wasn't a wild snake. A small black snake lifted its upper body off the ground as if to greet me. Glass scales covered its head and a small patch halfway down its back.

I kneeled down, recognizing it as a glass garter snake. "Oluk?"

The snake nodded.

"Are you in Survival Skills too?"

Another nod, then the garter dropped back to the ground, slithered a few feet away, and shifted into Oluk.

"All senior glass and bone familiars are in this class together," Oluk said, even as he was still forming a human mouth—the *s*'s in his words elongated like a hiss. "I figured you must have been put in a lower grade when you didn't show."

"No, I just got lost. Where is everyone else?"

"Searching."

"Searching?"

Oluk pointed at a piece of paper tacked to a nearby tree. I walked over to it and read the scrawling handwriting aloud: "*Welcome to Survival Skills, students. You have until lunch starts to find me. Good luck. Madam Bai.*"

Madam Bai. Where had I heard that name before?

Pink and yellow flashed in my mind. That's right, one of the women who rode in with the glass students.

"Is Madam Bai a glass familiar?" I asked Oluk.

He nodded, the same quick up and down he'd done in his snake form. "She can shift into a glass vine snake. Bright green. Venomous too, but she hasn't bitten a student in years."

"Right, okay." I hadn't expected this out of class, but it was called Survival Skills. Playing hide-and-seek with our teacher was a bit like hunting prey. "Any ideas?"

"I checked all the burrows around the clearing in case she went to ground, but I couldn't smell any signs of another snake. I know she's still at Witch Hall somewhere because Madam Kawak yelled at her last time she took students off campus. Other than that . . ." Oluk shrugged.

"Well, I guess we better get looking then."

"Together?"

"Is that okay?"

Oluk looked a bit surprised, but he nodded again, even quicker this time. "No, that's fine!" He shifted back into his garter form. I went horse, so I could look up at the tree branches and building rafters while Oluk searched the ground level. Careful not to step on my new friend, I trotted off in a random direction.

By lunch, Oluk and I ran into all of our classmates around campus, but none of us had found Madam Bai. We headed back to GR 2 only to find her waiting for us with a wide grin. "Better luck next time, kids!" she cackled. "See you tomorrow." With a wink, she shifted into a bright green snake. Even as I watched, she disappeared into a pile of brush and vanished.

I smiled before I could help myself. I loved a hunt, and that game of hide-and-seek had stirred the interest of all the predators in my heart. I already couldn't wait for tomorrow's class.

My happiness lasted only until I got to the dining hall and lined up for lunch. It felt like every student in school was staring at me. I hunched my shoulders and grabbed food without looking.

At the senior ice familiars' table, the squawking grated on my ears worse than usual. The predators in my heart were still primed, wanting to run, to chase. The attention was uncomfortable.

Toketie and her friends wanted to talk about my placement exam and Mister Voll slotting me in with the seniors. I managed to get by with short answers until they moved on to talking about one of the classes they'd had that morning. I ignored them as best I could, letting my gaze wander across the dining room.

I'd noticed that people all tended to sit in the same areas for every meal. The teachers had two round tables on the far right of the hall, slightly separated from the square tables for the students. The largest of the student tables sat sixteen, like the one I was at with Toketie and her suitemates, but the sizes ranged all the way down to two-person tables pushed against the far left wall.

Shaw and her friends sat at an eight-person table. It gave the four of them an excess amount of room, where most everyone else was bumping elbows with their neighbors. I'd assumed, the first night, that it was a way of rubbing their status in everyone else's faces. But I wondered if there was a subtler purpose too. A message to the familiars at the school that Shaw's entourage still needed to be completed.

But if they refused to court any of the interested familiars, wasn't that message more of a taunt?

Shaw looked up and I quickly turned away before she could lock eyes with me. My gaze ended up on the two-person tables at the wall. Unlike the group tables, I'd noticed those switched occupants more often. Pairs of witches and familiars, I figured. Having a more intimate meal, away from their friends, to get to know each other better. I saw more than one set of hands held across the table.

Except there was one table with only a single occupant. I doubled back to look again. Oluk sat by himself at a table in the corner. He ate slowly, methodically, without even a book to keep him company.

Where were his friends? He was so chatty during our shared stable duty, I'd been sure he had tons of them.

I turned to the ice familiars, interrupting whatever they'd been saying. "Do you know Oluk?" It took me only a second to remember his last name. Mister Jostein shouted it often enough. "Oluk Blackwell?"

"We do," Froya said slowly. "All the seniors know each other."

"Then do you know why he's sitting alone? Shouldn't he be with the other glass familiars?" I pointed, in case they didn't believe me.

The ice familiars went quiet, uncomfortably so. A few shook their heads.

"He always sits alone," Froya said. "I'm sure he's fine."

"But why?" I supposed it was possible that Oluk liked to eat alone, but he was so eager to talk with me as we fed the horses and filled hay nets and mucked stalls together.

Then I remembered his surprise when I asked to partner with him during our Survival Class. If the other senior glass familiars were in that class, shouldn't he have been searching with them?

"He's a scholarship student," one of the ice familiars mumbled, saying *scholarship* as if it were a bad word.

My stomach dropped. "So am I," I said.

Froya waved a hand. "You are not. You saved the princess's life and she's funding you in repayment. That's not pity money, that's a well-earned reward."

I scowled at Toketie. "You told them? About what happened in the Forest?"

"Why shouldn't I have?"

Because I didn't want to stand out. How could I keep my head down if everyone knew the whole reason I was at Witch Hall was that I'd supposedly saved the princess's life? Never mind that I hadn't cared about her at all—that if Toketie hadn't been there, I might very well have left Shaw and her entourage to their fate.

"Even if Oluk is a scholarship student, that's no reason to ignore him," I said, unwilling to give up the point.

"He's not exactly engaging company," Froya said.

"He's disgustingly dull," one of the ice familiars added.

"Barely passes his classes," another said. "He had to have remedial lessons for his first three years. Couldn't even read when he came here."

The fact that Oluk hadn't been able to read surprised me, though it shouldn't have. He'd said his parents couldn't read. Who would have taught him before he came to Witch Hall?

But that wasn't his fault, and calling him dull because of it was horrible.

"I truly have no idea how he filled out the scholarship application, or why they thought to give it to him over the other applicants," Froya said.

"Like you said, pity money," one of the other ice familiars said.

The group laughed at that. Not Toketie, but she didn't say anything against her friends either.

I opened my mouth to argue, but Toketie stepped on my foot. "Leave it," she hissed, then started up a conversation about the coming full-moon assembly, the first of the term.

I was still angry about the conversation when I went to my final class of the day.

Etiquette was taught by an ice witch named Mister Sorensen. He was tall and thin, with eyes as pale as his ice-blue shirt and wispy blond hair. As soon as I entered the clearing for class, he grabbed my hand and pulled me uncomfortably forward so he could peer at my palm. He smelled strangely sweet, like overripe fruit. I wanted out of his space immediately, but Mister Sorensen's grip was tight.

"What's this?" Mister Sorensen murmured. He traced a line on my palm with one long finger. "A thin romantic line suddenly thickens. You will struggle to find your witch, but the bond will be strong once you do." The witch paused and looked at me. "But this uncertain lifeline . . . you must be wary of indecision and doubt."

I shivered, unnerved. Mister Sorensen smiled and squeezed my hand. "Not to worry, I'm here to teach you the etiquette you will need to impress your future witch. By the end of the term, you shall know how to properly behave."

I hated everything he'd just said. "For my future witch, sir? I thought it was for court?"

"Yes, as you can clearly see, this class is for all the senior familiars," Mister Sorensen said. "Witches and familiars who graduate from Witch Hall occupy a particular social stratus and you must learn to properly navigate it."

I scowled, but Mister Sorensen had already turned away from me. Toketie caught the look and glared at me. I knew it was a warning, like stepping on my foot at lunch had been. I didn't know why she was trying so hard to fit in. It was obvious we didn't belong here. Not even ten years of Witch Hall would be enough to erase the fact that she was raised on a horse ranch.

Etiquette was my largest class yet. That seemed to be the only reason it was held in one of the outdoor classrooms—there were too many senior familiars to fit inside together. Both outdoor classrooms had seats in the form of logs spread around the clearing. A cluster of a dozen or so flower familiars sat in the eastern part, nearest to the slope that led down to the riverbanks. Toketie and her suitemates found spots together in the front. Sitting to their right were Charles and the other bone familiars. Spread out along the back were the ten glass familiars, including Oluk.

I didn't want to sit with Toketie or her friends right now, but I didn't get the sense that I'd be welcomed with the bone familiars, despite being their suitemate. Not a single one of them had said a word to me since I moved in on Saturday, not even a "Welcome to Witch Hall."

I chose a seat next to Oluk and stretched my legs out. The grass was long and silky against my ankles, the ground soft but not wet, and the weather beautiful—cooler than it had been in months. I was glad this class was held outside. I wasn't sure I would be able to sit through etiquette lessons otherwise.

"I'm surprised they don't find it undignified to sit on trees," I whispered to Oluk, gesturing to the other familiars. The desks and chairs in the indoor classrooms were made of polished wood, smooth enough to slide on. "Weren't they all born with silver spoons in their mouths?"

Oluk laughed. "You should hear the complaints when it rains. They don't cancel outdoor classes unless there's lightning in the sky."

Mister Sorensen coughed. "If you are done having your own conversations, it is time to start class," he said, staring at Oluk even though we were far from the loudest group.

Oluk flushed and looked down.

"Let us meditate!" Mister Sorensen said, clapping his hands together. "Close your eyes and listen to my voice. Let's find inner peace so that we may better remember today's class."

I folded my hands in my lap. Meditation was familiar to me. Pops had enjoyed it and often called the family to meditate together. After he'd died, Uncle Inge had taken up the tradition, though never as frequently as Pops used to. I closed my eyes, focusing on the breeze as it caressed my cheeks.

"Focus on your breathing," Mister Sorensen said, falling into the cadence of someone familiar with guiding meditations. "Breathe with me. In. Good. Now out. Yes. In. And now out."

I let myself fall into the meditation. My breathing steadied. In. Out. In. Out.

"Imagine another presence with you. They are breathing just beside you. Matching your breaths as you match theirs. They feel warm and safe."

In my mind's eye, I pictured Pops sitting down next to me. He was a young man, but just as strong and sturdy as I remembered him. He winked at me and crossed his legs. I wondered if it was just my imagination. Ever since Mister Voll had told me it was possible for bone familiars to sense ghosts, I'd been thinking about Pops. I felt a prickle of tears at the corners of my eyes. Together, we breathed. In. Out.

"Do you feel them?" Mister Sorensen asked. "Raise your hand if you can."

I raised my hand, still keeping my eyes closed. I knew if I opened them Pops would vanish. I still couldn't tell if he was really there, but I knew that I wasn't sensitive enough to see him physically if he was. A bone witch might be able to, but there was no way I was going to ask Shaw.

I wanted to believe this was real. I could practically feel his warmth. His pride in me. My heart grew with happiness and relief. Pops wasn't upset that I was at Witch Hall. He was just happy to be here, with me.

"Wonderful, wonderful. Remember their presence. You will feel it again. You will be drawn to them as they will be to you. Imagine their hand in yours. A full moon overhead. Imagine their fingers brushing along your neck, a soft promise for what is to come."

My eyes flew open. Pops's presence vanished. Mister Sorensen was circling among the students. He turned in my direction and I quickly closed my eyes.

"Yes," Mister Sorensen said. "Your witch. Your fated partner waits for you. All you need to do is find them."

My calm meditative state was completely gone. I tried to keep my breathing steady, but it was difficult.

"Focus," Mister Sorensen snapped. "Have you learned nothing of meditation these past terms?"

I opened my eyes again. Mister Sorensen had come to stand in front of me. For a second, I thought I was in trouble for having broken out of the trance. But then I followed his gaze and realized he wasn't glaring at me, but at Oluk.

Oluk flushed red, eyes on the ground. "I was, sir."

"Do not lie to me," Mister Sorensen said. I noticed several students had turned to watch. Some rolled their eyes, as if this was a common occurrence.

"I'm sorry, sir. I'll try harder."

Sorensen raised his hands in the air in dramatic exasperation. "What's the use? For years I've taught you. From Beginner Spirituality to The Basics of Bonding. Years of meditations and never once have you felt your witch's presence. I suppose it's too much to expect someone like you to find a bond."

Oluk said nothing, but the corners of his eyes glistened.

My anger from lunch returned like a flash flood. I raised my head and stared hard at Mister Sorensen. The ice witch didn't seem to notice.

"Useless," Mister Sorensen snapped. "I told the headmistress to rescind your scholarship. It's clear you'll never live up to Witch Hall's expectations. The headmistress is convinced you just need a bit more time. As if five years were not enough."

Oluk hunched down like he was trying to hide his face in his lap.

I couldn't just sit quietly and watch Oluk's humiliation. I wanted to shift, to get between Oluk and Mister Sorensen. I wanted to growl loud enough to scare this intruder away from what I had claimed as mine to protect. The wolf's voice rose with a ferocity so bold, I almost gave in to the shift.

"Excuse me," I said, and there was the rasp of a growl in my voice.

"Yes, Miss Rosamund?" Mister Sorensen said, and his voice held none of the vitriol he'd just directed at Oluk.

The tonal flip only made me angrier. "Maybe it's not Oluk's fault. If five years of the same technique has created the same result, then maybe it's the technique that's to blame. Or the teaching of it. Sir."

Behind Mister Sorensen, the familiars all gaped at me. Toketie buried her head in her hands. Charles smirked as if he knew exactly how this was going to end.

"Are you insulting the instruction at Witch Hall, Miss Rosamund?" Mister Sorensen said slowly.

My prey instincts began to wake up, but the wolf was still too close to the surface for me to care. "Well, I've only been here a few days," I replied, just as slow. "But it's not like *you* have taught me anything yet, since you've spent half of our class time yelling at someone who did nothing more than attempt to do exactly what you were instructing."

Mister Sorensen lifted his chin and looked down at me like I was worse than the mud on his shoes. "You are new here, so I am willing to overlook your ignorance. But your attitude is another matter. You will join Mister Oluk in page duty for one hour during the coming assembly. Is that understood?"

I met Mister Sorensen's gaze. "Yes, sir, it is," I said evenly.

Mister Sorensen went purple in the face. He spun around and stalked back up to the front of the clearing. "Let's start in on the etiquette!" he said, a touch too cheerily.

For the rest of the class, Mister Sorensen focused his attentions on me. He didn't snap at me like he had at Oluk, but his passive-aggressive comments were worse. I did everything wrong, apparently, from not bowing low enough during the mock formal introductions to not knowing the official stages of courtship. And he hovered over me during the ending meditation, as if just waiting for a chance to tell me off for fidgeting. This, of course, prevented me from being able to meditate at all, but at least he wasn't paying attention to Oluk anymore.

"Thank you," Oluk whispered once we were headed from class to the stable to feed the horses. "But you really shouldn't have. Page duty isn't a fun way to spend your first assembly, Rosamund."

"Too bad," I said. "We'll just have to weather it together and get on to the fun after. And call me Rosy."

Oluk frowned but didn't argue. I almost asked him what page duty actually was, but he was upset enough. The assembly was Friday evening, I'd figure it out then.

"Rosy!"

That was Toketie. I slowed so she could catch up to Oluk and me.

"Can I talk to you?" Toketie asked. "Alone?"

"I'll meet you at the stable," Oluk said quickly. He gave Toketie a nervous little smile, then rushed off.

"That was rude," I scolded my cousin.

"It's you who's been rude."

I reeled back at her anger. "What?"

"You can't talk to our teachers like that! You're new here but the glamour will only last so long, you know. This isn't like Forest's Edge."

"You're right, this isn't like Forest's Edge," I said. "Everyone here is a rich snob. You heard how your suitemates were talking about Oluk! Iktus's children wouldn't have known how to read either if Papa hadn't opened up his school."

"You can't go around saying that. Comparing us to the lowest of society," Toketie said. "Don't you realize what that would do to our social standing?"

"What, you agree with Mister Sorensen?"

"I don't have to agree, but I do have to learn from him."

"But why? What use is etiquette to us?"

Toketie scowled. "There aren't as many job openings for a lone ice familiar as there are for lone ice witches. My best bet is to find a bond, Mister Sorensen made that very clear. And if I bond with a strong enough ice witch, my future is set."

"You have a future at Forest's Edge! You were going to teach, Toketie!"

"That's not a future, that's a trap," Toketie snapped. "I don't want to spend my life stuck in the past, Rosy. That's your problem, not mine."

I flinched. "Tokey—"

"I don't know why I even try," Toketie said. "Look, just stay away from Oluk. For me? Don't associate yourself with the school's social outcast."

"He doesn't deserve to have to sit alone just because he comes from a poor family. That could have been you, Tokey."

"But it wasn't, because I learned how to fit in. I won't let you and Oluk ruin it for me after I've come this far."

"How have I ruined anything?"

"Face it, Rosy, you haven't made any attempt to fit in here. You publicly rebuffed the princess when she offered her notes—yes, I heard about that—and you completely ignore my suitemates' attempts to talk to you. I don't even think you know anyone's name!"

"I do. I know Froya."

Toketie gave me an unimpressed stare. "Great, now name

another one." I hesitated and Toketie rolled her eyes. "Do you even know the names of your *own* suitemates?"

I kicked the ground. I knew Charles, but that was it.

"This is useless," Toketie muttered. "Fine, if you're going to be like this, then make friends with the scholarship student. But leave me out of it. I can't have you bringing down my own reputation."

"Are you making me choose? Between you and Oluk?"

Toketie's eyes widened, as if she hadn't expected me to point it out. We stood in silence for several heartbeats, then her shoulders squared up. "Yes," she said. "I am."

I stared at my cousin, wondering what had happened to the girl who used to drag me outside to jump in rain puddles. She stared back, her mouth a thin line.

"Fine," I said. My throat felt tight. "If that's how it's going to be, fine. I'll stop bothering you."

Toketie sucked in a deep breath. "Good." She hesitated a second, and then she walked away and didn't turn back.

# Chapter 9

OLUK LOOKED SHOCKED WHEN I FOLLOWED HIM TO HIS little table in the corner for dinner that night.

"Do you mind if I sit with you from now on?" I asked. I deliberately didn't look over at where Toketie was sitting with her suitemates. I knew that if I did, I'd either start crying or yelling. Maybe both.

"If you want," Oluk said, but I could tell he was pleased, and that made me feel better.

Oluk and I compared schedules while eating. I already knew we shared two classes, Survival Skills and Etiquette, but we also shared both Friday workshops.

"That's right, you said you had two shifts!" I said. "It says Madam Xu teaches both?"

"She's brilliant," Oluk said. "She really helped me get consistent with my rattlesnake shift while we traveled back from the Desert after Lammas. That's the only reason I'm in Advanced instead of Intermediate Shapeshifting this term. She's a hard taskmaster though." He winced. "I just hope she takes it easy on us Friday. We're going to need our strength for page duty."

Unfortunately, even though it was the first workshop class of the term, Madam Xu did not take it easy on us.

Advanced Shapeshifting was held in the same outdoor class-room as Survival Skills—the one close to the waterfall and the teachers' cottages. It was a small class, only a dozen familiars in total, from all grade levels and classifications. Unfortunately, Charles Almstedt was one of them. Oluk and I sat as far from him as we could.

Madam Xu was an intimidating woman. Today she wore a white brocade tunic—the kind popular in Waiming, made for ease of movement—and loose black pants. She held herself straight and tall. From where we sat, she loomed over us.

"Welcome, familiars," she began. She spoke brusquely. Not snappishly like Madam Dyer, but to the point. "You are in this class because you have discovered, through accident or not, the true secret of us whom they call familiars. We are not mindless animals confined by one bestial form. For hundreds of years, it was not believed familiars could have a second shift. Does anyone know why Witch Hall is called such?"

She didn't even give us time to answer before continuing. "Because a century ago, familiars were not allowed to study here. Magical education was reserved for witches, who have always known that they could learn new techniques to hone their craft. It wasn't until the time of the last Witch Queen, may her spirit be at peace, that Witch Hall opened its doors to familiars."

Madam Xu looked to each of us in turn. "Hear this as a call to action. Each and every one of you has pushed past the barriers that once held all familiars back. You have learned the secret of shapeshifting. This term I urge you to push further. To prove that familiars can soar to even greater heights and achieve ever more power, just as our witches have."

I felt the strength of her words echoed by every voice in my heart. I remembered, as if from a dream, a story Pops had told me as a child. How he and Gran had been among the first familiars accepted to Witch Hall.

"She was a firecracker, your gran," he'd said with a laugh. "Never let anyone look down on us for it, even though neither of us ever figured out a second shift."

I hadn't intended to put any effort into this class, but a part of me wanted to now. To prove that I could. That the legacy my grandparents started was worth something.

"Now, everyone will go around and introduce yourselves one by one," Madam Xu said. "Your name and your shifts."

I soon learned that of the dozen of us, only Charles and one of the flower familiars, a girl named Lei Banks, had three shifts. Charles had a deer, a pronghorn, and a mountain goat. Lei had a mud crab, a hermit crab, and a river shrimp.

The others just had a pair of shifts. Oluk with his garter and rattlesnake, a flower familiar named Kwaddis Tenas with pike and chub, and so on.

Madam Xu pointed to me last.

"I'm Rosamund Holt. Horse and mouse," I said.

Madam Xu's mouth twisted in a strange little smile. "Is that all, Miss Rosamund?"

I froze. "Ma'am?"

Madam Xu turned to the rest of the class. "Can someone tell me what stands out about Rosamund's shifts?"

There was silence. My heart began to beat at double speed. What was Madam Xu referring to? For a second, I wondered if it was possible for her to hear the voices in my heart.

"I shall give you a hint, then," Madam Xu said. "My first shift was a python. My second, a boa."

Oluk let out a little gasp.

"Yes, Mister Oluk?"

He looked at me and bit his bottom lip, then turned back to Madam Xu. "Everyone's first shifts are similar. In the same family or related in some way. But a horse and a mouse don't have anything in common besides being prey."

"Exactly," Madam Xu said. "Miss Rosamund has not just discovered the secret of shifting, she has hit upon the art. It took me years to do so myself. I mastered every type of snake, but the lizard? The tortoise? They were as foreign to me as a fish or a bird. Until I discovered the art of shifting and learned to let go of my perceived limits. That is what I expect all of you to do, as I have expected of all my students in this course. Each of you will learn to shift into a creature outside the family of your first if you wish to pass." She paused to let us all digest that. "Now, shall we get to work?"

"Yes, ma'am!"

Madam Xu had us practice shifting from one of our forms to another. Most familiars felt they had to turn back into a human between shifts. That was again the difference between the secret and the art, Madam Xu explained. Once we all mastered the ability to pop from one form to another without the human in between, we could move on to trying to add more forms.

"Madam Xu," I whispered as she released everyone to begin practicing. "Can I talk to you for a moment?"

Madam Xu inclined her head and led me closer to the waterfall. The crashing of the water into the creek would help us from being overheard, but I kept my voice low anyway. "My first two shifts . . . they really were different."

I had a feeling Madam Xu knew I was hiding shifts, but she

hadn't outwardly said so and I hoped the rest of the students would just think I'd gotten lucky, discovering this so-called art between my first and second shift.

But though I didn't dare say that my first shift was a wolf, it didn't change that fact that my first two shifts were wolf, then horse. If Madam Xu was right, and it seemed she was in the case of the other familiars, then my second shift should have been a dog or a fox—something similar to the wolf.

"Were they?" Madam Xu remarked mildly. "I did have a student once, a glass familiar. Their first shift was a skink, their second a rat snake."

"So then—"

"We claim our shifts through empathy with the animal. An intrinsic understanding of them. This is why your horse is unsurprising. You grew up on a horse ranch, yes? You understand bone horses, their instincts, their desires. This same effect is why many familiars follow in the footsteps of their parents or grandparents. If they were exposed to their family's shifts at a young age, they often come to understand that animal as well."

My panic returned. Gran was the most famous wolf familiar in the kingdom. Was that why Shaw was interested in me? Even if she believed I couldn't shift into a wolf yet, maybe she thought it would be easy for me to gain that shift.

"But why does the second shift fall in line with the first?" I asked, trying to distract myself. "I was around horses all my life, but then I got my mouse shift when I found a nest of them in our grain room. They'd been stealing the horse feed for months without us knowing."

"And you empathized with that?" Madam Xu pressed. "That

sneakiness?" Madam Xu must have seen the panic on my face this time because she let out a laugh. "I am not here to force answers out of you, Miss Rosamund. I have shifts I no longer wish to use, for one reason or another. I ask only that you do not hide your capabilities in my class. You are correct that it is possible for a first and second shift to be distinctly different, but it is precisely because of our empathy for our first shift that we so rarely learn to see outside of that. That we lean toward shifts that feel similar. You are a rarity, Miss Rosamund. I expect you to be the first student in class to find a new form. To lead the rest by example."

"Yes, ma'am."

Madam Xu nodded and walked away. I took a deep, steadying breath, filling my lungs with the misty air. I had made a huge mistake coming to Witch Hall. I should have known it wouldn't be so easy to hide. Why else would Gran have asked me to stay home with her? She'd gone to Witch Hall, after all.

But my reasons for being here hadn't changed. I had to help Gran.

And so what if I was good at shifting? So long as I hid my predators, the wolf especially, I'd be okay. I just had to do poorly enough in Combat that they didn't think me capable of fighting . . . but not so poorly they failed me.

I buried my face in my hands to gather strength, trying to cling to the feeling that Madam Xu had inspired with her first speech. It was enough that I could ignore my worries, at least for a moment. Trotting back to the clearing, I found an open spot and carefully shifted between the horse and the mouse. There was no reason for me to hide that I could, since Mister Voll had seen it, but I made sure to do it slowly, just like the few others in the class who seemed to be capable of direct shifts.

I watched the other familiars in between my own shifts. The flower familiars splashed about the waterfall's creek, plants sprouting from their bodies the way bone protruded from bone animals. Lei Banks had petals that popped out of her crab shells, spilling into the creek like a tree in bloom.

The ice familiars shed icicles in much the same way. I watched a little ice sparrow dart around the clearing. I never understood why the ice growing on their feathers didn't weigh them down—but that was magic for you. Even the pheasant with huge ice shards replacing its tail had no trouble at all getting around.

Oluk came up to me in his rattlesnake shift, a glint of obsidian-glass scales covering his rattle. I shifted to the horse, my mouse too terrified to stay in the presence of a snake even if he was a friend. We touched noses, then Oluk disappeared back through the brush.

When Madam Xu finally released us for lunch, I was sweating. Shifting was not particularly difficult for me, but three hours straight was far more than I'd ever attempted before.

"Oh no," I said as I sat heavily down in front of my lunch.

"What?" Oluk asked through a mouthful of food.

"We have her again after lunch."

Oluk patted me on the hand. "Better eat up."

Our walk to Madam Xu's class after lunch was much slower than it had been after breakfast. I was far more anxious about Familiar Combat than Advanced Shapeshifting—and even more so now that I knew Madam Xu wasn't fooled by my shifts. What's more, I really didn't want to have to shift any more today, but I had a feeling we weren't just going to talk theory. Not with both Madam Xu and Madam Bai teaching.

Luckily, we didn't start with combat in our animal forms. Since every senior familiar was in the class, there were a good number with forms that were useless in combat situations.

Instead, Madam Xu and Madam Bai worked together to demonstrate hand-to-hand fighting techniques. Then we were paired up and set to practice.

"One of the feats tonight will be mock combat," Madam Xu said as we took a midclass break for water. "Your homework will be to compete in it."

Charles flicked the tail of his braid over his shoulder and smirked in my direction.

Oluk raised his hand. When Madam Xu called on him, he said, "Excuse me, Madam Xu. Rosy and I can't compete. We have page duty."

"Have you?" Madam Xu frowned at me.

"Just for an hour, ma'am," I said.

"An hour?" Madam Xu's frown deepened. "Well, you will be quite useless after that, won't you?"

Charles's smirk widened. I felt my cheeks flush red.

Madam Xu waved a hand. "Very well. We shall adjust the requirement. Everyone must compete in a combat feat at least once this term. Tonight, next assembly, or the one after. I do hope you will not be on page duty for all three."

"No, ma'am," I murmured at the same time Oluk said, "Thank you, Madam Xu."

Charles's smirk twisted into a scowl. He was probably hoping we'd fail the homework. I knew I couldn't afford to, but could Oluk? I turned to him. "What are the requirements to keep your scholarship?"

"Oh." Oluk looked embarrassed for a second. I tried for a

pleasantly curious expression. "I'm not allowed to fail more than two classes a year. I, uh, already failed one. Mister Sorensen's class last term. And I think he's going to fail me again, so I have to pass everything else."

Everything, including Combat. And Madam Xu's difficult-to-pass Advanced Shapeshifting workshop.

I bumped my shoulder against Oluk's. "Don't worry, I'll study with you. I'm not allowed to fail anything either, since I started late."

I hated the unfairness of it. Everyone else could fail five, which was plenty generous for all the rich children of nobility. But for the scholarship students, only two? No wonder Oluk was the only scholarship student in the upper years. All the others were probably pushed out. The fact that Oluk was still here just made me more proud to be his friend.

Madam Dyer came to the senior bone familiars' suite after dinner to escort me to the assembly.

"I was informed you were assigned an hour of page duty," Madam Dyer said. She raised a condescending eyebrow. "On your first assembly, Miss Rosamund. Impressive."

"I'm sorry, ma'am," I said, though I wasn't really. I didn't care to pander to snobs like Madam Dyer and Mister Sorensen.

Madam Dyer sniffed. "Well, let's hope this once is all you need. The headmistress takes discipline very seriously here at Witch Hall."

"Yes, ma'am."

"Follow me. Quickly now."

The moon was still low in the sky, but it had crested the tops of the trees. It was a harvest moon, large and butter yellow. It lit our way down the grassy slope.

The assembly took place across the entire eastern side of campus, from the waterfall, down the creek, and along the bank of the river. Most of the school was already milling about. There were several tables set up and a few pavilions. Madam Xu presided over a booth of snacks and refreshments. Next to her, a glass witch sat with what looked to be a bunch of deconstructed protective amulets and charms. A few students fiddled with parts at the table.

Under another pavilion, a group of ice witches sat at a long table, shuffling tarot cards or peering down at crystal balls. Down by the river, an obstacle course was set up in the water. Some flower familiars shifted and took their place at the starting flag while flower witches cheered them on from the finish marker.

At the large classroom clearing where Familiar Combat was held, a rope had been wrapped around the poles to make a barrier. Two senior familiars I vaguely recognized from my suite faced off inside. Madam Bai called for them to begin and the familiars shifted and went to attack each other. A crowd of other students cheered them on. I noticed a pair of adults in military uniforms watching.

I slowed. "Oluk said the school assembly was like a festival. With games and things."

"We call them feats," Madam Dyer said. "They are not games any more than Witch Hall is a playground. Our students compete to show off their strengths. Visitors come from across the kingdom to watch the competitions and, if they are impressed enough, offer jobs to the witch or familiar, or witch-familiar pair, once they graduate."

That explained the military presence. Maybe I should be glad to have page duty, then, if it kept me from having to compete in feats under the eyes of the recruiters. I didn't need or want to be offered a job. My future was set back at the ranch and I was happy with it.

Madam Dyer led me to a pavilion near the waterfall that overlooked the entire assembly. Oluk already waited outside the pavilion. Madam Dyer pointed for me to stand next to him. Inside the pavilion, a half circle of chairs sat alongside a table of refreshments. The headmistress, Madam Kawak, sat in one of the chairs, talking to a man who wore a brown military uniform, marked with a flower crest and a red sash. The sash meant he was a thane of the army and the crest marked the company he was assigned to. Given the flower, I guessed it was probably Multah's Company.

"Excuse me," Madam Kawak said to the thane. She stood and grabbed a bundle of cloth from one of the tables, then walked out to where we waited. "Thank you for bringing her, Moll," she said. "You may go to preside over your feat."

Madam Dyer nodded and, with one last disgusted look in my direction, she left.

Madam Kawak didn't look disgusted, but she definitely looked disappointed. "I had hoped none of our students would need to use these in the first assembly of the term. It does not look good for our visitors."

Oluk stared at the ground. I kept my eyes on the cloth, wondering what it was. Madam Kawak didn't keep me waiting long. She pulled the bundle apart, revealing two tabards.

Oluk put his on, and I copied him. The tabard was brown, the color of the military uniform, and slightly oversized on me. It fell halfway down my shins instead of to my knees like tabards were supposed to. I noticed there were runes etched around the collar, though I had no idea what they were for. I tucked it into my belt to keep it from flapping about.

"I know Mister Oluk is aware of the rules, but for Miss Rosamund's sake, here they are. While you wear that tabard, you are an assembly page. You must stay in sight and available. For the next hour, you will obey all orders given to you by other students, teachers, and our esteemed visitors. Should you receive conflicting orders, visitors will always take precedence, followed by teachers, then the students. I will come find you when the hour is up. Do not come to me before then. If you complain, I will extend your time. Understood?"

"Yes, ma'am," Oluk said, and I quickly echoed him.

"Good. Off you go."

Oluk headed down to the main thrum of the assembly, and I followed.

"That's it?" I asked once we were out of Madam Kawak's earshot. "It doesn't seem so bad."

"You say that now," Oluk muttered. "We shouldn't talk to each other. It's always best to look busy while you're on page duty, especially if you're not actually busy."

Before I could respond, one of the visitors called Oluk over. "You there, page boy! Fetch me a chair."

"Yes, sir," Oluk said, and off he went.

I crossed my arms over the tabard, uncertain what I was supposed to do to look busy.

"There you are."

I turned to see Charles approaching me.

"What?" I said, wondering why he'd been looking for me.

"Pages aren't to talk unless asked to," Charles said, his tone polite enough that I almost didn't hear the actual words. "Follow me, Rosamund."

I rocked back on my heels. A bad feeling formed in the pit of my stomach. "I'm not sure—"

"Pages obey without question," Charles said, still a touch too pleasant. "Or they get disciplined."

I scowled. "I'm going to go fetch some chairs for the visitors."

"I heard them ask Oluk to do it, not you."

I took a step away.

"Kneel," Charles said before I could take the next.

I had no intention of obeying, but I found that I didn't have a choice. The runes at the shoulder of the tabard activated and all of a sudden a massive pressure came down on top of me. A pressure that forced me to my knees, my forehead to the ground.

I could just barely make out the tips of Charles's boots as he stepped closer and crouched down next to me.

"You need to learn your place, horse girl," he hissed.

The pressure abated. I sprang back to my feet. Charles had the sense to back out of my reach, but not to wipe that self-satisfied smile off his face. "Follow me," he said again. "Unless you'd rather spend the rest of your hour acquainted with the dirt?"

I followed. I didn't have a choice, not unless one of the teachers or visitors requested something from me. But Charles was smart enough to steer clear of them. Instead, he took me to a set of tables and chairs where the seniors who weren't currently competing in feats all seemed to be congregated.

Then he commanded me to do a series of meaningless and

humiliating chores. I had to fetch food and he wouldn't let me stop until the tray was piled high. But then I was to take it back to him without spilling, a task I inevitably failed. After I was punished for the mess—more time kneeling with my face in the dirt—he told me to clean the food up. I got punished again for trying to wipe it up with the corner of my tabard.

"We're but animals on the inside, aren't we?" Charles said, still sugary sweet. "Use your tongue."

I glared and he punished me for the disrespect.

I almost wished the punishment were physical discipline. I'd rather be smacked than be forced to kneel again and again. It was humiliating. It was also exhausting. Whatever glass magic used to enchant the runes on the tabard drained me with each punishment. Every time the discipline ended and I struggled to my feet, I felt like I'd been forced to run a mile.

The worst part, though, was how everyone stared. Dozens of witches and familiars, students I had classes with, all sat around their tables and watched as I fought a battle of wills with Charles. Maybe if we'd been alone, I would have debased myself enough to lap up the food on the ground. Charles was right, we were animals on the inside, and I'd eaten enough food while shifted that I wasn't bothered by a bit of dirt.

But I couldn't make myself do it while the rest of the seniors laughed at me.

Charles sighed in mock disappointment. "Maybe I need to go tell the headmistress that you're having trouble obeying. She'd be thrilled to assign more hours of page duty, I'm sure."

It was a bluff, it had to be. Madam Kawak surely wouldn't agree with what Charles was doing.

But then, she had said not to complain. If I tried to explain myself, who would she believe? Me or Charles?

I swallowed roughly, wrestling with my pride. I glanced around at the crowd, trying to prove to myself that their opinions didn't matter. I'd never see any of them again after I graduated. I'd go home and they'd go on to their cushioned lives and that would be that.

Then I saw her. Toketie. Standing with her suitemates by a table in the back as the ice familiars all giggled and pointed at me.

I watched my cousin, not sure what I was waiting for, but sure that she would do something. Come tell Charles off, maybe. Be at my side like she always was, growing up. Even just the presence of someone who was horrified by Charles instead of amused would be enough.

For one second, I was sure she would. She opened her mouth, leaned forward as if she were about to approach.

Then Froya turned to whisper something to her and Toketie hesitated.

Up until that moment, I'd been sure Toketie was going to come around. That she'd realize how silly she'd been and join me and Oluk at our little dining table. Toketie and I had grown apart over the years, but we were still family. My cousin had never shied away from danger, even when she should have. I remembered too well how I'd gotten into this mess. That day in the Bone Forest. Toketie, wings outstretched, standing between Shaw's entourage and a rampant bull moose.

Except Toketie turned away from me. Turned her back to pick out some snacks with the rest of the ice familiars, and I finally realized what I should have known years ago. Toketie didn't feel the same way about me that I did about her. To me, we were best friends before we were cousins. To Toketie, I was a burden she was ready to leave behind.

That realization hurt more than anything Charles had done so far, even as he forced me to kneel again for my inattention. I pressed my forehead into the dirt and fought not to cry.

# Chapter 10

## SHAW

THE NECROMANCY FEAT WAS SIMULTANEOUSLY THE smallest and the best attended. There were only a handful of other bone witches besides Shaw who even had a passing skill at necromancy. Shaw knew all of them from the workshop Madam Dyer had taught last term, but the only one who kept her attention was the witch she now faced in the final round of the feat.

"Ready, Shaw?" Chao asked. He was one of the few students outside her entourage who'd earned the right to use her given name.

Chao Hu was the son of the bone witch and familiar of her father's entourage. Had Shaw been born an ice witch like her father, she would have chosen Chao to join hers. But they were both bone witches, so he occupied the rare space of someone she considered a friend, but not an advisor.

"I'm ready," Shaw said. "Are you?"

Chao grinned. "When facing you? Never."

Madam Dyer finished scattering the bones across the field and raised an arm. "On my count. Three . . . two . . . one . . . and begin!"

Shaw reached for her magic—for that intrinsic sense of death and darkness. The bones around her rattled as she sent a metaphorical touch across them. She called out to them, searching for the spirit that still clung to those old remains.

The first to answer was a bobcat. The spirit pulled toward its skull, all the way in the corner of the roped-off field. Shaw stayed where she was, but held a hand out in the skull's direction to help direct her energy. With a great push, she sent the spirit to inhabit the skull.

The bobcat's skull rose in the air as the spirit unfurled around it. The jaw opened, yowling in demand for the rest of its skeleton. Shaw let the spirit sink its claws into her magic, using her as a vessel to pull the rest of its bones to it.

A femur flew past her head. Ribs clacked together as they slotted into place along an unfurling spine. At last, the bobcat's skeleton had regained enough shape to move. She sent the spirit to attack Chao, to distract him from completing his own skeleton.

The next spirit to answer Shaw's call was a wolverine. As she began to assemble its skeleton, Chao dodged out of reach of the undead bobcat and finished assembling a fox. The two skeletons clashed together as Chao sent the fox to fight.

The necromancy feat was a test of speed and control. Shaw was faster—she assembled four of the skeletons in the time it took Chao to make two. But Chao's control over his two was solid. His fox and elk pair were close to demolishing Shaw's four.

Shaw went for the elk. It was hard to split her magic between maintaining her connection to the four skeletons and sabotaging Chao's, but this wasn't her first necromancy feat. Bit by bit, she picked at the bond between the elk's spirit and its skeleton.

Finally, just as the elk was prepared to stomp on her bobcat, Shaw pulled the last thread loose and the skeleton fell apart into a pile of bones once again.

Chao looked from his single fox to her four skeletons. He scratched the back of his head, grinning. "I concede."

A huge cheer rumbled through the audience. Shaw let go of the four spirits and their skeletons collapsed like the elk's.

"The winner, Princess Shaw Colchuck," Madam Dyer shouted over the roar.

A group of young soldiers to her left cheered the loudest. "Congratulations, Princess," one said as she passed by on her way to Madam Dyer. She nodded to them, but otherwise didn't acknowledge the congratulations. She didn't feel like she'd won yet.

"Madam Dyer, allow Chao's familiar to join us for a rematch," Shaw said.

Madam Dyer's face pinched. She wasn't a fan of Jingyi, mostly because she wasn't a fan of any bone familiar. Shaw couldn't tell if it was bitterness because Madam Dyer had never bonded herself, or some bullheaded belief that bonding didn't actually help a witch gain power or control. Perhaps both.

Shaw's father *was* the strongest ice witch in the kingdom. But he had been bonded once, even if he was no longer, and what was left of her mother's magic still lived in her father. All evidence pointed to the fact that bonding was the single best way to improve as a witch.

"Madam Dyer," Shaw repeated, when the teacher hadn't replied.

"Yes, very well," Madam Dyer said, just short of snapping. She raised her voice. "The princess has requested a rematch! Jingyi Wang, if you will join your witch on the field."

Jingyi was a boy today, his long hair done up in a traditional topknot and held together by a bright orange ribbon. He shifted into a bone fox to duck through the ropes around the field. With a running leap, he climbed up to Chao's shoulders. The witch-familiar bond was strongest when the witch and familiar were actively touching. Chao and Jingyi had practiced this method of Jingyi clinging to Chao's shoulders for months and it proved effective now. Bone foxes were larger, of course, than nonmagical foxes, so he sprawled awkwardly across both shoulders. But Chao was as wide as Einar, though he was nowhere near as tall, and he supported Jingyi without issue.

The next match was much harder than the first. Chao claimed half the skeletons from the start and assembled all three simultaneously. Shaw reclaimed the bobcat and managed to grab the elk, but even pushing herself, she could only make one at a time. She was still faster than Chao, but it wasn't enough. His three skeletons overwhelmed her two before she could begin to pull one of his apart.

Madam Dyer called the match in Chao and Jingyi's favor. Shaw clapped along with the crowd as Jingyi shifted back into his human form and gave Chao an enthusiastic kiss.

"Just imagine how powerful the princess will be once she bonds with a familiar," she overheard one of the soldiers say.

"Especially a strong one," another replied gleefully.

She turned away from them and headed to the other end of the field, where her entourage waited in the audience.

"You were close," Einar said, as if she needed the encouragement. "Perhaps next assembly—"

"We'll see," she said, not wanting to get into it with so many people around.

Her entourage knew her moods better than anyone. "Tea?" Yuyan asked, detaching the nearest rope so Shaw could step through.

"Perhaps we should head to the seniors' corner first," Aklemin said. "You did say that you wished to see Miss Rosy Holt confront the pyre, Shaw."

Shaw turned on her heel midstride and headed in the direction of the collection of tables the students like to call the seniors' corner. "Pyre, Aklemin?" She wanted Rosamund tested, but pyres were deadly—even metaphorical ones.

Aklemin looked up in the air for a second, as if consulting with the stars. "It could be," they said quietly. "If you leave it just a couple minutes longer."

She quickened her pace. This was what she'd been waiting for. She had to see how Rosamund reacted to the threat, before the threat grew actually dangerous. She had no problem testing her people, but she had a responsibility to keep them safe from real harm.

Shaw and her entourage rounded the corner of one of the dormitories and the seniors' corner came into view. It was easy to assess the situation. Rosamund in a page's tabard, kneeling in the dirt. Charles standing over her. Half the seniors of Witch Hall laughing. Shaw spotted Rosamund's cousin standing next to Froya, saw the way she had her back to the situation, and understood what Aklemin had meant by pyre.

Rosamund Holt was a mystery, but that, at least, had been entirely predictable.

"Are you listening to me?" Charles snapped as Shaw drew close enough to hear. "Kneel."

Rosamund's forehead smacked the ground. Several students noticed her entourage approach and drew back a few steps. Shaw stopped where she was and waited for the runes on the tabard to deactivate.

They did, and Rosamund pulled herself back up. Grass stains covered her forehead and mud caked her cheeks. She looked more like a ranch girl now than she had in that little village where Shaw had found her. Shaw didn't like it, though she wasn't sure why.

"Why are you doing this?" Rosamund asked. Her voice was strong, despite all reason for her to cower. She had not broken yet.

"Answer me this, Rosamund," Charles said, smiling a touch too wide. "Did you tell Mister Jostein not to offer me stable duty?"

Rosamund began to stutter out something of an answer, but Charles shook his head. "Haven't you learned your lesson by now? Address me with respect and answer me the minute I ask something of you. Honestly, you're slower than Oluk."

"You—" Rosamund tried, but it was too late. Charles told her to kneel again and down she went.

"Shaw," Yuyan murmured.

But she was already stepping forward. She'd seen enough and she didn't like the look of it. This wasn't trial by fire, this was bullying, clear as the full moon in the sky.

"Are you done playing with your food, Charles?"

Rosamund's back visibly stiffened as she heard Shaw's voice. Charles startled like the deer he was. He turned wide-eyed in her direction.

"Good evening, Princess. Did you want something from me?" There was an unsettling amount of hope in his voice. Shaw wanted to glare at him and the desire took her by surprise.

She didn't dislike Charles, though his lack of subtlety sometimes aggravated her. He was interesting if only because of the way he controlled the bone familiars at school, just as Froya controlled the ice. But she wasn't interested *in* him, not the way he wanted. A lifetime of worship was an appalling prospect.

"Not today," she said. "But I wouldn't mind stealing your page. I need someone to pour me tea."

"I would be happy to serve you," Charles said, a touch too desperate.

"I wouldn't want to keep you from your feats," she responded. With a flick of her eyes, she included the rest of the seniors in those words. More than one looked ashamed. She turned to head back to the main section of the assembly. "Come, Rosamund."

Rosamund wasted no time jumping to her feet and hurrying after Shaw. Shaw's entourage waited for her to walk up to Shaw's side, then closed ranks behind them.

The group walked in silence until they were far enough from the seniors' corner, then Shaw looked at Rosamund out of the corner of her eye. She walked directly beside her, even though a step behind would be more appropriate for someone on page duty. Her chin was raised high, her expression set in a mulish look. What was she thinking? Shaw couldn't tell.

"You made yourself a target, Rosamund," Shaw said, to try to get something out of her.

Rosamund looked at her, and only then did Shaw see the anger burning in her eyes. "Charles only targeted me because of you. Because he wants you, and you aren't brave enough to give him an answer."

Not brave enough? She'd never thought of herself as particularly brave, but no one had ever insinuated she was a coward either.

"What kind of answer would you have me give him?" she asked.

Rosamund rolled her eyes. "You know what he wants. You know what they all want. I've only been here a week and it's clear enough to me. Find a familiar to court and put the rest out of their misery."

"I'd think you'd want them to be miserable, after what I just witnessed."

Rosamund shook her head. "You're the one creating an environment that makes them think that kind of thing is right, you know. You're the princess. You'll lead the whole kingdom one day. What's Witch Hall if not your training grounds for that?"

If Witch Hall was Shaw's training for ruling the kingdom, Rosamund's tone implied that she was liable to fail. It was a strange feeling, disappointing someone who she hadn't even wanted to impress in the first place.

"Perhaps you're right. Perhaps I do need to take responsibility."

Rosamund looked startled, but she nodded. "Yes, you should."

They reached the tea tent. "I'd tell you to sit and rest, but you are still on page duty. Get us tea," she told Rosamund, wondering how far she could push before the familiar snapped at her again. It was almost refreshing, being told off. Not even her father did so anymore.

But Rosamund didn't snap. She turned to Shaw's entourage instead and asked them what kind of tea they would like, saving Shaw's preferences for last. Then she went to the back to get tea while the four of them sat around one of the tables.

Rosamund returned with their tea a few minutes later. Shaw took a sip of hers, then set it back down. "No, I don't think I want this blend tonight. Get me mint instead, one sugar cube."

Rosamund said nothing, merely headed back to the tea table.

"You're playing with a predator, Shaw," Aklemin said, smiling.

"Am I? I can't tell."

"I can't tell if you're trying to flirt, horribly, or if you're just in a bad mood," Yuyan said.

Shaw scowled at her. If she wanted to flirt, she wouldn't be horrible at it.

Einar cleared his throat, warning the group that Rosamund was approaching again.

Shaw took the tea, then sent Rosamund back to refill the empty kettles at the table with the large water jug in the corner of the tent. After that, she sent her to sort the tea leaves.

Not once did Rosamund speak up. She didn't even glare. She seemed perfectly content to be treated like a servant, despite refusing to respect Shaw's authority in every other situation.

"I don't understand her," Shaw complained under her breath.

"Give it time," Yuyan said. "People are complicated."

No, they weren't. But before she could disagree aloud, Oluk Blackwell came into the tent, looking harried.

"Oh," he said when he caught sight of Rosamund. "Are you okay, Rosy? I heard that Charles—"

"I'm fine," Rosamund said, cutting him off. "How about you?"

Oluk shrugged, though Shaw noticed it wasn't very convincing. She'd thought after the number of times he'd been given page duty, he'd be used to it. "I need to deliver some tea."

"To visitors? Teachers?"

Oluk shook his head.

Rosamund bustled over to the entourage's table. "Shaw," she said, completely ignoring any attempt at courtesy or formality. "You know Oluk, right? I mean, he's got stable duty too, so—"

Shaw raised an eyebrow, urging her to get to the point.

"He needs this break more than I do," Rosamund continued quickly. "Can you . . . ?"

Break? Was that why she wasn't reacting to Shaw's taunts? Most other students would be humiliated to be set to such menial tasks. Then again, compared to Rosamund's earlier humiliation, perhaps this quiet tea tent was a relief.

Shaw should have been upset, but instead she felt warm. Like she could bask in Rosamund's gratitude.

Well then. "Einar," she said.

Einar stood and walked over to Oluk. "This is not your first page duty," he said, staring down from his considerable height to the top of Oluk's bowed head.

"No, sir," Oluk said, proper as a page should be. His voice was thin. Shaw could tell that he was exhausted. Had he been forced to his knees too, or just run ragged trying not to be?

"Oluk didn't deserve this one," Rosamund interjected hotly. "Mister Sorensen was picking on him in class, and when I defended him, Mister Sorensen gave us both page duty. I know I was being disrespectful to a teacher, but Oluk did nothing wrong."

"That doesn't sound honorable," Einar agreed. "After you've delivered that tea, would you return to this tent, Oluk? You can tell them I've requested your service. Only if you wish to."

Oluk looked surprised to be asked. He nodded quickly, a small blush spreading over his freckled cheeks.

Shaw glanced at Rosamund, hoping to see gratitude again, but she'd returned to the tea table. Shaw watched her work while her entourage struck up a conversation about classes. It was soothing, the hum of their voices in the background while Rosamund sorted tea and lifted heavy jugs of water like they weighed no more than a woven basket.

Oluk returned and Einar sent him to help Rosamund. Shaw wanted them to talk, to gain some insight into Rosamund from their conversation, but the two worked in silence.

She was so lulled watching the familiars that it took her by surprise when Aklemin abruptly slammed down their cup.

"I'm going to go check out the cooking feat," they declared. "Coming?"

Shaw knew what that tone meant. She stood. Einar and Yuyan followed.

"I wonder if they're making stew this month," Aklemin said, leading the way out of the tent.

"Do you only ever think with your stomach?" Yuyan complained, falling into step with Aklemin.

Einar picked up two of the empty teacups. Shaw grabbed hers and the one remaining, then brought them over for Rosamund to wash.

"You're almost done. Stay strong," Einar whispered to Oluk as he handed his cups over.

Rosamund took Shaw's two cups. Her calloused fingers brushed over Shaw's skin. Her hand tingled at the curious sensation. She met Rosamund's gaze. Only now could she make out the color of her eyes. Brown from a distance, but with flecks of green hidden within. Hints of grass growing from mud. It shouldn't have been as striking a combination as it was.

Rosamund pulled away first. Shaw broke out of her contemplation, realizing Einar was already at the entrance of the tent. She left. Behind her, Oluk hissed, "Look busy, Rosy."

Madam Kawak was headed in their direction when Shaw stepped out of the tent.

"Are our wayward pages in there, Princess?" she asked.

"They are, Headmistress."

Einar held the tent flap for Madam Kawak and she ducked in to relieve the two of page duty. Shaw didn't bother to wait. She'd already decided on her next move.

She thought of the necklace she had in her room. The one her father had gifted her on her thirteenth birthday. The chain was short—it would sit high upon the neck. Visible like a warning.

Like a claim.

# Chapter 11

## ROSY

I SPENT THE ENTIRE WEEKEND AT THE STABLE. RIDING cleared my head better than anything else. The only horse Mister Jostein asked I didn't ride was Cow, the princess's bone mare, but I gave the rest of them a test run. With no surprise, I found one of the other bone mares, with a bright sorrel coat and exposed bone along her neck and ankles, was my favorite.

When I wasn't riding, I wrote a letter to my family. I started and restarted it several times, crossing out anything related to Shaw, Madam Dyer, Mister Sorensen, or page duty. I ended up with a simple letter about making a new friend, how nice the school stable was, and how I missed them.

On Monday morning, Oluk showed me where the courier's station was as we headed from the stable to breakfast. Toketie stood at it, slotting her own sealed letter into the mailbox. I told Oluk to go on ahead.

"Morning," I said. My voice came out more brittle than I wanted.

Toketie's shoulders came up almost to her ears. She slowly turned to face me. "Hello."

I swallowed roughly, but said nothing else as I swerved around her to put my own letter in. If Toketie wanted to leave me behind, fine. I wasn't going to spend any more effort on her. Gran would tell me to worry about myself, and it was time I listened.

Letter deposited, I turned to head to breakfast.

"Rosy, wait."

I stopped, but I refused to spin around. "What?"

Toketie said nothing. I gave in to the urge to turn so I could glare at her.

"What?" I repeated.

Toketie wrung her hands. "I'm sorry, Rosy. What Charles did was awful, and I'm . . . I'm glad the princess stepped in to help."

I nodded. Toketie paused, as if waiting for me to say something. But I wasn't going to give her the absolution she was looking for. Her betrayal wasn't the kind of thing a simple *sorry* could repair.

"How are your other classes?" Toketie asked finally. "Besides Etiquette and Combat, I mean."

"Fine."

"You're in Advanced Shapeshifting, right? Did you know that Madam Xu has over a dozen shifts—"

"I know."

An awkward silence settled over us. I knew I was being petty, but I couldn't help it. I had tried for over three years to maintain a relationship with my cousin after she went off to Witch Hall. I'd risked my life trying to save her in the Forest, only for her to refuse to help me stand up to a single bully. She didn't get to reach out only after the danger was over.

"Well," Toketie muttered, as if she could hear my thoughts. "Have a nice day, Rosy." She stalked away.

I watched her go, resisting the urge to run after her and ask about the rest of her classes. To tell her about Pops visiting me during Mister Sorensen's daily meditations, see if she thought it was really his ghost, like I was starting to believe. I wanted to talk with her like we used to when she'd come home for break. I wanted to know what else she was learning. Wanted to know if she was happy here, with the other ice familiars.

Instead, I waited until Toketie was out of sight before slowly making my way to the dining hall. I grabbed breakfast without care for what ended up on my plate and sat down heavily at the corner table Oluk and I had claimed as ours.

I'd only taken one bite when I saw Oluk look at something over my shoulder. He flapped his hand to get my attention, eyes wide.

"Rosy," he said. "Rosy, turn around."

"Why?"

Oluk looked panicked as he watched whatever was behind me. "The princess is coming this way," he hissed.

I turned in my seat. Shaw was indeed approaching our table. There was no mistaking it with the surety of her steps, the way she ignored every other table as she neared.

Oluk set his fork down as she got close, giving Shaw all his attention. I didn't want to do the same. I was still in a bad mood from talking with Toketie. I didn't want to play one of Shaw's games today.

I didn't have a choice though. Everyone in the dining hall seemed to be watching us—including the teachers. I slowly lowered my spoon back into my porridge.

Shaw thrust out her right hand. There was something shiny cupped in her palm. I stared. After what felt like the longest minute of my life, Oluk kicked me.

"Ow," I said, glaring at him.

Oluk glared back, gesturing at Shaw. The princess stood still and silent, as if she could easily wait all day for me to acknowledge her. Even her expression was patient. If anything, it was a touch amused.

This was another game, then. I should have expected something after the help she'd given me at the end of the assembly. It was shaping into a pattern. Give me something I wanted, then add a complication. Thank me for saving her life, then force me to go to Witch Hall. Convince Mister Jostein to let me try out for stable duty, then tell Charles about it.

Rescue me from Charles's humiliation, then . . .

I slowly reached forward, and Shaw deposited the item into my hand.

It was a necklace. Spaced evenly along a smooth silver chain were pieces of moonstone—each carved to look like miniature bones. I'd heard of moonstone, but it was so expensive that I'd never seen any in person. The pieces shone iridescent silver, as if it really were made of moonlight itself. I shifted the necklace around in my palm, captivated by the blues and greens and purples that reflected off the silver bones.

"Familiar Rosamund Holt, this is my official request to court you," Shaw announced. In the hush of the dining hall, her words echoed. "You hold a token of my intent willingly given. May you look fondly upon it until our courtship progresses."

"Shaw," I demanded, instantly furious. "What is this?"

Softer, so that only Oluk and I could hear, Shaw said, "You did ask me to take responsibility."

With that, the princess bowed, turned on her heel, and stalked back to her seat. The dining hall erupted in conversation.

My face felt hot, though I couldn't tell if it was from embarrassment or anger. I turned to Oluk, hoping he'd be able to make sense of what just happened.

"Rosy!" Oluk squeaked, sounding more mouse than snake. "That's so exciting! The princess has never courted anyone."

"So I've heard," I muttered. "But why now? Why me?"

Oluk looked at me like I'd asked a particularly ignorant question. Maybe to him it seemed obvious. I'd supposedly saved Shaw's life. She'd paid my tuition to come to Witch Hall. I was a strong enough familiar to be in Advanced Shapeshifting, even if I hid the full extent of what I could do from everyone.

To the school, it must look like Shaw was enamored. But I didn't believe that. She didn't have the look of someone in love. Not like my parents or Uncle Inge and Uncle Chetwoot. Not like Solemie, when he talked about his fiancée. She didn't even look like Toketie, blushing over her attraction to Aklemin.

No, this was just another complication in a game whose rules I didn't understand.

"How do I tell her no?"

Oluk eyes widened. "But why?"

Because she was Death's Heir. Because she represented everything I hated about this kingdom. All the reasons for Gran's pain and my family's suffering. Because she would lead us into war one day.

Because Shaw looked at me the way a predator looked at potential prey. Like she was trying to decide if I would be worth the effort to hunt.

"I don't want a witch to court me," I said, and that was true too. In all my daydreams, my Gravestown horse rival turned lover was never a witch. And even if I did fall in love with a witch one day, I imagined it'd be one of the many who hadn't been able to afford Witch Hall. Someone like Toketie's aunt. Not the princess. "Especially not *her*."

"I guess it's a lot of responsibility," Oluk said, a bit hesitantly. "If you bonded with the princess . . . you'd be Familiar Queen one day."

Theoretically, I'd known that, but hearing Oluk say it just made the whole thing much more real. No wonder the rest of the school kept throwing looks my way. I could predict the conversations happening at those tables. *Why her? What is it about that familiar that caught the princess's attention? How could a ranch girl help rule the kingdom?*

But they didn't see Shaw like I did. Shaw didn't actually want to bond with me. What she did want . . . well, I was still figuring that part out.

"How do I tell her no?" I repeated.

"You can't yet. You have to take a week to think on the offer. Everyone does, the first week of courtship. You're supposed to wear the necklace. Courtship tokens are imbued with the witch or familiar's energy. Gives the courted a chance to feel if your magic is compatible."

I frowned. "How would I know that?"

"If it makes you uncomfortable to wear it, then you're not compatible. It'll itch or feel too cold or too hot. If you're compatible, you'll feel it." Oluk shrugged. "I've never been courted, so I can't say for sure. But Mister Sorensen said it would be obvious."

I stared down at the necklace. It was, without a doubt, the most expensive thing I'd ever held. "I have to wear it?"

Oluk nodded. "Next Monday, the princess will approach you. If you take it off and give it back to her, she'll know your energies weren't compatible. If you keep it on, she'll proceed to the next stage."

Just a week. I could handle that.

I had to.

Slowly I undid the clasp and fumbled with it behind my head. It took me a second, but I managed to clip it again. The moonstones were smooth against my skin, the largest resting just above the hollow of my neck. The necklace was warm, but not uncomfortably so. I resisted the urge to fidget with it.

"The courter isn't allowed to talk to the courted during this stage," Oluk said. "So as not to influence anything. Of course, I think some people lie about the magical compatibility if the match is good enough. Or lie about it being incompatible if they want to politely say no." He lowered his voice. "I didn't think anyone would dare turn the princess down though."

I understood his shock. What small-town ranch girl would turn down the chance to be a queen?

"Well, I will," I said, just as softly. All I had to do was wait until Monday and return the necklace. Then everyone would just assume our incompatibility.

Maybe then Shaw would turn her attention to other prey.

Students began standing and taking their plates to the giant water tank outside the kitchen, to later be picked up by students with dish duty. I quickly finished my breakfast. The necklace swung forward. It was heavy enough that I couldn't ignore it. I wanted to tuck it under my school dress, but it was too short for that.

"Try not to let everyone's staring get to you," Oluk said as we headed to put our dishes in the tank. "Like I said, you're the first familiar Shaw's courted. You're the first familiar any of them have courted."

"Shaw's entourage?"

"Yeah. They're kind of famous for it. This is the longest any entourage has gone without filling in at least some of the other half."

I turned to watch Shaw and her friends stand from their table. The crowd parted as the four walked to the dish tank. Witches and familiars alike stepped aside for them. Even the witch I'd seen sit next to Shaw during The Dead and Undead stayed back, out of the group's way.

Yuyan brushed past a trio of unbonded flower familiars and they all giggled. She either didn't notice or didn't care, distracted by another bickering argument with Aklemin. Einar was the same, ignoring the glass familiars that tried to catch his gaze. He was caught up in chuckling over whatever Yuyan and Aklemin were yelling at each other about. Shaw walked in the rear of the group, head held high, gait strong. Untouched by the rest of the world.

As if she'd felt my gaze, Shaw looked back at me over her shoulder. Her expression was as smooth as a pond and, from this distance, I couldn't tell what hid behind those dark-as-night eyes.

*What do you want?* I asked silently. I didn't understand political games. What was Shaw trying to get out of giving me such an obnoxiously bright courtship necklace? What was she hoping would happen?

Shaw inclined her head, as if acknowledging something. Then she and her entourage put their dishes away and left.

The rest of the students flooded toward the dish tank in their wake, hurrying so they could get to their first classes of the day. Oluk and I entered the crowd. It took minutes before we finally reached the front.

Just as I was setting my dishes down, someone bumped me from behind. My whole arm splashed into the dirty water. The smell of bloated fruit and rancid milk wafted into the air like a three-year-old's attempt at cooking. Pieces of soggy egg clung to my sleeve as I pulled it out.

"Careful, Rosamund," Charles said from behind me. "The princess's familiar must show a certain level of grace."

Oluk pulled me away from the tank, glaring at Charles. "Ignore him, he's just jealous."

"He should take it up with Shaw, not me," I said, flicking egg off my arm with a grimace. "I didn't ask to be courted."

I wanted to go change into my spare uniform, but I didn't dare be late to Madam Dyer's class. I shook my arm clean as best as I could and hitched the strap of my small satchel higher up my shoulder.

When I entered the classroom for The Dead and Undead, Charles wrinkled his nose dramatically. I smiled back with all my teeth and made a show of adjusting Shaw's necklace. Charles went red in the face. The wolf in my heart huffed something like a laugh.

Except, when I bothered to look away from Charles to the rest of the class, I saw that Shaw had also noticed the movement. I quickly pulled my hand away and Shaw turned to face the front of the class.

"Sit down, Miss Rosamund," Madam Dyer snapped. I flinched and did so. "Everyone, take a paper and pass it down," she said without looking away from me. "I will be testing whether you managed to learn anything I attempted to teach you last week. Notes away, I won't have cheating in this classroom."

I put my journal back in my satchel, stomach sinking. I hadn't studied at all over the weekend. The tests were passed around by row. I grabbed the stack from the familiar in front of me, took a test, then handed the rest to the witch behind me.

"You will have ten minutes. Go."

I looked down at the questions. There were ten. One for each minute. I could do this. Working methodically, I wrote down my answers. Even without studying, I had listened to Madam Dyer's lectures last week. It wasn't perfect, but I came up with answers to all the questions on spirits, phantoms, and ghosts.

The last four questions were about specters. Only then did I remember Shaw's offer to lend her notes. They'd covered specters the first day of class, the one I'd missed. I stared at the questions, trying to remember anything about specters, a story from my childhood, a passing comment, anything.

All around me, the other students got up and handed their tests in to Madam Dyer.

I set my graphite stick to the page, pulled it away, set it down again. Should I make a guess? They were obviously a type of the dead. Were they more similar to phantoms? Fragments of emotions left behind?

Someone came to hover over me. I looked up.

Madam Dyer shook the small clock in her hand. "Time's up." She took my paper, the last four questions still blank. Her eyes darted over the page as she looked at my answers. "No matter how ... distracted you are, Miss Rosamund," she said, glancing from my test to my new necklace, "I still expect you to prepare for class. You will be giving the class a report on specters next Monday, and it best be thorough. Understood?"

"Yes, ma'am," I mumbled.

"What was that?"

A hot flash of humiliation flowed to my cheeks. "Yes, Madam Dyer."

"Good."

I didn't dare look up. I was sure Charles would be smirking. I didn't know what Shaw's expression would be and I didn't want to. For the rest of the class, I scribbled notes furiously in my journal, determined to retain everything Madam Dyer lectured about. None of it, of course, pertained to specters at all.

When class ended, someone came over to me as I put my journal and graphite stick in my bag. It was a bone familiar I recognized from our shared suite. I'd seen her alternate between the boys' uniform and the girls', but today she was in the white dress with her black hair loose down her back.

"Hi. I don't think we've been introduced yet. I'm Jingyi Wang." She smiled brightly.

"I'm Rosamund," I said, not sure whether to be friendly or wary. Had Jingyi been one of the seniors laughing at me during the assembly? I couldn't remember.

Jingyi kept in step beside me as we left the classroom. "Don't let Madam Dyer get to you," she said once the door was closed behind us. "She hates courtship spectacles."

"Why?"

"Who knows? Maybe she fell in love and was rejected. Maybe she just isn't interested. Of course, Madam Bai isn't interested in bonding either, but that doesn't change *her* behavior." Jingyi huffed. "Madam Dyer was horrible when Chao-er and I bonded. Didn't want to let me join her necromancy workshop, even though Chao-er does better when I'm there."

"Chao-er?" I asked.

Jingyi pointed to the big witch who usually sat beside Shaw in class. He walked next to her now, a few paces ahead of Jingyi and me. "Chao Hu. My witch."

I nodded. If Chao had been in a necromancy workshop with Shaw, he had to be one of the more powerful bone witches at school. Necromancy was a notoriously difficult skill, even for bonded bone witches. No wonder Shaw seemed to be friends with him, despite her distance from everyone else outside of her entourage.

Looking sideways at Jingyi, I wondered again why she was being friendly with me. And why now? Was this another of Shaw's ploys? Had she asked Jingyi to talk to me? Or was I overthinking things?

"Can I ask you a question?" I said, just to see how Jingyi would react.

"Of course! What is it?"

"How do I get one of the boys' uniforms like you have?" I didn't mind dresses, but it was nice to have the option to wear pants instead.

Jingyi looked at me for a few seconds, as if trying to assess the sincerity of my question. "Are you a boy?" she asked finally.

"Oh, no. I've always been a girl." My parents had asked me when I was younger. Apparently Mama had been the first person Uncle Inge had told, back when they were kids, so she'd wanted to make sure she was doing right by me if I didn't feel comfortable being a girl.

"Then, sorry, they won't give it to you. Old traditions, you know? I only get both because I'm a girl sometimes and a boy other times."

I thought about Aklemin's school uniform—how it was some strange combination of a dress like the girls' uniforms but with suspenders like the boys'. I'd thought it looked much more awkward than the robes they'd worn while we traveled from Forest's Edge to Witch Hall. Now I understood that they must not have had a choice in what to wear, if the school had such strict rules.

"How do I tell, for you? Just by your uniform?" I asked Jingyi. I didn't trust her, but that was no excuse for misgendering someone.

Jingyi gave me another of those long considering looks. "My hair, usually. I put it up when I'm feeling like a boy, and leave it down as a girl. Or braided, if I can't have it loose."

I nodded. Hair down, girls' uniform. She was a girl today, then. I made a note to pay attention, if I ever wanted to talk about her with Oluk or someone else.

"Anyway," Jingyi said, bright smile returning, "I know you missed our first day of class. On specters. Since you have that report, I wanted to offer to help you study."

I'd already turned down Shaw's offer by saying I'd ask one of my suitemates instead. It would look bad if I turned down Jingyi. "Sure," I said. "Thanks, Jingyi."

Jingyi gave me a little nod, then bounded up to her witch's side. Chao wrapped an arm around her waist without missing a step and pressed a quick kiss to her temple.

For some reason, that made me want to look at Shaw again. I couldn't imagine the princess ever acting like that toward her familiar. Public displays of affection seemed too undignified for her.

A flash of memory hit me—long fingers brushing over mine as Shaw handed me her teacup. The way her dark eyes had caught my own and held them trapped. The beating of my heart, all the voices inside silent and still as if waiting to see what would happen.

Jingyi twisted in Chao's arms to look back at me again. "Remember, Madam Dyer's not worth worrying over!"

"I wasn't," I called back honestly. Madam Dyer's words hadn't bothered me—it was the fact that I'd failed the test at all. I'd always been a good student for Papa. Never complained about any of his assignments, even when Solemie and Toketie had. It didn't sit well with me to be doing poorly in school. To be proving all the nay-sayers right, the ones who'd say it was because of my upbringing.

Well, I would just have to give Madam Dyer the best report she'd ever heard. Neither Charles nor Shaw nor anyone else would be able to distract me from it.

# Chapter 12

BETWEEN THE WHISPERS AND LOOKS, THE CONSTANT studying, and scrambling to do well in my classes, my second week at Witch Hall passed slower than the first. It felt like it had been a month by the time my last workshop on Friday arrived.

"We will start today by practicing quick shifts," Madam Xu said. "The difference of a single second may very well save your lives one day. Even if your form seems unsuited for combat, the ability to change shape, to shock or surprise your opponent, is invaluable when fighting. Partner up—you will be counting for each other."

I took off Shaw's courtship necklace and stored it in my bag. Because the necklace held its own magic—Shaw's magic—it wouldn't shift with me like my clothes and shoes did. I'd asked Oluk what most bonded familiars did and he'd mentioned an enchantment that glass witches could etch into the necklace that allowed it to change size as the familiar shifted. Shaw, it seemed, hadn't gone through the effort of getting that done on her courtship offering.

Necklace stored, I grabbed Oluk to be my practice partner and we got to work.

Before my placement exam with Mister Voll, I'd never tested how fast I could shift. I'd known it was easier to shift into my frequently used forms, but it was fascinating to hear Oluk say the numbers. My horse shift averaged two seconds, my mouse three and a half. I wondered what the wolf would be, if I were free to train with it.

A quick burst of anger came at the thought. If only I didn't have to worry about the army, about being conscripted to fight like Gran had been. I imagined the look on Charles's face if I shifted into my wolf. I had to put a hand to my chest to stop a growl from bubbling up into my throat.

"You should aim to get your shifts down to two seconds or less by the end of the term!" Madam Bai called as she walked past Oluk and me. "We'll be testing you at the start of each Combat session. An improvement from last week will be a pass, so practice on your own as homework."

By the end of the hour, I managed to shave off half a second from my mouse shift, but if my horse improved, it was too close to tell. Oluk wasn't doing better. His garter was at six seconds, but his rattlesnake shift took him a solid ten and actually got worse as class wore on. I wasn't sure if it was his obvious exhaustion or if he was overthinking it.

"I do believe that is enough practice," Madam Xu said. "Shall we test how much you've learned?"

I pulled myself to my feet, suppressing a groan. Oluk didn't even bother hiding his, but then, he wasn't the only one. Madam Xu didn't acknowledge it and Madam Bai just giggled at our misery.

"Miss Froya, Miss Jingyi," Madam Xu called.

Froya and Jingyi slowly walked up to the front of the ground, both sweating. There wasn't a single familiar who didn't look exhausted. No one, it seemed, was used to shifting so frequently. Especially for those of us who'd been in Advanced Shapeshifting—we'd already neared our limit before lunch.

"The scenario is this. You are on opposing sides of a conflict. You are both well-trained in combat and ready to kill. The first to shift will invariably be the winner. Let us see who it shall be. On my count."

My gut twisted as I watched Jingyi spread her legs slightly farther apart, as if to get herself lower to the ground. Froya arched her back, like she was getting ready to sprout wings. I could easily see the picture Madam Xu had painted, and I didn't like it. Why did we have to be trained like we'd one day need to kill each other?

"Three, two, one," Madam Xu counted. "Go!"

They both shrank. Gray fur engulfed Jingyi's dress and golden-brown feathers sprouted from Froya's. Nails turned into claws or talons. They both sprouted tails—Jingyi's bushy and tipped with bone, Froya's long and covered in ice feathers.

Jingyi was first, but only barely. Bone fox stared down ice eagle—both tense as if ready to attack at a moment's notice.

"Good," Madam Xu praised them. "Shift back. Miss Jingyi, step aside. You will move on to the next round."

I watched as, pair by pair, Madam Xu called up the class. I ended up facing off against one of Toketie's friends, an ice familiar who could shift into a blue jay. I went for the horse and settled into it a good second before his beak had finished growing.

The next couple rounds were similarly easy, even as Oluk and Toketie dropped out against their opponents.

Then in round four I was matched with Charles. He sneered at me. I'd considered going for the mouse, partially to test myself and partially because I didn't want to win. I'd done well enough to get a good grade for this class, and that was all I cared about.

But I couldn't stand the look on Charles's face.

Madam Xu called go and we both shifted. I grew into the horse as quickly as I could, skin and bones rapidly adjusting.

When my eyesight stabilized, Charles stood in front of me as a bone deer. He must have noticed I'd finished, because he threw his head back like an invitation to crash antlers. Except none of my shifts had antlers—female deer never did—and my horse shift remembered the fear of facing down the bull moose too well to want to meet the challenge.

"Mister Charles wins!" Madam Bai called.

I shifted back and turned away before I had to see Charles's smug face.

I should have been happy not to stand out. Instead, I hated it. Why did I have to lose to Charles? Anyone else would have been okay. Even Toketie. But Charles? I couldn't help thinking he'd rub his victory in for weeks.

Jingyi and Charles ended up in the finals. I still wasn't sure if I trusted Jingyi, but I cheered her on.

Madam Xu counted them off and they both shifted in a blur. Charles sprouted antlers in seconds, but he was disadvantaged by his primary shift being larger than Jingyi's bone fox. Shrinking was always easier for familiars than expanding, even if familiarity with a larger shift could mitigate that advantage. But between Charles's bone deer and Jingyi's bone fox, there was no contest.

"Good job, Jingyi!" I called as she walked past, beaming.

She winked and bounded over to talk to one of the other bone familiars. Charles glared at her, then at me. I lifted my chin, mimicking his earlier challenge. He sneered.

Madam Xu lectured us on combat techniques for the next hour while Madam Bai showed how a familiar could switch from animal to human to animal again, in order to throw off opponents.

Just as they were wrapping up the lecture, a group of students wearing black uniforms and pink belts—flower witches—approached our class. I recognized Yuyan. She nodded in my direction and I waved back, though I regretted it when several students noted the movement and began to whisper among themselves again.

"Oh good, they're here," Madam Xu said. "These fine students took Madam Tukwilla's Advanced Healing workshop last term. For the rest of class, they will be here to practice their flower magic on you. Yes, that means we expect you to get hurt." Madam Xu smiled, and it was frightening enough to make the prey in my heart shiver. "For this final half hour, we will spar."

With the flower witches there, Madam Xu gave us permission to go all out. The only rules—no killing or permanent injury. Everything else was fair game.

"If you get injured in your animal shift, you must not shift back," Madam Xu warned. "It will only exaggerate the injury to do so. Allow one of the flower witches to tend to you first. And if I call halt, you will stop attacking immediately. Understood?"

We all nodded and Madam Bai assigned us partners. Oluk was paired with Jingyi. I supposed they were less likely to kill each other than some other pairings. I would have worried about crushing Oluk in my horse form, and in my mouse a single bite would have done me in too quickly to be healed.

Unfortunately, Madam Xu paired me with Charles.

He sauntered up to me, hands in the pockets of his trousers. Still smug. I wanted to rip that look off his face.

Luckily, Madam Xu continued to give instructions before he could say anything.

"You will start as a human and may begin to attack the second you've finished shifting. Get ready. Set. And go."

I knew Charles was faster. I didn't dare shift into the horse only to end up already impaled. Instead, I went for the mouse and scurried to the side before I could be trampled.

The mouse wasn't happy to be faced with hooves again, but I maintained enough control to scurry under Charles. I shifted directly into the horse. Charles let out a bleat as I grew. He toppled over and shifted into a human as he hit the ground. I stomped hard in the dirt just next to his head.

"That's a kill for Rosamund," Madam Xu said, giving me a nod. "Reset and go again."

I shifted back. Madam Xu stepped away to watch another pair. Charles got to his feet. His face was covered in sweat and dirt. It felt good to see him like that. To be the one with power over him.

"I don't know what the princess sees in you," he said, visibly seething. "It can't be attraction. You look like a potato and your skin's splotchy. I'm surprised your hair isn't stained brown by all the horse shit you shovel. You certainly smell of it constantly."

I grimaced. I shouldn't let it get to me. Charles was jealous. Even if Oluk hadn't said so, it was as obvious as the sun in the sky. But I knew he wasn't wrong either, and to hear it said so bluntly . . .

Charles wasn't done. "It's not your looks. I doubt it's your class. A rancher's daughter? Hardly worthy of our future queen, and the Witch King won't approve once he finds out. Better to save yourself the trouble."

I wouldn't mind the Witch King stepping in to ban Shaw from courting me, but Charles didn't need to know that. I crossed my arms. "That's for Shaw and the king to decide, not you."

Charles stepped forward into my space. His voice was a low, angry whisper. "On Monday morning, you will take that necklace off and give it back. Or else I'll tell the princess your secret."

My heart skipped a beat. "What secret?"

"That you're just like that traitor grandmother of yours," Charles hissed. I only had half a second to panic before Charles gestured in Oluk's direction. "She married another familiar, didn't she?"

Pops and Gran had fallen in love and even though everyone had expected them to both find bone witches, they'd defied those expectations to be with each other instead. It was romantic, Toketie and I had both agreed on that from a young age.

If all Charles was insinuating was that I liked Oluk, then that was a relief. I didn't, not like that, but: "So what? It's not illegal."

"It should be," Charles said. "But really, no one will be surprised. A screwup like him? No wonder he's never been offered a courtship necklace. I guess he had to settle for an ignorant little ranch girl and a life of shoveling shit."

"Oluk doesn't have to settle for anything," I responded. "Even if he did marry another familiar, that's not settling. And my grandparents didn't settle either. They loved each other."

Charles laughed, cold and cruel. "Everyone knows your grandfather only married your grandmother after the Witch Queen turned him down. Apparently your family has a legacy of reaching above your station. You and Oluk have that in common."

The wolf in my heart growled, fierce and untamable. I dug my nails into my palms.

"No wonder your grandfather kicked the bucket so early," Charles continued, ignoring my rising anger. Or maybe relishing it. "He probably didn't realize his backup plan was so crazy when they married."

"Take that back!"

"I'll bet he took the most dangerous path down the Frozen Mountain on purpose. Just for the chance to escape her."

I shifted. Only years of Gran's warnings kept the wolf from coming out. But neither the horse nor the mouse would do. I wanted claws, sharp enough to rip Charles to shreds. To tear at his body like his words had torn at my heart.

The raccoon rose to the challenge with a high-pitched growl.

Charles stumbled backward and began to shift into his goat—perhaps hoping the thick hide would protect him. I latched on to his throat halfway through the shift, claws digging in as deep as they would go.

Rationality tried to return, reminding me that I couldn't kill Charles. I moved to pull back, but the raccoon's grip was strong. Its anger was fueled by the wolf's. The last time I'd hunted with Gran, I'd substituted the wolf for the raccoon. Now, the raccoon was taking on the wolf's feelings—the wolf's love of its pack, its protectiveness over Gran.

I was underwater and drowning in the raccoon's rage. Charles finished shifting and the raccoon climbed up the goat's neck, using the horns as handholds. It was aiming for the goat's face, ready to claw out its eyes.

"Halt! Miss Rosamund. That is enough!"

The raccoon ignored Madam Xu. Charles tried to throw me off, bleating wildly.

"The necklace! Someone grab the neckl—" Madam Xu shouted. The last words warped and then cut off, the way it sounded when I tried to talk in the middle of shifting.

I couldn't control the raccoon, trapped in my own mind. I could only watch in horror as I left deep scratches in Charles's face. Every second inched those claws closer to Charles's eyes.

Something struck me in the back. Teeth pierced my skin. The raccoon tried to cling to Charles, but whatever held it was too forceful. I was pulled backward, claws scraping through Charles's skin before finally releasing in a spray of blood.

It was a snake, I realized. A huge white snake held me tightly between its glass-covered jaws. Thick coils wrapped around my body. The raccoon shrieked, sure it was about to be crushed to death.

The anger had disappeared, but I was still trapped in the raccoon's terror. This sensation was more recognizable. I'd felt it as the mouse, back in the Bone Forest. I was feral.

Distantly, I wondered if I'd be trapped in this state forever.

Something warm wrapped around my neck. A hum sparked in my heart, as if another voice had joined the shifts that lived there. But it wasn't a bone animal. This hum was familiar. It called to me like a memory of brushing fingers and porcelain teacups.

The raccoon's terror retreated and my human mind regained control.

I shifted, shaking. The snake's scales pressed against me from all sides, the glass patches touching my heated skin like buckets of cold water being poured over my anger and mortification.

Madam Xu uncurled from around me and shifted as well. "Are you back, Miss Rosamund?" she asked.

"Sorry," I whispered, more ashamed than I'd ever felt in my life. "I'm so sorry, Madam Xu. I don't know what—"

Madam Xu reached forward and laid a cool hand on my head. "Calm yourself. Panic will help nothing now. Deep breaths."

I did as ordered, breathing in, and out, in, and out. After a moment, I realized Oluk was kneeling next to us. Was he the one who'd wrapped that warm thing around my neck?

I lifted trembling fingers and felt the edges of it. The necklace. Shaw's necklace. Oluk must have grabbed it from my bag and wrapped it around the raccoon while Madam Xu's snake form had me trapped.

I knew bonding helped to stabilize familiars in danger of going feral, but I hadn't thought a courtship necklace would have such a strong effect.

"When you are ready, you need a flower witch to look at those wounds," Madam Xu said.

I looked down. Blood stained my white uniform. I'd shifted even though I shouldn't have, and the bite wounds had grown in proportion. Each individual tooth mark was shallow, but they were wide and horrifyingly painful, now that I was aware enough to feel them.

Another set of hands touched me. I flinched, but the smell of mint and willow bark followed. Yuyan.

"Calm down, Rosamund, I've got you," Yuyan said.

I didn't trust Shaw's entourage, but Yuyan had healed me before and my body remembered it. I relaxed into her grip and let her flower magic take hold of me. As Yuyan worked, I looked over at Charles. Two flower witches were working in tandem on his face and neck, trying to heal the deep scratches my raccoon had given him.

"I went feral again," I whispered to Yuyan. "I can't, I don't—"

"You'll be okay," Yuyan said. "You remember what I said about my friend? Shantie? She's not a strong physical healer, but she's a prodigy at potions and poultices. Shaw almost chose her for the entourage instead of me. Shantie will find a cure, promise. You just have to deal with it for a little longer."

I took deep, unsteady breaths. "Can I meet her? Shantie?"

Yuyan was quiet for a few seconds. I watched the scratches on Charles slowly close through the combined effort of both flower witches. The pain of my own bite wounds faded as Yuyan's magic did its job. I grew too tired to keep my eyes open.

"Tomorrow," Yuyan finally said. "After breakfast. I'll introduce you."

My tongue was too heavy to respond. I tightened my fingers around the necklace at my throat. The warmth of Shaw's magic followed me into sleep.

# Chapter 13

I SLEPT STRAIGHT THROUGH DINNER AND WOKE MINUTES before breakfast began. Hurrying to get ready was complicated by my aching side and the newly healed bite scars. I jogged to breakfast and found everyone already eating. Oluk had two trays laid out at our usual table.

"Sorry I missed stable duty," I said, panting from the run. "Was Mister Jostein mad?"

Oluk shook his head. "I told him what happened. Are you okay, Rosy?"

"I—" I stopped and sat down with a heavy thud. My brain felt fuzzy still. What could I say? How could I fix this? Not only had I gone feral in front of all the senior familiars, I'd also shown off another shift. And a predator at that. I wanted yesterday to be a nightmare, but the pain in my side proved otherwise.

"Is that the shift you've been working on in Advanced Shapeshifting?" Oluk asked.

I nearly reached across the table to hug him. That was it. No one had to know how old my raccoon form was. I wouldn't even be the first from our workshop to gain another shift. Lei Banks had found her fourth—another type of crab. I *would* be the first to pass Madam Xu's requirement, if she believed the raccoon was new. It was wildly different from the horse and mouse. But even if she didn't, so long as she said nothing, no one else would know I was hiding shifts.

"Yes," I said quickly. Then, loudly enough that I knew the nearest tables would be able to overhear us, "Yes, Madam Xu wanted me to find a form that wasn't prey for our workshop. I saw a family of raccoons in the woods, past the creek, and it seemed like enough to work off of." Considering how few shifts most familiars had, I figured my ability to pull in new voices after only observing the animal once was rare. "I've been trying to get a voice to settle for days. I guess the spar was the push I needed." Softer, I added, "It scared me."

"Me too," Oluk said. "I'm glad you're okay."

"Thanks, Oluk."

I didn't want to talk about it anymore, and I was glad when Oluk chose another topic for the rest of breakfast. I let his soothing chatter wash over me, helping me calm down from the panic I'd woken up in.

Just as we were dropping our dishes off, Yuyan waved me over. Luckily, Shaw and her other two companions had already left to do whatever they did on Saturdays.

"Ready?" Yuyan asked.

I'd almost forgotten about my request. "Yes," I said. "See you in a bit, Oluk. Yuyan's going to help me with something."

Oluk looked like he wanted to ask but didn't dare in front of a member of Shaw's entourage. He gave a hesitant wave goodbye. Yuyan nodded to him, then led me to the flower witches' dormitory— apparently the one closest to the teachers' cottages. The seniors' suite was around the back of the building, facing the waterfall.

"There she is." Yuyan pointed as we walked inside the suite.

Shantie was a breathtakingly beautiful girl. I'd never known any-one to be prettier than Toketie, scars and all, but Shantie had her head back in laughter as sunlight fell through the smoke hole in the roof, highlighting her high cheekbones and her rich sienna skin. Her black hair had just the slightest hint of wave that bounced in time with her laugh.

"Oh, YuYu!" Shantie said, still fighting giggles. She waved good-bye to the flower witch she'd been talking to and walked over to us.

"Hi, Shantie," Yuyan said, a bit breathless, as if she too had been affected by the enchanting melody of Shantie's laugh.

Shantie smiled, turning from Yuyan to me. "Hi. You're Shaw's familiar, right? I'm Shantie Cosho."

Shaw's familiar. All my stunned attraction fell away in an instant. Shaw's familiar. Was that all I was to the school? A posses-sion? A pet the princess had claimed? No longer even the new girl or the rancher's daughter. *Shaw's* familiar.

"Rosamund," I said, trying to control my expression. I needed Shantie. Needed the cure she was developing. For Gran, but also for myself.

I couldn't bear the thought of attacking someone else like I'd attacked Charles. Out of control, vicious. What if I hurt some-one I cared about next time? I thought of my cousin's deep scars and it was enough to make me forgive Shantie's poorly worded introduction.

"Can we talk somewhere private?" Yuyan asked. I appreciated her discretion more than I was willing to say.

Shantie took us into her room. It was just as cramped as mine was—barely space for a tiny bed underneath a large hanging shelf where Shantie had her things stored in neat stacks. Yuyan closed the door behind us. Shantie sat cross-legged on her bed, patting the space next to her in invitation. I sat at the end of the bed, letting Yuyan take up the space between us.

"What's wrong?" Shantie asked, keeping her voice low. I knew from experience that the walls of the suites were thin enough that a loud voice was easily overheard, but a whisper was too muffled to make out even with a familiar's advanced senses.

Yuyan looked to me.

"I'm sure it'll be all over school by tomorrow. I'm shocked it isn't already," I grumbled. The students of Witch Hall hadn't seemed to be able to keep their mouths shut about me thus far.

"Oh," Shantie said. "*Oh*. You're the familiar who went feral in Combat?"

I winced. So the story had already spread.

Yuyan nodded for me. "Rosamund wanted to meet you. To ask about your senior project."

"The cure," I added. "If there's really a chance—"

But Shantie was shaking her head. "There's no cure."

My throat clenched. The voices in my heart began to shriek and squeal together, reacting to my horror. No cure? What was the point of this, of any of this, if there wasn't—

Shantie must have seen the look on my face, because she quickly raised her hands. "No, no, don't misunderstand me. There will never be a *cure*. That's not what I'm trying to make. Feralness is caused by animal instincts overtaking the human mind. Trying to cure that would be like trying to cure the intrinsic magic of shifting. It's just not possible. Even if it was, I wouldn't want to do it. The same effect that can push familiars feral is what makes them familiars."

"So what are you doing, then?" Yuyan asked. Her tone made it clear this was news to her too.

"I'm trying to restore the balance. Mitigate the symptoms." Shantie grimaced. "It's a bit complicated. Basically, I'm trying to figure out a way to mute the heavy emotions so the rational mind can reestablish itself over the animal. Bonded familiars are able to pull on the magic of their witch to achieve the same effect, so I'm trying to figure out how to mimic that or to supplement the bond, in severe cases."

I caught myself reaching for Shaw's necklace and dropped my hand back to my lap. "How would it work?"

Shantie shrugged. "For familiars who chronically go feral, it may be something they need to take every day, as a preventative aid. But for most, it would be used during a feral episode. Hopefully it will be enough to snap most familiars out of it. Do you know the most common time for a familiar to go feral?" At Yuyan's and my headshakes, she continued, "After losing their witch. Across the board, if a witch dies before their familiar, the familiar goes feral. It's the opposite for witches. We usually go catatonic if we lose our familiar, which is less dangerous overall. Going feral makes the death of their witch even more traumatic for familiars. I hope my potion will help make the grieving process just a little easier."

"That's brilliant," Yuyan said. "Really, Shantie, this will help so many familiars, all over the kingdom."

Shantie blushed and ducked her head. "That's the goal. I'm trying to perfect the formula now." She glanced at me. "I'll need test subjects soon. Familiars who are willing—"

"Yes," I said, before Shantie finished her offer.

This was what I'd been hoping for. If I could help Shantie complete the cure—or the aid, as she called it—then maybe she'd let me take some back to my grandmother. A daily potion would be expensive, but we'd make it work. If it was for Gran, my family would find a way. Especially if she could be brought home because of it.

"Great! That's great," Shantie said. "Thank you, Rosamund. I usually work on it during my free period right after lunch."

"That's when I'm free too!"

Shantie clapped her hands. "This is perfect. You don't need to come every day, but maybe once a week can you come here, to this suite? It'll be good to have another test subject. My familiar's been getting the brunt of it. He's too good for me." She let out a rueful laugh, and I smiled back.

Yuyan stood, abrupt enough to cut into Shantie's laugh. "I'm glad it worked out. Good luck, Shantie, Rosamund."

"Thanks, YuYu."

I stood too, feeling lighter than I had since coming to Witch Hall. Possibly lighter than I had in years. "I'll see you next week, Shantie."

Shantie said a cheerful goodbye and I left. Yuyan had disappeared somewhere—maybe to her own room. I'd have to remember to thank her.

"Don't worry, Gran, I'll bring you home soon," I whispered as I stepped out onto the sun-soaked lawn outside the flower witches' dormitory. I remembered Yuyan's words, what she'd said as I was shaking from my own feral moment. "Just hold on a little longer."

I WAS STILL RIDING THE joy of the talk with Shantie as I refilled hay nets for my before-dinner stable duty.

Unlike the massive pastures at my family's ranch, Witch Hall's horses had less room. The herd had demolished any grass inside their small pasture long ago. To supplement, Oluk and I tied hay nets along the fence line while the horses ate their evening grain.

I finished the last hay net and collected all the empty ones into my arms to carry back to the hayloft. The pile was precarious enough that I had to concentrate my entire attention on making sure one didn't slip out.

"Watch out!"

I stumbled back just in time to avoid getting kicked by Cow. The empty hay nets tumbled out of my arms to the aisle floor. The bone mare pinned her ears back.

"Cow," Shaw scolded, jerking on the lead rope. "Be nice."

Cow snorted but let Shaw lead her around me to the pasture. I watched them go, noting Shaw's casual clothes and the sweat marks on Cow's back and girth line. They'd just come back from a ride. It wasn't the first time I'd run into Shaw taking a horse in from or out to a ride, but it was the first time since she'd offered the courtship necklace.

I bent down to pick up all the hay nets. I told myself that my rapid pulse was because of nearly being kicked, not because of Shaw herself.

Shaw returned, harness and lead rope coiled up in one hand. With the other, she helped me pick up the nets. She said nothing, and I remembered that she wasn't supposed to speak to me. Her warning shout had broken the rules as it was.

"Thanks for the heads-up," I murmured. Was I not allowed to speak to her, or was it only forbidden the other way around?

Shaw inclined her head. I'd noticed that she wasn't naturally talkative, but the silence now was unnerving. I was all too aware of her necklace, the warmth of it against my skin. As the necklace was imbued with Shaw's magic, it resonated when Shaw was close, increasing the power it gave off by tenfold at least.

That power, that magic was enough to make me sway where I stood. I felt like I'd been wrapped up tight in a heated blanket. Warm and safe. Like nothing could possibly hurt me.

Did Shaw know about what had happened yesterday? About the raccoon and going feral?

The raccoon was my deadliest shift, outside of the wolf. Bone raccoons were nearly four feet in length and a good forty pounds. It was nothing compared to a bone wolf, but enough to kill a human if I wanted to. Enough to kill Charles, if Madam Xu hadn't pulled me away in time. If Oluk hadn't wrapped Shaw's necklace around my neck. If the magic of it, Shaw's magic, hadn't been enough to calm me out of the feral state.

Did Shaw know that? She had to. Yuyan had seen it all. I worried about the consequences of it. Not about the raccoon—I didn't think they'd force me into the army just for that. I had to hope they wouldn't, anyway. Raccoons weren't nearly as prestigious or powerful as wolves.

No, it was the other part that worried me. The way the necklace had broken the feral state. I had to give Shaw the response to her courtship offer on Monday. How could I claim that our magic wasn't compatible? What excuse would I have to turn down her courtship if half the school's seniors had seen how I reacted to Shaw's magic?

How would I be able to give the necklace back when the warm weight of it was the only thing keeping the terror away? The fear that I'd go feral any second and hurt someone I cared about?

Shaw reached forward and I froze like a startled rabbit. The humming in my heart, the humming that Shaw's magic had put there, reached a fever pitch.

Slowly, like she knew I was seconds from bolting, Shaw plucked a straw of hay from my hair. She gave me a wry smile as she set it on top of the stack of hay nets in my arms. Then she turned and walked away.

It took me several seconds to get my legs to move. I walked to the hayloft and dumped the nets unceremoniously on the ground.

I hated this. Hated that I couldn't trust Shaw. Hated that her magic had this effect on me, when at the same time she looked at me like a hunter looked at a potential meal.

Was I the kind of prey that would walk willingly into a trap just for a chance to eat the bait?

SUNDAY FOUND ME SCRAMBLING TO finish up my presentation on specters for The Dead and Undead. Jingyi Wang had agreed to meet me at the library after lunch. The librarian, Mister Voll, kept piling books on our table as we went over Jingyi's notes from that first class on specters.

"There's a reference in this one, page thirty-six. No need to stop what you're doing, I'll mark it for you," Mister Voll said, adding another book to the top of an already unsteady stack.

"Thanks, Mister Voll," I said for something like the tenth time.

Jingyi played with the long orange ribbon that held his hair in a bun, waving the end of it at a section of text. "I really think you need to include this part here. Madam Dyer put a lot of emphasis on it."

"It doesn't seem as common though," I said. "I don't really know how to tie it in with the rest of the report."

"Maybe if we can find an example," Jingyi said. "Mister Voll!"

"The red book!" Mister Voll called back, showing he'd been listening even from the other side of the library. A couple younger students shushed him before refocusing on their own studying.

Jingyi lifted the top books off the stack so I could grab a slim red volume from the middle. It was a diary some witch had penned a hundred years ago. Mister Voll had marked a few pages, entries describing an encounter the witch had had with a specter.

I began to write notes in my own journal, letting my thoughts flow directly through the graphite stick to the page. After a few minutes, I realized the only sound was the scratching of my graphite stick, the scurrying paws of Mister Voll's squirrel form, and the flipping pages of the other studying students.

Looking up, I met Jingyi's eyes. The senior bone familiar watched me silently, seemingly unconcerned with how I would react to an unblinking stare.

"Why are you helping me?" I asked, whispering softly enough that hopefully Mister Voll and the younger students wouldn't overhear.

Jingyi's eyes flicked down, just for a second, to Shaw's necklace. The gleaming moonstone claim wrapped around my neck. The anchor to my sanity and the weight that was pulling me down into treacherous waters.

"I know what it's like," Jingyi whispered back, eyes on my face again as if he'd never glanced down. "Being the new student. I came to the Cursed Kingdom last year, from Waiming. Showed up at Witch Hall halfway through a term, without any idea what to expect, what it meant to be an outsider here."

For some reason, Jingyi's words made me think of Toketie. I'd never considered before how hard it would have been for her, coming to Witch Hall late. Being from our little village, with no social standing. Uncle Chetwoot's side of the family, the ones who'd manifested ice magic, had never been able to afford Witch Hall. That was why his sister, Toketie's aunt, was only able to read small fortunes and barely made a living in Woodside. Our grandparents had been strong enough for Witch Hall to personally invite them when it opened its doors for familiars. They'd gained fame during the war afterward, but any prestige we held for being Pops's grand-daughters we lost for being Gran's.

"It's unfair," I muttered. "None of it should matter."

Jingyi's smile seemed more genuine than any of the beaming grins I'd seen him wear so far. "No. But it does."

I almost went back to my notes, but I stopped at the top of the next letter. Glancing back up, I said, "You didn't answer my question."

Jingyi laughed as if I'd told a joke. "I did though."

That still wasn't an answer. "I don't know if I can trust you," I said, perhaps too honestly. "All the other bone familiars—"

"You forget, I'm already bonded," Jingyi interrupted. "I don't want the princess, not like that. I fell in love with my Chao-er the moment I met him. I knew within the first week of our courtship that I would follow him to the farthest reaches of this world. But Chao-er loves this kingdom. He bows willingly to its princess. So it will be my kingdom too. I will bow to her, and to the familiar she chooses to rule with her."

My heartbeat picked up. I knew where this was going. I shouldn't have asked. I didn't want to hear this.

Jingyi leaned forward in his chair. "That's you, Rosamund. You came out of nowhere and suddenly you're the most powerful familiar in school. You dragged Charles from his imagined throne, when none of the rest of us dared to try. Finding your raccoon shift just proves it. You think we aren't impressed? Mouse and horse and raccoon. It's a wider range than anyone except Madam Xu. It proves that you have perspective. That you can lead us, all the familiars of this kingdom."

"I don't want to be queen," I said. I didn't care that my voice had risen above a whisper. Let Mister Voll and the other students overhear. Let them spread the word. "I don't want *this*."

I didn't really know what *this* meant. All of it, probably.

I'd never had a feral episode before Shaw arrived in Forest's Edge. Never felt this out of control. I wanted to flee. To run back home, to the ranch, to my family, to Gran.

I took a deep breath and turned my face away from Jingyi to hide my expression. I wasn't here for myself. Shantie was making a potion. Shantie's feral aid was all Gran and I would need. I wouldn't have to cling to Shaw's necklace and the peace her magic gave me. We'd find our peace at the ranch, Gran and me. I just had to make it through the rest of the year. Just three terms. By Beltane, I'd be a graduate of Witch Hall and our family would be better for it.

I tried to ignore the fact that it had only been two weeks and I already felt like I was falling apart.

"You may not want it, but that doesn't change who you are. Doesn't change that you're the one the princess chose." Jingyi reached forward and squeezed my hand. "I know it's scary. But the Cursed Kingdom does romance better than most. That necklace isn't a seal. Courtship isn't a binding contract, not till the end. The whole point is to see if things will work between you and your witch. To test it out."

"But—"

Jingyi grinned and cut me off. "Who knows? You might end up liking it, being the most powerful familiar at school. I know I will. This place could use an upset."

# Chapter 14

SHAW WASN'T AT BREAKFAST ON MONDAY, THE DAY I WAS to answer her courtship offer. I wasn't the only one looking around for her, but she was nowhere to be seen.

It wasn't Shaw but Aklemin who approached after I'd eaten most of my food. "I'll take you to her," they said, soft enough that only Oluk and I could hear. "She didn't want to do this publicly."

I wondered why. Did she know I was going to give her necklace back? But if so, why offer courtship in the first place? I couldn't help feeling like I was about to walk into the trap Shaw had so carefully set. I had no choice, though, so I nodded to Aklemin and took my dishes to the wash tank.

Aklemin led me to a building just past the eastern longhouse. I was a bit surprised to see the senior bone witches' suite looked identical to all the others I'd been in. A few rooms had their doors open enough for me to see that they were just as cramped as my own. I'd assumed they'd give Shaw special accommodations, but the only difference to mark that the princess lived there was a few small rugs spread around the suite's central firepit.

Shaw sat on a cushion at the back of the firepit, legs stretched out onto a rug. The fire was unlit, but Shaw stared at it anyway.

She didn't look up as Aklemin gestured for me to sit down. I stayed standing.

"Thanks, Aklemin," Shaw said. It was an obvious dismissal.

Aklemin looked between Shaw and me, brows furrowed. After a second, their expression smoothed out and they left.

"Shaw . . ." I began, then couldn't figure out what else to say. If this was a trap, the cage bars weren't obvious yet. I worried that I'd misstep and fall into a leaf-covered pit.

Shaw didn't look up. It felt strange, looming over her like I was, but she didn't stand. I wanted to rip the necklace off and leave. I wanted to hold the necklace close and stay. I pushed the second feeling aside and reached for the clasp at the back of my neck.

"I don't understand why you're going to give it back," Shaw said, still not looking at me.

Just like that, I could breathe again. "You don't understand why?" I repeated. "Because you can't fathom that someone wouldn't be interested in you? That I may not want you?"

Shaw finally looked up and caught my gaze as easily as a falcon spotting a hare. "You do want me," she said without a hint of uncertainty.

I gaped. A flash of anger burned away any embarrassment from Shaw's statement. "I don't want a witch. I don't want to bond. And I definitely don't want you."

I went to take off the necklace again. Shaw reached forward as if to stop me. She was too far away to touch me, but I paused anyway, wary of her hand stretched halfway between us.

Then Shaw let the hand drop into a fist on her lap. "Rosamund-the-girl may not want me, but Rosamund-the-familiar does. You cannot fake a magical connection."

"Shaw—"

Shaw stood. She was a solid six or seven inches taller than me, enough that I felt tiny as she took a step closer.

"My magic pulled you out of a feral rage. Just that trickle I'd imbued into the necklace. Do you understand how rare that is? Most familiars would need a bond for their witch's magic to affect them so strongly."

The necklace warmed with each step Shaw took to bridge the gap between us. The humming was a purr in my chest. I wanted to deny it. To scream in Shaw's face that she was wrong. But I couldn't.

"Bonds aren't the be-all and end-all," I said instead. "Pops was always able to keep Gran from going feral, and they could never bond the way witches and familiars do."

"They were bonded," Shaw said, stopping only a foot away from me. "Not in the same way, exactly, but my grandmother presided over a ceremony to marry their magics together."

That information was enough to pull me out of the fight-or-flight response that had been brewing in my body. "Really?" I asked, but even as I did, I knew Shaw had told the truth. It explained so much about how Gran had reacted when Pops died. Shantie had said how familiars suffered when their bonds were severed. "Why didn't I . . . I mean, I didn't know two familiars could bond."

"It's not common. It takes a powerful witch to marry the magic of two familiars, or a powerful familiar to marry the magic of two witches. Father lost his ability to perform the ritual when my mother died. I read my grandmother's journals so I could learn to do it. So I could teach my bonded the same, and all our future citizens would have the option if they desired it."

"That's really sweet," I whispered, and hated it. Why did Shaw have to be like this? So arrogant one second, then noble the next.

Why couldn't it be as easy to hate her as it was when I hadn't known her?

Shaw reached out and I forgot to flinch away. Her thumb brushed against the necklace, fingertips pressed lightly against the skin of my neck. The necklace heated enough that it was almost uncomfortable, as if it had been set on fire by Shaw's proximity.

"I didn't predict you," Shaw murmured. "Aklemin tells me surprise is a good thing."

"Aren't they an ice witch?"

Shaw chuckled, fingertips twitching against my neck. "Hypocritical, isn't it?"

I pulled back, though part of me didn't want to. Part of me wanted to draw closer instead, to burrow into the heat of Shaw's body like she was the lone sunbeam breaking through the Bone Forest's dense canopy.

Shaw's hand fell away as I backed out of range. She didn't try to follow me, and that was the only reason my tone was gentle as I said, "I can't bond with you, Shaw."

"Tell me, do you truly believe you would be happy in some backwater village when you are powerful enough to be Familiar Queen?"

And there was the arrogance again. I scowled. "I don't want that kind of power."

"You don't want the power, or you don't want the responsibility?"

"I don't want to be at your side when you raise an army of the dead and go off to war," I snapped.

Shaw stared at me, eyebrows furrowed as if I'd surprised her. I tried for a third time to undo the clasp of the necklace.

"Wait," she said. "I respect that you don't want to bond with me, but please keep the necklace. For your sake, if nothing else."

There it was. The trap had finally sprung. "Why?" I asked, though I didn't want to know.

Shaw lifted her chin, as if to avoid the blood splatter when she went in for a kill. "You may have fooled most, but not me, Rosamund. Your raccoon was not a new shift. It makes me wonder what else you're hiding."

My breath caught in my throat and I had to cough it out.

Shaw continued ruthlessly. "My magic calms you. I'll have Einar enchant the necklace so you don't need to take it off to shift. If you give it back now, what will keep you from falling into another feral rage? What will keep you from revealing another shift?"

"I have no other shifts," I said, but I knew the lie sounded weak.

Shaw didn't call me on it except to smile. "For my sake, then. There is no one else at this school I wish to court, and I don't want the speculation to distract me from my final year. Let me continue the facade of courting you."

I thought of Jingyi's words then. Of the power that would come with this offer. Power to keep myself safe from those who were suspicious. It would even, I realized, keep the military away. Why would they try to recruit me? If I were Shaw's familiar, I would follow her into war. They didn't have to know I'd be parting ways with her, and everything she represented, as soon as we graduated.

Those were all just excuses to make me feel better though. I knew the real reason I wanted to say yes. I would get to keep Shaw's necklace. Shaw wasn't wrong about its effect. I didn't want to go feral again. The mere idea of it was enough to make my pulse thunder in my ears and sweat bead along my palms.

"I will not trap you in a bond," Shaw said. I'd taken too long to answer, so she must have thought her argument wasn't enough. "We will simply be using each other. You are free to reject my courtship at any point and I will not press again. On my honor, Rosamund."

She held out a hand, palm up. It was a traditional gesture. Mister Sorensen had talked about it in class last week. For someone of higher status to turn their palm up to someone lower, it signified an offer to share power.

Shaw didn't need to do it. Such an offer was more weighty than this deal. A version of it was used in bonding ceremonies, or by a jarl when appointing a new advisor. But this wasn't either of those things.

But then, that was the facade, wasn't it?

"Fine." I paused, still staring at Shaw's upturned hand. "Fine," I repeated, "I'll keep the necklace for now."

I slowly put my hand on top of Shaw's. Her palm was warm—like the necklace. She slid her hand up so that she could squeeze her fingers around my wrist, completing the gesture. My skin tingled long after she pulled her hand back.

"We should get to class," I said, trying to subtly shake my arm. "I have a report to give to Madam Dyer."

"I look forward to it," Shaw said. She held out an arm.

I frowned. "Are you serious?"

"It will be expected."

Fine then. I tucked my arm into Shaw's and let her escort me to The Dead and Undead.

"One more thing," Shaw murmured as we exited the suite. "My entourage refuses to entertain their own matches until I have made mine. I would be grateful if you didn't let them know of our deal."

"You want them to find familiars?"

Shaw hummed in agreement. "Even if it takes me some time to secure my own, I would like our entourage to expand as it should.

I don't wish the familiars of the kingdom to feel unrepresented by my future rule."

"Yes, fine, I won't tell anyone." I knew my tone was rude, but I was done with this whole thing and ready to move on. Shaw had helped solve some problems but she'd also introduced a good dozen more.

For now, I pushed it all to the back of my mind in favor of mentally reciting the report I'd prepared. Even when Shaw led me to sit next to her in the front row, I focused only on reviewing my notes and internally practicing my speech.

Madam Dyer wasted no time. As soon as class started, she looked pointedly at me. "Rosamund, I believe you are our instructor today."

"Yes, ma'am," I said.

It was a quick walk to the chalkboard from my new front-row seat. When I turned to face everyone, I couldn't help seeing that all eyes were on my neck—on the moonstone necklace still resting just above my collarbone.

Jingyi grinned. Chao nodded. The other bone witches gave me their full attention, like I was suddenly more worthy of their respect than before. Half the bone familiars looked jealous, the other half excited.

Charles's expression was the worst. It was blank, so much so that I might have been fooled into thinking he didn't care. If I hadn't seen the split second when I walked into the room on Shaw's arm. If I hadn't caught the expression of pure anguish, of a dream being violently ripped away. After what happened at the assembly, the blankness that followed made me nervous.

I looked to Shaw, the only person in the class not staring at the necklace. She raised an eyebrow as if to say, *Well? Get on with it.*

"While ghosts, spirits, and phantoms are all related, spec-ters are in their own category," I began. "Ghosts are imprints of people and sometimes animals who died in regret. They are the most autonomous of the dead. They turn into spirits if they lin-ger in the mortal realm for too long without passing on. Spirits lose their physical forms and become embodiments of emotional energy. This is why spirits are able to possess people, especially those who echo the same emotions. Phantoms, in comparison, are things that have left an emotional imprint, often in response to sudden loss, such as an amputee's phantom limb or the phantom of a wedding ring."

I paused, wishing I'd thought to bring water. I wasn't used to speaking for so long without interruption. The poignant silence of the class unnerved me.

"Specters," I continued, "are like none of the other types of dead. They exist completely in the physical world, but are halfway between living and dead. They are caught in the same emotional feedback loops as spirits and phantoms, but while spirits and phan-toms eventually dissipate, specters never will. Nor can they choose to let go of their regrets and move on, like ghosts. What's more, specters are always malevolent. They exist forever in a state of rage, attacking any living creature that comes near them."

I continued from there, explaining how specters were often cre-ated in a spiritual possession gone wrong, or made on purpose by a curse. Only very strong bone witches were capable of separating the two combined souls, allowing them both a chance to move on. Most of the time, specters had to be killed instead and their energy dissipated through strong cleansing rituals.

The report went pretty well, I thought. Madam Dyer didn't have anything negative to say about it, at least. By the end, everyone in the class had refocused on my face instead of the necklace. The only holdout was Charles, but I tried to ignore his blank stare the best I could.

At the end of class, Shaw stood at my desk before I could escape. "Let me walk you to your next class?" she offered.

"Must you?" I asked, too low for anyone but Shaw to hear. The stares got worse when we were together.

She held out her arm without answering. I wondered how long I'd be able to stand this before I threw the necklace away.

Luckily, Shaw didn't share my second class—Survival Skills with Madam Bai—so we separated outside the clearing. I quickly found my usual seat next to Oluk.

"You decided to accept after all?" he asked brightly.

"Yeah, well, Shaw convinced me to give it a try." I pulled my notebook out of my bag, avoiding Oluk's eyes. I wanted to tell him that it was all for show, but I'd promised Shaw I would tell no one. "We'll see how long it lasts," I said instead.

Oluk's lips twitched, like he was holding back a smile. "If you say so."

"I do." I flipped to the section of my journal I'd been using to take notes on Madam Bai's various and scattered Survival Skills lectures. There was no rhyme or reason to her classes, but they were without a doubt my favorite at Witch Hall. Even though I'd spent six years hunting in the Bone Forest with Gran, Madam Bai still managed to teach me something new every day.

She wasn't there yet and there was no note for us to begin without her, so I turned to Oluk. "Will you tell me what to expect? What's the next stage of courtship?"

"The test of companionship. The first stage was the test of compatibility. Now that that's been passed, you have to see if you can be good companions to each other. Walk together, work together, all that."

"How long does it usually last?"

Oluk shrugged. "There's no specific limit. A few months to a year. The school is small so witches and familiars in courtship see each other a lot. Some break off after only a couple weeks, but that's rare. Usually if the compatibility test is matched, then that means you'll be physically comfortable in each other's presence. So it takes a bit longer to figure out if there's other things that might get in the way of the relationship."

"Is there another stage after?"

"Yeah, negotiations. It's the shortest stage. The marriage contract, basically. Who will live with who, and who'll take whose name. Though usually that's decided by who the courter and who the courted is. Who has higher status."

"Right," I said. *Rosamund Colchuck.* I grimaced at the thought.

"The princess will be expected to give you gifts," Oluk said. "Three of them, total. The first is the easiest. Something to prove her power. I'm sure she won't have any trouble with that. The second is something that represents how she perceives you. It's usually the most sentimental of the courtship gifts. The final one is supposed to show that she understands your desires and is willing to help you achieve them."

"Then we move on to negotiations?"

"You give her a gift in return first. After you receive the third. It represents a promise. Nowadays, it's always the matching necklace. Haven't you seen how the bonded pairs wear complementary ones?"

I had noticed, but I hadn't paid much attention to why that would be. I was glad this whole thing was fake. There was no way I'd be able to afford a matching moonstone necklace.

It didn't matter. We just had to drag the fake courtship out through the rest of the school year. Maybe not even that long. Once Shantie finished her senior project, I'd remove the necklace. Even if we hadn't graduated yet, Shantie's potion would keep me from going feral.

Hopefully by then, Aklemin or Einar or Yuyan would have found a familiar to court. Shaw was right about the necessity of that. It would be good to have at least one familiar in Shaw's entourage. I'd happily let that familiar take all the attention once I stopped the courtship.

When I graduated and moved back to Forest's Edge, it wouldn't be long before no one remembered the ranch girl Shaw had tried to court. She'd find a different familiar to take to war with her and I'd bring Gran home.

Madam Bai breezed into the clearing long after everyone else had found their log seats. "Good morning, good morning!" she said. "It's a new week, no time to waste. Let's talk about all the things that are poisonous to our human forms and what your animal shifts may be able to ingest. Shall we get started?"

"Yes, Madam Bai," I answered with the rest of the class. Madam Bai was a stickler for class participation.

Our teacher did a little dance in front of the clearing. "Good, good! Let's start with hemlock." She pulled a plant out from the bosom of her dress. "Oh, wait, this is stinging nettle. Well, let's start with this one then."

Another good thing about Madam Bai's instruction style, other than her strange flavor of genius, was that it left no room for the other familiars in the class to stare at me or gossip about my court-ship with Shaw.

An hour later, Madam Bai flitted around the class checking how we were all doing on a plant-identifying worksheet. When she got to my log, she leaned down close, as if to check my answers.

"Hang in there, Miss Rosamund," she whispered.

I startled so badly my graphite stick went flying and smacked Oluk in the face.

Madam Bai straightened and winked at me. "Class, what is the number-one rule of survival?"

"Trust your instincts!" everyone replied.

Madam Bai plucked the graphite stick from where it had fallen at Oluk's feet and handed it to me. "Here, Miss Rosamund," she said. "You'll need it."

I knew she wasn't talking about the graphite. "Thanks, Madam Bai," I said. Then, with only a bit of hesitation, I asked, "What if your instincts are telling you two different things?"

"That is a good question." Madam Bai tapped her chin dramatically. "I suppose, find someone else you trust, someone who has never led you wrong, and listen to *their* instincts."

I returned to my worksheet, but I wasn't really seeing it. I was thinking of Gran. What would she say about the fake courtship?

Nothing good, I knew. But, for the first time in years, all the voices in my heart were in agreement. Wolf and horse, raccoon and mouse, otter and squirrel, and all the dozen large and small bone animals that I held like a herd in my chest. Giving up access to Shaw's necklace was unacceptable. The comfort of her magic was worth whatever obstacles would come.

# Chapter 15

## SHAW

HER FATHER'S LETTER OPENED WITH THE USUAL pleasantries. Updates on his court and the jarls' council. Discussions on the growing tension with Vinland and the army's new training maneuvers. Halfway down, he finally penned the reason for the letter.

*Biyu informed me of your courtship. A peasant, Shaw? You know I trust your judgment, but I hope you understand how this looks to the court.*

With the travel time of couriers, Chao must have written a letter to his mother the very day Shaw offered the necklace to Rosamund. It was foolish to feel betrayed by that. Chao wasn't a member of her entourage. He had no obligation to keep her secrets. He might not have even realized that she hadn't told the king about her plans yet.

*You need every advantage to prepare for the coming conflict. My scouts report significant unrest along the Vinland border. Their anti-witch propaganda spreads rapidly and calls to arms with it.*

*You will need a strong familiar to stand at your side when the spark finally lights.*

It was her own fault for not writing her father earlier. She'd been waiting to see what Rosamund's response would be. She had a letter drafted already, explaining herself. Telling her father that the courtship wasn't serious. That she'd wished to test the bone familiars at school, the way one tested hunting dogs with a juicy bone—to see if they'd keep their head in the hunt or get tempted by an easier snack. Publicly courting a familiar with no standing at school had already shown her an entirely different side to Charles Almstedt and several other familiars. It had been a good plan.

At least, until Rosamund had uprooted her expectations yet again. Until Yuyan had come running to Shaw's suite, just before dinner on Friday. Until she'd learned about the fight. The raccoon. The feral rage.

Until Rosamund had stood before her, ready to remove Shaw's necklace, and she'd realized that no one else at this school was ever going to catch her attention like this infuriating ranch girl had done so effortlessly.

Rosamund wanted a fake courtship, but Shaw was not raised to give in so easily.

She ripped her draft letter to shreds and grabbed a fresh piece of parchment.

*Dear Father,*
*Do not concern yourself. I am well aware of the threat across the border. Rosamund Holt may not be prepared for the politics of court, but I have come to believe that she*

*is the best choice to fight beside me. She is stronger than anyone at Witch Hall wishes to admit.*

Shaw considered what else she could add. In truth, her father was likely worried because he couldn't foresee Rosamund's future. Even the most powerful ice witches could only see the future of those they'd met. The Witch King might be having visions of Rosamund's effect on Shaw's future, but until he was introduced to Rosamund, they would be incomplete.

Though if anyone was able to glean the future from an incomplete picture, it was her father. She ended the letter with:

*As always, Father, I heed your words. Please write to me if your visions show danger or treachery.*

*With love and respect,*

*Shaw Colchuck*
*Heir to the Witch King*
*Princess of the Cursed Kingdom*

She closed the letter with her personal seal and imbued the paper with a touch of magic so her father would know her words hadn't been forged.

Aklemin fell into step with her as she walked to the campus mailbox. They both had their free period before lunch, but they rarely saw each other unless Aklemin wanted something.

"You should have Einar enchant that necklace soon," Aklemin said. "Rosy's definitely the kind of girl who appreciates actions more than words."

"She never gave you permission to use that nickname," Shaw reminded them, not for the first time.

Aklemin ignored her once again. "You'll need to be decisive. Your courtship will fall apart if you take too long to act on it."

Shaw hadn't told Aklemin about the deal she'd made with Rosamund, but she wouldn't have been shocked if they knew. They always seemed to know her secrets.

"Do you see her in my future?" she asked them softly.

Aklemin looked up at the sky, though Shaw knew cloud-seeing was not one of their talents. "There's crossroads still to come," they said.

"Aklemin."

The ice witch shrugged. "Perhaps, perhaps not. It's hard to say."

Shaw shouldn't have asked. When had Aklemin ever given her a straight answer about the future? She would be better off introducing Rosamund to her father.

Perhaps next term. There was no rush. Rosamund was still skittish as a newborn foal. Shaw had to go slowly. Show her appreciation through this courtship, get Rosamund used to her regard. Entranced enough by it that she wouldn't realize the courtship was real until it was too late.

The first step was to show Rosamund the support she hadn't given before.

Shaw and Aklemin walked to lunch. They were among the first in line for food. Yuyan was next to join them both—her class was close to the dining hall. Rosamund and Oluk were after. Shaw waited to see if Rosamund would come join her table, but she walked to her usual corner without a glance in Shaw's direction.

Apparently, it was a day for foolish disappointment. First Chao, now Rosamund. Shaw shouldn't have expected different from either of them. She knew she still needed to prove herself. Her tutors growing up had always praised her patience. She shouldn't let the first familiar who had really caught her eye change that.

Einar was the last to their table. He'd carved runes into the underside of the wood years ago. With a touch of glass magic, the runes would keep the nearby tables from overhearing their conversations. Shaw tapped the table to signal that she wanted privacy, and he activated the runes without a word.

"Something wrong?" Yuyan asked.

"I need to know the reactions to my courtship with Rosamund. How has the school taken it?"

"The twins think it's romantic," Einar offered, referring to the half siblings who ruled the year below theirs with iron fists and bright smiles.

Of course they did. Shaw expected nothing less from the twins. She turned to Yuyan.

"Kwaddis seems happy, but I think that's only because Charles isn't," she said.

Kwaddis Tenas's father and Charles Almstedt's mother were two of the most powerful voices on the jarls' council, and frequently sat in opposition on political matters. Most votes came down to Froya Falk's parent, who took a more neutral stance and convinced their power base to vote with Jarl Tenas or Jarl Almstedt depending on the issue.

"How has Froya taken it?" Shaw asked Aklemin.

"Cautiously pleased, I think," Aklemin said. "Not because of Miss Rosy, but because she hopes this means I'll choose a familiar soon."

"Are you going to court her?" Einar asked.

"Oh, no, she would despise me forever. Froya Falk will never accept having the lower status in a relationship." Aklemin waved a hand in the air, as if to dismiss the very idea. "But she needs me to court a different ice familiar so that she's open to court whoever she has her eye on."

"Jarl Falk would never accept it if Froya courted someone before Aklemin made their choice," Shaw said, because Einar still looked confused. "Not if there was a chance that Aklemin would choose her, no matter Froya's feelings about it."

"But you dance with her at every ball!" Einar protested.

"Well, I have to entertain myself somehow, don't I? She gets so mad. And she can't let anyone know, lest it get back to the jarl. Last Beltane, she *accidentally* stepped on my feet five times in a single song." Aklemin chucked fondly at the memory.

"You are the most ridiculous person I have ever had the misfortune to be friends with," Yuyan told the ice witch.

"I suppose we know how the bone familiars feel," Aklemin said, ignoring Yuyan.

"Most, certainly," Shaw agreed. "Jingyi threw her lot in with Rosamund last week."

Aklemin whistled. "If Jarl Hu—"

"I'm not sure," Shaw interrupted. "Chao wrote his mother a letter and she shared the news with Father. He wasn't pleased."

"That doesn't mean Chao's letter wasn't optimistic," Yuyan noted. "Only that the king isn't convinced."

That was true. Regardless of her father's uncertainty, Chao hadn't outwardly dismissed Rosamund. He hadn't stopped his familiar from helping her with the specter report. Jingyi's support of Rosamund was a statement of its own. She was the only senior bone familiar to have bonded and one of only a few among all the bone familiars at Witch Hall.

Shaw's chosen familiar would take the familiar's throne one day. Even before she became Witch Queen, they would likely assume all the duties of the most powerful familiar in the kingdom. With Shaw's mother long dead, there hadn't been a familiar royal in years. She expected more familiars would find a way to show their support of Rosamund before the end of the term.

Rosamund didn't know, Shaw thought, just how much power she held. Power to influence her entourage's own choices of familiars. And by their choices, power to influence the political tendencies of Shaw's future rule. Shaw had her own beliefs, and she'd chosen her entourage to fit with them, but new voices could easily tip the balance on positions she and her entourage were neutral on.

Her entourage did not agree with her on every topic either, and it was her duty as future queen to listen when they didn't. Their familiars would have just as much of a voice in that. Her own familiar most of all.

A gaping hole had been left in the power structures of the kingdom when Shaw's mother died. The other familiars of her father's entourage had done what they could to fill that gap, Chao's mother especially, but it was only ever a temporary fix.

Shaw wanted to see Rosamund rise to that position. She wanted to learn her beliefs, hear her thoughts, be swayed and sway her in turn. Time would show her if all they had was magical compatibility or if her instincts were right, that Rosamund had the strength to claim the throne that had sat empty since the day of Shaw's birth.

"Will you support my choice?" Shaw asked her entourage. "My father doubts Rosamund's viability as future queen because he has not met her. It's you three whose words I'll listen to, if you doubt it too."

Yuyan was the first to shake her head. "I like her."

"She's good for you," Einar said. "I believe that with my whole heart."

Aklemin took the longest to answer. "She walks her own path," they said finally. "You won't succeed trying to pull her off it. You must choose to walk it with her, or to step off and return to your own."

"You're losing your touch. That was almost blatant," Yuyan said.

Before the two could start another argument about Aklemin's cryptic teasing, Shaw asked, "Will her path lead me away from my own, or can we walk parallel, and hold hands across the gap?"

"Perhaps for a time," Aklemin said. "But there are crossroads ahead."

"Yes, you did say that, didn't you?" Shaw pondered their words for a few seconds. Should she be concerned? She wasn't. Anticipation drowned out everything else. What would the crossroads be and how could Shaw and Rosamund make it across together?

"Here is the plan," Shaw said. "Yuyan, continue to prioritize Rosamund when she needs healing. Don't let another witch tend to her. Cheer for her during spars if you'd like. Talk up her potential to the other flower witches and familiars, especially the jarls' heirs."

Yuyan nodded. "No problem."

"Aklemin, keep an ear out for rumors. I want to be ahead of the school gossip. And try not to make Froya angry. We need her on our side."

"Oh, very well."

"Einar, I need you to enchant Rosamund's courtship necklace so that it will adjust to the size of her shifts. How long will that take you?"

"I'll need you to feed some magic into the runes so the necklace won't reject the enchantment, but it won't take more than an hour."

"Good. Let's do it publicly. In the library tonight should work. I need you to ask Rosamund at dinner. Make it loud and apologize for not having time to do it before I gave her the necklace."

Einar frowned. "You didn't ask me to."

"I know. Is that okay?" Einar despised lying, but Shaw expected that his desire to help Rosamund's social standing would outweigh a misleading statement on his scale of honorable actions.

Einar thought it over for a second before agreeing.

"Thank you." Shaw looked from Einar to Yuyan, and finally to Aklemin. "All of you."

"We support you, Shaw," Yuyan said. "It's about time you found a familiar who's capable of standing up to you."

Was that what this was? Shaw thought of Rosamund's scowl as she accepted her courtship offer. Was she merely interested in the first familiar who'd played hard to get?

But no, that wasn't what Yuyan had meant. Rosamund Holt wasn't afraid to stand her ground before Shaw, but she never ignored her. That was how Shaw knew she could win her over. Rosamund was as drawn to her as she was to Rosamund.

"I want her," Shaw said, and it was the first time she'd admitted it out loud.

"Shall we plan your first courtship gift?" Einar asked.

"Oh, I know—" Aklemin began.

"For the last time, no familiar wants cake for any courtship gift! Let alone their first," Yuyan snapped back.

"Not just any cake," Aklemin retorted.

Shaw gestured for Einar to remove the privacy enchantment as Yuyan and Aklemin began to argue loudly about the proper protocol for courtship gifts. Let the school overhear them. The gossip would run rampant as everyone speculated about what she would give Rosamund.

She already knew, of course. She'd had her first courtship gift selected since long before she ever met Rosamund. She'd need to adjust the measurements—Rosamund was shorter than the average familiar—but all that took was a letter to the royal tailor.

She'd contemplated the look of it on a number of bone familiars over the years. None of those mental pictures had felt as right as the one she had now of Rosamund, swathed in red and glory.

# Chapter 16

## ROSY

I forced myself to wait until Wednesday before checking on Shantie during our shared free period. I didn't want to seem too eager. Einar had enchanted my necklace earlier that week, so my excuse for wanting the feral aid had dwindled.

Shantie wasn't in the senior flower witches' suite when I arrived, but someone else was. By his white uniform and pink belt, he was a flower familiar. He was handsome, with short black hair ending in artful bangs. I'd been at Witch Hall long enough to know to check his neck and, sure enough, he wore a beautiful necklace marking him as a courting or bonded familiar.

"Hello," I said as I stepped fully into the suite. "Here to help Shantie too?"

The familiar shrugged, then peered at me. "Is that what you're here for? To help?"

I couldn't tell if the flower familiar knew who I was. Strange that I'd gotten so used to everyone recognizing me after only a few weeks.

"I'd like to," I said. "The potion she's making is important, you know?"

"Useful, certainly," the familiar agreed. "Especially for those with a tendency to go feral."

He definitely knew who I was. "It is," I said more firmly. "No one should have to feel trapped by their own magic and ostracized by their community for it."

"Strong word, ostracized," he said, and deliberately looked at my necklace.

I hadn't been talking about myself, but before I could say anything, Shantie walked out of her room and into the common area of the suite.

"I thought I heard talking. Hello, Rosamund. Has my brat of a familiar introduced himself yet?"

I shook my head. Shantie's familiar adopted a sheepish look, but it was too dramatic to be real.

"Guanyu Cosho," he said, holding out a hand. He and Shantie were already bonded then, since they shared a last name.

"Rosamund Holt," I returned evenly.

Shantie hung a small pot from the hook above the fire. "Guanyu, would you—?" She didn't even finish her question before her familiar was there with flint to light the fire.

"I'm not a fan of open flames," Shantie confessed to me as Guanyu got the fire going. "Silly, for a flower witch who brews potions, but I can't help it."

"It's not silly," I said. No witch who feared fire was silly, just as no familiar who feared hunters was. Witches and familiars had been killed for the crime of being born for thousands of years.

"Ready, love," Guanyu said.

Shantie began to pour vials of liquid into the pot, standing awkwardly so that she was as far from the fire below it as she could manage. "I've almost refined the potion," she explained as she poured in a bright green liquid, and then a clear one. "The only issue is how to make its effect proportional to the magic of the familiar in question."

"Why not just prescribe a different amount?" I asked.

"Unfortunately, I can't. If my calculations are correct, for powerful familiars, they'd have to drink three times their body weight before it even started affecting their magic. And at that amount, some of the ingredients in here can become fatal."

That certainly didn't sound good. I eyed the fumes coming up from the pot. Was it my imagination or was the steam glowing purple?

"So I've been experimenting with magnifying agents," Shantie continued. "Ingredients that boost the effect of potions. Most of them haven't reacted well, but this week I figured out that a couple pinches of frozen ash just at the start of boiling . . ."

As if on cue, the potions began to bubble. Shantie opened a small drawstring pouch and took out a pinch of ice-blue ash. I watched as she sprinkled it over the potion. The liquid sparked, as if Guanyu had just struck his flint over it, then the bubbles simmered down, leaving an eerily calm surface.

Shantie grabbed a cloth, then carefully pulled the pot off the fire. With a small grunt, Shantie set the pot on one of the tables in the corner of the suite's common area. She carefully ladled the potion into a teacup.

"Here," she said, handing the cup to me. It was shockingly cold to the touch.

"You haven't told her what you need her to do, love," Guanyu said.

"Oh. Oh! Sorry, Rosamund. I'll just need you to drink that and shift. It doesn't matter what form. Don't worry, it's perfectly safe. The worst that will happen is, well, nothing."

"How will I know if it worked?" I wasn't feral right now, and I didn't know how to make myself feral.

"You may find it harder to shift," Shantie said. "The goal of this potion is to reestablish your rational human mind over the instinctive animal one. So if I got the balance wrong, you may find your inner voices silenced. You'd still be able to shift—it's not possible for anyone to block that magic once a familiar has unlocked it—you just wouldn't be able to feel your inner animal. Or animals, in your case."

"If you're used to drawing on their voice to shift, you'll find it difficult. But your ability to do so won't be gone," Guanyu elaborated. I could tell he knew what I was feeling—the thought of being cut off from the voices in my heart was terrifying. "And it isn't permanent. It'll wear off after a couple hours."

I stared at the potion in the teacup. I relied so much on the voices in my heart. Silencing them felt like a type of betrayal, even if it was temporary. I understood now why no one other than Shantie's familiar had volunteered to help test her project.

But this was for Gran. I had to be brave. I took a deep breath. "Okay. So I just have to drink this and shift?"

Shantie looked relieved, as if she'd been expecting me to refuse. "Even if you don't feel anything, I can assess how your body is reacting to the potion. And it will be easier to assess you than my Guanyu."

"I have to go down to the river to shift," Guanyu said. "Even the creek's too shallow, unfortunately."

"He's a flower salmon," Shantie explained.

I whistled. Flower salmon were easily five feet in length. "I can shift into my mouse, if that's easiest?"

"Yes, perfect!"

"Ah, one more thing," Guanyu said. "You'll need to take your courtship necklace off. We don't want the princess's magic to affect Shantie's assessment."

"Right." That shouldn't have been any scarier than the threat of the voices being silenced, but I hesitated a touch too long before undoing the clasp and stuffing the necklace in my bag. "Now?"

Shantie nodded. I gathered whatever courage I had and drank the potion.

Nothing happened at first. I waited a couple seconds, but I couldn't sense anything different. The voices in my heart were still there, several actively curious about the proceedings.

I shifted into the mouse and held still as the flower witch kneeled down and put a single finger on my head.

"Nothing," Shantie muttered. "Traces, but it's nowhere near strong enough. Go ahead and shift back, Rosamund. Guanyu, get me another cup. Let's see if adding the crushed lavender will help."

Just like that, we were off. Drinking the potions got less scary over time, as even the strongest doses weren't enough to completely silence my voices. At most, they sounded muffled, like there was a blanket covering my heart, but that one wore off only ten minutes later.

For over an hour, Shantie tested different combinations of ingredients and brewing methods. By the end of it, I felt exhausted. But not like I'd done too much work, more like I was sleepy and couldn't be bothered to put any effort into anything. The voices in my heart grumbled, their displeasure softened by the same lethargy I felt.

Guanyu laughed as he looked at me sitting on the ground, disinclined to move. "I think we should call it a day, love," he said.

"Oh, yes, you're probably right." Shantie wrote down a few more notes in her journal, then came to sit beside me. "Let me encourage your body to burn through those potions. I think the combination of them all is working against you right now."

Guanyu kneeled in my line of vision as Shantie placed a hand on my forehead and got to work. "So, Miss Holt, what are *you* doing for your senior project?"

"Don't know yet," I admitted. I'd been holding out for Madam Dyer to come around. I'd thought that maybe after the report, she'd soften toward me. I still wanted to learn if it was possible for unbonded familiars to commune with the dead, especially since I was pretty sure Pops's ghost *was* visiting me when I meditated. But what other teacher would be able to advise me on that? Madam Dyer was the resident expert. I'd already tried asking Mister Jostein, since he was a bone witch too, but he'd said he wasn't good at dealing with the dead and he couldn't give me any advice.

I'd only just started coming around to the idea that I'd need to choose a new project. Vaguely, I knew I should be worried about that, but it was hard to care about anything with the potions muting my feelings.

"Oh, I see, the lavender of the second try and the chamomile of the fifth have been amplified by the frozen ash," Shantie muttered.

"I'll figure something out," I told Guanyu.

"Best do it soon," Guanyu said. "Have you found a teacher to supervise you yet?"

"Should have burned through the earlier attempts before moving on. We'll have to redo those last few again next week. Silly of me," Shantie continued muttering.

I was beginning to feel a bit more alert. I sat up straighter, nearly dislodging Shantie's hand from my head. "No, that's the problem.

Madam Dyer turned down my first idea." I scowled, annoyed at the memory now that my emotions were less muted by the potions. "What about you? What's your senior project?"

"I created a business where I sell potions by mail to villages without a resident flower witch. I had to prove that I could sell a hundred potions before Madam Ipsoot accepted, and now I'm asking the villages for reports on how the potions are affecting their communities to create my final project report."

"Isn't he clever?" Shantie said. "He's already saved two lives, if the letters we've gotten back are to be believed."

Guanyu ducked his head, though not enough to hide a pleased smile. "You're the one supplying the potions," he murmured.

"And I would never have thought to send them out by mail. Or had the sense to make it a successful business while still keeping prices low enough to actually support small villages," Shantie said.

"Have you reached out to Forest's Edge?" I asked. "My uncle, Chetwoot Holt, he works as the doctor for our village. I'm sure he'd love to have more potions stocked in case of emergencies."

"I'll add him to my list of contacts," Guanyu said.

I left the flower witch suite feeling a horrible combination of successful and panicked. Even though Shantie hadn't found the right recipe for her potion yet, it felt good to be helping in the process. And I now knew how I could get Shantie's potion to Gran. Once the potion was complete, I'd just have Uncle Chetwoot include orders for it alongside whatever other healing potions he'd buy from Guanyu for the village. We wouldn't even need to go out of our way to find a flower witch to make it, if the potion could just be sent to us by mail courier.

With things looking up for my plan to help Gran's feral episodes, I had to focus on graduating Witch Hall so I could petition the jarls' council to get Gran released. Which meant, on top of doing well enough to pass my classes, I also had to figure out a senior project.

If I couldn't do my first idea, I had nothing else. I didn't have any skills that I could use, not like Toketie's organizational or Guanyu's marketing abilities. I had no product I could make, like Shantie's potions. What kind of senior project *could* I do?

That evening during stable duty, I asked Oluk what his senior project was. I didn't expect him to immediately look upset.

"What? What's wrong?" I asked when he didn't say anything.

"It's just . . . Mister Jostein approved my project, but I don't know that I'll be able to do it. We even had to get special permission from the headmistress for him to advise me, since Mister Jostein isn't a teacher. She'll be so disappointed if I can't do it, and Mister Jostein will too—"

"What's the project?"

Oluk gestured around us. "I came up with a plan to redesign the school stable. It hasn't been updated since familiars started being allowed into Witch Hall, and there's never enough room for all the horses and carts. It's worse when we have visitors. You remember how much cleanup we had here after last assembly?"

I nodded. I hadn't minded the work at the time, shaken as I was from the assembly itself, but I could see how that would be tough to deal with every month.

"Mister Jostein approved the plans and we're going to start renovating next term. The problem is, my design requires some enchantments. To do things like replenish the horse troughs and keep them clean."

"Like the tubs in the bathhouses," I said. The baths were a luxury I'd never known before. There were even runes that warmed the water.

"Yes, like that!" Oluk set his empty grain bucket down with a solid thump. "But every glass witch I asked to help said no. I even figured out a way I could cut down on the number of enchantments. But I need at least some, or the whole design doesn't work."

"What do most people do?" I asked. "Shouldn't there be a way to force a witch to help a familiar, if they need it? Or give them extra credit or something?"

Oluk shook his head. "No, it's more of a . . . I think it's how they encourage us to bond or at least start courting in school."

I thought of how Guanyu was helping Shantie test her recipe, and how Shantie was giving Guanyu the potions for his business. "That's not fair to the ones who don't want to bond," I muttered.

"I mean, you can always come up with a project that doesn't need help," Oluk said quietly.

That was true, I supposed. Toketie's project didn't require an ice witch's help. "So why'd you make a design that did?"

Oluk looked down. "Because I, well, I guess I hoped . . ."

There was a sheen to Oluk's eyes, like he was about to cry. I closed the lid to a chest full of curry combs and brushes, then tugged him to sit down with me. "What's the problem?"

Oluk rubbed at his eyes with the back of his sleeve. "Sorry, Rosy."

"You don't need to apologize. Just talk to me."

He stared at his knees, still visibly fighting back tears. "I want a witch like Mister Jostein, one day."

"What, brusque and intimidating?"

"No! Strong and . . . you know." Oluk blushed.

"Handsome?"

"It's not about appearances," Oluk said. "Haven't you seen how he treats Mister Voll?"

I remembered the first day I'd met them. That long kiss, Mister Voll's laugh. "Yeah, I've seen some."

"They're partners. Both of them do their own things, and they're okay with that. It's not always just one supporting the other."

"They respect each other."

"Exactly." Oluk smiled, but it was a small thing. "That's what I want out of a witch, most. One who will respect me."

"Just because no witch has seen your worth yet, doesn't mean one won't," I said firmly. "The people here are all too focused on status and background, instead of what really matters."

"What?"

"What's in here," I said, poking Oluk in the chest. "And I don't mean your shifts either, though you do have two strong snake shifts and some glass witch will notice that, someday. What matters most is that they also notice the rest of you."

"Enough to forget that I'm the son of illiterate obsidian miners?"

"Enough to appreciate that you are. Your upbringing is what made you *you*. You wouldn't be my friend if you were some snobby jarl's son, you know."

Oluk sniffed and rubbed at his eyes. "I'm glad we're friends, Rosy."

"Me too. And because we're friends, you're going to help me come up with a senior project while we muck the stalls."

I thought for a second that I'd miscalculated. That putting the focus on me was rude, not helpful. But I'd noticed that Oluk didn't like it when people gave him too much direct attention, and sure enough, he brightened at the thought of changing the subject to my own senior project.

We threw ideas back and forth across the barn aisle, each more ridiculous than the last. It was only as we were putting our muck rakes away that Oluk said, "What about shifting?"

"What about it?"

"Madam Xu's the strongest familiar in the kingdom. There's no one better to teach Advanced Shapeshifting. But the basic shifting workshops aren't very good. If you could figure out how to teach familiars the trick of getting their second shift . . . especially the art of it. You're the only one in the class whose first two shifts were so different."

That was a thought. Shifting was definitely my best talent. I'd gained so many shifts that the memories had blended together, but I distinctly remembered what it had felt like to shift into the horse for the first time, after a year of only having the wolf's voice.

"Do you think Madam Xu would agree to advise me?"

"I'm sure she would! Especially if you came to her with a theory."

It was worth a try. "Thanks, Oluk. You really are a good friend."

Oluk's smile then was much wider than earlier. I resolved to think about a way to help him with his project too. The only glass witch I knew was Einar, but maybe . . .

I thought it through while Oluk and I headed to dinner. "Do you mind if we sit somewhere else tonight?" I asked as we went through the line together.

"Sure?"

"Come on."

Oluk followed me as I walked to the middle of the room. I could hear his steps hesitate as he realized where we were going, but to his credit he didn't stop.

I hoped this wasn't a big mistake, but it was too late to back out now. I stopped at the edge of Shaw's table and waited for my fake-courting partner to invite us to sit down.

# Chapter 17

AKLEMIN WAS THE FIRST TO NOTICE US. THEY NUDGED Shaw. The princess looked up from the soup she'd been stirring. The only sign that she was surprised to see me standing there was one slow blink.

"Oh, there you are, Rosamund. Did stable duty run long?" she said, as if she'd expected this. As if we'd planned it beforehand.

Shaw was better at this whole fake courtship thing than I was.

Aklemin slid down, leaving obvious space between them and Shaw. On the other side of the table, Yuyan did the same, so that Oluk could sit across from me—between her and Einar. Good. The whole reason I was here was for Oluk. Let the glass witches see him being accepted by Shaw's entourage. Let them wonder. Let them want.

"A bit long," I said to Shaw's question, and sat as close to her as I dared. I didn't want to be the weakest link in our game of pretend. "Oluk and I got caught up chatting about our senior projects. Did you know he has a plan to redesign the stable?"

Shaw and her entourage all turned their attention to Oluk, as did most of the witches and familiars sitting at the tables around Shaw's.

Oluk was obviously uncomfortable, but Einar patted the open

seat Yuyan had made in invitation. Slowly, Oluk sat down, his face red. Einar didn't seem to notice, turning back to his food even as the other tables broke out in incredulous whispers.

I was about to nudge Shaw, but she spoke before I could. "A redesign is long overdue. That's a commendable senior project. Will you tell us about it?"

There it was again. That side of Shaw that I could actually find myself liking. I looked at her out of the corner of my eye as Oluk, stuttering a bit, began to answer her question. She looked every bit as attentive as she did during class, like Oluk's words stood between her and graduation.

I worried it would make him more nervous, the princess's undivided attention, but it seemed to do the opposite. Oluk sat up straighter and his nervous stutter began to fade.

It wasn't the attention he didn't like, I realized. It was the negativity. Attention when he was feeling useless or ignorant. But here, now, the princess and her chosen entourage were seeing Oluk at his best—discussing a design that he'd obviously spent countless hours perfecting.

"What rune sequence did you intend for the aisles?" Einar asked. At some point Oluk had pulled his journal out of his bag and now he and Einar were bent over some sketches, food forgotten.

"Oh, I'd thought this"—Oluk flipped back a few pages and pointed—"but Shugh told me it was too difficult and no glass witch would want to put that much effort into . . ." He trailed off, obviously unwilling to finish the sentence.

"It's just this part here that's difficult," Einar said, tracing a rune. "But if you flipped it here, so the power of this rune helps make a connection between these two elements—"

I turned my attention away from the two glass students, too

lost to follow their conversation anymore. "What are you doing for your senior project?" I asked the rest of Shaw's entourage.

"I'm apprenticing under Madam Tukwilla at the school infirmary for the year," Yuyan said.

"Yuyan's healing is the best in the school, so Madam Tukwilla is working with her directly on improving it," Shaw added.

I frowned. I remembered that name vaguely. She was the witch in charge of the Advanced Healing workshop. It made sense that she ran the infirmary too. But, "Why does everyone call her Madam Tukwilla? Isn't Tukwilla a given name, not a surname?"

"Same reason Mister Jostein doesn't go by Mister Voll," Shaw said. "Madam Tukwilla is bonded to Madam Ipsoot. They can't both be Madam Ipsoot, so Madam Tukwilla goes by her first name."

"I still think it's ridiculous that bonded or married couples are expected to have the same surname," Yuyan said. "In Waiming, we keep our family names."

"There's no law that you can't keep your family name here. Jingyi Wang chose not to take Chao's surname, no matter what Jarl Hu thought of it," Shaw said, a touch amused. "I don't think Madam Xu would have taken her witch's name if it weren't for the opposite problem."

"Oh, because Madam Bai is her sister?" I asked. "So there would have been two Madam Bais?" I couldn't imagine calling Madam Xu by her first name. Though I suppose, judging by their personalities, we'd have been calling Madam Bai Madam Xiaoqing instead.

"Yes, but it only worked out because Mister Xu has the higher status between them," Yuyan complained. "If he'd been lower status than Madam Xu, they would have been Mister Bai, Madam Bai, and Madam Bai. So it's a ridiculous tradition either way."

"I wouldn't mind keeping my family name," Oluk said, putting away his journal. It seemed he and Einar had finished going over his design for the stable. "I know I'm going to be lower status than any witch I bond with, but I don't want to ignore where I came from. I don't want people I meet to forget that I started out as a Blackwell. Too many people in my family have sacrificed their lives to the obsidian mines for me to turn my backs on their legacy just because I was lucky enough to break free of it."

"That is more than admirable," Einar said, and his expression was soft as he looked at Oluk.

I frowned. Oluk might have been the whole reason I wanted us to sit at Shaw's table, but I hadn't intended this. I wanted Oluk to find a witch who would respect him, wanted that dream to come true for him. Maybe I thought Einar would help him on his project, but I should have known that Einar would like Oluk. Who wouldn't like Oluk once they got to know him?

I wanted the best for Oluk, but Einar was not the best. No member of Shaw's entourage was the best, for all that I had come to like them as people. All of them had made a choice steeped in blood when they joined Shaw's retinue. Their familiars would have no choice but to be dragged into it.

I didn't want Oluk to break free from a legacy of illiterate miners only to die in Shaw's coming war.

Shaw turned her attention to me, noticing my frown. I tried my best to control my expression. There was nothing I could do, not now. From what I knew of Einar, he wasn't the type to rush into anything. He wouldn't start courting Oluk after a week, like Shaw had with me. There was time still. Time for Oluk to get help on his project without the pressure of courtship. Time for him to realize, once the glamour wore off, that Shaw and her entourage weren't worth going to war for.

August bled into September, bringing cool breezes to counteract the summer sun. Friday afternoon was so pleasant I wished I could take a nap along the riverbank instead of attending my workshops.

In Advanced Shapeshifting, Madam Xu had us working so hard that the flower familiar named Kwaddis Tenas eventually complained aloud, "What's the point of finding another shift now? Once we all bond, won't it be easier?"

The hairs on the back of my neck bristled as Madam Xu turned from where she'd been giving Charles advice and stared at Kwaddis. "And why would a bond make it easier to find another shift, Mister Kwaddis?"

Kwaddis looked like he knew he'd put his foot in his mouth, but he continued anyway. "Everyone knows bonding makes you stronger. Witches and familiars."

"Everyone knows that, do they?" Madam Xu stepped to the front of the clearing and gestured for all of us to sit down on the usual log benches. "Let me tell you a story," she said. "It is the story of my early years, when I still lived in Daming, the great nation across the ocean."

I sat, interested. Oluk joined me, looking just as entranced. I guessed that Madam Xu didn't tell this story often.

"I discovered my first shift as a young girl," Madam Xu began. "It was a massive white python, and I was chased out of my own village because they saw me as a demon. I spent years learning how to defend myself. I practiced all forms of martial arts, begging anyone who'd be willing to teach me. I learned other shifts too. Mostly constrictor snakes, at first, then venomous species. I was lonely for many years, until at eighteen I rescued a small green snake from decapitation by a farmer. The green snake turned out to be another shifter cast out from her home, and Xiaoqing and I became sisters. You see, in Daming, many rural villages believe all shapeshifters to be embodiments of evil. To the upper class it was different, as it is here in the Cursed Kingdom, but we had no status then."

I shivered, imagining my family kicking me out. Imagining my entire village turning against me. What Madam Xu went through was terrifying to even consider.

"Xiaoqing and I traveled together. We were never able to stay in one place long. I had learned to control my shifts, but Xiaoqing was younger than me and still struggled not to shift when consumed by emotions. One day, our training was interrupted by a young man. He'd seen us and wanted to know how we were able to shift into animal forms. This man was Xu Xian. Xian Xu, you would say here. He had a gift for creating protective charms and amulets, but there was no formal school for magic in Daming then."

Madam Xu explained how she shared what she knew with Mister Xu, but unbeknownst to them, another familiar eavesdropped on their conversation. A tortoise shifter by the name of Fahai, who knew that if he bound himself to a witch, his own powers would increase. He followed Xian and attempted to force the bond.

There were gasps all around. Madam Xu nodded. "Yes, to force a bond is a truly immoral act, but Fahai was obsessed with power. He cared not for A-Xian's objections. But I was stronger than Fahai, and I fought him until he conceded. From then on, A-Xian, Xiaoqing, and I journeyed together. A-Xian and I fell in love and eventually we stumbled upon a bond of our own. We made enemies, however. Word of our power traveled. Princes paid A-Xian to set up magical wards around their palaces and courts. Where A-Xian went, so too did Xiaoqing and I. But the same power struggles that led to many families fleeing to the Waiming Territories also hunted us. I had to protect myself against the various assassins sent after me and A-Xian. At least, until I got pregnant."

No one else seemed surprised at this news. I wondered if Madam Xu's child was here at Witch Hall. I imagined they would be either a glass familiar or witch. I looked over the glass familiars in the class, but none of them looked like Madam or Mister Xu.

"I would have stayed. Our life was not safe, but it was good. We had enough work, now that our reputation had grown. We were invited to many splendid palaces and poisonous courts. It was as glamorous as it was dangerous. But Xiaoqing wished for a child of her own, and A-Xian became worried about our vulnerability. Staying was not worth the lives of our children. He begged me to agree to travel across the ocean to the Territories, and from there to the land we'd only heard about in passing. The Cursed Kingdom. Eventually, I agreed. Xiaoqing and I birthed our children on the ship, but we were safe. The headmistress was willing to offer us a place here, and so here we have been for sixteen years now."

Madam Xu's story ended and we all sat in silence, digesting her words. After some time, she asked, "Now, why do you think I told you that story? Mister Kwaddis?"

"To give us a break, because we were getting tired?" the flower familiar said.

"Perhaps," Madam Xu said in a tone that told us he wasn't right at all. "Miss Lei?"

"To inspire us to work harder? Because you trained enough that you were able to rescue your witch when he was in danger of being forced into a bond?"

"Closer," Madam Xu said. "Mister Oluk?"

Oluk wrung his hands in his lap, but he spoke clearly. "I think so we could remember how lucky we are, being here in a place that accepts us and teaches us and helps us find our witches like you found yours."

"That is true," Madam Xu said. "Witch Hall is not perfect. There are things I would change about the system here. But you are clothed and fed and taught. You are impressed with a sense of duty. You live in a kingdom that seeks to protect you from the frightened and the angry, and you are allowed the chance to join that fight."

She paused and met my eyes suddenly and unexpectedly. "But what I want you all to remember is that bonding with a witch, or another familiar, is not the ultimate goal. Bonding is not a magical cure that will grant you power, grant you shifts. It may grant you security, and a larger pool of energy, but I had dozens of shifts before I ever met my A-Xian. Our bonding only brought more complications into my life, for all that I don't regret it." She paused. "Maybe that is the question. Why do I not regret it, if bonding with my witch was such a difficult journey?"

"Because you love each other." Surprisingly, it was Charles who said that. He had his arms crossed, looking defensive as the rest of us glanced at him. "Because you're a team and you make each other stronger. Not just magically, but as people."

"Indeed, I think that is the lesson I was trying to impart after all." Madam Xu smiled. "Now, enough chitchat. Back to work!"

I walked up to Madam Xu as the rest of class went back to practicing their shifts. "Madam Xu, can I talk to you for a second?"

"Yes, Miss Rosamund?"

"I'm looking for an advisor for my senior project. You keep telling us how important it is for familiars to have our own power, outside of our witch. I was thinking of doing my project around shifting. To help familiars figure out the trick to unlocking their second shift."

Madam Xu beckoned me closer. "What is your theory, then?"

"Emotions? We talked about how shifting comes from connecting emotionally with an animal. Relating to it. So maybe the problem for familiars with only one is that they're too emotionally attached to their first shift?"

"Then how would you propose fixing that issue?"

"I think, if a familiar can figure out what it is about their first shift they emotionally connect with, that will help them look beyond it."

Madam Xu nodded slowly. "It is an interesting thought, but just that. A thought. If you bring me proof of concept, I will gladly sign off on the project."

"What do you mean, proof of concept?"

"Teach a familiar how to unlock their second shift and journal the process. Come to me once you have succeeded."

I MULLED OVER MADAM XU'S order all weekend. Unfortunately, Oluk already had two shifts, so I couldn't use him. The only other familiar who came to mind was Toketie, but we hadn't spoken since our argument.

This was the longest I'd ever gone without speaking with my

cousin. Even when she was at Witch Hall without me, we wrote letters. I was angry at her still, but I missed her too.

Could I use this as a way to mend whatever had broken between us? Toketie didn't need me anymore, that much was clear. She didn't think our family was worth holding on to. But if I could show her how to get another shift, that would be valuable to her. That might prove that turning her back on me, on our whole family, was a mistake.

Decided, I tried to find a time to catch Toketie alone. Only she was always surrounded by her suitemates. Were it not for our last conversation, I would have just walked up to the group and asked to talk to her. But I worried that, after our argument, she'd say no. I didn't want the mortification of being rejected by my own cousin in front of the biggest gossips at Witch Hall.

I thought I could pair up with her in Etiquette, but Toketie was undeniably Mister Sorensen's favorite student. We'd started a dancing unit and Mister Sorensen always called her up to be his demonstration partner.

On Monday, I watched as Mister Sorensen led Toketie through a minuet, with small steps timed precisely to each count he made.

"The leading partner will then bow or curtsy, then the following partner will do the same. From there, it's on to the second verse. Watch closely now, because this dance is tricky. On the second verse, the leading partner will turn counterclockwise while the follow steps to their right. Everyone will end up in front of new partners. Understood? Let's practice."

Mister Sorensen told us to find our partners. I'd been pairing with Oluk, usually as the lead for the first half of class, then the follow for the second. This was the first dance we'd learned where we'd switch partners. Hopefully I wouldn't step on my new partners' feet like I did the first couple classes I danced with Oluk.

The count began. "One, two, three, one, two, three," Mister Sorensen chanted. "Left and right. One, two, three. Right, now left. Good! Second verse is coming, one, two, three, and switch."

I spun and danced, keeping an eye on Toketie's location. In one more verse we'd end up across from each other. Two, three, and turn. There.

I'd been so focused on watching Toketie that I tripped over my own feet as I got into position. Toketie grabbed my arm to keep me up, still moving to the count like nothing could interrupt her perfect dance.

"Thanks," I murmured. "I've been wanting to talk with you about something."

Toketie hummed, less like an agreement and more like a question. I stepped left, then right, knowing I needed to figure out how to make the request quickly, before the verse ended and I was down the line to another partner.

"Do you want a second shift?" I asked. "Because I've been working on a way to teach familiars with only one how to unlock their second for my senior project, and I thought, maybe—"

"I don't need your pity, Rosy," she said. "I'm not Oluk Blackwell, begging for your favor."

"Oluk has never begged me for anything."

Mister Sorensen called for us to switch. I watched Toketie step away, feeling like something I didn't even realize I'd grasped was now slipping through my fingers. "Just, Tokey, don't you want—"

"I got this far on my own," Toketie snapped back. "I don't need you."

Froya bumped into me, hard enough to be deliberate. "Forgot to turn, Rosamund?"

I quickly rotated to my new partner, still stinging from Toketie's words. I found myself across from Guanyu.

"Chin up," Guanyu whispered, making it clear he'd heard everything. "Don't let them see the pain, it will only make it worse."

This was exactly what I hadn't wanted. By tomorrow, everyone at school would know that Toketie wanted nothing to do with me. And even though I'd called her on her behavior first, it hurt.

But Guanyu was right. I did my best to mask my disappointment and fall into the steps of the dance.

"I need to tell you something," Guanyu said as we bowed to each other. "Meet me by the river dock tomorrow during our free period?"

I was instantly suspicious. I didn't know Guanyu well. We'd interacted only the one time so far and he hadn't been particularly friendly at first—though he'd warmed up by the time I was on the floor about to fall asleep from Shantie's potions.

"Fine," I said. "I'll be there."

Guanyu nodded and we spun away to face our new partners.

I ASKED OLUK WHAT HE thought of Guanyu during stable duty that evening.

Oluk thought about it for several seconds, before he finally said, "I think he's a bit like you, Rosy."

"Like me?"

"He plays by his own rules." Oluk shrugged. "He's a strong flower familiar. Kwaddis and Lei have more shifts, but Guanyu's got more raw power. If he were anything like the rest, he would have waited to see if Yuyan would choose him before moving on. But he choose Shantie instead."

"How do you know he's got more power, if he only has the one shift?" I asked. "Shouldn't that mean Kwaddis and Lei are stronger?"

"Not really . . . have you heard of the concept of anchors? Magical anchors, I mean."

I nodded. "I know bone wolves anchor bone magic."

"Just as ravens anchor ice magic, and pythons glass, and whales flower," Oluk listed off. "But do you know why?"

That I didn't know and I said as much.

"It's because those are the animals that channel the most magic. They keep the magic anchored to our world, or else it would, how did Mister Sorensen explain it . . . disappear, basically. There used to be magic all over the world, right? But when people started killing off witches and familiars and even just normal magical creatures, those wells of magic went away. Now there are only a few sanctuaries left. I know there's a huge well of flower magic in the western islands."

"I've heard of those. Supposedly there's a dozen whale and shark familiars patrolling the waters around those islands so nonmagicals can't get close." The western islands were one of the few other magical sanctuaries in the world, outside of the Cursed Kingdom. I'd heard stories of the ships they'd capsized, though it was hard to imagine a familiar who could shift into something *that* massive.

"Yes, exactly. I don't think we've ever had a whale familiar in the Cursed Kingdom, though I heard there was a shark familiar who lived here about a hundred years ago. He could only turn into a small shark, but still. We've never had a whale familiar because there's not enough flower magic to sustain one, but if we ever did have one, they'd be able to anchor a bigger well of flower magic. Right now, flower magic is actually the weakest of the four in the Cursed Kingdom, since it's confined to Lake Bloom and doesn't really have space to grow."

That I understood. The Bone Forest used to be a lot smaller, but it had grown over time to take up the entire southern border of the kingdom and then some. The Obsidian Desert was the same, though it grew east. The Frozen Mountain, too, had grown. The center of the magic used to just be at the very top, but now it encompassed the entire mountain.

"I know that familiars who can shift into anchor animals are powerful," I said, trying to ignore the wolf's amused huffing in my heart. "Like Madam Xu."

Oluk nodded. "She's a python. It's part of why she has *so* many shifts. She has enough magic inside her that she can hold dozens of voices in her heart."

I wondered what that meant for Gran. If she ever learned how to unlock a second shift, would she become like me and Madam Xu? Would voices come to her as easily as they did to us? I was even more interested in my new senior project now. Would it help Gran to have more voices in her heart? It was certainly hard for me to wallow in loneliness with how loud mine always were.

"Okay, but that doesn't answer my question. How do you know Guanyu is powerful? He's a salmon, not a whale."

"It's because he's a salmon. You can usually guess how much magic a familiar has based on their first shift. Every bone animal anchors bone magic, right? Wolves the most, but mice and squirrels and all of them help. Same with glass and ice and flower. Some witches came up with a system, a while ago, to categorize how much magic each animal anchors. We had to take a class on it and memorize the rankings in our third year. There's a book in the library if you're interested."

I was interested. "So Guanyu . . ."

"Flower salmon are much higher in the ranking than crabs and pikes," Oluk confirmed. "That's part of why everyone is impressed by you, Rosy. Horses are pretty highly ranked too. Your horse and Charles's stag are basically even in base power, so everyone's waiting to see what other animals you shift into to gauge how much magic they think you have. Your raccoon is definitely higher on the list than Charles's pronghorn or goat."

I grimaced, then tried to redirect Oluk's attention away from me. "What about you? How do your snakes rank? Probably pretty high for your rattlesnake, right?" I assumed the fiercer predators were ranked high, though maybe that wasn't always the case. Eagles were bigger than ravens, just like sharks were scarier than whales, but there was no disputing that ice ravens and flower whales were the anchors to their type of magic. I vowed to look through the book Oluk mentioned when I had a chance.

"Yeah, everyone was pretty shocked about my rattlesnake," Oluk admitted. "It's rare to get a second shift that's higher ranked than your first. Not unheard of, but rare."

"So what does that mean? Where do you rank among the glass familiars at school?"

Oluk blushed. "Uh, first. Technically. At least among the seniors. There's a younger student with a Gila monster shift, so that's higher."

I knocked my shoulder into Oluk's, grinning. "Look at you!

Showing up everyone who ignored you because of your scholarship. I bet most of them wish they'd been your friend from the start, huh?"

Oluk was bright red now. "Yeah, maybe. But back to Guanyu." I grinned, because he was redirecting away from himself just like I had. "He is essentially the head of the flower familiars, at least until Yuyan chooses one of the others for the entourage. Lei and Kwaddis tussle over who's in charge, but if Guanyu steps in, they both listen to him. He's not like Charles or Froya. He doesn't try to rule them, not really. But there's a reason the flower familiars give Yuyan so much space. Guanyu's witch is Yuyan's best friend. I think he tries to make sure her choice will be respected."

"Why wouldn't it be? Didn't you tell me she has to be the one to court her familiar, not the other way around?"

Oluk grimaced. "That's how it's supposed to be, but outside of the princess, Yuyan doesn't have any status here. She moved from Waiming about five years ago. I think her family is important there? But the Cursed Kingdom has always kept to our own when it comes to things like that. Kwaddis is the son of Jarl Tenas, and the Banks family—Lei's family—practically owns the trade up the river. If they wanted to, they could both pressure Yuyan."

"Is Guanyu from a powerful family, then?"

"That's the thing, not really. His dad is our ambassador to Waiming, but like I said, the Cursed Kingdom doesn't care as much for external politics. And he didn't gain much status bonding with Shantie either. Her parents run a healing clinic in Multah. That's why I said he's like you. His power comes from him, not from his family. I think, if you'd come to Witch Hall as a kid, it would have been the same. I don't think Charles would have been the undisputed leader of the bone familiars if you'd been here, no matter your family."

I shook my head. I didn't want to think about what-ifs. The truth was, Oluk was probably right, even though he didn't know the real reason why. If I'd come to Witch Hall when I first shifted, I would have come as a bone wolf familiar.

"What do you think Guanyu wants to tell you tomorrow?" Oluk asked after a few minutes of working in silence.

"No idea." I finished tying the last hay net and threw three of them over my shoulder. "I guess we'll see."

# Chapter 18

IT WAS A RELIEF TO HEAD DOWN TO THE RIVER TUESDAY after lunch. The weather was too nice to be spent in the library for my entire free period.

Guanyu was already seated on the riverbank next to the small school dock. He had his shoes and socks off, feet kicking lazily in the water. I slipped off my shoes to join him, toes squelching mud until water lapped it away. Across the huge river, dark cliffs marked the border to the Empire of Vinland. On the shallow banks nestled at the base of those cliffs were tiny fishing villages. I saw a few fishermen cast their nets on the other side of the river, staying far clear of the magical wards that kept them from paying too close attention to Witch Hall.

"Lovely day, isn't it, Rosamund?" Guanyu said, staring out over the water even as I turned from the fishermen to face him.

"What did you want to talk about?"

"Not one for pleasantries, are you?" Guanyu lifted his face up to the sky. "I want to talk to you about your cousin."

"What about Tokey?"

"Ah, Miss Toketie Holt. I admire your cousin. I truly do. I don't think you understand what it was like for her, the first couple years."

I frowned. Were Guanyu and Toketie friends? I hadn't seen her interact with anyone outside her suitemates. "What do you mean?"

Guanyu finally turned to look at me. "If Oluk Blackwell hadn't been in our year, she might never have made it. But vultures always go for the easier prey, and Toketie worked hard to make sure it wasn't her."

"You mean she screwed Oluk over so she could be popular."

"Popular? Toketie is not popular. Not like you're thinking. She has no social power. No clout of her own. Her standing is reliant entirely upon Froya's affection. If she steps one toe out of place, Toketie knows she will lose that. Then it will be back to how it was before."

I wasn't sure I wanted to know, but I couldn't help asking, "How was it before?"

Guanyu looked at me silently, long enough that I thought he wouldn't answer. Then he shrugged. "She was such a forgetful child, her first year here. Missing homework, though she claimed it had been in her bag. Tangles in her hair so bad they almost had to cut it all off. Did they tell you the rule about only getting your first two uniforms free? Toketie Holt was always having to repair hers. So many rips and stains. And all the while her suitemates laughed and made comments that we shouldn't expect more out of a little ranch girl."

I didn't realize I'd stood until Guanyu pulled me back down. The wolf in my heart was furious—as furious as the first time the jarl had threatened to take our family's ranch away.

Toketie wasn't forgetful. She'd never been forgetful. She'd brushed her hair every morning and every night since she turned ten and convinced Uncle Inge that she should be allowed to grow it out long. She was smart and organized and too careful to ruin two uniforms without outside *help*.

"Why would they do that?" I asked, hoping Guanyu would ignore the rumble in my throat.

"Because even as a gangly fourteen-year-old, she was beautiful. Pretty as a doll, with an elegant and powerful shift. By innate power, only Froya's eagle beats your cousin's swan."

That couldn't be right. I'd looked through the book Oluk mentioned last night and I knew that, while swans did rank high, most birds of prey ranked higher. "But what about the familiar with the falcon shift?"

Guanyu shook his head. "Toketie consistently scores higher on any test that covers ice magic. She scores as well as some witches on dream interpretation. She can't actively see the future, of course, but just as you bone familiars are sensitive to the dead, ice familiars can feel the touch of destiny. And Toketie Holt certainly does. Most of us wouldn't be surprised if, when she unlocks a second shift someday, it's a hawk or an owl. The witch who bonds with her will get a significant power boost."

"And so will she," I said, getting it.

"So you see. Toketie has never made a friend outside of her suitemates. She makes herself small and lets them have control. She's smart enough to keep them appeased. To keep Froya appeased. And it worked. She has never had a single private conversation with an ice witch, but she will graduate as one of the best students in our entire year, even if most won't realize it. She turned a living nightmare into something she could survive and did it so well that most of her suitemates don't even remember why they ever struck at her in the first place."

I thought of Toketie's expression during that first argument. How she'd looked when she told me I didn't understand. "Why are you telling me this?"

"Who knows?" Guanyu crossed his legs under him and turned to face me fully. "I heard what you said about your senior project. It's a wonderful idea. If you're looking for a test subject, I volunteer."

"Why? We barely know each other."

It's not that I didn't understand why Guanyu would want a second shift, but, after my talk with Oluk and an evening spent looking through the rankings, I knew salmon were considered one of the most powerful flower shifts. Especially here in the Cursed Kingdom, where flower familiars were confined to rivers and lakes, instead of the open ocean. Sure, a second shift would help, but unlike Toketie and Froya, Guanyu's ranking was far above that of Kwaddis or Lei. And he was already bonded with one of the strongest flower witches in school. I couldn't help thinking Guanyu's offer was made out of pity, instead of a true desire for a second shift.

"You're helping my witch with her project. It's only equal exchange for me to help with yours."

I tried to look for the trick in his words, but Guanyu seemed genuine. He wasn't wrong—I was helping his witch. Maybe he thought he owed me?

"If you don't mind," I said finally.

"How about we meet here Thursday, then? Spend our free period working on your project?"

With no better option, I agreed.

JUST LIKE THAT, MY LIFE settled into something of a routine. I helped Shantie every Wednesday and Guanyu helped me every

Thursday. Oluk and I ate most meals with Shaw and her entourage, though I made a point of pulling him back to our old table occasionally so we could have some time to talk without the witches. People eventually stopped whispering, whether they saw us on our own or at Shaw's table.

Before I knew it, the fall term was already halfway over and our teachers announced that it was time for midterms. A test, I learned, that would count for nearly a third of my final score in each class.

I spent the week before my midterms frantically studying for The Dead and Undead with Shaw, Jingyi, and Jingyi's witch, Chao. Oluk and I danced the steps for Etiquette in the aisle of the stable every afternoon until Mister Jostein barked at us to get on with the mucking. When we weren't dancing, Oluk and I practiced sparring for Combat. I spent several late nights helping Oluk sort through his memories of the various glass animals he'd observed over his years in the Desert, before finally Oluk was able to find his third shift—an impressive glass tortoise. If the rattlesnake hadn't claimed his place as the most powerful glass familiar among the seniors, that would have. I'd seen more than one glass witch give Oluk considering looks, but none of them approached him that I could see. I wondered if they were all waiting, like I was, to see if Einar was going to do something about his obvious, growing infatuation.

The Dead and Undead's written test went better than I'd expected. Afterward, Jingyi and I walked to Survival Skills, a class we shared with all the senior bone and glass familiars.

Madam Bai wasted no time, ushering us away from the outdoor classroom and across the waterfall's stream, into the deep woods on the other side of it. The woods here were untouched by the residents of campus and wilder for it.

She stopped in a small clearing, indistinguishable from all the other clearings this wood held except for a huge gong set up in the very center. We'd done a few practical lessons among these trees, but I'd never seen that gong before.

"Who feels ready for today's test?" Madam Bai asked, bouncing on the balls of her feet.

I raised my hand. I hadn't done much studying for Survival Skills, but Oluk, Jingyi, and I had run through memory cards on the different poisonous plants in the area. I didn't figure Madam Bai could throw anything worse at us.

"Put your hands down!" Madam Bai snapped her fingers, as if scolding a pet dog. "What did you do? Draw some plants? Study some descriptions?"

I exchanged a look with Oluk. He was visibly nervous. He'd told me that Madam Bai was an unpredictable teacher.

"How can you know if you are ready, unless you put that knowledge into practice? Did anyone come out here to study? Traverse these woods and try to survive them?"

"We're allowed to come here without a teacher?" one of the glass familiars whispered to her friend.

"I don't think we are," her friend whispered back.

Madam Bai ignored them. "Well, I suppose we'll see how ready you truly are. You have the next hour to set yourself up for survival. When time is up, I will clang this gong." She demonstrated, and the sound was loud enough to make me and the other familiars clasp our hands over our ears.

"—go on."

It took me a second to realize that had been permission to get started. I looked around at my classmates, wondering if I'd missed a step of the directions. But everyone looked as confused as I did.

Well then. *Set yourself up for survival.* What did that even mean?

But I did know what it meant. I'd been taking this class with Madam Bai for five weeks now. Step one, shelter.

I shifted into the horse. My best bet was to gain some distance between myself and my classmates.

I set off in the direction of the waterfall, where the sound of crashing water would help mask my hoofsteps. I found what I was looking for after about ten minutes—a fallen tree. The branches were easy enough to break off with a couple well-placed stomps. Once they were free, I shifted back to human and set about building a makeshift wooden hut.

After that, I focused on food.

The wolf in my heart wanted to hunt, but with a touch of regret, I pulled up the raccoon instead. Raccoons weren't made for hunting like other predators, but I'd done this song and dance enough times to be proficient. I found a rabbit and surprised it from above.

I dragged the rabbit's body back to my shelter. I stored it between two leaning branches and covered it in wet leaves, hoping that would be enough to hide the scent from other predators for a few minutes.

That done, I shifted into the horse and cantered down to the river. I didn't know how much time I had left, so I ripped out as much cattail as I could fit in my mouth. It was a slower process to get back to my shelter this time, because the cattails were long and I kept losing them against trees as I wound my way back. The gong rang out just as I made it back to my little stash, loud enough to send several nearby birds flying.

I left my cattails and headed to the clearing where Madam Bai was waiting.

"Good? Everyone survived. Wonderful, that's no fails yet, then."

Madam Bai laughed at her own joke. "Let's go one by one. Show me what you did."

Most students showed off burrows and tree hollows where they could rest in their animal forms. I hadn't even thought to do that, but I was glad of it when Madam Bai shook her head at each of them.

"You assume you're alone, I see," she said after the third. "But most of you aim to have a witch. What will you do then?"

"What if I don't want a witch?" asked one of my suitemates. I'd made a point of learning their names after Toketie had called me out on not knowing them. This one was Ragna, a tiny girl with extraordinarily pale hair and a weasel shift.

"Well, I certainly can't begrudge that. I've never wanted a witch myself," Madam Bai said. Judging by the grins, most of the students knew that. Then she added, "But what if you're injured? A wound too small to kill you as a human, but that would put your animal body into shock if you shifted? You must know how to make a shelter big enough to survive in."

Most of the students had gathered enough plants and berries to create makeshift salads. A few had collected nuts. Ragna, when we finally got to her setup, had managed to catch a river bass. A couple others had smaller fish alongside their own pile of cattails.

Oluk got the best marks so far by showing off a camp he'd made at the base of a large tree, complete with firepit, a skewered rat, and a few medicinal herbs.

"There we go!" Madam Bai crowed. "That is what I want. Take note. Lucky knows how to be prepared."

"It's Oluk, Madam Bai," Oluk said, with the tone of someone who'd made that correction a dozen times before. Seeing as Madam Bai had called him Mister Luck since the first day of class, I thought it was more likely a nickname than a mistake.

Charles, however, topped Oluk's score by showing us to a small cave near the waterfall where he'd collected firewood, a fistful of hazelnuts, and a rabbit. It didn't have the medicinal herbs, but it was better shelter and more filling food, which Madam Bai was quick to commend.

I was up after Charles. I walked the class back to my own hut. I figured I'd get one of the better scores. My little hut wasn't pretty, but it was functional, and I'd collected just as much food as Charles.

Except, when we arrived, my cattails were scattered everywhere. The prey in my heart nudged me. I quickly scrambled inside my hut and dug my fingers into the wet leaves.

But the rabbit I'd caught was gone.

"I'm sorry, Madam Bai," I said. "I caught a rabbit, but I think a fox or something grabbed it while I was gone."

"Wasn't me," Jingyi said, pouting as if I'd accused him directly.

"A wild fox," I corrected him.

"Well, no shock there," Madam Bai said. "Did you take note of Lucky's setup? He had that rat skewered. Not as easy prey for a fox as a rabbit on the ground."

Madam Bai gave my setup a pass, but my face was still red in embarrassment as the class moved on. Oluk hung back and nudged my arm with his elbow, trying to cheer me up. I shook my head, then shifted into my raccoon.

A sniff was all it took to figure out what had come into my camp. It wasn't a fox, but something larger. Feline.

"Are there bobcats in these woods?" I asked Oluk once I shifted back.

"Maybe?" Oluk frowned. "I'd be shocked to see one so close though."

"Me too." Bobcats normally avoided humans, and these woods were too close to the hustle and bustle of Witch Hall.

"Rotten luck, Rosy. Charles's rabbit wasn't nailed down either, but his didn't get stolen."

We caught up with the rest of the class and I resolved to put it out of my mind. It could have been worse and I needed to focus on my Etiquette test that afternoon.

The sting of embarrassment didn't fade until long after I'd passed the dance practical, finished my stable chores, and sat down for dinner with Shaw and her entourage. It was only after Shaw leaned over and asked, "Rough day?" that I was able to shake myself out of my mood.

"I've had better," I said honestly.

"Best put it out of your mind, or tomorrow will be worse," Shaw warned.

"Why?"

"Fall senior brawl," Yuyan and Aklemin said together, as if they'd rehearsed it.

"Oh no, is it a brawl again this year?" Oluk asked, horrified.

"What are you all talking about?"

"Every fall, the seniors are put into Combat workshops," Einar explained. "All the witches, and all the familiars. The midterms and finals of those Combat workshops tend to be a class-wide competition of some sort. Last year, all the seniors played a game of combat hide-and-seek for their midterm and had a free-for-all brawl for their final."

"It likely won't be a brawl," Shaw assured Oluk. "They rarely reuse ideas. At least, not for many years."

"What will it be, then?" I asked.

Shaw, Yuyan, and Einar all looked at Aklemin. "Why are you looking at me? I don't know!" the ice witch protested.

"Not a single dream?" Yuyan asked wryly.

Aklemin's smile was hardly convincing as they said, "Not one. I suppose we'll all have to find out together."

THE MIDTERM TEST IN ADVANCED Shapeshifting was done in three parts. The first, timing the speed of our shifts. The second, shifting directly between them. The third, showing off any new shifts.

I went first. I'd gotten faster at shifting, though I still wasn't the quickest in our class. Shifting between my forms was no issue, but for the first time, I felt guilt as I passed off my raccoon as a new shift. I'd seen how hard everyone in my workshop had been working for their third or fourth shifts and I hadn't even tried.

"Excellent, Miss Rosamund," Madam Xu said. "You may spend the rest of class practicing. See if you can find another shift."

I walked away from the group, struggling with my guilt. I didn't want to show off here. My purpose hadn't changed. I already attracted enough attention as Shaw's familiar, I didn't need to give people more reason to look at me.

But no one had to know if I found another shift. I could nestle another voice in my heart without showing it off to everyone. And it would make me feel better, like I'd actually earned the grade I would get in this workshop.

The problem was, there were no bone animals at Witch Hall. Not wild ones, anyway. I'd never had to claim a new voice without directly observing the animal. Living on the outskirts of the Bone Forest had made that easy. But everyone else in the class had been forced to connect with the memory of an animal. It was only fair that I learn to do the same.

The real trick was finding an animal that I hadn't already learned to shift into. It took me a good ten minutes of thinking before it hit me.

My first shift had been the wolf. I'd never seen a wild bone wolf, but I'd become the wolf anyway. Because I had seen Gran. Because she'd been grieving, the night of her husband's, her bonded's, funeral, and I'd wanted to be there for her. To be her pack.

I tried to think of the other bone familiars, the ones who had shifts I didn't. I immediately dismissed Charles. I already had a deer shift and I didn't want to claim his pronghorn or goat. Jingyi came to mind next. A fox would be useful, even if I'd have to be careful to hide it from everyone at school. I knew now that foxes ranked higher than horses and deer, though for some reason Jingyi didn't claim to be the most powerful bone familiar at school. Maybe because she was a latecomer too and hadn't bothered to unseat Charles from his throne. Or maybe it was just because Charles had more shifts and Jingyi only had the one.

I sat down to meditate. Once I'd cleared my mind and settled my emotions, I planned to focus on the memories I had of Jingyi's shift.

Before I could, I felt a stirring in the energy around me. Pops's ghost had arrived.

I kept my breathing steady so as not to disturb the energy. He rarely stayed long, but our meditation sessions were only a few minutes in class. Maybe he'd stay long enough to communicate this time.

*I miss you*, I thought. *We all do.*

I got the sense that Pops was smiling at me. I couldn't really see him, though at times like this I wished I were a witch instead. How much easier would Gran's grief have been to handle if I could summon Pops's ghost to talk with her?

*Are you disappointed in me? For being here? For not being with Gran?* I asked.

Pops seemed to frown at that. A foreign emotion welled up in me, something like pride. Was that Pops? Could I feel him that well?

Shaw's necklace was warm against my neck. I wondered if the magic she'd imbued it with was helping me now.

"What are you doing?"

I snapped my eyes open. Charles was leaning against a tree just a few feet away, watching me.

"Go away," I growled at him, then tried to swallow down the wolf.

"Don't think I can't feel the death in the air," Charles said. "Surely it's cheating to ask a spirit to give you a new shift?"

"Just because you can't do it, doesn't mean it's cheating," I snapped.

"Oh, so that *is* what you were doing?" Charles laughed. "Go on then, show it off. What powerful new form have you collected now?"

I'd meant to find a fox's voice, but a new idea came to me. Pops was a familiar too. He had a badger shift. I remembered it vaguely. Huge and sturdy, with long claws and a thick white stripe down the center of his head. It churred at me. The voice was soft, like a half-forgotten memory—the warmth of Pops's lap as he rocked me to sleep when I was a little girl.

It was foolish to be taunted, but I wanted to honor Pops's memory. Wanted to feel that sense of home again, if only for a second. I reached for that voice, trying to pull it to my heart.

The badger turned away.

I frowned, nudging at it. The wolf's voice rose up instead. I felt it tugging at me, whining to be let out. But no matter Charles's taunts, I wouldn't give in to that shift. The badger was one thing, the wolf something else. I pictured pushing the wolf aside, gently, and holding out a hand for the badger.

And yet, it refused me.

"Having trouble?"

I scowled. "No."

There was still too much of the wolf's growl in my voice. I cleared my throat.

"I knew it was a fluke that you were the first to find another shift." Charles scoffed.

What could I say? I'd never had a voice refuse me like this before. I tried again, trying to cling to the feeling of Pops's warmth. Tried to open my heart for the memory of his badger to settle in. The badger dug its metaphorical heels in and refused.

Charles laughed again, long and mocking. He walked forward and the prey in my heart urged me to flee. I scrambled to my feet.

"You know, it took me a while, but I finally figured it out. The princess's interest. She was bored, so of course she'd be drawn to something new." He brushed past me. "But the shine will wear off soon enough, and then she'll realize just how worthless you truly are."

I turned, my prey instincts screaming not to let Charles walk behind me. I didn't understand why they were so scared. They hadn't even reacted like this during the assembly.

Charles waited until he saw me looking, then he shifted. Not into the stag or the goat or the pronghorn. No, instead of hair, he grew fur. Instead of hooves, he grew claws.

I stepped back as the bobcat Charles had shifted into grinned at me. His mouth opened wide, whiskers twitching as if in laughter, and then he bounded off.

I put a hand on my chest, trying to calm my racing heart.

"He's going to be insufferable."

Oluk had arrived, frowning after Charles.

"More than usual?" I let my hand drop.

"Of course he will. Bobcats are much higher ranked. I told you it was rare for a familiar to claim a shift that's more powerful than their first."

Right. I'd been so startled by my voices' reaction that I hadn't really thought about what the bobcat meant.

"He'll be horrible in Combat, once he learns to fight with it," I muttered.

"He's already horrible. Rosy, don't you remember what stole your rabbit?"

I should have realized immediately. It made more sense than a wild bobcat so close to campus. "He sabotaged my midterm."

Oluk's shoulders slumped. "You won't be able to prove it. Even if you could, I bet Madam Bai would still say you should have put up defenses or something. It's awful. He's such a jerk. He could have gone and caught his own. He probably tried and failed."

"He's not worth getting mad over," I said, trying for dismissive and failing.

"He deserves a kick in the rear though."

"Well, I've heard there's going to be a brawl after lunch," I said, only a touch dry. "So maybe I'll get a chance."

Oluk grinned. "I'd pay to see that."

The Combat midterm was not a brawl. At least, not in the traditional sense. Madam Xu, Madam Bai, Madam Tukwilla, and Mister Xu gathered all the seniors together and began to split us up into groups of four.

As Madam Bai and Mister Xu counted off the familiars and witches, respectively, Madam Xu addressed the group.

"Today, we will be observing your skills, your determination, your ingenuity, and most of all, your teamwork. You will be split into units, each comprising a fighter, a guard or healer, a scout, and a leader. These roles can be filled by witch or familiar, but your role has already been selected for the purposes of this midterm. Do not bother arguing."

Madam Xu raised an eyebrow, as if daring someone to say something. The entire group was silent. Madam Xu nodded, satisfied. "Alongside your role, you are being given a number. You will have ten minutes to find the other members of your unit. Once those ten minutes are up, the midterm will begin. The goal for each unit is simple. Inside these woods, from the creek to the marked boundary, we have hidden leather pouches. There are thirty in total. Once a pouch is found, someone in your unit must visibly wear it. Your grade for this midterm will be determined based upon how many pouches are in the possession of your team by the end of the hour, and how well you fought to keep them safe."

Madam Xu paused and Madam Tukwilla took over. "Hiding your collected pouches is not permitted, but stealing from other units is expected. This is Combat, we expect fighting, but keep to nonlethal blows. Attacking with an intent to kill will mean automatic disqualification from the practical and failure of the exam. In contrast, you will be awarded bonus points for succeeding in your assigned role and contributing to your unit. Are there any questions? No? Good. As soon as you know your role and number, you may begin searching for your team members."

Madam Bai handed me a small scrap of paper with the number one on it. My role was a fighter. My stomach sank as I read the word.

"Not a scout?" I asked. I didn't want to be a fighter, but I could scout as the mouse or even the raccoon.

Madam Bai smiled and winked. I swallowed down my arguments.

Oluk, surprisingly, was given the role of guard. We wished each other luck and split up to find our groups. I held up a single finger to indicate my number and began to walk around. A witch found me after a second. "Healer," he said when I looked at him.

"Healer?" His uniform colors definitely meant he was a glass witch, not a flower witch.

He grimaced. "I'm best at enchanting good luck charms. Mister Xu said it was closer to healing than guarding."

"Right," I said. Closer to healing, but not as useful as an actual healer. Nor as useful as a true guard. My group was already at a disadvantage.

"Are you our fighter?" the glass witch asked.

I frowned, a bit uneasy. I didn't like that he'd assumed that, but then again I did go feral while fighting Charles a couple weeks ago. "I am," I said, touching Shaw's courtship necklace to comfort myself.

We were soon joined by an ice witch scout. Once again, I was less than impressed. I'd rather a familiar with an inconspicuous shift than a fortune-teller.

Shockingly, the ice witch took one look at me and nudged the glass witch with a smile. "We lucked out, huh?"

The glass witch laughed.

I understood their ease a second later, as our assigned leader walked up. I should have guessed. Of course they would pair courting witches and familiars in the same group—it wasn't a good practical otherwise.

Shaw looked over the two witches, then her eyes landed on me. "I can work with this," she said. "Will you listen?"

The witches were quick to agree, both obviously thrilled to have the princess lead them. I kept my tongue. Combat was the one class I absolutely didn't want to do well in. All I needed was the bare minimum to pass.

"Trust me," Shaw said softly.

Our teammates looked between us, as if anticipating gossip. I couldn't outwardly disagree. Shaw watched me like she was already queen, eyes as dark as the night sky and skin that glowed like a sunset.

Well, fine. I supposed it would look worse if I didn't try at all, especially on the midterm. I nodded.

Shaw smiled, soft and satisfied. It made my stomach flip.

"Good," she said. "Then this is how we'll do it."

# Chapter 19

When Madam Xu called for the exam to begin, I shifted into the mouse and darted into the woods. It took only a minute before I found a pouch hidden among the exposed roots of a red oak. I tried to carry it in my mouth, but the pouch was too heavy for the mouse so I shifted back to human.

The shift came just in time. An ice falcon dove through the trees, just barely missing me. I held tight to the pouch and shifted into the horse. The falcon screeched as I cantered to where Shaw had said we would set up camp.

Shaw must have explored these woods in other classes, because she quickly claimed the same little cave that Charles had used for the Survival Skills midterm. It had a narrow opening, making it easy for our glass and ice witch teammates to keep an eye out for attackers. Since our scout wasn't a familiar, Shaw decided that it would be up to me collect the pouches and up to the witches to keep them safe.

I did my best to avoid everyone as I trotted toward the waterfall. I kept my eyes out for another pouch. The horse had wider vision than I did as a human and that peripheral sight was a blessing as I spotted a pouch hanging from a branch to my right about five minutes in.

I tried to grab the second pouch with my teeth, but dropped the first in the process. The prey voices in my heart protested as I shifted human, grabbed both pouches, stuffed them in my mouth, and shifted back. The prey encouraged me to run quickly—they felt like I was being followed. I sped up.

Whether I was actually being followed, I wasn't sure. I reached Shaw's camp without issue. With my enhanced hearing, I heard our scout of an ice witch say, "It's Rosamund," before the cave even came into view.

When I arrived, I found the ice witch hunched over a bowl of water. Scrying. I still would have preferred a scout who could help me collect pouches, but I supposed that was more useful than I'd assumed.

The glass witch took the pouches from me and attached them to his own belt. He'd painted his clothes with the mud from the creek, each stroke part of a sloppy rune.

"Here, let me give you a good luck charm," he said once the pouches were secure. He pressed a muddy finger to my cheek and drew something on it.

"Thanks," I said, fighting the urge to wipe the mud off. Shaw, I was delighted to notice, had a mud rune of her own smeared across her forehead.

"Rosamund, look," the scrying ice witch said.

I went over to his bowl and peered inside. I saw Yuyan sitting with her legs crossed—a meditative pose. Attached to her belt were three pouches.

"What's she doing?" I asked Shaw.

Shaw leaned in over my shoulder, her hair tickling my neck. "Healing trance. She'll heal as quickly as she gets injured, like that. Who are her teammates?"

The ice witch concentrated and the image in the bowl changed. First, a glass familiar I didn't recognize, shifted into a gecko, then Chao and Jingyi together.

"Perfect," Shaw said, pulling back. "We have time still. Rosamund?"

"I'm going."

I turned into the horse and ran through the trees to the make-shift hut I'd made for the Survival Skills midterm. I had to become human again so I could kneel and look into it. As I'd suspected, there was a pouch hidden inside. I reached within and just barely managed to close my fingers around it when the wolf in my heart growled a warning.

I threw myself to one side. A bobcat landed on top of the hut. Wood flew into the air as the branches collapsed inward. I'd been about to shift into the mouse, but at the sight of flying bark, it balked. The mouse remembered too well the pain of what had happened with the bull moose.

The hesitation was nearly my undoing. The bobcat pivoted on the collapsed log and lunged at me, teeth bared. I tried to dodge, but the back of my dress caught on something and I was jerked in the opposite direction. Luckily, the bobcat had moved to intercept my original path and its teeth clamped down on air instead of my arm.

Even more lucky, the miss catapulted the bobcat past me and it collided with a nearby tree. I scrambled to my feet as the bobcat shook itself, dazed.

"Charles?" I asked. I recognized the pattern of exposed bone on the bobcat's back.

Charles-the-bobcat turned to glare at me and in the next second he shifted into his deer form. He was smaller than a bull

moose, but a bone stag was frightening in its own way. His antlers were encrusted with exposed bone, each ending in a sharp
point.

The mouse in my heart squeaked harder, terrified. The wolf
reared up, wanting a chance to fight like I hadn't given it in the
Bone Forest. I shifted into the horse, grabbed the pouch firmly in
my mouth, and bolted.

I heard the thundering of hooves as Charles ran after me. Deer
were more agile than horses, but with his antlers weighing him
down, I was faster. The sound of hooves stopped. I slowed. I didn't
want to show Charles where our camp was—I'd make sure to lose
him before returning to Shaw and our teammates.

Something sharp pierced my side and I let out a scream that
became a high-pitched neigh. I shifted out of shock and the pouch
in my mouth fell into the leaves. Charles had shifted back into the
bobcat. He darted forward and picked the pouch up, tail flicking as
if to taunt me, then bounded into the undergrowth.

I took only a second to assess my injury. Charles's claws had
sliced just above my right hip. Fresh blood began to spread across
my torn white school dress. It looked bad, but the scratch was shallow. I could risk another shift.

I'd never wanted to shift into the wolf more badly in my life,
but I called for the raccoon instead. It was quick enough to catch
up to Charles. There weren't any teachers watching our section of
the woods—surely Charles wouldn't have dared to attack me so
aggressively if there were. I was safe to enact revenge.

The raccoon responded and I shifted. I scurried up the nearest
tree and darted across the branches, following after Charles. Blood
splattered leaves in my wake, but I did my best to ignore the way
my paws grew slick and my hip ached. Bone raccoons were big, so

though the wound hurt more in this form, it wasn't as dangerous as it would have been in something smaller.

It didn't take me long to find him. Like most predators, bobcats were designed for sprinting, not long-distance running. He'd slowed down to a jog, ears flicking back and forth like he was listening.

I jumped off a branch just over his head. I came crashing down on top of Charles, two-inch claws clinging to his shoulders to prevent him from escaping.

Charles flipped around, snarling loudly. His rear claws tried to rake my legs, but I clung tight to his back. The bobcat outweighed me, but the raccoon had room to maneuver. I used all that advantage to get my mouth around his neck.

Charles froze as my fangs scraped his fur. I pressed harder—not enough to break skin but enough to be a serious threat. He could try to shift, but a bite to the neck could kill any of his forms.

This wasn't like our previous fight. I wasn't feral, wasn't even close to it. I'd never felt more in control in my life and I reveled in that power.

"There you are."

Charles twitched. I didn't let him go, didn't even look away, as footsteps shuffled through the fallen leaves. Shaw bent down and picked up the discarded pouch.

"Leave him," she said once the pouch was attached to her belt. "We have better prey to hunt."

I saw it the second Charles realized the depth of Shaw's indifference toward him. His eyes—the bright yellow eyes of the bobcat—dulled in anguish. All the fight left his body and he slumped to the ground, defeated.

I pulled away and shifted. As a human, I turned my back to Charles and walked over to Shaw. The prey in my heart hated turning their back to a predator, but that was exactly why I did it. Charles would know what it meant.

"Where are we going?" I asked when we were far enough that Charles wouldn't be able to hear us even with enhanced senses.

"To claim victory," Shaw said. She glanced at me out of the corner of her eye. "Are you still able to fight?"

I had a hand pressed to the wound Charles had given me, trying to stanch the flow of blood with each step I took. I wished our team had a real healer.

"I can fight," I said. I gestured with my free hand to the dry mud on my cheek. "I've got a good luck charm."

Shaw let out a laugh, then covered her mouth with a hand as if it had startled her. I grinned, feeling satisfied to have broken the princess's careful control.

Luckily, it wasn't a long walk to our destination.

"I'll need you to keep the fox busy," Shaw said just before we broke through a thick section of trees into a clearing. I saw Yuyan sitting in meditation just like what was shown in the scrying bowl. Jingyi was helping a familiar I assumed was their scout wrap what looked to be a bruised ankle.

Chao turned to face us. "Here for round two, Princess?" he asked.

I looked at Shaw. "Round two?"

Shaw waved a hand like it didn't matter. Then with the same hand, she twirled her fingers.

All the animals in my heart fell silent. Something dead—dead and *hungry*—had joined us in the clearing. I couldn't see what it was, but I could sense it.

Chao raised his hands and a clattering sounded from a few feet behind him. I watched, fascinated, as a skeletal deer rose from the ground. It was missing a good number of bones, but it still had its antlers.

I knew, without having to think about it, that fighting a skeleton stag would be worse than fighting Charles. Charles could be stopped by threats of pain and death. The undead could not.

Everyone in the clearing was focused on the fight about to begin between the two necromancers. Jingyi crouched low and I watched as he shifted into a bone fox. I was about to call upon the raccoon when I caught sight of my teammate at the other end of the clearing, half hidden by a large bush.

It was our glass witch healer, covered in mud runes. Shaw must have left the ice witch alone at camp to guard our other pouches.

The glass witch's eyes were on Yuyan and the now four pouches in her lap. Shaw turned and caught my gaze just as Jingyi's ears flicked in the glass witch's direction.

Now I understood what my purpose was for this fight. Shaw and I were the distraction.

I shifted into the horse and reared up in the air, as if I were preparing to slam my front hooves down on Jingyi's head. Jingyi darted away, climbing up Chao's side to perch on his shoulders. Chao's deer skeleton charged and I got between it and Shaw, using the exposed bone on my shoulder to catch the deer's antlers. With a crack, one of the prongs shattered.

Whatever spirit Shaw had called upon had terrified the injured scout. He scrambled out of the way, putting distance between himself and Yuyan. Chao and Jingyi were less affected—but then, like me, they were used to the feeling of death magic.

"Break his concentration," Shaw said as the skeleton regrouped.

I shifted into the mouse and scurried to bite Chao's ankles. He cursed and kicked me, but I was too fast. Jingyi hopped down, teeth bared. I called upon the raccoon and we went tumbling away from the two bone witches.

I caught Jingyi by the scruff. The bone wolf inside me wanted to shake him like half-dead prey, but the raccoon just clamped down harder. Jingyi yipped and I let him go, worried I'd hurt him unintentionally.

"Jingyi!" Chao cried, and the skeletal deer collapsed.

Jingyi turned to his witch, as distracted by the cry as Chao was by his yelp. I shifted back into a human and used my body weight to hold Jingyi to the ground.

Shaw managed to get the skeleton under her control. With a click of her fingers, the spirit she had summoned combined with it and suddenly I could see dark fog begin to accumulate in the missing parts of the deer's skeleton.

"Chao, make it stop!" the glass familiar yelled in panic.

But it was too late. The possessed skeleton let out a shriek and the opposing team all flinched back.

The distraction had worked. Our glass witch snagged three of the pouches from Yuyan's lap and held them up high in the air. Before anyone could react, the ending horn blared.

Yuyan's eyes flew open and she clutched her team's remaining pouch to her chest. "Shaw!"

"Apologies, Yuyan," Shaw said, not sounding sorry at all. With a wave of her hand, the spirit dissipated and the skeleton collapsed as a pile of unmoored bones.

I slowly pulled myself off Jingyi. He shifted back and I held out a hand to help him to his feet.

Yuyan looked ready to scold Shaw some more, but then she caught sight of me. "Rosamund, you're bleeding," she said, and dropped the pouch to rush over to my side. Chao picked it up, scowling at our glass witch as if daring him to steal another one.

Now that the midterm was over, I felt horribly dizzy. I shouldn't have shifted so much with an open wound, especially not with such drastic size changes. The way the wound had grown and shrunk between the mouse and horse only made it worse. I barely remembered the walk to the creek where our teachers waited. The last member of our team showed up as Yuyan fussed over my wound.

"You're lucky this didn't go any deeper," Yuyan grumbled. "I'll do enough to stop you from bleeding out, but once class is over, I want to put you in a healing sleep."

"Thanks," I told her, then we had to be quiet as the teachers collected all the pouches from each team. Shaw gathered the three from our glass witch, the two from our ice witch, and the one she had on her belt, before handing them in.

"We have a clear winner here," Madam Xu announced. "Team One worked together with ingenuity, foresight, and no small amount of luck." Her lips twitched. I glanced at our glass witch, who smiled sheepishly. Next to him, the ice witch grinned.

"Together," Madam Xu continued, "Team One claimed six pouches. A pair more than the next-best teams. Congratulations, you will all earn perfect marks for this midterm exam."

Oluk grinned at me. I grinned back, flying high off the energy of my fights with Charles and Jingyi. Shaw looked at me, something glittering in her eyes that I couldn't place. My grin dropped. Shaw turned to the teachers.

"If I may, Madam Xu?" she said. Madam Xu inclined her head. Mister Xu put a hand on his familiar's back as she retreated to his

253

side. Madam Tukwilla didn't look up from where she was healing some of the students who'd gotten injured in the exam, but Madam Bai bounced back on her heels.

Shaw gestured and Einar approached with a bundle of red cloth in his arms. She took the bundle.

"I'm not done yet," Yuyan snapped from where she kneeled working on my injury. She sounded like she knew what was going on. I felt like I was trying to breathe underwater. It was hard to think. I tried to figure out what I was missing.

"Just for a moment," Shaw said. She held out a hand in front of me.

Yuyan sighed and sat back, letting Shaw lift me to my feet.

"What are you—" I began, but Shaw just smiled, warm and bright, and I couldn't find the rest of my sentence.

"Rosamund Holt, since the day I met you, you have proven your tenacity and courage in the face of ever more dangerous obstacles. Our success today would have proven impossible without you. This victory is yours."

Then she unfurled the red bundle and swept it over my shoulders in one smooth gesture.

It was a cloak, I realized. Made of crimson wool and lined with white fur, warm enough to protect against even the coldest nights. Shaw did the clasp—a huge piece of metal shaped like a bird. I stared down at it.

Not just any bird. The silver clasp was a raven, with three eyes carved out of the metal and set with small rubies.

This was the kind of cloak that jarls would run their people ragged to afford. The kind of cloak meant for royalty.

What had Oluk said about the first courtship gift? That it was meant to show Shaw's power?

I stumbled several steps back, away from Shaw. I was sure my face showed my horror, but Shaw wasn't looking at me. She'd turned to face everyone else. The entire senior class.

"I made my choice, but I ask of you all now—will you kneel for it?"

"No," I whispered, but the words didn't carry. I couldn't figure out how to speak properly. To shout at Shaw, for making such a spectacle when we both knew this courtship was fake.

Shaw's entourage were the first ones to move. Einar sank to one knee, as did Aklemin. Yuyan was already on the ground, but she lifted a leg up so that she was also kneeling properly.

Everyone else still stood in stunned silence. Shaw drew herself up higher and said, "Will you accept Rosamund Holt as you've accepted me?"

Then, before I could stop her, Shaw spun on her heels and kneeled for me too.

"I would," the ice witch on our team said, breaking the suddenly painful quiet. "I would follow you both to war and call you both my queens by the end of it."

And then he kneeled. Followed by the glass witch covered in muddy runes, and then the team standing behind them. Then Chao, and Jingyi, and their glass familiar scout. Oluk fell to his knees next to Einar, beaming at me as if I somehow wanted this.

Froya kneeled, and when she did, so too did the rest of the ice familiars. Toketie bowed her head as she went down, refusing to meet my eyes. Madam Xu, Madam Bai, Mister Xu, and Madam Tukwilla kneeled too, though the flower witch kept one hand on the wound she was healing.

By the end, only Charles was still standing. Shaking visibly, hands covering his face like his world had just ended.

I figured it out then. This wasn't for the fake courtship. This wasn't Shaw making a statement about bonding with me. This was Death's Heir, collecting the power she'd need to ride into battle.

I wanted to close my eyes. To believe this was all a strange dream. My head was fuzzy from the effects of Yuyan's healing magic, but it wasn't enough to avoid this. Avoid seeing the look in the other students' eyes, the belief that this was right. That one day I would lead them to war beside Shaw, and that we would come out victorious on the other side.

The red of the cloak, I realized, was the same red as the sashes that thanes wore to mark their position as officers of the army.

"No," I said, and it was stronger this time.

Shaw was there even before the word left my mouth. I hadn't seen her stand until she stepped between me and the rest of the seniors, her back to them like they didn't matter. But they did matter. They all mattered. Even Charles. Even Froya and the rest of Toketie's suitemates. They all mattered, and war would ruin them. Kill them, like Pops had died. Hurt them, like Gran was hurt.

"No, Shaw," I said. "This is not a victory."

Shaw reached forward to brush a loose strand of hair behind my ear. She looked worried. She didn't get it. Why would she? She'd been raised for this. From the moment she was born and her future was decided, this was her destiny.

But I wasn't made for war.

I'd messed up. Let my anger at Charles blind me and the thrill of the fight pull me along. This entire midterm had been a test of war, and I'd let Shaw use me to win.

I turned away. I couldn't be here. I wasn't meant to be here.

Ignoring the barely healed scratches in my side and the cloak weighing down my shoulders, I ran.

Guanyu found me at the spot by the river where we normally met on Thursdays. Those peaceful afternoons testing my shifting theory seemed so far away now.

"You do yourself no favors, wearing your heart on your face," Guanyu said.

"I'm not in the mood," I told him, head buried in my arms.

Guanyu sat down next to me. "You asked me, several weeks ago, why I shared Toketie's story with you."

Guanyu knew me well by now. Well enough to know what would catch my attention, anyway. I lifted my head up to look at him. "Why did you?"

"You came to Witch Hall six weeks ago," Guanyu said instead of answering. "Barged your way in here with no regard for the power plays the rest of us have navigated all these years. Within a few days, you befriended the social outcast, alienated the most powerful bone familiar in school despite the danger of sharing a suite with him, and caught not only the princess's attention, but the attention of her entourage. It took the princess a week to offer courtship. A week. And then Yuyan Yao is introducing you to my witch in a way that kept all the power in your hands. Chao Hu and Jingyi Wang are publicly placing themselves on your side. Einar Ottosen now sits with Oluk Blackwell every shared class they have. Aklemin Alki warned Froya Falk from spreading gossip about you. Rosamund, I need you to understand the power you have."

"I told you to call me Rosy," I muttered. I'd offered my nickname to him and Shantie weeks ago, while gagging on one of Shantie's test potions.

Guanyu gave me a look like I'd just proven his point.

"So what? What's the use of this power you say I have?" I took a breath and it shuddered in my lungs. I was crying. When had I started crying? I pressed shaking hands to my eyes, as if I could hold the tears in. "What should I do? I didn't ask for this."

Guanyu hesitated, then he put an arm around my shoulder and pulled me to his side. I breathed in lavender and lily. Flower familiars always smelled floral, residue of their shifts sticking to their human skin.

"It's a heavy burden, that necklace you wear," he murmured, the ends of his bangs tickling my forehead. "Don't let it pull you under, Rosy. The kingdom could use someone like you, keeping us honest. All these politics will be the death of us. If Vinland doesn't kill us first."

I blinked away my tears, staring out at the other bank, those dark cliffs across from us and the fishing villages before them. "My papa's parents are from Vinland. They cut him off when he married Mama. Because her parents were familiars. I never met them."

"Shantie's family lives in Multah. They say there are anti-magic protests across the river in Vingate every other day now. No word on if the emperor wants war, but Shantie and I have talked about it. What we would do. My parents would move back with my grandparents, to Waiming, and they said they'd take Shantie's family. She has a little sister, only eight."

"What about you two? Would you go with them?"

"I can't. Shantie would never run. She feels the responsibility of her power too strongly. Even if she's not the best healer, we could supply the army with potions. Do our part."

*Responsibility of her power.* Shantie hadn't asked for it either. It wasn't right, forcing someone to fight just because they had the power to do so.

My hands felt cold and I tucked them under my arms, scooting even closer to Guanyu. "I'm terrified of war," I whispered.

I thought Guanyu would point out that I was wearing Shaw's necklace. That war was inevitable. Instead, he tightened his arm around my shoulders.

"Have you told her that?" he asked softly.

I shook my head.

"Maybe you should."

"Why? She can't do anything about it."

That was true. I hadn't really considered it before, but Shaw was as trapped as the rest of us. She hadn't asked for the coming war. The prophecies had started the day she was born. I wondered what she thought of the nickname the common folk had for her. Death's Heir. Did it please her? Did she hate it?

"She may not be able to do anything about the war, but she's courting you for a reason, Rosy. She should know how you feel about all of this."

Shaw wasn't courting me for the reasons Guanyu thought she was, but he was still right. I reached for the beautiful cloak I'd dropped in the mud next to the river. I'd need to clean it off before I could wear it. If I would ever wear it.

"I'll talk to her," I promised. "Thanks, Guanyu."

"Don't mention it." Guanyu let me go and stood. "Really, don't mention it. I never wanted to get involved in entourage politics."

"Really?" I frowned up at him.

Guanyu smiled, which wasn't an answer. He walked away without another word, leaving me and my bright red cloak to stare at the border of Vinland in solemn silence.

# Chapter 20

## SHAW

REGRET WAS AN UNFAMILIAR FEELING. SHAW RARELY HAD time to wallow in her mistakes. She learned from them as much as she could, but she never lingered over them. It was best to fail now and figure out a better path than fail in the future and see her people die for it.

This was different. Regret that she might have stumbled, tripped when she needed to be running. She'd pushed too quickly with Rosamund, and spooked her like a wild horse sent galloping to safety.

Only Shaw wasn't sure why Rosamund had spooked. Once again, her inability to read the familiar irked her. Was it the attention? It had never seemed to bother her before. The fight? Had Shaw asked for too much, having Rosamund distract Jingyi while injured? Or was it the cloak? But Rosamund had said nothing when Shaw put it on her.

Had she seen something on Shaw's face, when she touched her? Shaw had always prided herself on masking her emotions. Her circumstances were too public. She'd learned quickly to hide her thoughts from prying eyes.

Perhaps her excitement over their success during the Combat

midterms had cracked that mask. Might have allowed Rosamund to see too much. Did she realize this wasn't fake, to Shaw? Did she know what Shaw expected, what she hoped for?

There was no use wondering. Shaw could watch the scene a thousand times and not glean anything new. For all her powers of observation, she understood Rosamund best when talking with her. Each word was a treasure to hoard, and Rosamund was too honest to hide herself away like she should.

Shaw knew that Rosamund had a habit of riding each Saturday morning on Madam Dyer's sorrel bone horse. Pyre was the mare's name. A testimony to what Madam Dyer escaped from when she fled the Colonies to come to the Cursed Kingdom. She thought the mare suited Rosamund more—Rosamund looked good in red.

Shaw got to the stable early and tacked up Cow and Pyre. By the time Rosamund arrived, she could hold out Pyre's reins for the familiar like a peace treaty.

"Shaw—" Rosamund began, and Shaw thought from her tone that she was about to reject the silent offer.

"Will you do me the honor?" Shaw asked quickly. "Please."

Rosamund stared at Pyre's reins for long enough that the bone mare grew irritated. She threw her head, attempting to pull her reins loose. Cow went to bite Pyre's shoulder and Shaw had to turn away to reprimand her horse. Cow settled down, but Pyre only grew angrier.

"Oh, fine," Rosamund said. She took Pyre's reins from Shaw and pulled the mare out of Cow's reach. Pyre stomped a hoof, just barely missing Rosamund's left foot. Rosamund laughed, more comfortable facing a raging bone animal then the rightful respect of her classmates. Shaw still didn't understand her.

They both mounted once Rosamund calmed Pyre down

enough for it. Shaw let Rosamund lead them out of the barn aisle and down to the river. She waited until they'd turned along the riverbank, heading toward the creek, before speaking.

"You were upset yesterday."

"Yeah," Rosamund said. Her casual way of speaking had grated on Shaw's ears at the beginning, but it was a comfort now. Formality was Rosamund's way of putting up walls.

"Will you tell me why?"

Pyre pranced a bit, obviously wanting to cause a fuss, but Rosamund kept control of the reins and the mare settled down. Shaw waited, even when the silence stretched on for several minutes.

"Everyone says war is inevitable," Rosamund said finally. "Even the ones who wish it wasn't. They think it's inevitable, so they do nothing to stop it. You all act like the game is already set and we're just waiting on our opponent to start playing. And this school . . . this school is the worst of it. Homework assignments about how to use what we learn in class on the battlefield. A required Combat workshop that teaches us the best ways to kill. They disguise army training as midterms. They don't do anything about the bullying or the politics because desperation breeds and they need willing soldiers."

"Witch Hall has always been this way," Shaw said. "This isn't because of me."

Rosamund laughed. "Witch Hall has only been this way since familiars were introduced. Because of war. Your grandmother's war. And it hasn't changed since then, even when it should have, and now no one dares to try. Because of you and your war."

"Everyone compares me to my grandmother," Shaw said, then stopped herself. She hadn't meant to talk about this. She avoided talking about the late Witch Queen. Not even her father knew the feelings she held deep in her heart.

But Rosamund was turning to look at Shaw for the first time since they'd started this ride. "It's an easy comparison to make, isn't it?" she asked, but her voice was gentle. As if she could tell this was an open wound, even though no one else ever had. "A bone witch set to rule the kingdom. Who faced war before she was even truly an adult. Whose power was unmatched, until you were born."

Shaw shook her head. "Everyone forgets that my grandmother did not fight alone. My grandfather powered her army of the dead, and kept her safe to wield it while the enemy surged to stop her. When he was finally felled, she collapsed alongside him. Were the enemy not already retreating, our history would look very different. I know war is terrible, Rosamund. I *know*."

"Then why do we call it inevitable? Isn't the reason ice witches can see the future so we can change it? So we can exert free will upon our own destinies?"

"That's true when the future sits at a crossroads, but—" Shaw stopped suddenly, hearing her own words. Crossroads. Was this what Aklemin had meant?

But there was no crossroads about the war. About when it started, perhaps. About who it was with. But war *was* Shaw's destiny. It has been since the moment she drew her first breath.

"I will not be my grandmother," Shaw said instead. "Her war was bloody and it nearly destroyed the Cursed Kingdom. History praises her army of dead, but ignores that more than half of it came from our own people."

"Half the dead were ours, but we faced an army ten times our size," Rosamund said. "My grandparents respected yours, you know. Even now, Gran mourns your grandmother's death day. The Witch Queen did her best with a terrible situation. A situation her own parents created and handed over to her with their premature deaths. She's not at fault for your destiny."

Shaw closed her eyes, feeling as though Rosamund had just struck a fist through her chest. How did this ignorant ranch girl see the buried resentment inside her? Shaw's grandmother died the same minute she was born, the same minute Shaw's mother bled out from a hemorrhaging womb. Shaw had inherited that bloody legacy. She felt that truth in her bones.

"I am not my grandmother," Shaw whispered. "I am myself and only myself. If I must have war, then I will not let it be like hers. I will not hesitate in an attempt to broker peace where none exists. I will use *everything* in my power to strike hard, and fast, so that none will think to attack again. So that our people can be saved from this cycle of hatred and bloodshed."

A soft touch had her opening her eyes. Rosamund had reached across the gap between their horses and put her hand on top of Shaw's.

"I believe you," she said. "I wish you didn't have to fight, but I believe that you'll do everything you can to save as many people as you can. You have the potential to be such a good queen, Shaw."

Shaw moved Cow's reins to her left hand so she could tangle her fingers with Rosamund's. The familiar's fingers were short and thick, calluses along each pad. Nothing like what she'd imagined and yet somehow better for it. Had she once thought this girl plain? Shaw had to stop herself from lifting that hand up to kiss each knuckle. She settled for squeezing their palms together instead.

"I can't be a good queen alone." She hoped Rosamund could hear the plea in her voice. Hoped that she would understand what Shaw was asking. "I need help. I need you."

But Rosamund wasn't listening. Her attention had been caught by something going on at the center of campus. Shaw followed her gaze. A few geldings grazed near the library building. Well outside the pasture they were supposed to be contained to.

"I didn't leave the gate open," Shaw said, sure of it.

"Does Mister Jostein ever graze the herd freely?" Rosamund asked, but Shaw could tell she already knew the answer. Shaw shook her head anyway.

The geldings lifted their heads seconds before Shaw heard the thunder of hooves. The rest of the horses from the pasture rounded the corner of the central hall. The geldings reared up, quickly joining in with the stampede.

"Whoa. Whoa!" Rosamund cried, yanking her hand back from Shaw's to grab Pyre's reins tighter.

Too late. Pyre's haunches bunched up and she bolted. Shaw watched, horrified, as Rosamund slipped off backward and fell to the ground with a heavy thud.

"Rosamund!" Shaw threw herself off Cow and fell to her knees beside the familiar. Carefully, she turned her over. Rosamund winced, but she sat up as Shaw helped her.

"Anything broken?" Shaw asked, looking over her as best as she could.

"I don't think so," Rosamund said between gasps. "Just winded and—"

She winced again, one hand clamped around her side. The scratches. She'd never let Yuyan finish healing them. Blood soaked her shirt. The wounds had reopened.

Rosamund's head came up, staring over Shaw's shoulder. "Cow!"

The warning came too late. Cow tore her reins from Shaw's hands. With a loud neigh, she bolted after the herd. With ease, the horses parted for her, so she galloped in the front with Pyre hot on her heels.

s were, and the mare slowed to a walk, looking back

ler.

now, there's no food that way," Shaw said. "Let's go get

ed, but she stopped moving. Shaw dismounted from
areful to avoid her wounds, and approached. Cow's
ngled. Shaw carefully pulled them apart. Pyre had
Cow had, but she stood farther away, less trusting

aw got Cow situated, Rosamund shifted. She walked
ard Pyre. Shaw worried about the mare taking off
lly since Rosamund smelled so strongly of blood. But
as a deft hand with bone horses and she caught Pyre's
ore the horse made the decision to run.

Rosamund remounted their mares and turned them
us. The rest of the herd followed the bone horses, as
hey would.

low going. She didn't want to trot, too aware of
injury, nor did they want to start another stampede
rses following behind. Several stopped to graze along
they always caught up once Shaw and Rosamund got
d.

ly, they arrived at the main path, then went through the
the stable. Madam Kawak and Madam Dyer waited for
with Oluk. The group watched as Shaw and Rosamund
orses into the pasture—gate wide open.

eir tack off and brush them down," Madam Dyer
Oluk.

ded toward Shaw, but she told him to get Pyre first.
amiliar looked nervous, but his steps were steady as he

The stampede tore

watched them gallop past

the road that led to Multa

"Help me up," Rosamu

There was no time to

Rosamund's arm and lifted

dangerously for a second, b

make Shaw's own head hu

This wasn't the time to get

"We need to go after the

Rosamund took a few s

a bone horse. The scratches

gushing freely. With a whick

for Shaw to climb on.

"Be careful," Shaw said, bu

pulled herself up.

Rosamund waited barely

she was charging after the h

ing her torso close to Rosamu

wind.

They caught up with the her

circled around them, neighing. 1

to stop following Cow, slowing

Only Pyre and Cow kept going.

"Cow!" Shaw called, projecti

"Cow, come!"

Rosamund tilted her head to

clear in the way she flicked her e

when called, and bone horses les

way few thing

over her shoul

"Come on

some fresh ha

Cow snort

Rosamund, c

reins hung ta

stopped wher

than Cow wa

While Sh

sideways tow

again, especia

Rosamund w

reins just bef

Shaw and

back to cam

she'd hoped

It was s

Rosamund's

with the ho

the way, but

too far ahea

Eventua

entrance to

them, along

rode their h

"Get th

snapped to

He hea

The glass

"I'm fine," I said. Madam Kawak hadn't approached me, even though I'd seen her at the dining hall for dinner, so I hoped that meant she'd decided not to blame me for the horses after all. "What are you all planning on doing tonight?"

"Yuyan has to go watch the flower familiars' feat," Einar said. "Even though she doesn't want to."

"I don't want to give any of them the expectation that I might be interested," Yuyan explained. "But Madam Ipsoot is insisting I go, since I skipped it last assembly."

"Madam Ipsoot wants to see you become the best healer in the nation," Shaw said. "Which means bonding."

Yuyan rolled her eyes. "Madam Ipsoot can kindly keep her nose out of my personal life. I know we'll need a flower familiar for the entourage eventually, but that doesn't mean I have to bond with them."

"It doesn't?" I asked. When I glanced at Oluk, he looked just as thrown as I did.

"It *has* meant that, historically," Aklemin said, sauntering up to our group. The feat, it seemed, had ended. "Yuyan's just a rebel."

"Not interested in first place today?" Yuyan asked, side-eyeing the young ice witch being congratulated behind Aklemin.

Aklemin gave an exaggerated pout. "First place? In lithomancy? If only I were so talented."

Yuyan snorted. "Sure."

Shaw shook her head and moved closer to me. She held out an arm and I took it. I wanted to grumble, but I was tired still. It was a relief to let Shaw lead.

We headed to the flower familiars' feat—an obstacle course in the river. The river floor had been lit by glowing stones, likely enchanted by glass witches so that viewers could actually see the feat.

"There you are," Shantie said to Yuyan as we approached. "Madam Ipsoot wanted me to make sure you came."

I expected Yuyan to roll her eyes, but she looked contrite instead. "Sorry, Aklemin was finishing theirs."

Shantie waved it off, turning to face the flower familiars at the starting line. "Bet on first place?"

"Winner copies class notes for Herbs and Poultices?"

"Deal." The two flower witches shook on it.

To my surprise, Shantie didn't bet on Guanyu. She named Lei Banks. Yuyan named Kwaddis Tenas.

The feat began. Einar and Oluk weren't paying attention, caught up in a quiet conversation about rune sequences. They'd been working on Oluk's senior project the past several weeks. Aklemin cheered and clapped as the flower familiars shifted and dove into the water, apparently enthralled by the race. Shantie yelled encouragement to Guanyu, stopping only to complain to Yuyan whenever Kwaddis pulled ahead of Lei.

A heavy wind rushed across the river, bringing with it a faint smell of smoke. I shivered as the wind bit through the thin sleeves of my school uniform.

"Cold?" Shaw murmured in my ear.

"A little," I admitted.

"Perhaps if you had a warm cloak—"

"Shut up."

Shaw let the insult slide, probably realizing that I'd get actually angry if she pushed it. But instead of backing away, she stepped closer to me, arms slightly out like she was asking for a hug.

People were watching, I could feel the prickle of their glances on my back. I let myself lean into Shaw. I tried telling myself that it was no different from hugging Oluk. But it felt different.

Shaw's breath was warm on my head as she pulled me closer, arms wrapping around both shoulders and coming together just under my collarbones. I didn't love being short, especially when I needed to reach something in the stable and had to climb like a barn cat to get it, but it was nice to feel encompassed by Shaw. Like she could protect me from the wind and the stares both.

"Do you smell something burning?" I asked her softly.

Shaw was silent for a few seconds, then she nodded. "Another fishing village, across the river. You can see the embers on the horizon, to our left."

Shaw was right. There was a subtle glow to the northwest. "Isn't that close to Vingate? Has the port caught fire?"

Vingate was the largest city on Wimahl River and Vinland's main port for trade from the western ocean. The capital of the empire was an eastern port, all the way on the other side of the continent, and from all the stories Vingate just didn't compare. But it was still triple the size of Multah and more densely populated than any town in the Cursed Kingdom.

"I don't know," Shaw admitted, though it sounded like it pained her to say.

I watched the distant orange flickers. A number of small Vinland fishing towns had burned down in the past several months. Consequences of a dry, hot summer. I knew from Papa's rants that the Cursed Kingdom had offered to trade fireproof runes and enchantments, but Vinland's anti-magical majority had spat on the offer.

"Faster, I know you can move faster than that!" Shantie cried, bringing my attention back to the feat.

The flower familiars were nearing the end of the course. I understood now why Shantie hadn't bet on Guanyu. He was in the middle of the pack. His salmon shift was huge and powerful, but he slowed down considerably at every obstacle that required precise movement. Meanwhile, Kwaddis's pike shift darted through the rods and reeds with ease while Lei's crab shift scurried along the river floor.

The final stretch was just open water, a pure race to the finish. "Kwaddis has it," Yuyan said as he and Lei reached the end of the final obstacle at the same time.

I would have agreed. A pike was faster in open water than a crab. But I knew that Lei had been working on a fish form during Advanced Shapeshifting. If she could control the shift, she had a chance.

Just as I was thinking it, Lei shifted directly from crab to flower bass. With a powerful flick of her tail, Lei sped ahead of Kwaddis and across the finish line.

"There it is!" Shantie crowed.

I clapped with the rest of the crowd. Shaw didn't, arms still wrapped around me. I moved my shoulders in a silent request for her to let go. She pressed her nose to my hair instead.

"Are you smelling me?" I asked, incredulous.

"Your hair smells as it looks. Like freshly dried hay."

I felt heat rush to my cheeks. I remembered Charles's taunt, almost a month ago, about how I smelled like the stable. But Shaw didn't sound disgusted. She took another deep breath, as if she wanted to get more of the smell.

"Shaw," I said, uncomfortable now.

She finally let go, but not far. She held out her arm again. "Where shall we go next?"

I bit back a sigh as I looped my hand around Shaw's arm. "Oluk and I have to do Madam Xu's feat for class."

"I look forward to seeing it."

Shantie and Guanyu joined our group as we walked to the base of the waterfall where Madam Xu was setting up. I was disgusted to see a military recruiter among the crowd waiting for the feat to begin.

"Nervous?" Shaw asked.

"No." Not about the feat, anyway.

I went to pull away from Shaw and head to where the other familiars were waiting, but Shaw tugged me back. With quick fingers, she adjusted my necklace so that it sat a little higher on my neck.

"Going to pee on me next?" I asked, irritated now. Then, quieter, "You don't need to sell it this hard. Especially not after your little stunt on Friday." I'd refused to wear Shaw's cloak out of protest, even though the nights were getting colder.

"I put you in a difficult situation, courting you. I simply wish to make it clear that, while you choose to wear this"—Shaw brushed a thumb over the largest moonstone—"you are under my protection."

"I don't need your protection."

To my surprise, Shaw grinned at that. "No, you don't. Perhaps that's why you're the first to wear this necklace."

I didn't know what to say to that, so I turned away and joined Oluk with the other senior bone and glass familiars. The flower familiars joined soon after, still dripping from their feat, and the ice familiars followed from whatever they'd been caught up doing.

This feat was simple enough. Madam Xu had it set up bracket style, like it was the beginning of Familiar Combat. A good handful of familiars were still visibly recovering from the midterm, sporting mostly healed cuts and bite marks. I realized that must be part of the focus of this assembly. The news about the midterm results would spread, if it hadn't already, and visitors would learn who came out on top. The military would learn.

I pressed a hand to my side, but Madam Tukwilla's healing had done its work. I was scarred and the newly healed skin pulled when I stretched too far, but it wasn't painful anymore.

The competition went by quickly. It was merely a measure of fast shifts after all, so each bout took seconds. I chose the mouse more to test myself than anything else. I was faster as the horse, but expansion would tug at my new scar. The raccoon was closest to me in size, but I didn't want to show it off with that soldier watching.

Despite my exhaustion, I ended up making it to the finals. Oluk had fallen away in the quarterfinals—I made a mental note to set some time aside to practice fast shifts with him. I knew he could do better than that and I wondered if the crowd made him nervous.

It was only when I went to face off against Jingyi, dressed in his male uniform with hair tied in a topknot today, that I realized Charles hadn't been in the competition at all.

"Where is he?" I asked softly. Jingyi would know who I was talking about.

"Page duty," Jingyi said. "It must have been something big, he's been wearing the tabard for over an hour."

Before I could ask any more questions, Madam Xu shouted at us both to shift. I took a deep breath and called the mouse out of my heart again. The world grew larger around me as I squeezed down into the mouse's small body.

"Once more!" Madam Xu called. I looked up the now long distance to her face, confused. "It was too close to call, do it again."

I shifted back. Jingyi gave me a little bow as we reset and I quickly copied him.

We shifted one more time, but the mouse was tired of being

made to perform. I knew I should switch to the horse, but I was stubborn enough to push through the mouse's discomfort.

When I finally shifted, I knew I'd been too slow to beat Jingyi.

Jingyi was thrilled at his victory. Chao jumped the rope that marked the boundary of the feat and lifted his familiar up. Jingyi laughed freely as Chao spun him around in a wide circle. When Chao set him down, he pressed a quick kiss to his witch's lips that Chao turned into a longer one.

I headed back to the group, shrugging as Oluk said, "So close, Rosy!"

Guanyu watched the bonded witch and familiar. "They certainly won't struggle to get an offer," he said to Shantie.

"Offer?" I asked.

"By a jarl," Shaw said, coming again to stand a step too close to me. It was only getting colder as the night wore on, so despite my earlier irritation, I leaned into her body heat.

"Why wouldn't they have gotten an offer? Isn't Chao the best bone witch in school, after you?"

"He is, which is why people were upset when he bonded with Jingyi last year," Guanyu said, speaking low to prevent Chao and Jingyi from overhearing us. "Jingyi has no family, not since he left Waiming. I'm not sure if they died and that's why he immigrated or if they disowned him when he moved."

"The second, I think," Yuyan said. "I offered to send a letter to his family when I paid a courier to take one to mine a few months after he arrived, and he looked like he wanted to accept, but eventually said no."

"The army doesn't care, do they?" I asked pointedly. "Jingyi's a fox, that's deadly enough, and Chao's a necromancer."

"It's best for them to have options," Shaw said. "The army will accept any witch or familiar who wants to enlist, but if they wish to go in as officers, they need negotiating power. Chao's parents are part of my father's entourage and his mother is a jarl. That would have been enough before he bonded with Jingyi, but now he has to negotiate for both of them, which changes the equation."

"So if they get other offers, then it gives them the ability to negotiate," I said, understanding.

"And the power to choose a different option, if they don't wish to fight," Oluk murmured. I knew that he worried about that too. That his only option after school would be to enlist in the army, especially as an unbonded glass familiar with no social clout.

"And you? I assume you'll be an officer?" I asked Shaw.

Shaw nodded. She said nothing, but I could hear her unspoken words. Chao and Jingyi would have options, but she would not.

"We'll go in as thanes," Einar said. "It has already been offered to the four of us, and any familiars we bond with." He paused, glancing sideways at Oluk. "No matter their status."

I wasn't surprised, even if the blatant favoritism was aggravating.

"How about some tea?" Yuyan asked, obviously wanting to change the subject.

We all agreed and walked together toward the tea tent. It was halfway there that I spotted Charles. He kneeled before a group of giggling twelve- or thirteen-year-olds.

"Have you figured it out?" Aklemin asked, drifting over to stand at my other side. The side not attached to Shaw.

The punishment ended and Charles looked up. He met my gaze and sneered, but the twist of his lips couldn't hide the humiliation on his face. His eyes flicked to where my arm was pressed against Shaw's and the humiliation turned to despair.

I turned away. "He's the one who set the horses loose, isn't he?"

"He is," Shaw said. "The headmistress informed me yesterday. Set them loose, then reported to her and Madam Dyer the lie about you wanting to leave. He's on page duty until the assembly ends, with no breaks."

Aklemin looked up at the black sky above and its moonlit clouds like a painted ceiling far above our heads. Their eyes took on a familiar distant look—seeing a glimpse of the future as only ice witches could. "There is still misery on the horizon. Step carefully, Rosy."

"I never said you could call me that," I muttered, but my heart wasn't in it.

Aklemin didn't seem to hear anyway. They sped up to join Einar and Oluk at the front of the group, muttering something about how there would be cookies at the tea table.

"Don't let them get to you," Shaw said. "Aklemin thrives off of being cryptic."

"Most ice witches do," I said. "Why does Aklemin always pretend to be less powerful than they are?" The lithomancy today was a prime example.

"They've been like that all their life," Shaw said. "We grew up together. There weren't many kids our age on the Frozen Mountain. It's not an easy place to live. Falconridge has a strong community, but those with families live in Multah until their children are too grown to easily freeze to death. Chao's parents did that. His mother didn't take him up the Mountain to Father's court except during the summer months. But Aklemin's parents were different. Their father is jarl of Falconridge and he refused to send Aklemin away, like my father with me. We only had each other, Aklemin and I, until we both went to Witch Hall."

"Oh." I watched Aklemin as they flailed their hands about,

trying to accentuate some point about oatmeal in cookies. "It's good that you had them. Better than growing up alone."

"What about you? Were there many children in Forest's Edge?"

"Our village is small," I said. "Tokey and I were the closest in age. We only really had each other, too, growing up."

"You don't seem to talk with your cousin much anymore."

Shaw probably knew all about what had happened in Etiquette. My throat grew tight. "Yes, well, we have different priorities."

"You argued?"

I shook my head, unwilling to get into it. I hated this. I missed my cousin. We used to keep each other up late at night, huddled for warmth on the big bed we shared back home, chatting about everything we could think of. As little kids, we'd make up stories together and act them out in the pasture. Our relationship changed when I shifted for the first time, and again when she did, but I still loved her.

Until I came to Witch Hall and finally realized how much our relationship had fallen apart.

"It's not fair, the way everyone treats Oluk and Tokey, just because they aren't the children of jarls or wealthy or whatever."

"I know," Shaw said. "I've told both Madam Kawak and my father that I disagree with the current scholarship system. I've always believed that *all* witches and familiars should be allowed to come to Witch Hall."

My heart ached. I'd known that Shaw and her friends didn't hate scholarship students the way others seemed to, but it was different to hear Shaw speak of it so openly. Because she would be able to do that, when she was queen. She could make it so that money or status would never keep someone from Witch Hall.

And if all the small-town witches and village familiars came, the political structure Guanyu had spoken about would change.

It wouldn't just be one or two outcasts anymore. The lower-class witches and familiars would outnumber the rich ones, eventually.

"Just make sure they're all given opportunities after," I said. "It's not enough to give them Witch Hall if their only option will be to enlist in the army. There need to be choices for everyone, Shaw."

Slowly, almost reluctantly, Shaw nodded. "Yes, you're right. I'll work on it. I promise, Rosamund."

"I believe you," I said, and found it to be the truth.

We arrived at the tea tent and ducked through the flap.

"Oh, Mister Sorensen is doing tarot readings," Yuyan said, gesturing to a table in the corner of the tent where the ice witch was seated, a deck of tarot cards in front of him. A sign on the table said LOVE READINGS—SHOULD YOU BOND OR NOT?

"That could be interesting," Shaw said. "Rosamund?"

"Is that a good idea?" I asked, glancing at the sign. Would Mister Sorensen be able to tell from the cards that our relationship was fake?

"It may be good to know," Shaw said, like she was responding to my thoughts as much as my words.

I didn't have any good reason to argue with that, so I shrugged. I knew Shaw well enough that I was sure she had an excuse ready if the reading went poorly. "Sure, if you want. Let's see what the cards say about us."

# Chapter 22

DESPITE SHAW'S OBVIOUS INTEREST, SHE INSISTED WE GO last for the tarot reading. After some conferring, Einar sat down at the table first.

"Think of your future familiar. Your hopes and dreams. Picture your ideal partner," Mister Sorensen instructed as he shuffled the deck. "Ready? I'll draw. First, that which represents the current state of your love life. Ah, the Knight of Cups. You already have a partner in mind, I see. You are optimistic about them, perhaps willfully ignorant of potential problems. But they make you happy, that much is clear." Mister Sorensen tapped the card and raised an eyebrow at Einar.

Einar went pink, but he nodded. I glanced at Oluk. He watched the reading with wide eyes, shoulders tense like he was ready to bolt at any moment.

Mister Sorensen continued. "Let's see, the Three of Pentacles is your future. Your teamwork will be tested, your relationship attacked by external forces and . . . Oh, oh no, the Nine of Swords. There is trauma in your future together. Deep pain and, above that, shame. You or your future familiar will be beset with hopelessness."

Einar said nothing, but his face said enough. Aklemin looked troubled, staring blankly at the far wall of the tent. Yuyan stepped forward to put a hand on Einar's shoulder. "What does that mean?" she asked.

"I say only as the cards tell me," Mister Sorensen said. "They warn of the pitfalls, but they also give the answer to saving it. Mister Einar's potential bond is one of true honesty. This is a rarity, let me assure you. The pain, when it comes, will be overwhelming. But if you and your future familiar work together, you may make it through to whatever is on the other side."

"Thank you, sir," Einar said, standing. He looked at Oluk, visibly torn. Guanyu might say that I wore my heart on my face, but Einar was just as bad.

Oluk smiled, small though it was. "Tea?"

Einar took the offer with obvious relief. The two went to the tea table together. I looked after them. All I wanted was for Oluk to be happy. Mister Sorensen's reading did not inspire much confidence. Except Mister Sorensen had to know that Einar was interested in Oluk. It was obvious to anyone who spent more than a minute in the presence of both of them. Considering how much Mister Sorensen hated Oluk, I had to think he would have recommended Einar not pursue that relationship if he had any reason to. The fact that he'd hadn't, that he truly believed that Einar and Oluk would make it through to the other side of whatever trauma the cards saw in their future, meant something.

No need to guess what that trauma would be. Shaw's prophesized war loomed ever heavy over the horizon.

"Aklemin? Yuyan?" Shaw asked.

Aklemin blinked a few times, coming back from whatever daze they'd fallen into. "I'll go. Those cookies are calling me."

Mister Sorensen reshuffled the deck. Like with Einar, he told Aklemin to think of their future familiar, their ideal partner.

"Let's start with the present. A King of Swords in reverse. Someone is lying. Perhaps to themselves, perhaps to you, perhaps you to them. And here, the High Priestess. Now that's interesting. Your future lies in your ability to intuit the future. But you must take care not to get lost in the possibilities. You must choose a path forward before, let's see, the Hanged Man, oh dear. If you stay sedentary, you will fall into darkness. Your refusal to make a decision may prove your undoing." Mister Sorensen looked up, frowning. "But you knew that already."

"Your words of wisdom are appreciated," Aklemin said. Unlike Einar, it was hard to figure out what they were thinking from their expression. Then they stood and bounced over to Yuyan as if the solemn silence that had spread over the rest of us weren't there at all. "Cookies?"

"Here," Einar said. He'd returned with Oluk, both of them holding a tray full of steaming teacups and plates of cookies.

Aklemin grabbed an oatmeal cookie with a dramatic gasp of joy. "Your turn, Yuyan," they said with their mouth full.

Yuyan frowned. "Shaw?"

"Your choice, Yuyan," Shaw said.

Yuyan hesitated for a moment, then she sat at the table. Mister Sorensen did his same speech about thinking of her ideal partner. Yuyan nodded and Mister Sorensen flipped the first card.

"To start with we have the Hierophant in reverse. You wish to push back against these long-held traditions, perhaps around the witch-familiar bond, perhaps around the method by which you are to court your future intended. Or is it that you don't wish to bond at all? No, here this next card is the Two of Cups. You long for the partnership of a bond. The thing you must watch out for is, ah, the Tower. Disaster will strike. Before you can find success in your future relationship, you must first weather a tragic upheaval."

There was a clear pattern in these readings and I hated it. All of Shaw's entourage had pain in their future, all of them had tragedy coming. Was this because they'd chosen to follow Shaw? Or worse, was this the reality of all the witches and familiars in the Cursed Kingdom? The truth that we didn't like to say aloud, the darkness that war would bring.

Yuyan stood. She looked troubled. Einar balanced his tray on one hand and gave her one of the teacups. She took it without a word.

Shaw grabbed a chair from one of the other tables and placed it next to the one everyone had sat in. "Shall we?" she asked me.

"I'm really not sure this is a good idea," I said. After hearing the readings Shaw's entourage got, I wasn't sure I wanted to hear what was in store for Shaw and me.

"Please, Rosamund."

Apparently, I had a hard time saying no when Shaw unbent enough to beg. I dropped down into one of the chairs and Shaw joined me at the other.

"Well," Mister Sorensen said, shuffling his cards again. He looked as unsettled as I felt. I was sure he hadn't expected all this when he set up a table for giving witches and familiars love advice. "For a joint reading, you'll need to hold hands. Princess, if you'll put your palm up. Yes, like that. Miss Rosamund, you may place your hand atop hers."

I did as Mister Sorensen asked. Shaw's palm was warm and she squeezed our fingers together just like she'd done when we held hands while riding on Saturday. I tried not to fidget and focused on Mister Sorensen's words as he instructed us to think about each other and our hopes for our relationship.

I considered, briefly, thinking of something else. Tarot readers of Mister Sorensen's power were entirely accurate, but their readings only worked if the participant, well, participated. If I thought about someone else—Toketie or Oluk or whoever—then Mister Sorensen's interpretation would be inherently wrong. But even as I considered throwing the reading, I knew I wouldn't.

What would the cards say about Shaw and me? What kind of future would we have, if our courtship was real?

I knew the reading would predict pain. How could it not, with Shaw's war? I needed to hear it. Needed a reason to hold on to, something to help me remember that I was smart to refuse Shaw's courtship. We were only using each other.

But, just for a second, I looked at Shaw and let myself want her. Want to feel that warm touch, those gentle fingers caressing my skin. Want to see that smug smile, be embraced by the protection of that casual arrogance. Want to ride the thrill of battle together, victorious against our shared enemies. Want to constantly smell the vanilla and pine from whatever expensive soap Shaw used to wash her hair—a scent that reminded me of the Bone Forest.

For just one terrible second, I let myself want the promise of that blood-red cloak.

Mister Sorensen's hands stilled. He laid the deck flat in one hand and carefully pulled three cards from the top. He flipped the first to reveal the Moon and tapped it with his finger. "This is what brings you both together. The Moon represents intuition, especially intuition in the face of your own challenges. Your instincts draw you together, a feral promise of what could be."

He flipped the next card. The Four of Wands, upside down. "But your future together is unstable. Four of Wands in reverse represents problems at home. A desire for belonging that is not being met."

He flipped the final card.

"Death," Shaw whispered.

Mister Sorensen's voice grew hoarse. "Death symbolizes change. Great change, sometimes painful and terrible, but also renewing and rewarding. This relationship will push you to your limits. To succeed, you must both shed the trappings of your former selves and be reborn."

I shuddered. I wasn't sure I liked the sound of that at all. I definitely didn't like the way Mister Sorensen stared, as if trying to see what it was about me that meant I would have such a future with the Witch King's daughter. I wished I could tell him not to worry, that this future would never come to be. It was all in the cards, I wanted to say. Sure, I could bond with Shaw. But I would never be the same after. I would lose who I used to be—the me who supported my family and tamed bone horses and hunted with Gran in the woods. If I gave in to Shaw, I would be forever trapped by her bloody destiny.

Shaw pulled her hand out from under mine. I turned to her, wondering what she thought of the reading, but like I so often did, I found myself trapped in her dark-as-night eyes. It was only when she glanced down that I realized I'd been using my free hand to clutch the moonstone necklace.

AUTUMN APPROACHED WITH DARK NIGHTS and biting winds. I learned from Oluk that Witch Hall always had a feast during the solstices and equinoxes, but since the autumn equinox fell on a Saturday this year, there would also be a ball to celebrate.

"Is *that* why we've been learning dances in Etiquette for the past month?" I complained.

"It hasn't quite been a month," Oluk said. He wasn't fast enough to hide his laughter when I turned to scowl at him.

It wasn't that I disliked dancing. I'd grown up on country dancing, whenever there was a reason for our village to celebrate. Dances where everyone would link hands in a circle and kick up our legs or clap to the music. Sometimes we'd be in two lines instead, weaving in and out, linking one arm, then the other.

But the dancing of the upper class was a different beast entirely. Bows or curtsies every verse. Gently held hands, carefully timed steps intended to look like you were gliding across the ground. It was precise in the way country dancing never was, which meant country dancing was fun in the way noble dancing wasn't.

Besides, I'd be expected to attend the ball with Shaw. We'd been courting for more than a month, if you counted from when Shaw gave me the necklace. She'd made our entire year kneel for me. She'd defended me to the headmistress and Madam Dyer. Charles, my greatest competitor in the eyes of the school, had served page duty for an entire assembly.

The problem was, I still didn't know how I felt about any of it. I was at Witch Hall to save Gran. These kinds of games were leagues away from the politics I would need to play to save my family's ranch from our jarl's greed.

I'd known Shaw was dangerous from the start, but I hadn't seen the whole of it until she'd offered me courtship. Until she'd persuaded me to keep it going. I'd let the trap close around me and even now I salivated over the bait instead of scrambling for a way out.

The feast was a glamorous affair. Roast duck and braised pig. Baskets of hot bread. Individual mince pies. Fresh greens and neatly chopped vegetables dribbled with honey. I piled my plate high and filled a cup with spiced apple cider.

At our table, Aklemin was already halfway through their plate and eyeing the food line like they wanted to go back for more. Oluk and Einar kept playfully stealing each other's food. Yuyan had her head in her hand, chewing viciously like it could distract her from the foolishness.

Shaw leaned away as I climbed onto the bench between her and Aklemin, then leaned closer again once I was seated. "Will you allow me the honor of escorting you to the ball tonight?" she asked without preamble.

"What if I want to go with Oluk?" I challenged, because I couldn't not.

Oluk squeaked, turning red.

"Einar already asked him," Yuyan said, exasperation in her voice.

"Oh," I replied, a bit dumbly. "Oh."

Oluk blushed redder. "You, um, haven't changed, Rosy?"

I looked down. I was still wearing the simple linen blouse and skirt I wore most weekends. Oluk had changed into a green shirt with embroidery around the shoulders. I'd never seen him wear it before, which meant he saved it especially for events like this ball.

It wasn't just Oluk. Einar's shirt looked like it was made of silk and his leather suspenders shone like he'd polished them. Yuyan wore a fitted dress instead of her normal shirt-and-skirt combo. Aklemin's robes had what might have been actual silver thread woven through the hem.

Shaw, however, looked no different from normal in her black dress. I'd never seen her wear another color. Black for her school uniform and black for her casual weekend clothes—though it was easy to see that her casual clothes were better made than anything the school could provide.

"I thought we might both change after dinner," Shaw said, like she knew I'd come in the same clothes I'd worn for horse chores and hadn't wanted to embarrass me. "I'll meet you outside your suite?"

I nodded and spent the rest of dinner trying to figure out what I'd packed that would look halfway decent.

I still hadn't figured it out by the time I was in my suite, digging through my chest. I only owned one dress, outside of my school uniforms, but it was a plain thing with three-quarter-length sleeves and a frayed hem.

I put the dress aside and found my nicest blouse instead. It tied in the front with ribbon, so I didn't wear it to the stable in case one of the horses decided to chew on the ribbon ends. To pair with it, I chose a blue skirt dark enough to hide whatever wrinkles or stains it probably had.

Even with Shaw's moonstone necklace glittering at my throat, I knew I would look like a peasant next to the princess. It shouldn't have bothered me. I was a rancher's daughter, not a jarl's. I had no use for fine clothing.

My eyes drifted to the corner of my room and the bundle of red there. Slowly, I walked over and picked up the cloak Shaw had gifted me. I'd beat the dirt and mud off it before storing it in the corner, vowing never to wear it. But it was cold enough that a cloak would be a welcome addition to my attire.

I looked over the crimson-dyed wool. The neat, professional

stitches. The three-eyed raven clasp, mark of the royal house. The lining, white enough that I knew the fur had been sun-bleached.

That lining was familiar. I didn't recognize the exact pattern, but I knew the type of fur. Knew it from years of burying my face in Gran's side. The lining was made from a bone wolf's pelt. The touch of bone magic was still heavy in each strand as I ran my fingers through it.

Hungry now for something I couldn't name, I brought the fur to my nose and inhaled. The soft smell of vanilla and pine clung to the wolf's fur. I'd thought it was Shaw's soap, but maybe it was something else. Maybe the bone magic that flowed through her lingered in a different way. The smell of the Bone Forest. Of Gran and my home away from home. It was enough to make me cry.

Decided, I threw the cloak over my shoulders and did the clasp with fingers I tried to pretend weren't shaking. I rubbed my face, hoping to hide any hint of tears, and let my hair fall loose. I'd kept it braided all day, so it was less tangled than normal. It would have to do.

Shaw waited for me outside the suite when I stepped out. She'd changed into a deep blue tunic that came to mid-thigh and black breeches that clung tight to her legs. Gleaming leather boots covered her calves, the buckles made of shining silver. Her own cloak was the same blue as her tunic with a black satin lining and a three-eyed raven clasp nearly identical to my own, except with sapphire eyes.

Blue and black were the colors of the royal house. I hadn't thought about it when I chose my dark blue skirt, but there was something in Shaw's eyes as she looked from it to my cloak. Something I didn't want to name.

I said nothing as I took Shaw's offered arm like I'd done it a hundred times. I *had* done it a hundred times. The warmth of Shaw's body, the way her magic echoed in my necklace, was achingly familiar now.

Yellow-speckled leaves framed Witch Hall's waterfall like a painting as we walked to the section of campus that had transformed into an outdoor dance hall. The sun had only just set and the sky was the kind of blue that existed for storybooks.

Torches lined the dancing area and pavilions with chairs and tables took up the rest of the space between the creek and the teachers' cottages. Most tables were full, though no one was dancing yet. We weren't the only couple arriving slightly late. Just ahead of us, a glass witch and familiar stopped by Mister Voll, who stood at the entrance of the festivities. He nodded, then announced their names loudly. The pair proceeded through the dance floor and across to a table where their friends clapped for them.

Then it was our turn. Mister Voll grinned and gave me a wink. "Ready, Miss Rosamund?"

I wasn't sure what I was supposed to be ready for, but I nodded.

Mister Voll turned to face the rest of the school. This felt different than the Combat midterm or even the assemblies. Everyone was here—all the teachers, and all the students from seniors down to the early years. At least there were no military recruiters. The only outsiders were a small group of musicians sitting underneath their own pavilion, waiting for a signal to start playing.

"Princess Shaw Colchuck, daughter of the Witch King, heir to the Cursed Throne," Mister Voll declared. "Escorting Rosamund Holt of Forest's Edge."

I didn't have to wonder what we looked like. Shaw had done most of the work, between my necklace and cloak. I met Guanyu's eyes at a table under the leftmost pavilion. He tapped his chest, then his cheek. Was I wearing my heart on my face again? I tried to control my expression, to keep it looking calm and serene as I walked beside Shaw onto the dance floor.

We didn't walk through the dance area to the table where Shaw's entourage sat though. Instead, Shaw stopped us in the center.

"No," I hissed, but it was too late. The musicians began to play, and Shaw bowed.

At least they'd chosen one of the less complex minuets. I did my best to keep my scowl off my face and dropped into a curtsy in time with the music. Then Shaw held out her hand and I put mine on top of it and off we went. Slow steps, stop, turn, step again.

It wasn't terrible, dancing with Shaw. Even with the eyes of literally everyone at school on us. This dance was a game of chase, where one partner walked away and the other followed, only to turn around and do it in reverse.

Following Shaw was easy. Even when she made a game of it, stepping outside of my vision, I knew where she was. I had fun with it, stepping sideways instead of forward, doing a little spin until I came to my place in front of her. Shaw bowed, I curtsied, then it was my turn to leave first. I made my steps long, getting all the way to the other end of the dance floor.

I ended with my back to Shaw. The hairs on my neck bristled as she came after me. I felt stalked like prey, but it wasn't a bad feeling. The voices in my heart were excited. They all wanted out, every single one. To frolic and play for Shaw's amusement.

The dance ended with Shaw taking my hand and bowing over it. My heart pounded as I curtsied back. My gaze moved over her face, eyes catching on the way the torchlight reflected off her cheekbones. She really was beautiful, especially with her eyes softened and a smile tugging at her lips. Her future familiar would be blessed to wake up beside that every morning.

The roaring in my ears was so loud, I almost didn't realize everyone was applauding until Shaw let go of my hand.

"I'm impressed, Rosamund," she said, a touch teasing.

The spell broke. I rolled my eyes. "I guess Etiquette is good for something."

It seemed everyone had been waiting for Shaw and me to open the floor, because on the next dance several dozen pairs joined us. I let Shaw lead me through two more songs before I begged off to rest.

Yuyan was the only one at the table when we sat. She nodded without speaking, caught up in watching Shantie spin Guanyu around the dance floor. I poured cups from the water pitcher at the center of the table for Shaw and myself, then looked around the dancing couples for the rest of the entourage.

Einar and Oluk were near the center of the floor, eyes fixed on each other's faces even when the dance had them turning away. They looked good together. Oluk was only about four inches taller than me and leaner than I was, while Einar was massive, with broad shoulders and a chest that would only widen as he aged. The way his huge hands wrapped around Oluk's—gentle, like he was something precious—was clear even across the dance floor.

Aklemin, in contrast, wasn't attached to any partner. They accepted the hand of any ice familiar who asked but switched to the next after each dance. I watched for a good half dozen dances, but Toketie never asked Aklemin. When she danced, it was with Froya or another one of her suitemates. Most of the time, she sat at their table and watched the revelry go on around her.

Einar and Oluk finally left the dance area and Aklemin followed them, eyes glinting like they knew something the rest of us didn't.

That something became clear a moment later, as Einar didn't sit down when Oluk did. Instead, he grabbed something from his pocket and kneeled before Oluk's chair, offering it up from the palm of his hand.

The tables around us had caught sight of what was happening. Several younger witches and familiars stood, trying to get a better view of the spectacle. Einar and Oluk ignored all of it, still focused on each other.

I had the best angle to watch as Oluk first paled, then blushed. "Are you sure?" he whispered, and I knew what he was referring to. Knew the tarot reading sat heavy between him and Einar.

"I have never been more certain. Oluk Blackwell, I've never known a familiar as stalwart as you. Your determination impresses me every day and your charm makes it hard"—Einar coughed— "hard to speak, sometimes. Whatever challenges our future brings, I would face them at your side. Will you do me the honor of accepting my courtship necklace?"

Oluk nodded, looking too overwhelmed to speak. Einar stood and fastened the necklace around his neck. It was a beautiful piece of brown leather, the exact shade of Oluk's hair. Gold-painted runes glimmered across it, turning a simple choker into a work of art.

I wasn't sure how to feel. Happy, for Oluk. Scared, for what it meant.

But it wasn't a night for worries. I'd decided that when I put Shaw's cloak on. I stood and walked over to my friend, hand out.

"Come on," I told Oluk. "You can't be seen talking to him for the next week, can you?"

Oluk laughed and, after sending one more meaningful look Einar's way, he accepted my hand and let me draw him back out to the dance floor.

I danced the rest of the night. First with Oluk, then Aklemin, then Guanyu. I saw Shantie pull Yuyan from our table, the torchlight casting a red glow on her cheeks as she danced with her fellow flower witch.

The musicians called the last dance and Shaw broke away from where she'd been dancing with Aklemin to get to me. I curtsied, she bowed, and together we swept across the floor.

That night, I laid my cloak across my bed and buried my face in the wolf fur. The weight of the cloak let me pretend, if just for a moment, that Gran was there.

I dreamed I was the wolf. Shaw ran long fingers through my fur, smiling down at me.

"You're beautiful like this, Rosamund. I knew you would be," she whispered.

When I woke up, I was crying.

# Chapter 23

OLUK ACCEPTED EINAR'S COURTSHIP THE NEXT SATURDAY. He did it publicly, during dinner, and when he said yes Einar swept him into a tight hug like he'd been terrified that Oluk Blackwell, school outcast, would turn him down.

I wished he had. I wished he'd been selfish and walked away. Einar had already helped enough with Oluk's final project for the stable. Oluk wasn't desperate anymore. He could have said no and let the other glass witches in our year get to know him as Einar had.

But I knew Oluk would never do that. He was as smitten as Einar was, it was plain as day. It didn't help the guilt I felt as I saw them smiling at each other. I couldn't help worrying over Einar's tarot reading and what it meant for Oluk's future.

I tried to imagine what it would be like in the entourage when I left. What if Shaw bonded with Charles after all? What would it be like for Oluk, who Charles hated nearly as much as he hated me? And what if Aklemin bonded with Froya? Would Yuyan choose a flower familiar from a powerful family, like Kwaddis Tenas? Oluk would be the social outcast again, except this time there'd be no end, no graduation to look forward to. It would be like that for the rest of his life.

I didn't have much time to think about how I could convince

Oluk not to rush into bonding, because the next Wednesday I walked into the flower witches' suite after lunch to see Shantie jumping up and down like a child, squealing with excitement. Guanyu watched her with so much affection on his face that I felt like I should look away to give them privacy.

I hadn't seriously considered bonding before coming to Witch Hall, but these past weeks had made me think about it. I wanted something like what Guanyu and Shantie had, one day. Uncomplicated, full of love and mutual respect. I understood Oluk now, when he'd told me of his dream witch. Except he'd forgotten to add the desire for a simple life in his qualifications. Without politics or war to ruin everything.

"Rosy, Rosy, there you are!" Shantie said. "I figured it out. It's been staring me in the face this whole time, I was just too distracted to see it."

"Figured out— You mean the potion? Shantie, did you get it to work?"

"I still need to test it, but I figured out the scaling agent. The one that will help it work, regardless of a familiar's level of power or type of magic."

I let my excitement drown out all my other worries. This was it! Even if I had to wait two more terms before petitioning the jarls' council to free Gran, I could start sending her the aid. She'd be free of her feral episodes and the rest of our family would feel safe visiting her again.

"What are we waiting for, let's test it!" I said, rushing fully into the suite.

Shantie's face fell even as Guanyu shook his head. "It's not that easy," he said. "It's a pretty rare ingredient, found in the deepest parts of Lake Bloom. Only a few specialty buyers sell it."

Rare meant expensive. Expensive ingredients meant expensive potion. I tried to convince myself it would work out. Even if we couldn't afford a daily dose for Gran, even just having one on hand for when she did turn feral would help immensely.

"I don't think anyone will sell it over mail," Shantie said. "I'll need to find a seller in Multah over the break and buy it. We'll have to test the formula next term."

"Why can't we go to Multah this weekend?" I asked. "It's not far."

"Students aren't allowed to leave campus without permission," Guanyu said. "And I don't think Madam Ipsoot will give it just for this. There are only a few weeks left of term as is."

I wasn't ready to give up. I wanted to be able to bring the cure to Gran when I went home. To prove to her that going to Witch Hall hadn't been a mistake after all.

"What we need is a reason to go to Multah outside of buying the ingredient," I mused.

"Like what?" Shantie asked.

An idea came to me. "Mister Jostein," I said. "He goes every Saturday to get supplies for the coming week. If we offered to help him load and unload, I bet he'd let us."

Shantie looked at Guanyu, still bouncing on the balls of her feet. "No harm in asking, is there?"

"I suppose not," Guanyu said. "And everyone knows he favors Rosy here. I bet he'll agree if she does the asking."

"He doesn't favor me," I protested.

"He let you be a stablehand even though bone familiars were forbidden," Shantie pointed out.

"There were tryouts, and Shaw's the one who— You know what, never mind. That doesn't matter. I'll ask him tonight and let you know at dinner."

I composed my argument for Mister Jostein all through Etiquette, but when it came time to ask, he just shrugged halfway through my first point and said, "Sure, if you and your friends want to help. Make the work go by faster. Since that incident with the freed horses, Madam Kawak doesn't want me to be gone from campus so long anyway."

I was so excited, I gave Mister Jostein a hug, then did my best to ignore his wide-eyed look and the subsequent awkwardness. At dinner, I stopped by the table where Guanyu and Shantie sat with a few other flower witches and familiars. "This Saturday. Meet at the stables after breakfast, ready to work."

Shantie clapped and Guanyu grinned. "We'll be there," he agreed.

IT TOOK US AN HOUR to get to Multah by horse and cart. We passed the outskirts of the town first—a few ranches and farmland. Then the houses grew closer and closer together until we walked through whole neighborhoods of individual cottages and communal longhouses. We clattered over a small bridge and at the crest, I could see the city. The southern outskirts of Multah surrounded Lake Bloom. Small bridges crossed the various creeks and streams that fed into the Lake. The northern part of town was a dedicated port for Wimhal River, but just as much of Multah's commerce came from Lake Bloom as it did from the river docks.

The Saturday market was held a couple blocks from Lake

Bloom, in the main town square. Mister Jostein parked our cart along a row of similarly parked carts and wheelbarrows. "Help me with the large produce first, then I'll see about giving you a second to wander off," he said. He knew about our errand and hadn't cared much so long as we put effort into helping him.

Guanyu, Shantie, and I followed Mister Jostein obediently through the first couple stops. One was to a farmer who sold us several bags of cabbages and potatoes. Then we picked up five massive baskets of apples from the orchard owner and a few kegs of unfermented apple cider.

Once we dropped those purchases off at the cart, we moved on to the butcher to get huge slabs of smoked meat, then to the fisher to get the daily catches. I'd noticed Witch Hall typically served fish on the weekends and now I knew why.

It took us over an hour to load the cart with everything Witch Hall would need for the next week. Mister Jostein was particular about how to pack it, which made sense once I realized the sheer volume of food we were buying.

Finally, Mister Jostein cleared his throat. "I've only got small things now. How about you lot grab some lunch and meet me back at the cart in an hour?"

"Thank you, sir," Shantie said earnestly, and dragged both Guanyu and me away by our wrists.

We did go for lunch first, exhausted from the morning's work. My respect for Mister Jostein had grown with each minute of it and I promised myself that I'd volunteer to come with him more often, to give him a hand.

Lunch was a cheerful affair. Shantie told hilarious stories of her and Guanyu's time in the early stages of their courtship. I couldn't tell if the flush on Guanyu's cheeks was from embarrassment or delight, but he laughed freely and held Shantie's hand the entire time.

As we were finishing, Shantie checked the angle of the sun. "We've got time still. Guanyu, darling, why don't you show Rosy the Lake. You've never seen it up close, right?"

Guanyu looked pleased with the idea. "You'll be all right getting the quills?"

"If someone has them in stock," Shantie said, then waved a hand. "But one or three buyers won't make a difference. They're hard to get, so if no one has them in stock I'll have to place a special order. I'll deal with it. Go have some fun. You both deserve it, for how much you've helped me with this project."

I wasn't sure that was fair, since Shantie had certainly helped Guanyu more with his and Guanyu had been trying to help with mine. But I wanted to see Lake Bloom, so I didn't protest.

Guanyu led me through a series of neighborhoods to the edge of the Lake. We ended up at a quiet part of the Lake's shore. Up close, Lake Bloom was massive—certainly wider across than I'd want to swim in most of my forms, human included. It also smelled strangely sweet, like a berry pie or a heavy spray of floral perfume.

Guanyu plopped down on the shore, uncaring of the wet reeds and their vibrant, multicolored flowers. I'd never seen reeds flower like that, but then none of the trees in the Bone Forest looked normal either.

"We have a plan, Shantie and I," Guanyu said, staring out over the deceptively calm water. "After Witch Hall, we'll get a place here. Not too big. We don't want children, so it'll just be the two of us. Her family lives on the other side of Multah. Close enough to visit, far enough away that we'll have some privacy. We'll continue our mail-order potions business. Shantie will make them, of course, and I'll dive into the Lake and collect the ingredients she needs. We'll be known across the kingdom as the best place to buy quality potions. Maybe we'll even be able to retire before we're too old and gray. Teach some new Witch Hall graduates what we do and live out the rest of our days watching the sun rise and set over the Lake."

"That's a beautiful dream," I said, and I tried to squash the vicious jealousy that welled at his words.

"Ah, but that's all it is. A dream. Shantie's the best potion-maker in the entire kingdom and what am I? Prideful, useless—"

"Whoa, Guanyu, why would you say that? You're not useless!"

Guanyu let out a bitter laugh and shook his head.

I tried again. "Who even came up with the idea for mailing potions? That was you, not Shantie. If not for that, she'd be selling her potions in the Multah market for the rest of her life and we both know she'd never succeed nearly as well as she will with your idea."

"You don't get it. I'm supposed to get her ingredients. That's the purpose of flower familiars here. We're not strong like the ones out in the ocean, so we have to be smart instead. To brave these treacherous waters and return with life-saving ingredients. The amount of money we'll lose having to outsource the collecting . . ."

Guanyu angrily threw a rock into the Lake. The water didn't ripple as it landed. It was as if the Lake opened a hole just large enough to swallow the rock, then just as quickly closed it again. The water remained too still, too serene.

"Why can't you get the ingredients? You've got a salmon shift. Surely there's not much in the lake that can hurt you in that form?"

"True, but I'll never be able to maneuver the garden at the Lake floor as a salmon. Never have the dexterity to collect those hard-to-find ingredients. The salmon's too noticeable to trap any of the native creatures of Lake Bloom and too big to catch them if they stay under the cover of the plants."

I remembered the feat at the assembly then. How not even Shantie had bet on Guanyu's success. I remembered, too, the freedom I'd felt when I got my first small shift. My first two had been bone wolf and horse, both large and, as Guanyu said, noticeable. The first time I'd become the squirrel, it had felt like flying as I scurried up into the trees.

"That's why you were so quick to offer yourself for my project. To get a second shift," I said.

"Not that it's worked," Guanyu muttered, angry.

That was true. We'd been trying for weeks, and Guanyu had said he practiced on his own, but no matter how much we meditated or I talked him through his memories of other flower creatures, he hadn't come close to finding another voice.

"It's not your fault. I think my theory is wrong," I admitted.

I'd thought it would help once Guanyu figured out his connection to the salmon, but we'd gotten that the first week. To him, the salmon represented pride. A beautiful shift, strong, majestic. His own inner pride had manifested into that form. But now he saw the pride as his weakness, thinking himself incapable of opening up to another flower animal because of it. I hadn't wanted that. Connecting with a new animal didn't mean ignoring the first.

I jumped to my feet, suddenly sick of it all. Guanyu was wallowing in his misery and if I sat here any longer, I'd start thinking about how it was almost the end of the term and I might not graduate if I didn't figure out my senior project. We both needed a distraction.

"You said what Shantie needs is quills, right? What kind of quills?"

"From a flower lamprey," Guanyu said. "They have a mane of sorts, except it's made of super thin petals that we call quills because of how sharp they are. It's a lucky find when you see a shed quill on the Lake's floor."

"Why not just catch a lamprey and skin it?"

"Because they're terrifying. The flower lampreys are more similar to the ocean ones. Normal river lampreys are tiny, but these ones are easily three feet long."

"Well, you're near double that, as a salmon," I pointed out.

"I can't catch one alone," Guanyu protested.

"You're not alone." I walked up to the very edge of the Lake, trying to tell myself I wasn't scared of diving past that smooth surface to explore the depths beyond.

Guanyu tugged me by the arm. "Rosy, no, the Lake's too dangerous. Humans don't survive. That's why flower familiars are the only ones who go in there."

"I may not be a flower familiar, but I survived for years in the Bone Forest for a reason." I took a deep breath and hoped I wasn't being reckless.

Then I reached into my heart and drew up a voice I'd only been able to use once before. The otter yipped in delight as it merged with me.

I took one look over my shoulder at Guanyu, who stared down at me with his mouth hanging open, then I dove into Lake Bloom.

The world was muffled underwater—the otter's natural instinct was to close the flaps over its ears. I had about five minutes of breath before I'd need to surface again. I swam a bit deeper, just as Guanyu dove in where I'd been. He truly was huge as a salmon and the flowers growing out of his fish scales danced like they were alive.

Guanyu swam a few feet in front of me. He flicked his tail back and forth, obviously unsure. I kicked down to head into the depths of Lake Bloom. Like I'd hoped, Guanyu followed.

I swam along the Lake floor with Guanyu as it gradually sloped deeper and deeper. Reeds gave way to flowering vines. I didn't know Lake Bloom like I knew the Bone Forest, so I followed Guanyu's lead as we descended deeper.

After a few minutes, I lifted back toward the surface, avoiding a field of orange flowers that fluttered gently in the water. They smelled like peaches, so delicious my otter instincts wanted to try to find the fruit.

My human mind knew better. The trees of the Bone Forest were sentient. Magic gave them a level of awareness other trees didn't have. They could create an unnatural fog or complete darkness. They could shift and make people forget which way they'd come from. They didn't have exposed bone like the creatures that lived there, but they were cursed all the same.

I could only imagine this garden in Lake Bloom was similar. And a bone otter, no matter my natural swimming ability, did not have the same instincts or immunities to whatever the Lake could do.

I kicked up just as my lungs started to contract. Large lily pads floated all around me, their huge stalks stretching up from the lake floor all the way to the surface. I followed one stalk up and surfaced right next to the lily pad to take a deep breath.

A frog croaked in my ear. I startled, shying away. It was a flower frog—about the size of my otter's head. Its skin was bright green, the same color as the lily pad it sat on. Like all flower creatures, it had a plant literally growing out of it. Tiny little purple flowers littered its back and in the center of each one was a small bud, like the start of a fruit.

The frog croaked at me again. I chittered back, amused.

A couple of the little buds on its back burst. I watched as small specks of purple dust flew through the air. Pollen? A few specks landed on my nose and I sneezed.

Something tugged hard on my back paw. I dove under to see that Guanyu had me caught in his mouth. He pulled me away just as my nose began to hurt. I rubbed at it with my paws. Guanyu tugged me farther from the lily pads.

Right, avoid the flower frogs, message received. My nose eventually stopped burning. Guanyu circled around me, then bobbed up and down. I nodded back at him, a bit contrite.

Guanyu must have understood, because he darted forward and bumped my side with his nose. I knew this game. *Tag, you're it.*

I raced after Guanyu. He swam away, keeping just above the veritable jungle that spread across the Lake floor. Some of the flowers were tall enough that I had to dodge clear of them even several feet above the floor. Their faces turned to watch me as I swam around them. I tried not to let it bother me. The flowers were no different than the Bone Forest's trees, I told myself, though the thought wasn't nearly as comforting as I wanted it to be.

I caught up with Guanyu and snagged him by the tail, then turned in the other direction to avoid being tagged back. My lungs began to protest. I looked up to find a spot on the Lake's surface clear of lily pads. Guanyu caught me as I came up for breath.

Determined to win this game, I dove again. I caught up to him almost immediately and was about to chitter in victory, only to realize he had stopped swimming. I followed Guanyu's gaze and saw something moving toward us. I tried to peer through the gloom made by distance. What was it?

Guanyu dove down just as the shadow crystalized. A school of bass raced toward me. Like Lei's new shift, the bass all had small sets of pale yellow flowers on their sides with pollen stalks that trailed out alongside their fins. I figured the fish school would catch sight of me and veer in the other direction, but within seconds they were mere feet away with no indication that they cared that I was there.

I had just enough time to tense up and then the bass surrounded me. I closed my eyes and curled up in a ball. I felt several bass slam into my side, pushing me into another fish until I was like a ball bouncing off the walls. It was over in seconds, but I had a feeling I'd be covered in bruises tomorrow.

Opening my eyes, I caught sight of the reason for the school's panic—and very nearly panicked myself. A large *thing* came barreling toward me. It was a good three feet long and almost completely black, except for a mane of spines and one huge red blossom on top of its head. But the terrifying part was its mouth. A perfect circle, displaying sharp teeth that pointed in all directions.

# Chapter 24

I BARKED IN FEAR, BUT THE STRANGE FLOWER CREATURE completely passed me by. I spun underwater in time to see it catch one of the bass at the back of the school. With terrifying efficiency, it burrowed inside the bass. Blood clouded the water as it came out the other side of the fish. It darted back to its prey, this time burrowing down the length of its body. Chunks of flesh and bone drifted to the Lake floor.

When Guanyu said lampreys were terrifying, I hadn't thought they'd compare to a feral bone wolf. But those teeth and its mane of quills were scary enough to fuel my nightmares for days. I understood why Guanyu hadn't wanted to face it alone. Considering how easily it had torn into the bass, it would have no trouble burrowing through Guanyu's salmon shift.

But there was no time to panic. Guanyu was darting past me with powerful strokes, heading straight for the creature. I'd promised I'd help him get those quills.

I dove to get underneath the lamprey, cutting off its escape path as Guanyu attacked it from behind.

The lamprey didn't seem to care about Guanyu until he was right next to it. Maybe it was used to being top of the Lake's food chain. It wasn't until Guanyu had its mouth around those sharp quills that the lamprey reacted. It lunged at Guanyu and I kicked up. Guanyu drew back, bleeding at the mouth from where several quills had punctured him. The lamprey didn't try to run, going after Guanyu again like it had fallen into a feral rage. Maybe it had. I didn't know if flower and glass and ice animals raged like bone animals did, but it made sense that they could. All types of familiars could go feral, after all.

Guanyu whipped around and whacked the lamprey with his body. It flew back just over me and I took the opportunity to get my teeth around its middle.

The lamprey was three feet long, but it was slender. It took only two sharp bites for me to break it into two pieces.

Guanyu grabbed the top half, careful of the quills, and then drifted toward me. My head was starting to hurt from lack of air. I gestured up to the surface. He turned his back to me and I grabbed hold of his top fin. With a powerful push of his tail, he propelled us toward the surface.

I broke through the water, gasping for breath. Guanyu swam downward and I let him go, not ready to dive again. But when I looked at him through the water, he made large jerking gestures with his tail, like he was trying to tell me something.

A croak rang a few feet from me. I froze. Another croak echoed the first. Then another, and another.

I turned slowly. A huge collection of lily pads spread out across the surface of the Lake in front of me. On each lily pad, a frog sat— tiny purple flowers fluttering in the wind.

Then, one by one, the buds in the center of the flowers began to burst.

I dove back into the lake. Guanyu shook his head, the lamprey's quills fluttering about him like a horse's mane. I felt the sudden urge to laugh. We swam deep enough to avoid the poisonous frog pollen, all the way back to shore.

"You're brilliant, Rosy!" Guanyu said as we both shifted and collapsed onto land. The lamprey's bleeding body lay on the shore between us. "Absolutely brilliant. With this many quills, the potion's practically made itself."

"You're still bleeding, stop talking," I said, but I couldn't stop laughing while I did.

Guanyu put a hand to his mouth and grimaced as it came back bloody. The puncture wounds weren't big and it was almost comical, the way the little waterfalls of blood covered his mouth. He licked them and grimaced again.

I looked back at the Lake. I wouldn't be diving in for a repeat anytime soon, but it had been wonderful to experience it. The center of all flower magic in the kingdom. It wasn't my home, not like the Bone Forest was home, but it was special in its own way. Special, and deadly.

"What were those frogs?" I asked. "What does that pollen *do?*"

"We call them king frogs, 'cause they rule over the surface of the Lake. Nothing hunts the adults, not even humans, though the pollen's useful in some potions. Deadly though. You're lucky you were able to wash off that small amount so quickly."

"Yeah," I said, still remembering how my nose had burned. I had a thought and glanced sideways at Guanyu.

"What?" Guanyu asked, wiping his mouth.

"King frogs, huh? Like your king salmon?"

Guanyu stared at me, then looked out over the Lake to the lily pads only barely visible. "They are, aren't they?" he said, as if to himself.

"Let's try it. Right now. Try to shift into a frog."

Guanyu shook his head. "Did the lamprey burrow through your brain? It won't work."

"Just trust me. Remember those frogs, how proud they look on their lily pads. Please, Guanyu."

Guanyu frowned, but he closed his eyes.

And then, despite weeks and weeks of nothing, he shifted.

I clapped, overjoyed. "I wonder if you could do the lamprey too, after our duel with it. That thing was certainly proud enough." I kicked a bit of mud at the corpse on the ground.

Guanyu shifted back, grinning even though it made him bleed. "Take it one step at a time. Why did it work this time, when it didn't before?"

I shrugged. "Shifting is easier when you're here, isn't it? The home of flower magic. I should have realized before. Oluk told me he got his second shift while all the glass students were visiting the Obsidian Desert for Lammas. I'm not sure if he ran across a rattlesnake, or if he had as a kid and just remembered it, but he was there. In the Desert."

Guanyu held a hand up to stop me. "Wait, slow down. What are you saying?"

I didn't realize I'd talked without breathing until I had to pant a few seconds to be able to speak again. "I'm saying that in order for familiars to get their second shift, they should come to where the magic is strongest. Experienced familiars, those with multiple shifts already, we can sometimes push for it. That's the art of knowing the difference between your voices and how to tell when a new one has joined you. But my project's about familiars finding their second shift and I think this is it."

My mind was already racing ahead. If I talked to everyone in our Advanced Shapeshifting class about where they were when they got their second shift, maybe the same pattern would exist. I knew it fit for me. After all, I'd grown up on the edge of the Bone Forest. No wonder it hadn't even been a year before I found my second shift. And now with Guanyu's success, I had clear evidence. I didn't know much about the nation of Daming, across the ocean, but I wondered if Madam Xu had been living in a place that teemed with glass magic when she got her second shift.

It was a better lead for my senior project than anything so far. I could be wrong. I might be wrong. But something about this felt right in the way none of my other ideas had.

"We should get back," Guanyu said, obviously still confused. "But, Rosy, however it happened, thank you. A flower frog's exactly what I needed. Salmon for the power, frog for the small spaces. It's perfect."

"You'll need to practice, to get consistent with it," I warned him. "But I'm glad. You deserve it. You really do."

Guanyu picked up the lamprey's head. "Let's get this back to Shantie, shall we?"

I was about to reply when I noticed the prey in my heart were uneasy. It had been long enough that they should have calmed down from our adventure in the Lake, but if anything, they were only getting louder.

Then I smelled it. Alongside the sweet scent of Lake Bloom was another, thicker smell. Something was burning.

I spun on my heels, frantically searching the horizon.

"Rosy, what?" Guanyu asked.

"There's smoke in the air. Is it from Vingate?" Vinland's port was directly across the river from Multah. If Vingate was on fire—

Guanyu grabbed my arm in a death grip as we both spotted it at the same time. An ominous billow of black smoke rose up into the sky. It wasn't coming from Vingate, but from the direction of Multah's market.

WHEN GUANYU AND I ARRIVED at the market square, we found an entire row of stalls on fire. People shouted for water buckets. Others yelled, fists in the air, spewing obscenities. Even more people cried for help.

"We're under attack!" one woman screamed. "The war has begun!"

"What?" I tried to ask, but the crowd pushed her away.

One of the stalls tipped forward. I watched, horrified, as the beams holding the awning collapsed into the next row. With a sound like an animal's roar, the stall it had fallen on erupted into flames. The awning itself fell in burning clumps onto the crowd.

"Shantie!" Guanyu yelled, high-pitched and terrified.

The wolf howled. The other predators in my heart told me to run—that this was not a fight we could win. The prey were frozen still, so scared they couldn't even panic anymore.

I lost sight of Guanyu as the crowd surged, all trying to flee. Screams filled the air. Guanyu wasn't the only one calling out for a loved one.

I felt as though I were dreaming. I'd never seen fire like this. How had it gotten so out of control? There were runes to stop this. Enchantments to prevent fire from spreading. A city like Multah should be covered in them.

Someone slammed into me from behind and I fell to my knees.

The fire spread rapidly from stall to stall. Out of the corner of my eye, I saw a woman frantically trying to beat out the fire that ran up her son's sleeve, unaware that her own skirt had caught fire too.

"Mama!" the kid screamed, and I scrambled to my feet, determined to help them.

The crowd surged once more, pushing me away. I struggled, trying to break free of the elbows and knees. I stepped on something and was horrified to realize it was a person, trampled by the stampede, face turned purple from bruising. Once again, the crowd pushed me away before I could try to help.

Then I heard Guanyu's voice again. "Shantie, we need to leave!"

I clawed at the panic in my heart, mentally yelling at my voices to get it together. One brave voice met me and I shifted into the squirrel. I launched myself from people's heads and shoulders to get to my friend. I found him and Shantie several yards away. The smoke billowed thick and black. They both were crouched down low. Shantie was frantically helping a girl who'd caught fire. She screamed as Shantie grabbed an entire jug of some blue-colored potion and used it to douse the flame.

"Guanyu, give me some energy, I need to heal her," Shantie said.

I leaped down and shifted into a human, regretting it a second later. The smell of burned fabric and cooked meat was horrifying, and squirrels couldn't vomit. I'd killed animals without remorse for most of my life. Skinned and gutted mammals of all shapes and sizes. I'd just torn a flower lamprey in half. The sight of gore had never affected me much, but now my stomach rolled. The girl's dress had melted onto her skin, chunks of black mixing with fresh red blood. I came dangerously close to spewing my lunch all over the ground.

"Bring her with us, we need to go," Guanyu insisted.

"She's dying!" Shantie snapped back.

There was a crack as the stall behind us collapsed. The fire roared higher, the heat oppressive. My eyes began to water. Soon, I knew, my lungs would be full of smoke—if they weren't already. It was so hard to tell. I felt as though my body were detached from the rest of me.

Shantie forced a potion down the girl's throat and she began to cough, spitting most of it back up. "Guanyu!"

Guanyu put his hands on Shantie's shoulders and she pressed a palm to the girl's side. Her hands shook. I remember Shantie's fear of fire then. She had to be forcing herself to ignore it completely, so she'd be able to heal the girl. But this wasn't a fire that could be ignored. I watched the blaze spread and knew we had minutes, if that, to flee the market square.

Horse steps clattered across the cobblestone. I looked up just in time to see a trio of men on horseback. They looked Vinish, light hair and fair skin.

"There's another one!" one of the men called, pointing at one of the few stalls that hadn't caught fire.

Another man took a sword and began to hack at the awning until the charm that had been tied to it fell to the ground below. The third man uncorked a bottle and dumped what look like oil on the awning, then took his lit torch and set it.

Only then did I realize that woman had been right. This fire hadn't been an accident. It was an attack.

The first man turned, preparing to canter off, and then he saw us.

"Witch," he spat, staring at Shantie.

One voice drowned out all the rest in my heart. A growl I knew like the back of my own hand. A fury that matched my own. I could no longer hear the roaring of the fire, the screaming of the crowd. I couldn't even hear Shantie, trying frantically to save the girl's life, or Guanyu, urging her to flee.

"Let this be a warning to your tyrannical king of magic," the man announced as the two men riding beside him raised their lit torches. "We will not stand idly by and let your evils spread to our borders. Tell your king that Vinland bows to no witch. He wishes to set our kingdom ablaze?" The man smiled, cold enough to freeze my heart. "This is our answer."

My wolf surged up, desperate to protect. I wanted to shift. I should shift. These men were dangerous. I was more scared than I'd ever been before. Not even when Gran attacked Toketie, or when I went feral and tried to kill Charles.

But if I shifted into the wolf here, I was trapped. Not physically—I knew how I could win. A snap at the nearest horse's ankle, to make it spook left. A leap to the man on the right, to bring him down. A quick bite across the throat, and then I could move on to the next.

I could kill these men, but what then? Guanyu and Shantie were here. They'd have no reason to hide what happened from school. From Shaw.

I was frozen in indecision, but the men were not. They circled us. One took his uncorked bottled and dumped oil directly over Shantie, Guanyu, and the girl they were trying to save.

"No!" I shouted, turning toward them.

Guanyu met my eyes. I understood immediately what he planned, just as I had in the Lake. *No*, I wanted to shout again, but it was too late. The torch came down.

Heat blossomed over my right side so fierce I thought I'd been caught in the fire. I stumbled forward, horrified, even as the smoke burned my tear ducts. The dying girl had caught fire first. Her body, already charred, ignited into an inferno. Guanyu pushed Shantie away, but he was too close. The fire latched on to the oil covering his skin. He began to scream—loud, tortured screams.

The men on horseback were laughing. Shantie was petrified, frozen by fear. I rushed forward. I didn't know how I could beat out a fire that big, but I was ready to try. I was stopped by the cold press of steel. One of the men had drawn a sword and held it to my throat.

The wolf rushed up again. I was ready to shift now, ready to tear these men apart.

The only thing that stopped me was a name. My name.

"Rosy!" Guanyu yelled, between his screams. "Rosy, go!"

I stumbled sideways, away from the man and his sword. I had just enough time to watch as Guanyu shifted into the salmon. The flames had begun to leap from Guanyu to Shantie, but with a huge whack of his tail, the familiar beat them away. Shantie fell forward, thrust several feet by the force of Guanyu's tail.

I caught Shantie with a grunt.

*Move*, the wolf in my heart said. My ears were ringing and my throat burning and my eyes watering. My fingers scrambled to find a grip on Shantie's oil-covered arms. I knew what Guanyu wanted. The man with his sword drawn looked angry. He only needed one witness and Shantie was the witch. They'd wanted her to burn, more than anything.

I threw Shantie over a shoulder and shifted into a horse. Doing my best to keep Shantie balanced on my back, I ran.

We were almost to the other side of the market when Shantie shattered. I felt her fall from my back and quickly shifted back to human. She screamed like Guanyu had screamed. I had no idea if those men were chasing us. We needed to keep moving. I touched her, trying to calm her down.

As soon as my fingers met her skin, I knew. I was a bone familiar—I had an intimate connection with death. The bond between Shantie and Guanyu had broken.

Guanyu was dead.

"There you are!"

I looked up to see Mister Jostein rushing toward us, looking frantic. He picked Shantie up, cradling her in his arms like she was a child. He didn't ask about Guanyu. He was a bone witch, he could tell like I could. He could feel the emptiness at the other end of Shantie's spirit. I gripped Shaw's necklace with both hands, gasping for breath as I followed Mister Jostein to our cart.

"No, wait, wait," Shantie said, barely coherent enough to talk. "We need to go back."

"The army is here," Mister Jostein said. "They'll do their best to contain the fire. They'll catch who did this."

"Guanyu, we need to get him," Shantie cried. "Where is that silly brat? Guanyu, come on, we're leaving!"

Mister Jostein carefully placed Shantie in the back of the cart, gentler than I'd ever seen him. Shantie tried to climb out, as if she'd realized we weren't going to help her find Guanyu. Mister Jostein caught her by the shirt and held her close. "Can you take us back, Holt?" he asked me.

Only then did I realize the two horses we'd taken with the cart were missing. I hoped Mister Jostein had set them free to run back to campus. I put one of the harnesses over my chest and then I shifted back into the horse.

The leather dug into me—it wasn't attached properly—but I didn't care. Mister Jostein usually took two drafts to lug the cart, but bone horses were stronger than regular beasts and I was running off pure fear. I set my shoulders and lunged forward.

It took several hard pulls to get the cart moving behind me. I could hear Shantie yelling, screaming at Mister Jostein to let her go, shouting for Guanyu. I broke into a trot and finally the cart moved freely.

I didn't know how long it took me to haul us back to Witch Hall. I didn't even remember arriving. All I knew were Shantie's screams, my agonized lungs, and the burning pain in my heart. Darkness flickered at the edges of my vision, threatening to overwhelm me, but I couldn't give in until we were safe.

It wasn't until I saw Shaw, the only clear face in a sudden crowd of people all shouting for explanations, that I finally let myself collapse.

# Chapter 25

## SHAW

SHAW WATCHED YUYAN SLOWLY WORK HERSELF TO DEATH, trying to keep Rosamund alive. She didn't know how to help her friend. Wouldn't help, if it meant Rosamund dying, even as the bags under Yuyan's eyes grew deep enough to cut into her skin like canyons.

Madam Tukwilla, Madam Ipsoot, and the other flower witch teachers were all in Multah trying to help with the injured, which left Yuyan and the others in the Advanced Healing workshop to hover over Rosamund, Shantie, and Mister Jostein.

Mister Jostein had only needed a bit of work to clear his lungs, so he was out of the infirmary by Saturday evening. Shantie had woken up the next day. She'd refused to speak, even while Yuyan tended to the scattered burns on her arm. The pain of a lost bond had left her acting lifeless, like a broken doll. Shaw couldn't bring herself to figure out how to fix that either. Rosamund was still unconscious.

It was after class on Monday now, more than forty-eight hours since Rosamund had collapsed. Since she'd shifted from her horse form back into a human in the middle of pulling the cart. The leather had nearly strangled her, and when she managed to avoid that, the cart had rolled over her shoulder, iron wheels cutting into her like a knife through cheese.

Yuyan hadn't slept since. Shaw knew, because neither had she. But where Yuyan had been hunched over all night, draining the smoke from Rosamund's lungs and knitting her muscles back together, Shaw had been useless. Sitting, staring. Sitting, waiting. Sitting, seething.

The Vinlanders had gone too far with their anti-magic protests. They'd taken the aggression from their side of the river and crossed the boundary to the Cursed Kingdom. They'd burned. They'd killed.

"Princess."

Shaw blinked, eyes painfully dry, and looked up to see Rosamund's cousin. She'd been in and out of the infirmary, but they'd had nothing to say to each other. Toketie Holt's worry was a mirror showing Shaw's fractured reflection. It was too painful to look at her.

Except, she touched Shaw's shoulder. As if she had the right, now that they both shared these days of misery.

"I can sit by her for a while, if you want to rest."

Rest? What rest was there to be had in the face of this? Vinland had committed an act of war. She'd already written her father, asking for news. Shaw knew her father well. Even now, she expected he was talking with Vinland's ambassador. Demanding reparations for this act of terrorism.

If the Emperor of Vinland refused, the Cursed Kingdom would be forced to send the declaration of war. They couldn't afford not to, or these anti-magical attacks would only grow. There was too much hatred over the border to turn a blind eye.

The war Shaw had been promised would come, years before she was ready. Before any of them were ready.

Shaw looked over at Yuyan again, kneeling beside Shantie's bed.

She had one hand over the other flower witch's, not to heal but to comfort. She was so still, Shaw wondered if she'd fallen asleep like that.

"I've got her," Einar said.

Shaw's head spun. When had Einar arrived?

The glass witch went to Yuyan's side and picked her up. Yuyan protested, but Einar shushed her. "You cannot help them if you're too weak from exhaustion," he told her gently. "We will keep watch and fetch you the second something changes."

Oluk took Yuyan's seat at Shantie's bedside, a cup of tea clutched between his hands. Toketie still hovered over Shaw's shoulder. Einar gave Shaw a look. She stood and followed him out of the infirmary, letting Toketie take her place.

Einar took Yuyan to the senior flower witches' suite. Shaw didn't wait for him to return and pester her to her own bed. She walked past the dormitory, across the waterfall's creek, and to the woods on the other side of campus.

She walked until she felt the first taste of death, then she stood and held up both hands.

Bones clacked and scraped against one another. Spirits resisted the call until Shaw pushed hard enough that they could no longer. Ghosts moaned like the wind, pulled from their undead mourning to do Shaw's bidding.

Shaw forced every last inch of her power to spread out over these woods. She commanded and ordered until skeleton after skeleton ran and flew and ambled to her side.

When at last she opened her eyes to see the results, she was disappointed to count only fifteen. The best was a skeletal bear, though she thought the spirit inside of it was a familiar, not a wild bear. There were raptors and songbirds both, half a dozen on the trees over her head. Deer and squirrels and a fox. A half-built feline skeleton hobbled in the back, just barely kept upright by the ferocity of the spirit inhabiting it.

"It's not enough," Shaw said.

"Wasn't your record seven before? You've more than doubled it."

That was Aklemin. Shaw shouldn't have been surprised. The ice witch took a step closer, so that they were within Shaw's line of sight.

"At the height of her power, my grandmother could control fifty corpses at once, and pull together another fifty just seconds after the first set collapsed."

"Fifty corpses of the recently dead. Of furious ghosts and untamed spirits. Necromancy is a different beast on the battlefield, Shaw."

Shaw knew they were right, but she didn't want to hear it. "How are we to survive this? My grandmother fought the Colonies, whose army had some two thousand miles to reach us, and even that was near enough to overrun us. The Vinland Empire? We'll be crushed."

"War will not start tomorrow."

Shaw knew that. Her father would demand reparations first, as he must, but they both knew Vinland would refuse to meet them. It might take months, but war would start sooner than any of them had hoped.

"I thought we'd at least get to graduate," Shaw muttered, bitter and angry. "If nothing else, I would have liked to complete our education. We're not ready."

"Nothing is certain," Aklemin said. "Not our victory, but certainly not our defeat. There are choices yet, Shaw."

Shaw turned to face the ice witch fully. "What choices? What is there left to decide?"

Aklemin said nothing. With a sharp wave of her hand, Shaw let the skeletons collapse and the spirits go free. She turned her back on the pile of bones and stalked back to campus.

Shaw ducked into the senior flower witches' suite and headed to Yuyan's room. The door was open. Einar looked up as Shaw approached. Yuyan was curled against his chest, crying. Shaw hesitated and Einar shook his head silently. Shaw had chosen her entourage deliberately. She needed three witches she could fight beside, could die beside without regrets. They were the only ones she'd let into her heart, until Rosamund arrived. Now her heart was torn and she didn't know what to do.

Aklemin tugged her away, back out of the suite.

Shaw turned to them. "What's wrong?"

"You know Yuyan's in love with her," Aklemin murmured, serious in a way they so rarely were.

"Who?"

Aklemin gave Shaw a look. Her exhausted mind finally connected the dots. Of course. Yuyan had loved Shantie for years in silence. Never wanted to get between her and her familiar. There were so few witches who were interested in a witch-witch bond, instead of the traditional witch-familiar one.

Yuyan had been adamant that Shaw choose Shantie for her entourage. Talked up all of Shantie's good qualities, her skill with potions, her eagerness to help, her laugh—as if Shaw would choose her entourage based on how pleasant they were to listen to. When she still refused, Yuyan told Shaw that she would never love a familiar and Shaw told her she didn't care.

She still didn't care. She thought it would set a nice precedent, if a pair of the royal entourage had a platonic partnership. When Yuyan had finally agreed, Shaw had put the issue of Shantie out of her mind to focus on more important things.

Shantie's familiar had died at the Multah market. Rosamund had yet to awaken, but Mister Jostein had told them. He didn't know how the boy had died, but they could all guess. All that was left was recovering the body.

There was no telling how Shantie would react to the broken bond. Some never recovered. She was young still and they'd only been bonded for a short while, comparatively, but it all came down to Shantie's will to live. Without that, she would waste away no matter how much Yuyan tried to heal her.

Shaw hadn't cared about Yuyan's feelings for Shantie when she'd learned of them because she hadn't understood them. She'd never known that bone-deep admiration, that unending affection, that trust that love could conquer all.

Now, though, she felt wounded. Like someone had punched the deep bruises that already littered her spirit and carved out another piece out of her heart.

"Come," Aklemin whispered. "You need sleep."

Shaky from more than just physical tiredness, Shaw did as Aklemin suggested. Stumbled through the too-bright sun of a pleasant autumn afternoon. Trod across the well-worn grass to her suite. Fell onto the blankets that covered her bed.

Aklemin grabbed her cloak to cover her, then closed the door to her room behind them.

She lay in bed, staring sightlessly at the ceiling. This was useless. There was too much to do. She wished her father was at Witch Hall, or that she were home. She wanted the comfort of his presence, the surety that came when they were together, working for the betterment of the kingdom. She and her father didn't agree on everything, but they respected each other. Trusted each other.

This silence was torturing her.

Was war truly just around the corner? It had always been there on the horizon, but she'd thought she had years still. Despite how tension with Vinland had been building, she couldn't fathom facing the might of the entire northern empire. All her power meant nothing to a hundred thousand witch-burning fanatics.

But if she wasn't ready, then that fanatical fire would not stay across the river. Multah had only proven it. Her people had already died. Guanyu had died. Rosamund had—

No, Rosamund was not dead. Would not die. They had hit those crossroads Aklemin had seen and fallen to their knees, but they would get up together. For all Rosamund's distaste of war, Shaw knew she would understand. She had to understand, after what she'd seen. Those horrors Shaw had studied but had yet to face.

Shaw had already lost so much of her legacy to war. She didn't want to lose her future too.

She rolled over and gathered her pillow in her arms. She wished Rosamund were there. Wished she could hold her close, be assured by her steady breathing. She wished her entourage were at her side, a comforting presence. She wished her father were just beyond that door. She wanted him to tell her that they would get through this together. Wanted him to meet Rosamund, the familiar she'd chosen, and to see her as Shaw did.

Shaw wanted more time. But war did not wait and her time was up. She knew what her father would say, if he were there.

*You are strong enough to face this.*

Tomorrow, she would be strong. She would be an example for all her classmates. A pillar for them to lean on. Tomorrow, Rosamund would wake up and Shaw would be there for her, and together they would face the future.

Tomorrow, she would be Princess Shaw Colchuck, Daughter of the Witch King, Heir to the Cursed Throne. Tonight, she was just Shaw, and she let herself grieve the final remnants of her childhood.

# Chapter 26

## ROSY

THE FIRST THING I SAW, WHEN I OPENED MY EYES, WAS Toketie. She was kneeling beside my bed, both hands clutching one of mine. Tear tracks stained her cheeks and her waist-length braid was frazzled and unkempt.

I tried to say something, but all that came out was a painful croak.

Toketie's eyes flew open. "Rosy!" She quickly scrambled to her feet and put a hand in the middle of my chest. "No, don't get up. You're still recovering."

"Water," I said, or tried to.

Toketie understood me. She bustled beyond a curtain hung from the ceiling and returned with a glass of water. I didn't recognize where we were. It wasn't my room, though the bed was the same as the ones in the dormitories. There was another bed on the other side of the room, though it was empty.

Someone had changed me into my sleep dress. My shoulder was bandaged tight. I didn't remember injuring it. I tried to move my arm and winced from the flare of pain it caused.

Toketie helped me lift my head and carefully sip the water.

"What happened?" I asked. My voice was still hoarse, but at least I could talk again.

"Madam Tukwilla went to Multah to help the wounded there, so Yuyan had to heal you. She said she cleared the smoke in your lungs, but she couldn't completely heal your shoulder. You have to take it easy the next couple days until Madam Tukwilla returns."

Toketie talked too fast. It took me a second to figure out what she was saying. "My shoulder?"

Fresh tears rolled down Toketie's cheeks. "Rosy, I was so worried. When you fell to the ground, and the cart rode over you. The wheel cut you. Any more to the right and it would have sliced your neck. There was so much blood." She began sobbing in earnest. "I thought you were dead."

My memories suddenly returned. The fire in the market. The men. The torches. Guanyu. I couldn't breathe. I couldn't breathe. I couldn't—

"It's okay, calm down, you're safe," Toketie was saying. "You're back at Witch Hall, we're safe here. Deep breaths, Rosy, you're okay."

I breathed in too quickly and my lungs protested. I coughed furiously for a minute, Toketie still frantically trying to calm me down.

"Shantie," I said, between coughs. "And Mister Jostein, are they—"

"They're both okay. Better than you."

The coughing died down. "We were attacked," I said. "The fire was intentional. Guanyu, and so many people— They died, Tokey. They all died."

"I know," Toketie said, soft and solemn. "They're saying it was a group of merchants from Vinland. Or at least, they pretended to be merchants. Apparently, they blamed us for the fires, you know

332

the ones? The fishing villages that burned down, and that whole section of Vingate the other week. So they tried to burn Multah in retaliation. It's horrible, Rosy. They planned it deliberately, attacked during Market Day so they could do the most damage. The Witch King says it was an act of war."

I tried to sit up and almost knocked my head against Toketie's. War. I had lived with the knowledge that war would return to the kingdom for most of my life, but I never could have imagined it like this.

"War?" I repeated. "Against Vinland?"

"Well, not yet," Toketie said. "But it's clear that the Vinlanders can't be trusted anymore. Parts of Multah are still burning. Over two hundred dead, and bodies are still being counted."

"But—" We weren't ready. Shaw hadn't even graduated yet. Vinland stretched across the entire continent. How would we survive such a war?

Toketie squeezed my hand. "The king sent a company from the Frozen Mountain to stand guard over Witch Hall. They're on constant patrol around campus. If the Vinlanders truly do mean to start a war, they wouldn't dare attack us here."

I hadn't even been thinking about that, but now that Toketie had said it, I feared fire spreading over campus as it had over Multah. For a second, Toketie's body took Guanyu's place in my memory.

"We need to go home," I said. "Tokey, let's go home."

Toketie's fingernails cut into my palm. "We'll be okay, Rosy," she said.

There was a knock on the wall next to my curtain and Yuyan poked her head in. "Hey, Toketie, they're loading up another cart to take to Multah and Froya is asking if you can help organize the medical supplies."

"Will you stay with her?" Toketie asked, already standing.

Yuyan stepped into my room and took Toketie's place at my bedside.

"Wait," I tried to protest. "Tokey—"

Toketie gave me a watery smile. "I'm so glad you're okay, Rosy."

I tried to follow her as she left, but Yuyan wouldn't let me.

"Shit, it started bleeding again," Yuyan muttered, then, louder, "Hold still, Rosy. The wheel sliced clean through muscle and it's not knitting together right."

"Tokey!"

"I told you to hold still!" Yuyan pressed down hard over the bandages on my shoulder.

Pain reverberated through me so suddenly that I almost screamed. I passed out instead.

YUYAN FINALLY LET ME LEAVE the infirmary for dinner on Sunday. She helped me walk to the dining hall and led me over to our usual table. "I'll get you food," she said. "Just sit."

Oluk was the first to come hug me. I hugged him back, hard enough that my wound pulled too tight and pain flared through my shoulder.

"We're glad you're okay, Rosamund," Einar said sincerely, coming to stand at Oluk's shoulder.

Then Oluk stepped back and suddenly Shaw was in front of me. She raised a hand to my cheek, fingers shaking, and brushed her thumb under my eye. I wondered if she was trying to brush away a tear—except that my eyes were painfully dry. I wanted to cry, but I couldn't seem to do it.

"Rosamund," Shaw whispered.

I wanted to say something. Wanted to lean in to Shaw's embrace. Wanted to let myself be comforted. But I didn't feel like I deserved comfort. I'd had a lot of time to think, in the infirmary. A lot of time to imagine what I could have done differently.

If I'd let the wolf out, would Guanyu still be alive?

I pulled away from Shaw. Aklemin held out a hand to help me sit down. I almost ignored it, but I felt weak. I let them help me sit.

"I'm sorry," Aklemin said softly, so that only I could hear.

*There is still misery on the horizon*, Aklemin had said.

"Did you—?" I began. Had the ice witch known?

Aklemin shook their head, but before they could say anything another person came up to our table. Toketie. Her grip on her dinner tray was white knuckled. She looked from me, to Shaw, to Aklemin, then back to me.

"Can I sit with you?" she asked.

I stared at her. Sit with us? But what about her suitemates?

Toketie gave me a bitter smile, like she could read my thought. She probably could. Guanyu always said I wore my— I cut the thought off before it could wound me more.

"I nearly lost you," Toketie said. "I couldn't fall asleep last night thinking about it. I nearly lost you, and we haven't talked all term without being mad at each other. I had a whole month to make it right and I didn't. Rosy, I'm sor—"

I interrupted her. I didn't need to hear Toketie's apology, not anymore. "Just sit down, Tokey. Please."

Aklemin scooted over, leaving an open space between them and me. I had to move closer to Shaw as Toketie sat. I noticed that

Shaw took care not to bump my injured shoulder as she cut into her food.

Conversation began. Aklemin and Toketie shared a few ice-specific classes. Yuyan asked them what the ice witch teachers were saying about the war. It had been foretold for years, but no one had divined exactly how it would start.

"—just rotten luck that Rosy was there the exact day it began," Toketie was saying.

I didn't want to listen. Rotten luck. Was that all it was? Rotten luck that I'd convinced Mister Jostein to take Shantie and Guanyu and me to the market? Rotten luck that Guanyu and I had gone to mess around at Lake Bloom instead of going back to Witch Hall the minute lunch was over?

Was it just rotten luck that I'd pushed the wolf down? That I'd been too slow to save my friends? That I'd sat back and done nothing while Guanyu sacrificed himself to save Shantie?

I turned to look at the table where Guanyu and Shantie normally sat. Shantie was there, her face in profile. I couldn't read her expression at all. There were none of her usual smiles, that infectious cheer. Her friends—all flower witches and familiars—fussed over her. She didn't respond to anything they were saying. The plate in front of her was still full of food.

I wanted to go over to her, but what would I say? What could I say? I couldn't help feeling like her pain was my fault. I could have saved Guanyu. Even after he caught on fire, he didn't die immediately. I could have shifted into the wolf instead of the horse, ripped that man's sword out of his hand. Could have beat the fire from Guanyu's skin, helped Shantie heal him.

I couldn't stomach another bite. Out of the corner of my eye, I noticed Shaw watch me put my fork down, but she said nothing and neither did I.

School felt irrevocably changed that week. The conversation between classes was stilted, too loud or too quiet. Soldiers were stationed outside every longhouse and the doors of the stable when Oluk and I did our morning duty. I was slow to do the chores, kept to the easiest tasks by Mister Jostein and Oluk. My body was sluggish. I hadn't been able to sleep—woken by nightmares of fire and death.

Classes either dragged on too long, or I didn't remember them at all. Toketie took to sitting with me at every meal, and at Etiquette. Shaw was a silent shadow at my side in all of our shared classes and outside of class time. Oluk stayed close as well. In the stable, Mister Jostein watched me with sad eyes, none of his usual gruffness in his voice at all. The rest of Shaw's entourage tried to talk loudly and about inane things—as if faking cheer could make everything better.

Shantie wasn't at breakfast on Wednesday. I noticed Yuyan look over at her usual spot multiple times. During my free period, I went to the flower witches' suite, but Shantie wasn't in her room.

By Thursday, with no sign of Shantie, I asked Yuyan.

"She said she was going home," Yuyan said, and there was a resonance to her voice that reminded me of the pain in my own heart.

"But doesn't she live in Multah?"

Yuyan nodded. I saw the gleam of tears in her eyes, before she looked down at her plate. I could tell Yuyan thought the same thing I did. Shantie shouldn't go yet. She wasn't ready to face where her familiar had died, even with her family to comfort her.

The guilt I felt was overwhelming.

"I've got her," I heard Shaw say.

Then I was led away from dinner and toward my suite. I wanted to shake Shaw's hands off me, but she was so warm and I felt cold. Cold enough to freeze everything around me, though Shaw didn't flinch when she rubbed my frozen fingers between her palms.

AT THE STABLE THE NEXT morning, as Oluk and I hauled hay out to the pasture together, I finally let the words I'd been holding in tumble out.

"Is this the rebirth, do you think?"

Oluk looked startled. "What?"

"Mister Sorensen's tarot reading. The Death card. He said I'd be irrevocably changed." I tied a hay net. Cow chased off the other horses approaching it and began pulling the straw out through the gaps. Her chewing sounded too loud to my ears.

"I know it hurts, but this isn't the end," Oluk said softly. "You're going to get through this. Mister Jostein said all you needed was time."

"What will time do?" I asked.

Nearly fifty years and Gran still hadn't healed from the scars of the past war. Was I to be the same as her? Except, instead of being trapped in the wolf's feral mind, I was trapped by my own guilt. My own inability to act. Ever since I'd woken up with my wound bandaged and Toketie's hand in mine, the voices in my heart had not spoken a word. Not even the wolf.

I spun on my heel. Oluk flinched back, startled. I grabbed him by the shoulders.

"You still have time, Oluk."

"What?"

"Einar's fortune. Don't you remember? Trauma in his future. Deep pain."

I knew pain now. Knew it like I knew nothing else. Pain had taken control of my body and it would not let go. I could barely breathe from the weight of it.

Oluk looked stricken. "What are you saying?"

"Walk away. Take that necklace off and walk away."

Oluk's hand flew to the courtship necklace Einar had given him. "I don't understand," he said.

I shook his shoulders hard. "You need to leave!" I yelled at him. "Now, before it's too late. Save yourself from this forsaken war. Go home to your parents and their obsidian mine and don't come out till it's all over."

But Oluk was shaking his head, hand still clutching his necklace tight as if he was afraid I would rip it from his neck. "I know it'll be hard," he said. "I know what Mister Sorensen said. We'll be hurt. Perhaps it will even happen tomorrow. I wish we had more time, if we really are going to go to war with Vinland . . . I know that it will hurt, Rosy. But I can't walk away. I won't walk away. Please don't ask me to do that."

"It's not worth it," I whispered.

Oluk pulled away and my arms fell in the space between us. "He is worth it, to me. No matter if the pain comes today or tomorrow or years from now. I won't give up what we've started because of fear."

Oluk didn't talk to me for the rest of our stable duty. I was angry at him, and afraid for him. He'd only been courting for a few weeks! Why risk his life for that?

I didn't follow Oluk to dinner and he didn't make me. Left alone, I stood in the center of campus and stared up at the sky.

"Okay, Rosamund?"

It was one of my suitemates. Ragna, the pale one with the weasel shift. I stared at her blankly. Two and a half months and this was the first time she'd ever said a word to me. Okay? How could I possibly be okay?

Ragna hesitated. "Do you want me to get the princess?"

I shook my head, but when my suitemate turned away, I knew she was going to get Shaw anyway.

I walked aimlessly. I reached the creek and stared across it at the deeper woods. The company charged with guarding Witch Hall had pitched tents among the trees. Most of the animals that once called that section of campus home had fled—their chirps and squeaks replaced with the grunts and groans of human soldiers.

I almost turned to follow the creek down to the river, then remembered the soldiers stationed at Witch Hall's dock and stopped. Instead, I walked upstream to where the waterfall crashed down upon the creek.

I waded toward the waterfall until I was up to my ankles in water, then sat down in the mud and dead reeds. My fingers squelched through the muck. A bug scurried over my thumb. I leaned back, staring up at the waterfall, and imagined it as a lance about to strike me through.

There was a shuffle of footsteps, then Shaw sat down in the mud next to me. She didn't seem to care how undignified it would look for the daughter of the Witch King to be covered in stains. I tried not to remember that the last person to sit in the reeds with me was Guanyu.

"It wasn't your fault," Shaw said firmly.

I didn't look away from the waterfall. "We should never have been there."

"You didn't set the fire. Rosamund, look at me."

I tore my eyes away from the cascading water. Shaw looked furious. The last time I'd seen that fury in her eyes, she'd been defending me against Charles's attempt at sabotage.

"Listen to me closely," Shaw said, tight, controlled anger laced through each word. "It was not your fault."

"It was though. You don't understand. I should have done something. Isn't that the point of our Combat class? I could have fought."

"Class is not a battle and games are not war. No one blames you for being scared. Not even Shantie."

"She should!" Shaw flinched at my yell, but I didn't care. "Don't you get it? I could have saved them both. Maybe even that girl they were trying to heal. I could have killed those men, Shaw."

"Then kill them next time," Shaw whispered.

I let her words settle into my heart. The wolf rose up to meet them. It growled, harsh, and I realized it agreed with Shaw. Slowly, the other voices joined in. The horse. The badger. The squirrel and the mouse and the raccoon. The voices flooded in until I couldn't easily distinguish between them.

The otter's voice, I noticed, was missing. I closed my eyes and searched for it. Tried to call up its playfulness. A near-forgotten memory of splashing in a Bone Forest creek. A warm afternoon playing tag with Guanyu. A mad duel with a lamprey with terrifying teeth, tumbling to the shore, heart pounding, but laughing.

There was no playful chitter in my heart. The otter would not speak.

I began to cry. Ugly sobs that shook my whole body. I could barely breathe through it. I pulled my hands from the mud and rubbed my face, trying to get the tears to stop. The mud smeared over my cheeks instead. I remembered the glass witch who'd been on my team during the Combat midterms. If he'd covered Guanyu's face with good luck runes, would we have made it out of Multah safely? I sobbed hard.

Shaw hugged me. Her body was like the sun—as warm as a summer day. I fell against her and let myself cry freely into her neck.

Shaw held me long after my sobs turned into silent tears, even long after they stopped. She held me as the sun set and the moon rose, and through it all, the only thing she said over and over again was, "I'm here. I've got you." And with each repetition, the bone animals in my heart joined in, louder and louder until they drowned out even the crashing of the waterfall.

I didn't know how long it had been, but my tears had dried into stiff tracks along my cheeks. I could feel the indents of Shaw's clothing on my forehead, the weight of her arms on my back. I took one breath, then another. Enough to get the strength to pull back.

Shaw's hands moved to my shoulders so she could help steady me as I sat up. One hand came up to my cheek then, rubbing my tear tracks away with a thumb.

I turned my head and pressed a kiss to Shaw's palm. It was only after I'd completed the motion that my actions caught up with me. I scrambled to my feet, putting my back to the princess.

Shaw said nothing. She merely stood and waited. I faced the

waterfall and let the mist cool my heated face. Finally, I gathered enough courage to say, "Thank you."

"I am here for you, Rosamund," Shaw said. "Whenever and however you need me."

I spun around to look at Shaw, pulled like a flower turning up to face the sun. Her face was sincere, her eyes fixed on mine.

"I'm not worth the effort," I said.

"Isn't that for me to decide?"

I supposed so. I supposed Shaw had decided I was from the very beginning. It would be so easy to sway forward, let her arms close around me again. To take the comfort that was being offered. To take Shaw, as she offered herself.

The heat from her courtship necklace was the only comfort I'd had, this past week.

Before I could untangle the grief and affection and terror and need in my chest enough to figure out what I even wanted, another unwelcome interruption strode up to us. It was Madam Dyer, her usual frown fixed upon a weary face.

"Princess, there's a visitor for you at the main entrance."

"A visitor?" Shaw asked, already moving to follow the teacher.

I trailed behind, as if Shaw had me on a tether. I wasn't ready to part from her yet.

"Sent by your father," Madam Dyer said. "I think you will be most pleased. I am. The Witch King does not leave anything to chance."

There was an officer standing at the road leading into campus, an escort of four soldiers at their back. They had the typical red sash of a thane, but theirs was hemmed with gold to denote an even higher rank. They bowed as Shaw approached, but straightened quickly. "Princess, it's good to see you again."

"General Tepeh, this is a pleasant surprise!" Shaw turned to me. "Rosamund, this is Kiwa Tepeh, general of the Royal Company."

The highest-ranked officer in the entire military. I dipped into a little curtsy as General Tepeh looked me over. I was sure I looked a mess, mud on my face and my clothes, my hair windswept, but the general showed nothing on their smooth face.

"Pleasure to meet you, Miss Rosamund," they said instead.

Their voice was rich and their enunciation sharp. I couldn't tell their preferred gender—army uniforms were gender-neutral and the way the thane's blue-black hair was pinned up out of their face didn't speak to any gendered style. There were two silver stars and three bars on the breast of their military jacket, indicating twenty-three years in service, but they didn't look old. The black stripe on the side of their pants said they were a witch. I wondered if they'd joined the army as soon as they'd graduated Witch Hall.

Pops had that role, once. General of the Royal Company, military advisor to Shaw's grandmother. Until the Witch Queen died and the Witch King stepped into power and promoted a new general, possibly this Kiwa Tepeh, to take Pops's place.

I was too exhausted to be angry about it. Even when General Tepeh turned to Shaw and explained that the entire Royal Company was to be stationed at Witch Hall for the foreseeable future, taking over for the small company that had been here this week, who would head to Multah to join the soldiers there.

"Your father is taking no chances. Not while negotiations with Vinland's ambassador are so contentious," General Tepeh said quietly. "He asked me to give you this."

Shaw took the letter the general handed over but didn't open it yet. "We welcome you," she said instead. "Have you met the headmistress? Let me introduce you."

I stayed put as Shaw, Madam Dyer, and General Tepeh headed off to the teachers' cottages. Shaw looked back once, to see if I would follow, but I shook my head. She hesitated, visibly enough that General Tepeh looked startled. They glanced from Shaw to me and back. I turned away from them both and told myself the chill was from the autumn wind, even though I knew that was a lie.

I headed to the stables. Working with the horses, at least, never changed.

# Chapter 27

TWO WEEKS AFTER THE MARKET DAY FIRE, WITCH HALL held its final assembly of the term. In lieu of obstacle courses and pavilions, the student body of Witch Hall quietly gathered in the clearing between the river and the creek to listen to a school announcement.

Madam Kawak stepped onto a crate that had been brought out as a makeshift stage. General Tepeh stood on the ground to her left. Standing in an arc around them were all the staff and teachers of Witch Hall. Not even eccentric Madam Bai or optimistic Mister Voll were smiling.

Madam Kawak did not speak for several seconds, looking over us. I couldn't help noticing the lines around her eyes were more pronounced than ever.

"Mars is bright and Pluto warns of dangerous secrets," the headmistress said finally. "All the constellations weep for the horrors that have passed, and for those that have yet to occur."

Madam Kawak took a deep breath and clasped her hands together tightly. I stood at the front, with Shaw on my left and Toketie on my right. Close enough to notice that the headmistress's fingers trembled.

"The term is nearly over. If you plan to return to your families, we wish you a quick and safe journey. For those who want to stay over the break, Madam Xu and Mister Sorensen will be organizing volunteer groups to aid with relief efforts in Multah and help the company stationed here with border patrols."

Most of the teachers at Witch Hall were bonded, and as Madam Kawak talked they all seemed to drift closer to each other. I saw held hands and pressed shoulders, side hugs and long looks. Madam Bai stood at her sister's side, hands fluttering around her waist as if she wanted to do something with them, while Mister Xu wrapped his arm around Madam Xu's back.

"For our bone students," Madam Kawak continued, "Madam Dyer will lead the yearly pilgrimage to the Bone Forest for Samhain. The resentful dead will be numerous. It is more important than ever that the Samhain rituals all over the kingdom do their part to calm the wronged. As such, this year we will be limiting this trip to only the senior bone students. Younger students are free to sit vigil at home, or perform a smaller ritual with Misters Jostein and Tupso Voll here on campus."

Madam Dyer's arms were wrapped around her middle like she was trying to comfort herself. Next to her, Mister Voll was half turned to his witch, his cheek resting against Mister Jostein's chest.

"Here at Witch Hall, our aim is to prepare our students as best we can for the futures we can foresee, but especially for the futures we cannot," Madam Kawak said. "Our destinies are ever-changing, evolving as new variables are introduced, new choices are made. Never forget that for all the stars and cards and visions, your futures are in your own hands."

With that, Madam Kawak stepped down from the crate. General Tepeh replaced her, standing straight-backed, arms at military rest.

"Moon's blessings upon you," the general said. "I am Kiwa Tepeh, general of the Royal Company. The king sent me here to keep you safe and to take joint command of the northwestern front alongside the general of Multah's Company. I have been given permission to brief you on the potential for war."

Toketie reached out to take hold of my hand, her palm cool against mine. I glanced over, but she wasn't looking at me. Beyond her, Einar had his arms wrapped around Oluk from behind, holding him to his chest. Yuyan's arms were crossed, one foot jittering against the trampled grass. I looked to my other side, to Shaw and Aklemin standing shoulder to shoulder, their faces identical masks.

When Shaw saw me glance at her, she reached over and took my other hand. My palm tingled. I didn't know whether to feel comforted or coddled.

"As of yesterday, no articles of war have been sent, but the Witch King wishes his people to prepare. Witches and familiars have been fleeing from Vinland for years now, and more cross the river daily. As much as we may wish otherwise, we must be ready to face the Vinlanders head on. Vinland's military is a mighty force and our other neighbors may well take advantage of the situation to launch their own assaults. This conflict will not be over quickly, nor easily."

The general paused to let us digest their solemn warning.

"To that end, the Witch King has given me permission to begin training you now, so that, should you join our forces upon graduation, you are prepared to defend this kingdom with all your strength. All students over the age of sixteen may pre-sign the typical two-year service contract, with the amendment that your service does not officially begin until you graduate. For these pre-service students, starting next term, half your classes will be replaced with the standard military training camp. I have worked with Madam Kawak so this training counts toward your graduation requirements."

General Tepeh gestured and one of the nearby soldiers came forward with a bundle of papers, which they set in three separate stacks on top of the crate.

My stomach rolled. I didn't like this. I didn't like it at all. Recruiting students so callously, right after admitting how terrible this potential war would be? Guilting everyone over the age of sixteen into signing up, when no one here yet understood the terror they'd be signing themselves up for?

Why was the war a foregone conclusion? Where were the Witch King's diplomats? The attempts to negotiate reparations? Just because Shaw's war had been foreseen, it didn't have to be this one. It didn't have to be now.

And, if it did, why were the students of Witch Hall obligated to fight it? If war with Vinland was to erupt within the next year, would the Witch King really send sixteen-year-olds to the front? But then, that was Witch Hall's sinister purpose, wasn't it? The reasons for Combat and even for classes like Survival Skills. Making mock battles a fun competition was tricking us into thinking war was a game.

My classmates would sign up, and countless would die. Those who didn't would never be the same. Stuck in silent grief, like Shantie, or embedded trauma, like Gran. It was wrong. This was all wrong.

Then Shaw pulled her hand out of mine. I watched, horrified, as she stepped up to the crate. The general held out a hand and helped her jump on top of it.

Shaw turned to face the rest of the school. "It will soon be the fiftieth anniversary of the Battle of a Thousand Corpses, the day my grandmother ended our last great war and ushered in a new era of peace for the Cursed Kingdom. Now that peace is threatened. I have known since I was young that I would one day stand before the enemies of magic and face my reckoning."

The other students were still, even quieter than they'd been watching Madam Kawak or General Tepeh. Shaw raised her chin. "No matter the face of the enemy, I was born to protect this land from those who would harm it. I will fight for you with everything I am. I stand here now, before my friends and classmates, and ask that you do not leave me to face this threat alone."

She paused, surveying the crowd like she was already their queen. Without raising her voice, she asked, "Will you join me?"

As one, a roar rose up all around me. Louder and louder as Shaw jumped off the crate, her black dress lifting into the air like dark smoke. When she landed, she turned promptly on her heel to the stack in the center of the crate—just below the general's feet. With an exaggerated flick of her wrist, Shaw signed her name on the topmost service contract, then handed it over to the waiting soldier. The soldier bowed to her and Shaw bowed back.

Aklemin was the next to step up, then Yuyan and Einar walked over to the other two stacks. Oluk got into line behind Einar and slowly more witches and familiars joined.

The crowd's roar quieted as what looked to be every student over the age of sixteen pushed their way into the lines. The wolf in my heart began to howl. A long and mournful howl, like it had the day of Pops's funeral. Like it had when it became the first voice that ever nestled in my heart.

"Come on, Rosy," Toketie said, pulling me to get into one of the lines.

"Come on?" I dug my heels in, bile in the back of my throat. "Tokey, no. We can't."

Toketie stopped trying to push into the line and turned toward me instead. She took both my hands in hers. "Yes, we can," she said softly.

"You'll be hurt. You'll be *killed*. Tokey, please."

"Deep breaths, Rosy, it's okay. Breathe with me."

My head hurt, my heart raced. My hands slipped through Toketie's, too sweaty for a good grip. I watched Toketie take deep breaths in and out. I struggled to match her.

Gran would get Toketie to see reason. When we went home for the fall break, Gran would make Toketie see how idiotic it was for her to sign up to go to war. She was just an ice swan. She would be killed. Like Guanyu. Like the girl he and Shantie had tried to save. Like all the people who'd died in the market square that day.

Would Toketie even listen to Gran? She hadn't willingly interacted with her since she was attacked, that day she first panicshifted into the swan.

A horrible realization struck me like a sucker punch to the gut. Guanyu was dead. Guanyu was dead and Shantie was gone and with them any hope of finishing the potion to help Gran had died too.

"Rosy, Rosy, look at me."

I took three sharp breaths, blinking away the black spots that danced in my vision. Toketie had moved her hands to my face, trying to get me to focus on her.

"Listen to me. I'll be okay," Toketie said once my breathing was mostly steady. "My senior project impressed General Tepeh. The way I organized the storage here. I know I'm not much good for combat, but they said the army always needs quartermasters. I'll be training to purchase and organize the company's supplies. I won't be on the front lines, I won't be fighting directly. But I need to do this. I need to help, in whatever way I can. Can you understand that?"

I couldn't. War had taken so much from our family. I wanted to flee. To shift into something small and burrow myself deep in the hollow of a tree. I wanted to go to sleep like it was the dead of winter and wake up long after the war was over.

"I can't," I whispered. "I just want to go home."

Toketie pulled back. Her face was twisted in some hybrid of sadness and disappointment. "That's your choice. If you don't want to do this, I won't make you. But you have to let me make *my* choice."

I'd told Shaw once that all I wanted was for the witches and familiars of Witch Hall to be allowed a choice. To be able to choose what they wanted out of their own futures. How could I say that then and not agree now?

I looked over at Oluk. Einar had his arms wrapped around him as he, Shaw, Aklemin, and Yuyan talked. As I watched, Oluk waved his hand through the air like he so often did when trying to make a point clear. Shaw smiled at whatever he was saying and Einar inclined his head in agreement.

Oluk looked like he belonged there, in Einar's arms. In Shaw's entourage. He didn't look happy, but he looked relaxed, with none of the nervous fidgeting that he'd had when we first met, or when we'd first joined Shaw's table. He'd made his choice, and despite what the cards had said, he seemed better for it.

"Okay," I said finally. "If that's what you want, Tokey, then I won't try to stop you. Just, be safe."

Toketie pulled me into a tight hug. I hugged back, burying my face in her shoulder. My heartbeat sped up again. It was hard to let go. Hard to watch as Toketie got into the line. Painful to see her sign that paper and hand it off.

"Rosamund."

I turned. Shaw had broken away from her entourage to find me. I said nothing to her, watching Toketie stop to talk to Froya and her suitemates. Everyone who had signed was still lingering around the clearing. Some talked with the soldiers there. Others clustered in groups, pale faces and determined expressions. More than a couple lingered near Shaw and me, looking between us with wide eyes. I wondered how many had eavesdropped on my conversation with Toketie. I couldn't bring myself to care if they had.

"I grabbed this for you," Shaw said when it was clear I wasn't going to respond to her. She held out a paper.

I took it automatically, then stared blankly at it. It was one of the contracts. Shaw had already written my name. All that was left was for me to sign.

"How many students do you think signed up just because of your speech?" I asked flatly.

"I can't be sure," Shaw answered. "I hope it inspired—"

Just like that, the numbness receded. Betrayal burned in my gut. But that was silly. What reason did I have to feel betrayed? Hadn't I always known this about Shaw? What had she said? *I will not hesitate in an attempt to broker peace where none exists.*

I took the paper and tore it in two. Shaw reached out, face going slack in shock. "Rosamund, wait. What are you doing?"

I jerked backward so Shaw wouldn't touch me and ripped the paper again for good measure. "I will not sign. I am not a tool for the army to use and discard."

Shaw's eyes widened. I'd never seen her look so uncertain. "But I thought— You were there. You saw what they did. Don't you realize—"

"Yes, I was there!" I interrupted, rage growing with each word

Shaw said. "But no one is asking *why* the Vinlanders set the market on fire. No one is asking if the Vinland government ordered it, or if it was the work of a few angry men."

"My father will have investigated—"

"It's been two weeks! Why is the Cursed Kingdom so quick to jump to war? People will die. And you just sentenced our classmates to the same fate."

"I don't wish for anyone to die," Shaw said. "That's exactly why we need everyone to contribute. If we allow ourselves to be overrun, we will lose far more than our lives."

I swallowed hard and acid burned my throat on the way down. "We're just kids, Shaw. You might have been signed up for this war before you took your first breath, but the rest of us weren't."

Shaw took a step closer to me. "We may be young, but we're strong. You're strong. I don't know if I can fulfill my destiny without you."

"I see," I said. My rage abruptly morphed into cold, hard fury. The trap I'd been ignoring for months now clanged around me. "You never planned on letting me go, did you?"

Shaw flinched, eyes darting to the students who were now all watching us. "I merely hoped you would change your mind on your own."

"You merely hoped I would decide to bond with you," I said, sharp and mocking. "That I would be your loyal guard dog. Your source of power. That I would be like your grandfather, valiantly protecting your life while you siphoned all my energy to call upon your army of the dead."

"It isn't like that," Shaw whispered.

But I was done listening to Shaw's excuses. I grabbed the

moonstone necklace, curling my fingers around the warmth that I'd been so comforted by.

Shaw's attention snapped back to me, noticing the movement. "Calm down, don't act rashly. Let's talk this through."

"I am calm," I said, and I was. I was no cornered prey, no loyal dog. I was a wolf, and I would not be tamed. "I should have done this a long time ago."

"Wait!" Shaw cried, taking a step forward. "You asked me what my dream was. It's you, Rosamund Holt. From the moment I saw you in the Bone Forest, facing off against that bull moose, I had an inkling. It's only grown to surety since. You are my dream."

My hands shook. "You're not mine."

I ripped Shaw's necklace off, hardly noticing the pain as the metal clasp dug into my neck before shattering. I threw the moonstones in Shaw's face, the carved bones flying wildly through the air. Shaw flinched as one end rebounded off her chin. I stayed just long enough to see her scramble to pick the pieces of the necklace up off the ground. Then I turned on my heels and stalked off.

The other students parted for me like fish for the lamprey. Several were in tears, like I'd somehow hurt them alongside Shaw. None of them had a right to look like that. To echo what I was feeling in my own heart.

I missed the warmth of Shaw's magic already.

None of it mattered anymore. I had nothing to show for my time here at Witch Hall except anger and heartbreak.

I just wanted to go home. Back to my family. Back to the ranch. Back to Gran.

A student stepped in front of me, blocking my path. It was Charles.

Charles had glared at me a hundred times before, but none of them had looked like this. Like I had punched a hole in his chest and ripped out his heart.

Like he was afraid of me.

"How dare you?" he said, and his voice shook.

"Move out of my way."

"How dare you!"

"This has nothing to do with you, Charles. Move."

I tried to push Charles aside, but he grabbed me by the arm hard enough that I knew it would bruise. "Listen to me well and good, Rosamund, because I won't say this again. Shaw Colchuck is our only hope for surviving this war. Even with her father having visions of future troop movements and enemy action, we will not win a war with Vinland if she cannot fulfill her destiny."

"What does that have to do with me? I'm not Shaw."

"No, you're just the familiar she chose. And I hate you so much, because you don't even seem to realize what a blessing it is to be loved by someone like that. Someone with the weight of the king-dom on her shoulders, who was coddled and pushed in turn, and who still grew up to be noble and smart and so damn determined to do right by the rest of us."

"Shaw doesn't love me," I said, shocked out of my rage at Charles's words. "She just wants to use me."

"Sure." Charles rolled his eyes. "Keep telling yourself that. Run home with your tail between your legs and tell yourself it's okay, because *Shaw doesn't love you*. But remember the rest of us when you do. Those of us who will fight in your stead and die for it."

"I didn't ask any of you to sign up for this war! I'm not respon-sible for this!"

"You are responsible. You will be responsible. You gave them hope, you idiotic horse girl. You are the most powerful familiar this school has ever seen. Don't think we aren't aware, no matter how much you try to hide it. After all, you're the granddaughter of General Holt and Ylva the Red Wolf, two of the most powerful bone familiars of their generation."

"And where did it leave them? Dead and imprisoned for their services." I wrenched my arm away from Charles. I could tell he was ready to yell at me some more, but I was done hearing it. I was done with it all. This argument, this farce, this school.

I shifted into the horse and reared up. The students nearby all scrambled out of my way, even Charles. I launched off my back legs and galloped away. I didn't bother grabbing a cart or my trunk, didn't bother saying goodbye. A spooked horse always bolted for its stable and, in the end, I was no exception.

I ran home.

# Chapter 28

I RAN ALL DAY. SEVERAL SOLDIERS TRIED TO STOP ME AS I thundered past their patrols. I ignored their shouts and raised arms.

I passed the guard tower on the cliff where Toketie and I had eaten lunch with Shaw's entourage nearly three months ago. Now the tower was surrounded by tents and flags. Ice familiars flew in the skies above the river gorge, keeping an eye on Vinland's border while their witches waited in the tower for their reports.

I kept running. I didn't stop for food and only stopped for water when my legs trembled from the exertion.

Sometime in the middle of the night, I stumbled and nearly fell to my front knees. I found a grove of trees and slept for a few hours. At the first sign of dawn, I began again.

Without a cart to slow me down, I reached Forest's Edge in just three days. I wished it had taken longer. I didn't like the reminder that this kingdom was so small. Especially compared to Vinland, which stretched from one side of the continent to the other.

My chest heaved as I came to a stop on the hill between Forest's Edge's village square and my family's ranch. I walked the final steps to the crest and there, just beyond the hill, saw the ranch. It seemed nearly identical to how it had been when I left. Tempest in the

pasture with his herd. The foals with their mothers. The stable with its thatched roof half hidden behind the long log-and-clay ranch house where my family slept.

Someone was at the front of the house, stacking firewood under the awning. I trotted down the hill and saw that it was Uncle Chetwoot. He looked up as I approached and his face split into a huge grin.

"Ida, Sigmund, Inge, Solemie! Come quick, it's Rosy!"

I shifted just as Mama burst out the front door with Papa, Solemie, and Uncle Inge hot on her heels. Mama swept me up into a tight hug and I nearly burst into tears right then and there.

Papa came up to my side, hugging both Mama and me close. "We're so glad you're home," he said. "Our baby girl, we missed you so much."

It felt like hours before my parents finally let me go. I missed the comfort of their hugs as soon as they did, but then Uncle Inge was replacing them, fussing over my messy hair and dirty face. "I'll run you a bath later. Heat some water in the fire so it's nice and warm," he said.

"Why the rush?" Mama asked, worry putting lines on her forehead. "Where's Tokey?"

"Still at school," I said. "I just . . . I couldn't stay anymore. I'm sorry."

Uncle Inge exchanged a look with Uncle Chetwoot. "Tokey wrote us about the fire," he whispered, as if just bringing it up might be enough to break me.

"We're so glad you're okay," Papa said, hugging me again. "Bless you for coming home."

THAT FIRST MORNING, WHEN I woke early to feed the horses, I found Mama had already beat me to it. I went to fill the hay nets instead, only to remember after having filled three that we only used hay for the stabled horses—the mares about to give birth or the recently gelded. When I went to check if there were any who fit that description, I found Uncle Chetwoot already in the stalls taking care of them.

I headed out to the bachelor herd instead. They were few in number. Most had been sold already. Papa told me the army had requisitioned a good dozen horses.

The ones that remained were still being trained. I took a lunge line to several and spent the morning putting them through their paces. Several yearlings tried to fight me—bone horses were bone horses no matter what was going on in the world. Playing that ordinary game of dominance would have been more comforting if every move hadn't reminded me of working the stable at Witch Hall. Of chasing after the horses with Shaw. Of everything I'd just left behind to burn like Multah's market had burned.

The scent of smoke overwhelmed my nose. I spun on my heel, startling the colt I'd been working with. He raced back to his group of yearlings, but I barely noticed.

Something was on fire.

The memory of the market stalls overlaid the ranch house. I saw towering flames, consuming the walls and roof. Saw Mama, her skirt on fire, trying in vain to beat the flame eating at Papa's arm. Saw Solemie burning as Guanyu had burned. Toketie on the ground before him, charred like the girl Shantie had tried to save.

Then I blinked and the house was fine. The smoke came from the chimney—just Uncle Inge cooking breakfast for all of us. Everything was normal.

I sank to my knees in the middle of the pasture. My hand grasped uselessly at my neck, trying to find the comfort of a necklace that wasn't there.

"Toketie's not even here, idiot," I said. The sound of my own voice rasped in my ears.

"Rosy!"

That was Mama. I scrambled to my feet, but it was too late. She'd seen me.

"What are you doing?" she asked, a touch brusque, a touch worried.

I smoothed out my skirt. "Just tripped."

Mama didn't look like she believed me, but she walked past to collect the halter from the yearling I'd been trying to train. "We switched the rest day, for training. They're not meant to be worked today."

She said it gently, but it felt like a slap all the same. "Sorry, I didn't know," I said. The words meant nothing. Of course I didn't know, I hadn't been here.

Mama looked uncertain. I'd always seen her as a pillar of strength, the backbone of our family. The matriarch, ever since Gran had been imprisoned in the Forest. But after months of trying to read around the masks people wore at Witch Hall, Mama's emotions were all too clear on her face.

"What do you need help with?" I asked. I felt desperate for it. I wanted my routine back. But my routine had changed and so had the ranch's. It was clear in the way Mama hesitated, trying to come up with something for me to do.

They didn't need me anymore. Mama and Uncle Chetwoot had worked out a new system with the horses and it didn't immediately fold me back in.

"Come," Mama said, gesturing me toward the house. "It's almost time for your uncle Inge to take Ma her food for the day. Why don't you take it instead? She'll be glad to see you."

It should have been a relief to know our family had taken care of Gran in my absence. Instead, it was just another reminder that they'd been doing fine without me.

Still, I was glad for the job. I'd put off going to see Gran yesterday. Guilt was still a heavy weight in my gut. I knew I needed the excuse to get it over with. To confess my crimes to the only person I knew would scold me like I needed.

I headed to the Forest with a basket full of food—enough to last Gran and me all day. The outer woods were silent and still, red cedar watching me pass. Until I reached the boundary of the Bone Forest and the bone pines replaced them.

"I missed you too," I murmured as branches came to caress my head. Pine needles prickled my cheeks and hands. I set the basket down and reached out to hold on to the nearest branches, hugging them to my chest.

A whine interrupted our reunion. I looked up to see a familiar white wolf approaching. I didn't have to think. I reached into my heart and a howl rose to meet me.

Shifting into the wolf was like stepping into a warm bath after a hard day's work. I'd forgotten how much I loved it. I felt my fear fade away, consumed with puppylike happiness.

I bounded into Gran. We fell in a tangle of fur and limbs, both yipping. Gran licked my face, my ears, my ruff. I couldn't hold still, circling her, checking for visible signs of injury or pain. But Gran looked just the same as when I'd left her.

Finally, Gran shifted. I was reluctant to join her. I would stay as a wolf forever if I could. Live in the Forest and be free of human worries. But we had breakfast to eat and I had a confession to make.

"Welcome home," Gran said as I shifted. She looked me up and down. "You look a right mess."

Not as much of a mess as I had yesterday, but I didn't think Gran was talking about my clothing or hair.

"I failed, Gran," I whispered.

"What are you babbling about, girl?"

"I was trying—" My words failed me. I cleared my throat. "I was trying to—"

"Spit it out."

"I just wanted to save you," I blurted, then grimaced. That wasn't what I'd meant to say.

Gran didn't growl at me though. She just sighed, world-weary, and tugged me to sit down on the Forest floor with her. With gnarled fingers, she unpacked breakfast for both of us.

The silence worried me. I began to explain, about Shantie and the potions. About my plan to petition the jarls' council. I explained how foolish I'd been. How I'd had no control from the start. I explained about Shaw, the games, the courtship. About going feral, and letting myself cling to Shaw's magic.

Finally, I told her how it had all ended. The fire. Guanyu's death. Shantie's withdrawal. Shaw's speech. My leaving.

When I was done, I felt lighter. I knew Gran would yell at me for being so reckless. She'd be right to. I'd made too many mistakes. I was only lucky to have left before my biggest secret could be revealed.

But instead of yelling, instead of the look of disappointed fury I'd expected, Gran instead reached forward and took my hand.

"I don't need to be saved, Rosamund," Gran said. "I never needed to be saved. I just need this." She waved a hand to encompass the two of us and the breakfast we were eating.

"But you're trapped here. And when you go feral—"

"I struggle with going feral because, for a long time, I didn't care to stop myself," Gran said bluntly. "Not until I hurt Toketie and remembered there were more important things than my grief. I'm working on myself. It was never your responsibility to fix me."

For all of Gran's words, I knew she would have accepted the potion, if I had it. There was no shame in asking for help. Still, "You're not broken."

Gran laughed. "Otto would say the same thing."

Otto. *Pops.*

"I saw him, at Witch Hall," I said, a bit hesitant. When Gran didn't react, I continued, "When I was meditating, he came to visit me. I've been trying . . ."

I trailed off, putting my free hand to my chest. I remembered, then, Madam Xu's lesson. The same lesson I'd tried to adapt for my own senior project. Every familiar connected with their first shift in a special way, and it was that connection we could use to make room for other voices.

I hadn't truly reflected on what connected me to my wolf. I hadn't thought I needed to, with how easily voices came to me. But the badger hadn't, and I knew why. I had been desperate to connect with it, so desperate I hadn't tried to figure out what, exactly, I was connecting with.

The first time I'd shifted into my wolf, it was for Gran. Because she was mourning and she needed me. My wolf's voice represented pack. And all the others were the same. I'd found the horse's voice while watching Tempest run back to the herd. The mouse's when I'd seen that clever nest hiding in the barn. The squirrel's during mating season, as they'd raced each other around and around the trees.

Badgers were solitary creatures, but to me, the badger wasn't a territorial animal crouched in its den. To me, the badger spoke in Pops's voice.

Just like that, the voice settled in my heart with a sigh. I reached for it like a hug and it rose to meet me.

I looked down, shaking my head to adjust to a new line of sight. My hands had become paws and my nails, claws. Massive claws, made for digging deep burrows. I felt strong as the badger. Solid, like nothing could hurt me. I wasn't an agile fighter like the wolf, but I was a predator nonetheless.

"Oh, girl," Gran said. She reached forward and stroked my head. "He would be so proud of you. I wish—" She stopped, took a deep breath, then started again. "I wish he were here to see this."

My eyes landed on the band around Gran's ankle. I didn't know how to free Gran, not physically. But Samhain was only a couple weeks away. I'd learned a lot at Witch Hall. Samhain was the day of the dead, the time of remembrance. I wasn't a bone witch, I couldn't talk to Pops's ghost normally. But I knew he was lingering, watching us. Perhaps, when the veil was thinnest, I could find a way to bring him forth.

Gran had never been allowed closure. This, at least, I could do for her.

FOR THE NEXT WEEK, I did my best to research Samhain rituals—tried to use what I'd learned from Madam Dyer's class to adjust them for my and Gran's bone magic. More than once, I wished I were back at Witch Hall, if only for the library. Mister Voll would have known which books to read.

I missed Witch Hall for other reasons. If Oluk were here, I'd be able to talk with him. Bounce ideas back and forth, like we so often did during stable duty. Of course, I wouldn't have needed to. Shaw would have offered to do a ritual. No matter that Gran had attacked her, Shaw would have called Pops's ghost over because it was the right thing to do. Because Gran had been a friend to Shaw's own grandmother, and a tide-turning force in the Witch Queen's war. Shaw was not like her father. She knew what it meant to reward service, even in the face of grief.

I tried to sit down with Solemie after lunch one day, to talk it through with him, but half an hour in, he grimaced.

"Sorry, Rosy," he said. "I just really don't have time. It's a sweet idea, don't get me wrong, but we're all up to our necks."

"Why?"

"The jarl's coming for our assessment in a few days," Solemie admitted. "No one wanted to tell you. You've got enough to worry about."

I felt furious, suddenly, that our family had decided to treat me like a child. Hadn't I helped with the jarl's inspections for years? Just because I was still working through my own grief, my own fear, didn't mean I was too young to be of use.

For all Gran's words about helping herself, the fact of the matter was that without an official pardon from the jarls' council, our family's reputation was still on rocky terrain. I understood that even more deeply after my months at Witch Hall. With the threat of war so close, we'd need an impeccable defense to keep the ranch. Jarls all over the kingdom would be consolidating their resources to answer the Witch King's call for troops and supplies.

Thoughts of preparing for Samhain moved to the back of my mind. There'd be time after the jarl left. "What do you need me to do?"

And then we were off. I understood more about Gran and Pops's relationship with the former Witch Queen than I ever had before, thanks to Shaw. I used that to help my family prepare a case for why the Witch Queen's gift of land should be honored, despite Gran's imprisonment.

I didn't bother trying to write an argument that Gran wasn't dangerous, as I had in years past. I knew better now. This wasn't about danger, it was about control. Our jarl never would have cared about Gran's feral episodes if they'd targeted his enemies. Even if they'd targeted a bystander, she would have been given a pass so long as she was still his willing soldier.

No, the jarls' council stepped in because Gran refused to dance to their tune, that was all. Nobility did not like to hear the word *no*.

But none of that should give them a right to take our land. The Witch Queen gifted it to Otto and Ylva Holt in exchange for a tax of horses or income off horse sales sent to the jarl of Woodside and Forest's Edge. Our family had never failed to deliver on our side of the deal.

I helped Mama and Papa build an argument to that effect. Solemie balanced the accounts for supporting evidence while Uncle Inge and Uncle Chetwoot cleaned the ranch and the horses till they practically shined.

The day our jarl was set to arrive, we received a letter from Toketie. She wasn't coming home for fall break.

"Too much to do at the school," Uncle Inge said as he read the letter. "She's helping to get supplies ready for next term. Apparently, there's going to be some changes to the curriculum?"

"Army training," I said, grumbling.

Solemie leaned over Uncle Inge's shoulder, reading on. "She says she'll make it home for winter break though, no matter what."

"Your sister wouldn't miss your wedding for the world," Uncle Chetwoot assured him.

Mama grumbled, just as Gran liked to do. The older Mama got, the more I could see Gran in the wrinkles on her face. "It's probably for the best. We don't have time to plan another homecoming."

It was true. I tried not to worry about Toketie, though it was hard. I wondered what her suitemates had thought about her sitting with me and Shaw and the entourage, that week before I left. Would Froya punish her for it somehow? Would Shaw or Aklemin protect her? I couldn't be sure. They tolerated Toketie's presence because of me, but I'd thrown Shaw's necklace in her face in front of the entire school.

I regretted that now. Not leaving, but how I did it. I'd let my emotions win again and now Toketie might be paying the price for them.

Jarl Snass arrived around noon. Iktus's son ran to warn us that he was nearly finished meeting with Iktus about the farm. The jarl had approved their continued use of the farm without fuss. I hoped that meant he wasn't going to fight us either. Maybe he realized he'd need our supply of horses for the months to come. Or years. However long this war would drag on.

Jarl Snass rode in a carriage, escorted by three soldiers from his own company. One held the door open for him and another helped him step down from the carriage.

I stood with my family in front of our house. Mama had a scroll in hand, the argument we'd written up. She'd spent all morning memorizing it so she could give the argument verbally if the jarl preferred. Jarl Snass could be finicky, depending on his mood. He was a short man, barely taller than I was, and blunt to the point of rudeness. I would have liked how no-nonsense he was, except for how difficult it made things for my family.

"Jarl Snass," Mama said, bowing. She held out the scroll like an offering. "We've taken the liberty of compiling our accounts in this report. Would you like some tea while you read?"

"No," Jarl Snass said.

Mama straightened. "Then would you like me to summarize the report for you? My brother made fresh biscuits just an hour ago if you'd like a snack while I talk."

"No," Jarl Snass said again.

"Then—" Mama began once more.

"I'm sorry, Ida, but I'm not here to listen to you argue or plead with me," Jarl Snass said. "The Witch King has demanded each jarl give up a portion of their land in preparation for the coming war. There won't be many troops stationed here, considering our distance from the northern border, so I've been tasked with managing supplies. Unfortunately, your family's land is the largest single parcel I have."

"Sir—" Uncle Chetwoot began, outraged.

Jarl Snass held up a hand. "I can give you until the end of the day to pack your belongings. I understand you still have your ancestral house?"

"Our ancestral house is a one-bedroom cottage that's been swallowed by the Bone Forest and fallen to ruin," Mama snapped.

"And that's my fault?" Jarl Snass raised an eyebrow.

"Can't we be allowed to stay?" Uncle Inge said, voice shaking. "We'll keep the horses to a small pasture and the army can use the rest. We can help the organizing of supplies, even."

The jarl wouldn't meet our eyes. "I'm afraid your family cannot be trusted with such a task. Past events being what they were—"

"Horseshit," I said. "We have always delivered quality bone horses to you and our buyers. No, say it plainly. You're punishing us because of Gran. Because she went feral six years ago and scared a thane into pissing his pants."

Jarl Snass's face tightened. "The decision has been made. I will hear no more on the subject."

I took a step forward, outraged. His guards sneered at me, hands on their swords. I wanted to shift into my wolf and attack them for the insult. But just the thought of that made me cold. Made me remember the last time I should have let the wolf attack, and didn't. How could I kill a few guards for sneering when I hadn't killed a few terrorists for burning my friend to death?

I turned my back on the jarl so I could look at my family. "I'm sorry. This is my fault."

"No, Rosy," Mama said fiercely. "Don't blame yourself. This has been coming for a long time."

But she didn't understand. None of them did. I'd only told Gran about Shaw. Maybe Toketie had written to them about it, during the courtship, but none of them had asked. None of them had pressed.

I knew though. If I still wore Shaw's necklace, I knew Jarl Snass wouldn't have dared to do this to my family. We wouldn't have been the easy target anymore. He'd have found some other land to give. He might even have done the proper thing and just asked for each family to give up a small amount, to share the storage of supplies evenly.

"I'll start gathering the horses," I told Mama.

"You will not," the jarl cut in. "Your horses live on this land and thus are the property of the kingdom. I will not allow blatant stealing of the kingdom's property."

I turned sideways, eyes on the guards. They hadn't drawn their swords yet, but they were ready to.

It wasn't fair. None of this was fair. I looked at Jarl Snass and tried to think.

There had been a week in Etiquette when we'd learned about land-use laws. It had been geared toward understanding how to ask a jarl for a parcel of land, but there had been plenty of advice mixed among that for my family's situation. It had been one of the few times I'd been invested in Mister Sorensen's teaching and one of the few assignments I'd earned perfect marks on in that class.

"You can't take the herd. The land is yours, but the horses are ours. Caught and bred and trained by us," I said, starting slow but gaining speed as the memory of Mister Sorensen's lectures came to me. "The kingdom's bylaws state that land is loaned by the region's ruling jarl in exchange for citizen labor. By taking our land, you are declaring you have no need for our labor. You'd be the thief if you took our horses."

"And what will you do with your horses without land? Let them go free just to spite me?" Jarl Snass scoffed. "The kingdom will soon be at war, Miss Holt. There's no time for pettiness."

"I agree," I said, and let it be clear on my face that it wasn't *me* being petty. "But those horses represent three generations of the Holt family legacy. We can tie a line through the trees for now, until we can build a pasture. The Forest likes me. It will let us."

"The Bone Forest is public land," Papa said, stepping up beside me to add his support. "We are within our rights to expand our property there."

"And like the hunters who make a living catching game in the

Forest, we have a right to sell the horses we raise within it without your approval," Uncle Inge added.

"You will not last," Jarl Snass said. "There is a reason even the hunters pay for homes in Woodside or Gravestown, for all that they travel to the Forest. Those cursed woods are no place for the living."

"My mother has lived there just fine for six years, as the jarls' council well knows," Mama retorted. "Now, if you'll excuse us, it appears we must pack."

As one, my family turned our backs on the jarl and his soldiers. We headed back into the house that Pops had built and Gran had turned into a home. Where Mama and Uncle Inge had been raised. Where my cousins and I had been born, taken our first steps, spoken our first words.

I tried not to think about what Toketie would say as I packed up the room we'd once shared. Now I'd be sharing a room with my entire family, at least until we could build some additions to the cottage.

My hands shook as I packed another bag. Guilt and anger warred.

"I won't let this break me," I said to the barren room. "I won't let this break my family."

# Chapter 29

LIVING IN THE BONE FOREST WAS NEITHER EASY NOR comfortable. The cottage had been scrubbed clean floor to ceiling, but it would take more than a week's work to fix the broken walls and leaking roof.

The table had been moved outside, because bedding for all seven of us filled up most of the floor space, even when we piled it into the corner during the day. We didn't even need to light the fire at night—the warmth of so many bodies in such a small space was enough to ward off the autumn cold.

The hardest part was the horses. Gran had been eager to help, after so long being unable to work the ranch, but she was more wolf than human these days and the horses reacted poorly to her.

The temporary picket lines we'd tied the horses to lasted as long as it took Tempest to plant his feet and pull. I begged the Forest to help for hours until the wind blew like a sigh and then the clearing surrounding the cottage was closed off by a hundred bone pines.

"Will we be able to leave?" Uncle Inge asked me, nervous, as he eyed the too-neat circle of trees blocking any exit from our clearing.

I remembered how the Forest had trapped me with Shaw's entourage and a bull moose. For all that these woods liked me, they weren't a tame pet. The Bone Forest was old and wild and when it played games, there was no forfeiting.

"We'll be fine," I said, instead of giving voice to my worries.

I made sure to thank the Forest every day, especially when it opened up a gap just large enough for Gran and me to leave, closing the gap behind us before any of the herd could escape.

Gran and I had to hunt food for the whole family. I hadn't explicitly told my family about my other shifts—my wolf or raccoon or my new badger. But I didn't hide them either. The time for secrets was long over.

Madam Bai's Survival Skills class came in handy as I foraged for edible roots. I found caches of nuts that squirrels were saving for winter and, with a small apology, stole the lot. Gran and I weren't able to find large prey easily, so I showed my family what Madam Bai had taught me about cooking small game so that you got the biggest amount of meat out of it.

We had enough to survive, but it was hardly comfortable. There were few fruits and vegetables we could gather in the Bone Forest. We would have to buy produce at Forest's Edge market, but we needed income to do that. All my family's hard-earned money was being saved for building supplies so we could expand the cottage.

"We can sell half a dozen mares," Mama said, eyeing the horses grazing all around us. "We need to thin the herd anyway. There's not enough room."

No, there wasn't. Tempest had been particularly vicious in reaction to how crowded it was, and humans were an easier target than his fellow bone horses. It made me miss the beautiful stable at Witch Hall, with its corrals and the long pasture that sloped down to the riverbank.

In truth, I thought about Witch Hall a lot. Maybe it was

because we'd been forced to leave the ranch, but every night when I tried to get comfortable on a pile of bedding, crowded by my family, I dreamed of my little room in the bone familiars' suite. When I tried to pretend I wasn't listening to another argument between my parents or my uncles, I thought instead of those silly arguments Yuyan and Aklemin always had. I wondered what advice Madam Xu would give about my family's situation, wondered what joke Madam Bai would say to cheer us all up. I even thought about Madam Dyer, every time I looked at Gran. She would sneer and say that we'd brought this upon ourselves, but then she'd turn around and give us some lecture about bone magic that would inspire me to try a new way of communicating with the Bone Forest.

Somehow in the three months I'd been there, I'd grown comfortable with Witch Hall. The good and the bad. I longed for the routine of classes and stable duty. Even the schoolyard politics were easier to deal with than this.

If I wrote to Shaw, what would she say? If I promised to go back, to fight this war with her, would she demand the jarl give my family our land back?

"Don't sell to Jarl Snass, he doesn't deserve them," I said, trying to shake myself out of my thoughts. I was tired and hungry, and it was making me think things I shouldn't. I needed to focus on the here and now.

"No. We'll ride them up and see if the Gravestown Company wants them," Papa said. "Gravestown's jarl is a reasonable woman and her general even more so."

I found it ironic that Papa thought Charles's mother was reasonable, when I'd found Charles to be anything but. I didn't say that though. We didn't have many options.

"We should stop by Woodside on the way back," Uncle

Chetwoot said. He looked at Uncle Inge, then both of them looked at Solemie.

"What?" Solemie asked, scowling. "I don't want . . . I want to wait until we're more settled."

"She's probably already heard the news," Uncle Inge said gently. "Sole, we want to ask Lilly's family to take you in. They didn't want her to leave anyway. They'll take you both."

I bit back my instinctive disagreement. If Solemie married into his fiancée's family, he would no longer be a Holt. He'd take their last name and join their family's legacy. Just like Uncle Chetwoot and Papa had done when they took the Holt name and came to the ranch.

"I don't want to make shoes!" Solemie protested.

"Nonsense. You have a head for numbers, not leather. Make a place for yourself doing the bookkeeping," Papa said.

Neither he nor Mama looked surprised by Uncle Inge's suggestion. I got the feeling they'd discussed it together beforehand. I wasn't sure when, since it was hard to find privacy in the clearing. Maybe yesterday, when Solemie and I had been trying to decide if the patch of mushrooms I'd found was safe to eat.

"But—" Solemie tried again.

"Don't make a fuss, boy," Gran said. There was a deep scowl on her face, but she gestured to Solemie to come closer to where she sat on the only working chair, her back leaning against the stained table.

Solemie came and kneeled down in front of Gran. She stroked his hair like he was still a child.

"I'm sorry," she murmured. "We had such high hopes for this family, your pops and I. He lost his parents so young and I never liked mine. We wanted to do better for our future. The day we moved into that ranch was one of the happiest of my life. Next to only the days my children were born, and the days my grandchildren were."

Gran moved her hand to Solemie's cheek, forcing him to look at her. I wanted to kneel down beside him, like we used to do as children when Pops was telling a story. But I stayed back and tangled my fingers in Tempest's mane to keep him from interrupting Gran with another of his frequent tantrums.

"I let my grief and my rage ruin all of that," Gran continued. "I have no one to blame but myself for our family's fall from grace. Your pops always chided me for rushing forward without thinking things through first. I forgot that when he died, and I don't believe I'll ever forgive myself for it."

"Gran," Solemie choked out. "Please don't—"

Gran put her hand over his mouth. "Quiet while your elders are talking. Where are your manners, boy?" She didn't give him a chance to reply. "That Sapolill is a good girl who loves you as deeply as you love her. You are not abandoning us by going to her. Do you understand? You will always be a Holt, even if you become a Klahn. But you and your sister and your cousin, you three are our legacy and we would see you happy and comfortable. No matter what it takes."

I was no ice witch, but I saw the shape of the future stretched before me. Solemie making a living in Woodside with Sapolill's family. Toketie, if the war didn't kill her, rising through the ranks until she was in charge of the entire army's supply line. Until she had the social clout to find a witch who deserved her, and eventually retired with them on the other side of the kingdom.

And me, here in the Forest, helping my family. Jarl Snass had been right—this was not a safe place to call home. One by one, age

377

or illness or injury would take them all until I alone remained. The last of the Holts.

Here, in the Bone Forest, I would live and I would die. Once, I'd longed for this kind of life. Now, it tasted bitter.

My family left a few days before Samhain. My parents rounded up seven of our mares and rode to Gravestown, Mama to control the horses and Papa to sell them. He'd worked for Gravestown's jarl once. Hopefully that would be enough to earn our family some grace, even if Charles had written bad things about me to his mother.

Uncle Chetwoot, Uncle Inge, and Solemie all headed for Woodside. They'd stay with Uncle Chetwoot's sister, the ice witch who told fortunes, while they renegotiated with the Klahn family.

Gran and I stayed behind. The presence of Tempest and the herd kept me from being able to pretend that this was just a normal Sunday spent training in the Forest with Gran.

I thought more and more about Shaw, about her friends, about Oluk and Toketie. About everything I'd left behind. I wondered if it really would be better to join the army and fight as a bone wolf, rather than watch my family go through all this.

The Forest didn't help. I'd forgotten that Shaw was going to travel with the other senior bone witches and familiars to do a Samhain ritual in these woods. The Bone Forest hadn't. I knew the minute Shaw entered the Forest. The wind carried snippets of conversation from their camp. Madam Dyer preparing the students for the ritual. Chao and Jingyi, sitting with Shaw at meals. Charles, snapping at someone for bothering the princess.

*Give her time*, the wind whispered in Charles's voice.

*She should have courted you*, someone replied.

*It doesn't matter now*, Charles told them. *Focus on the ritual.*

The wind wasn't the worst of it though. Whenever I left our clearing to go hunt, the bone pines did their best to tug me in Shaw's direction. Her group was miles and miles away, on the other side of the Forest, but the pines didn't care. The Forest wanted me to go to her.

I almost did. I would have, if it weren't for Gran and the herd. I didn't want to leave her alone with the horses.

But the whispers on the wind brought a small blessing. Madam Dyer and Shaw spent many hours talking about options for their ritual and it gave me the final bit of information I needed to develop one for Gran and me.

Samhain dawned on the coldest day thus far. I took care of the horses as quickly as I could, then spent the rest of the day gathering what we would need from the trunks my family had stored under the eaves behind the house. Candles, a stick of cinnamon to burn, and mountain ash berries to ring the circle. Then I had to find something of Pops's that we could use to anchor his spirit while we talked. I knew Uncle Inge still had Pops's red-and-gold general's sash, but it took me most of the day digging through the trunks to find it.

The hardest part of the séance was getting Gran to join. She'd always refused to do any Samhain rituals before, even when our family had offered to come to the Bone Forest to do them with her.

"No," Gran snapped as I began to set the ritual up on the table. The sun was just starting to set, casting deep shadows across the clearing.

I'd never understood Gran's refusal before, but I thought I knew it now. She was afraid. Afraid it wouldn't work. Afraid to hope and be crushed.

"I can do this," I told her. "He's come to me before. I know I can do this."

Gran's whole body shook. I'd seen her struggle with bone rage enough times to spot the signs of it now. Her fingernails grew into claws and her face began to lengthen.

"Let me help, Gran," I whispered.

Gran took several deep, rasping breaths. The shift reverted. She twisted her fingers in her ratty dress, then nodded. "Just the once," she whispered back.

Gran sat on the only working chair while I stood at the table across from her. The horses grazed around us. We lit five candles, placed the mountain ash berries, then burned the end of the cinnamon stick and set it in a bowl at the center of the circle.

I placed my arms on the table, palms up on either side of the small ritual circle. Gran didn't look at me, eyes on the flickering candle flames. I waited as patiently as I could.

It took nearly a minute before Gran joined me. She placed her hands on top of mine, squeezing my fingers tightly.

"Oh little flame that burns so bright, be a beacon on this night," I murmured. "Light the path for all the dead, that they may see what lies ahead."

I took a deep breath and called the voices in my heart up to the surface. I'd never tried to bring up more than one before, and for a second my senses overwhelmed me. I focused on my sixth sense, the sense of death.

Even with two powerful bone familiars anchoring the ritual, it wouldn't have worked on any other day. But Samhain had a special type of magic, and Pops wanted to be seen. Just like that, he stood at the table with us. He looked decades younger than he had when he'd died, but I would never forget that soft smile. The edge of his form wasn't entirely solid. Wisps of mist licked at his shoulders and played over his hair. But he was there.

"Otto," Gran said, her voice cracking.

I held Gran's hands tight, worried that if we broke the circle, Pops would vanish.

"My darling Ylva," Pops replied. "How are you even more beautiful now than you were then?"

I was shocked to see Gran's cheeks turn pink. "Quiet, you," she snapped.

"How can I be quiet? I've waited years to talk to you again." Pops drifted closer—not quite walking, but not really flying either. Translucent fingers traced the air over Gran's lips. "I miss you."

"You should have moved on years ago, old man," Gran said.

"How could I, when you're still here? Don't give me that look, darling, I'm in no rush."

"You risk losing yourself," I said, suddenly worried. The longer Pops stuck around as a ghost, the more likely he'd lose his humanity and become a spirit—reduced to whatever emotion he clung to the hardest.

Pops smiled at me, then at Gran. "Our granddaughter takes after you."

Gran glanced at me too. "She's got a bit of you in her too," she said. "Not as much as our other granddaughter though. Foolish girl."

"Yes," Pops agreed. "I watched over her at Witch Hall, when I could. May this coming war treat her better than ours treated us."

"You aren't angry, Pops?" I asked. "That Tokey is joining the army?"

"Did Ylva never tell you?" Pops asked, turning to me. "I volunteered myself, all those years ago. I never regretted my service, even after everything."

"They killed you," Gran growled. "Those cowards."

Pops shook his head. I held my breath. Perhaps this was what Gran needed. For Pops to tell her the truth of how he died, so she could finally let go of her rage.

But then Pops looked up at the half moon hanging in the sky above us and said, "They did kill me."

Gran's nails bit into my skin.

"What? Pops—"

"You were right, then? That idiotic theory. Did he find out?" Gran asked.

"It seems I was the rash one this time, my darling," Pops said. "I shouldn't have gone alone. Should have been more cautious."

"I don't understand. What are you two talking about?"

Pops looked at me. I couldn't tell what the expression on his face meant. "There was no avalanche, Rosy. They buried me in snow after, to cover up that they pushed me off the cliff. No, don't blame the soldiers. They were just following orders."

I wanted to stand, but I couldn't while holding on to the ritual. My arms shook. Gran's nails dug deeper into my skin. "Whose orders?"

"Who do you think, girl?" Gran snapped. "The Witch King's, of course."

"But why?"

"Because I discovered his plan," Pops said. "I wasn't included in those meetings, but I was a general nonetheless. I knew when I was being maneuvered around. I figured it out and I knew he would kill me for it." He crossed his arms, and for a second I saw Shaw in his expression. That same commanding presence, same quiet surety. "It's hard to counteract a man who can see every possible future any time he wishes."

"What was the plan? What was important enough to kill you over?" I demanded.

Pops opened his mouth to answer, but instead of words he let out a yell like something had hurt him.

Gran and I reflexively let go of each other, both of us trying to reach for him. Pops didn't vanish, but he did move away. It took me a second to realize he wasn't moving naturally. It looked as though he were being dragged from the center of his chest. Like some invisible hook had caught him by the heart and was now pulling him away.

"Otto!" Gran screamed, and then she was shifting into the wolf.

Pops vanished through the wall of trees, dragged faster now, still screaming like he was being tortured.

With wild eyes, *feral* eyes, Gran-the-wolf barreled after him. I had just enough time to bite out a startled curse, then I sprinted after them both.

# Chapter 30

## SHAW

As a little girl, Shaw dreamed of bonding—stuck on the Frozen Mountain those long, lonely winters when even Aklemin refused to come out of his manor and play. Her greatest wish as a child was for a companion. Someone who would be by her side, always. Who would never betray her. Someone who would fight next to her, unflinching and unafraid. But someone soft too. Who would not hesitate to love and be loved in return.

Shaw had so little softness in her childhood. Her friendship with Aklemin was forged out of necessity and sustained through memories. Her relationship with her father was built on mutual respect and strengthened with each year she grew. His court were people to impress and to observe. The ones who'd been soft to Shaw were the most untrustworthy.

Shaw liked to imagine that her mother would have been soft. Would have filled those gaping holes in her childhood. Maybe she would hurt less now, if she had her mother's love to return to.

Instead, she rode beside Madam Dyer with her classmates trailing behind them, and she ached like she had been stabbed. They were days into the Bone Forest already, traveling deeper and deeper as Samhain dawned. They'd reach the heart of the Forest soon. Shaw had until then to let the wound fester.

Once they stopped and began the ritual, Shaw would lance it. Let it scab. Let it scar. She would figure out how to move on.

Her great-uncle used to tell her the story of how he found his witch, her grandmother's younger sister.

"I knew I loved her from the moment I met her," he would say in the years before the unforgiving cold of the Frozen Mountain took him too.

"It was that fast?" Shaw asked once, bored by the same story.

"Love has no timeline. It can take years or it can take seconds."

"How will I know, then?"

"You'll know, dearest. A strong witch like you? I expect you'll know before your familiar does. You'll need to put effort into courtship to win them over. Promise me you'll wait for them, dearest. Even if it takes a while, you must be prepared to wait."

Shaw's great-uncle was an ice familiar, and times like that made her think he was feeling the edges of the future, like ice familiars sometimes did.

"I will," she'd promised.

Her father had pulled her aside after one of those evenings spent at her great-uncle's side. He'd warned her that her great-uncle was still grieving his witch, who'd died in the war. That because of his grief, he romanticized things beyond what was reasonable, even in his own memories.

"You will find a well-suited familiar one day," her father said then. "The more powerful the familiar, the more powerful the bond, the more power you will gain. But do not confuse the bond with love. The reality is more complex than that."

Years older and months wiser, Shaw thought they were both right. She'd been drawn to Rosamund from the moment they met, known she was the familiar Shaw wanted to rule beside only weeks after that. But compatibility did not create love.

She had seen the shape of their bond first, but the shape of love had crept over her like the slow melt of ice under gentle spring sunlight. It would have been so easy to let the last of it melt and fall headfirst into the kind of devotion her great-uncle had felt for his witch.

Rosamund did not love her. That much was clear from the start, but she had hoped love might grow between them. Shaw had tried to be courteous. She'd put as much effort into the courtship as she could, within Rosamund's own parameters. She'd tried to keep her promise, to be patient.

The shattered remains of the courtship necklace clinked against each other in her pocket with each step Cow took.

Maybe, in another life, in another world, it could have been different. Maybe if they had just been two normal girls, love could have blossomed naturally. It would have taken seconds for Shaw, but even if it had taken years for Rosamund, she would have waited.

But in this life, Rosamund had chosen freedom over duty, and Shaw was left alone once more. Her heart choked her still, but she would live. She did not need a familiar. Childhood dreams so rarely came true, after all.

Shaw was the daughter of the Witch King, and he was the most powerful witch in the kingdom despite losing his own familiar. She would harden her heart like her father had hardened his. Softness had no place in war.

Everyone was relying on her. Aklemin, beset with prophetic nightmares of what was to come. Yuyan, grief-stricken and already weary of the people she would not be able to save. Einar, determined in the face of his tarot reading, wanting to do right by his new familiar.

And not just her entourage. All the witches and familiars of Witch Hall needed her strength. The classmates she'd grown with for the past half decade. The ones who'd promised to fight beside her in this war none of them had chosen.

"We're here," Madam Dyer announced, pulling Pyre to a halt.

Shaw rode farther into the clearing and the bone pines bowed her forward. The dirt was so dark it looked black. Sun-bleached bones stuck up from the ground as if the Forest were growing skeletons instead of roots. She could sense hundreds more buried deep beneath. The bones stirred as Cow trotted over them. The spirits pressed in on her from all sides, hungry for recognition. Wanting freedom.

At the center of the clearing was a massive bone pine. Larger than any pine could reasonably get. It stretched so tall that Shaw couldn't see the top even if she craned her head all the way back. The trunk was easily twice the length of Cow and there wasn't a single imperfection in the bark.

Shaw dismounted and tied Cow's reins to the saddle so the mare wouldn't trip on them. Then she bowed low to the heart of the Forest. "Samhain's blessings upon you."

The skeletons in the clearing rattled like laughter. Cow stomped her foot and cracked the nearest bone clean in two. The rattling stopped.

The great pine did not move, but Shaw felt when the energy in the clearing changed. Some of the hunger abated, leaving only the welcome embrace of death. She wanted to step closer, but she had a duty to her people. She couldn't fall into the peace the Forest offered.

"We've come to calm the dead who haunt you," she said. "If it doesn't please you, we will find another ritual space."

It had been a risk to go to the heart, but Shaw and Madam Dyer had agreed it would be worth it. The heart of the Forest would have enough reach to pull the spirits who'd died in Multah. If they did the ritual in a different part of the Forest, they might not have the power.

Of course, there were other bone witches and familiars doing smaller Samhain rituals all over the kingdom, including a group in Multah. But Samhain rituals were always most effective when done in the Bone Forest, like the rituals of Lammas in the Obsidian Desert, Candlemas on the Frozen Mountain, and Beltane at Lake Bloom.

The wind came then, whistling through the pines. *Welcome, Princess. Welcome. Welcome back. Welcome*, it said, using the voices of a dozen travelers who'd passed through.

"Thank you," Shaw replied. The wind tangled with her hair as she turned to face Madam Dyer and her classmates.

"Well, let's get started," Madam Dyer said. She got off Pyre and stepped into the clearing to start the circle.

One by one, her classmates joined. They hitched the horses outside the clearing, to keep them out of the way, then found the places they'd rehearsed. Chao and Jingyi took the west point and the only other bonded pair among the bone students took east. Shaw took south point, across from Madam Dyer. Ragna Strand had volunteered to be Madam Dyer's partner in the north. Charles came to be Shaw's in the south.

Last year, at Samhain, Charles had stood too close. His hand had brushed against Shaw's a few times too often to be a coincidence.

He'd been visibly disappointed when the ritual ended and she'd stepped away without acknowledging him.

Now, Charles did none of that. He nodded once as he took his place next to her and set his shoulders as he faced Madam Dyer and Ragna. Ready to do his part.

It should be a relief. It *was* a relief. Yet, Shaw couldn't help wanting Rosamund to be in his place. To link hands with her like Chao and Jingyi were.

She wrenched her eyes away from Charles before she found herself imagining Rosamund in his stead. The rest of their classmates filled in the gaps in the circle, alternating witch, then familiar, then witch. She looked at each of them in turn.

These were the people she would fight for. Whose existence was denied and threatened by those anti-magical terrorists across the border. Rosamund had turned her back on all of them. So be it. Shaw didn't need a familiar. Her father had lost his queen, but his power had not stagnated.

Shaw would follow in his footsteps. She would be strong enough to save her people. She would turn her back on softness and learn to rule without love.

Madam Dyer raised her arms. "Let's begin."

# Chapter 31

## ROSY

THE TREES OPENED A PATH FOR ME AS I RAN INTO THE Bone Forest after Gran and Pops. The pines rustled, branches reaching out as if to grab me. I shifted into the horse between one stride and the next and pushed my gait to a gallop. Gran had a head start on me and Pops's ghost had vanished from my sight completely.

*Stop her, please,* I begged the Forest.

An unnatural fog began to gather about my legs. The white of Gran's wolf form blended into it. I flicked my ears forward, trying to listen for her loping run, but the Forest had blanketed me in an unnatural silence. I dropped the gallop, then slowed down to a trot as the fog grew thicker.

What was the Bone Forest doing? More branches stretched toward me, scratching my skin as they tried to hold me back. Trees moved between me and Gran, blocking my path forward. For whatever reason, the Forest was preventing me from following Gran.

*Please,* I begged again. *She needs me.*

With a creak, the trees to my right moved aside, opening a different path. Roots protruded from the ground and sharp branches hung low like skeletal arms. As though the Forest was warning me the road ahead was dangerous.

*Whatever it takes,* I told the Forest. *Please help me.*

The entrance of the path widened and I stepped onto it.

I didn't have to go far. A clearing opened up just in front of me. The rest of the Forest was blanketed in fog, but ahead I could see the trunk of a massive pine tree. I'd only ever seen it once, six years ago, when Gran took me to the heart of the Forest to help me gain control over my new wolf shift.

Amid the skeletal graveyard that made the heart's clearing, a circle of people stood chanting. I knew them at once. Bone witches and familiars from Witch Hall. All the seniors. The witches I recognized from my classes and the suitemates I'd been too stubborn to befriend. Madam Dyer was the only teacher. There was Jingyi and Chao. Charles and Ragna. And Shaw—her back to me, chanting loudly with the rest.

As they chanted, ghosts entered the clearing in waves, pulled by their chests like Pops had been. A dozen, then a dozen more. Ghosts of children, of adults. Many had their mouths open, as if trying to scream, but none of them made a sound. As I watched, the ghosts were all dragged to the center of the circle and trapped by whatever Samhain ritual the witches and familiars had decided upon.

I realized what had happened. They were calling all the dead, all those souls who had lingered after passing. There were hundreds of people who had met violent ends just a month ago. If left untended, the kingdom would be overwhelmed with vicious spirits out for revenge and unconcerned with who they possessed to get it.

Except Pops had also been caught in the web of the ritual. I looked for him among the ghosts already trapped, but it was nearly a minute before I saw him being pulled into the clearing. Somehow, the Forest had shortened my path, gotten me here ahead of Pops.

Ahead of Gran.

I stepped into the clearing just as Pops was pulled over Shaw's head and into the circle.

A loud snarl cut through the ritual chanting. Gran, as furious as any bone wolf caught in a rage. Gran, finally reconnected with her dead husband only to lose him again. Gran, who once attacked even her own granddaughter in the midst of a feral episode. Gran, who had already tried to kill Shaw once. Gran, whose husband had been murdered on the order of Shaw's father.

I was not the same girl I'd been in the market. I would not let indecision hold me down, only to watch another person die when I could save them.

"Shaw!" I yelled, the only warning I had time for. Then I gathered whatever courage I had left, ignoring the dozens of shocked eyes on me, and shifted into the wolf.

I lunged forward just in time. I caught Gran midleap and we both went down.

"Keep the circle!" Madam Dyer screamed. "We must not let the ritual fail!"

Her warning came too late. The students had already broken the circle, witches retreating, familiars shifting. As they did, all the ghosts they'd trapped in the center of the circle broke free. The dead spilled out over the clearing, their voices returned in a jumble of wailing.

Gran ignored them all. She pulled away from me, eyes fixed upon her target. Upon Shaw.

I grabbed her by the tail, biting down as hard as I dared. Gran's wolf didn't care. She lunged forward and chunks of fur and skin came free.

Charles shifted into his stag form and pushed Shaw aside. She went down, head banging hard on an exposed tree branch. Madam Dyer screeched and rushed forward, only to be stopped by a group of angry ghosts, all crowding around her with garbled pleas and demands.

Pops was freed, but even as he floated down to Gran's side, I knew it wasn't enough. She was deep in a feral state, too focused on her rage to be soothed. He tried anyway, crooning her name softly, but she snarled.

Charles pawed the ground, lowering his head to show off his antlers. I shifted into human and spat out the fur caught between my teeth. "Charles, your bobcat! Don't be an idiot!" Stag or no, it was too dangerous to face down a bone wolf as a prey animal.

"Rosamund?" Shaw said from where she'd been thrown.

"Stay down," I told her.

Gran went for Charles and he was smart enough to listen to my warning. He shifted into the bobcat, clawing at Gran to make her keep her distance. I kept my eyes on them as I rushed over to Shaw.

"Are you hurt?" I asked, running my fingers through her hair to see if she was bleeding. I couldn't find an open wound.

"I'm fine, just winded," Shaw said as I helped her stand. She already sounded steadier. "Is that your grandmother?"

Fear struck me as hard as Shaw had struck the root. Shaw was well within her rights to execute Gran for attacking. For interrupting the ritual. Never mind that Pops had been caught in it, the jarls' council wouldn't take that as an excuse.

I turned to give Shaw my full attention. "Let her leave," I pleaded. "Open up a path and I can get her out. Please, Shaw."

"I can try," Shaw said, as if I hadn't needed to beg at all. "We need to contain the ghosts before things get violent."

I knew Shaw was right. The clearing was a mess, with familiars trying to corral the ghosts back to the center and witches desperately chanting to keep them contained.

*Can you keep them here?* I asked the Forest. *Keep the ghosts in this clearing?*

I had no idea if the Forest was capable of doing so, but there was no time to check. "I'll get her out of here so you can fix this," I told Shaw, already turning back to Gran.

Only she wasn't where she had been. Charles was on the ground, clutching what looked like a bitten shoulder. A witch leaned down to help him up. He swayed as he stood but otherwise seemed okay.

"Rosamund," Shaw said. "You're a wolf."

"Yes," I admitted faintly, still looking frantically for where Gran had gone. It was hard to hear her growls through the wails of the ghosts. Maybe she'd run off? I would have thought she'd go for Shaw, once she beat Charles. I was only glad she hadn't killed him. I should have stayed and helped.

"Rosamund," Shaw said again.

"What do you want me to say, Shaw? It was my first shift. I know what that means. I didn't want you to know. I didn't want anyone to know."

Shaw began to say something else, but I didn't hear it. I'd caught sight of Gran. Chao and Jingyi had her trapped against the trunk of the massive pine. Skeletal snakes wrapped around Gran's middle, keeping her pinned. Jingyi, as the fox, crouched in front of her, ready to attack if she broke free of Chao's skeletons.

I dodged around the ghosts and students to get to them. "Chao, Jingyi, stop!" I called. "I'll take her!"

They were too far away to hear me through the noise in the

clearing. Someone else reached them before I could. Madam Dyer, her dark auburn hair a tangled mess around her head.

I began to run. I was just close enough to hear as Madam Dyer said, "I'll deal with this, go help the princess reset the ritual."

"Stop!" I screamed, but I sounded like just another ghost and Madam Dyer didn't even turn to look.

"You!" Madam Dyer said. She pointed at Pops. His ghost still flickered uncertainly, reaching toward Gran but unable to touch her. "Ghost, heed me! Kill the wolf."

"No!" I yelled.

Pops's love for Gran was strong. He didn't want to listen to Madam Dyer's command, but he was dead and Madam Dyer was a necromancer. The witch's hands rose, channeling her power, pushing her will onto his. He flickered, a purple glow igniting in the center of his chest.

Pops swooped down to attack Gran, Gran lunged to attack Madam Dyer, and I shifted back into the wolf.

My head collided with Gran's and we both went flying. We slammed into Chao, pushing him to the ground. Jingyi let out a yip of shock.

Gran snarled. She bit me, not a warning bite, but with intent to wound. I yelped as her teeth closed down on my front left leg. Jingyi leaped forward to tear Gran's ear in half. It was enough to make her let go of me. Jingyi and I fell back as Gran crouched to get ready for another attack.

"Kill it!" Madam Dyer commanded Pops once more.

Pops came for Gran and she jumped out of his path—and just into the reach of Madam Dyer. The bone witch took her athame dagger and slashed at Gran. A strip of flesh came off Gran's shoulder.

Gran responded by biting off Madam Dyer's hand.

Madam Dyer screamed. "A curse upon you, you mindless beast!" There was something animalistic about her expression, as if she'd taken Gran's snarls and implanted them onto her own face.

"No!" Shaw shouted, voice cutting through the chaos. "Rosamund, stop her!"

I leaped forward, but it was too late. Madam Dyer's athame came down in the middle of Gran's back. Gran reared up, snarling from the pain. With mindless determination, she pushed forward, breaking Madam Dyer's grip on the knife.

Before I could stop her, before I even realized what was happening, Gran's teeth tore through Madam Dyer's throat.

Dark energy erupted from Madam Dyer's body. It rose up like a wave, then crashed down upon Gran. Pops let out another unholy scream. He'd gotten caught in the backlash and sucked into the sudden whirlpool of dark energy. Then the energy hit me and I was consumed by Madam Dyer's rage—the curse she'd cast right before her death.

I cried out, mimicking Pops's scream without intending to. It was hard to stop—I couldn't seem to close my mouth. I felt stretched, like my body was unraveling at the seams.

Warm hands grabbed me and the horrible energy retreated. I didn't realize I'd shifted until Shaw had me by the shoulders, pulling me several feet away.

"What—?" I asked, or tried to.

"It's the curse," Shaw answered, eyes fixed upon the dark mass that used to be Madam Dyer, Gran, and Pops.

The darkness expanded outward, tendrils like wisps of smoke reaching out as if searching for something. Chao lifted Jingyi up and away, scrambling back behind Shaw and me. The wailing in the clearing had stopped, leaving an unnatural silence. All the ghosts had retreated to the edges of the clearing. It looked like the Forest was managing to contain them, or it was clear they would have fled. The students were no better, pale and horrified in the face of what Madam Dyer had done.

And then the bubble of darkness popped, with an unnerving sound like boiling water, and Gran was visible again. A white wolf edged in black energy. As she shook herself, her physical body seemed to distort as if I were looking at her through a broken mirror.

When Gran lifted her head, there was no human left behind her eyes. There wasn't even the intelligence of a true wolf. Her eyes glowed with the same translucent energy that all the ghosts had.

Her shadow, I realized with muted terror, was an exact match to Pops's ghostly form.

"A specter," Shaw whispered.

I understood then. Madam Dyer's curse had been to make Gran a mindless beast, but this was worse than that. Gran and Pops had combined. Half-alive, half-dead, they'd become a monster in the truest sense of the word. The grandmother I'd always known was gone, mutated by her own dead husband and a witch's death curse. The grandfather we'd both grieved, whose ghost had kept watch over us for so long, had disappeared completely.

The specter was all that remained.

I whimpered, echoing the wolf in my heart. The specter's head snapped up and it pinned me with the mindless gaze of a predator locked on prey. All specters cared about was killing, tasting the energy of death that had twisted them again and again until they were finally put to rest.

The specter took a step toward me. Between one blink and the next, it disappeared in a flash of dark energy.

"Get down!" Shaw pushed me away and I rolled to the ground just as the specter lunged at me from behind.

I shifted into the wolf. Hesitating would prove lethal. This was not Gran anymore. I bunched my back legs under me and sprang up. I went to dig my jaws into the specter's leg, but my teeth snapped on air. It had vanished again.

I fell ungracefully to the ground, my injured leg crumpling under me. The specter reappeared on the other side of the clearing. I understood now why specters were such terrifying foes. The many prey voices inside my heart screamed at me to flee.

I got to my feet. I would not flee. It was my grandparents who'd become this specter and even though Madam Dyer had caused it, I still felt responsible.

I kept a wary eye on the specter, waiting for it to disappear again. Bracing for the attack, I was startled when, instead, the specter sat back on its haunches and lifted its head to howl.

The howl was unlike that of any bone wolf I'd ever heard. It was a haunting sound, remnants of a ghost's wail mixed with the echo of a witch's ritual chanting.

The ghosts in the clearing reacted to it instantly. They floated as one toward the specter, crowding around it. Their translucent bodies began to glow brighter. Colors began forming. The red of rage. The green of envy.

"It's turning them into spirits," Chao said, despair in every word.

My mind flashed to what Madam Dyer had done to Pops. The way he'd turned purple, the color of regret. Ghosts couldn't hurt the living, but spirits could. They could possess people—take over their souls and overwhelm their bodies. People possessed by spirits could be influenced to turn against one another or against themselves.

That was what Madam Dyer had wanted to do to Gran. Pops's ghost was anchored to this world because of regret. If he'd become a spirit, had possessed Gran, that regret would have made her want to die. She would have walked willingly into Madam Dyer's athame if I hadn't run into her, pushed her away from Pops before he could sink into her skin.

But that didn't matter now, because Gran had been possessed all the same. Possessed and turned into this.

"How? Specters can't—" Charles said.

"It's Madam Dyer," Shaw interrupted. "She died to cast that curse. Her ghost would have lingered. It's part of the specter."

I understood what Shaw was saying. Madam Dyer was—had been—a necromancer. One strong enough, apparently, to force a ghost to become a spirit.

I shifted into human, turning to Shaw. "How do we stop it?"

It wasn't just me. All the seniors had shuffled closer to Shaw, waiting for her command. They wanted to run, I could see it in the whites of their eyes. But they waited for Shaw's word.

Shaw let out a shuddering breath. She looked away from the specter and the ghosts to us. Her eyes roamed over the group, landing at last on me. "We can't retreat," she said, like an apology. "That many spirits, they won't stay trapped in the Forest. They'll flood the kingdom. This is exactly what we were trying to prevent with the ritual."

"Well, not this exactly," Jingyi muttered. "No one expected a specter."

Shaw gave her an annoyed look and she held up her hands.

"We understand," Charles said, and he was right. With the number of restless ghosts that had been made in the last month alone, any number would have turned into spirits without intervention. It was our job, as bone witches and familiars, to safeguard the living from that.

I'd never felt the responsibility of being a bone familiar before. Not like this, like I did now.

"We don't have a lot of time," Chao said, eyes still on the specter. I looked over. Half the ghosts had become spirits by now, a rainbow of colors. It would have been beautiful, if not for what it meant. The specter's howl still had them trapped, but once it released them, those spirits would turn toward the first available targets. Toward us.

"You and I are the only ones who successfully turned a spirit back to a ghost, in class," Shaw told Chao. "How much energy do you have left?"

"Not enough," Chao admitted.

Shaw nodded like she'd expected that. She turned to the other witches. "We'll need a power-sharing ritual. Kalitan, I need you to lead it."

A witch I recognized as being one of the more attentive students in our shared class stepped up. She put a hand on Chao's shoulder. She held out her other hand and another witch took it. Quickly, all the witches grabbed hands. The final one placed his free hand on Chao's other shoulder, completing the circle.

"Jingyi, can you anchor me?" Chao asked. His familiar shifted into the fox and, with a running leap, landed on his shoulders. She settled down over the two witches' hands, nose nestled against Chao's neck.

"The rest of you will need to defend them," Shaw told the other familiars. "Bone familiars are naturally resistant to possession, we know that. It will take a good second or two before a spirit can settle inside you. Help one another distract the spirits. Keep moving. Shift between forms as much as possible, that will prevent them from getting hold."

"We've got this," Charles said. I glanced at his shoulder, where Gran had bitten him, but the blood was all dry. The wound must have clotted well. Shifting might reopen it, but we didn't have a choice.

"I have faith in you all," Shaw said, and I saw the effect her words had on the familiars. Their shoulders straightened and the fear left their faces, replaced with determination. "Watch for the change, when Chao turns them back. Don't waste your time on the ghosts. The remaining spirits will only fight harder, once they realize what's going on."

The familiars shifted into their various bone animal forms, spreading out to make a line in front of Chao and the witches. As they did, Shaw turned to me.

"Rosamund," Shaw said. "The specter is the main issue. I have a plan, but . . . I can't do it without you."

"I'm here."

Shaw took a deep breath. The specter's howl had reached a fever pitch. I knew we had only moments before the battle began. "Will you trust it? Trust me?" Shaw asked.

"I do trust you," I said, and found that it was the truth. Whatever Shaw's plan, I would follow it.

Shaw shook her head. "You didn't, though, even though you said you did."

Perhaps Shaw was right. I had hidden my wolf. Even as I'd come to believe Shaw would be a good queen, I hadn't trusted her with my secret. But . . . "I'm not hiding anymore. Not ever again."

Shaw was still visibly uncertain. Had I finally learned how to read her or had her walls dropped in the face of the battle to come? "Your arm—" she began.

"Shaw," I said, cutting her off. "Madam Xu made me your fighter for our Combat midterm and we won despite what I was hiding. But I'm a wolf and I've got two dozen more shifts besides. I can fight for you. I will fight for you. So, use me like you did then."

Shaw's shoulders fell back, straightening like the familiars' had. As if my words had given her resolve just as her words had given it to them. "I need to get my hands on the specter. I need to touch it. Without it killing me in the process."

"No problem," I said, though we both knew that was a lie. "Let's do this."

# Chapter 32

THE FIRST STEP WAS GETTING SHAW CLOSE ENOUGH TO the specter without the spirits overwhelming us. *Can you hide us?* I asked the Bone Forest.

The bone pines to my left beckoned. I grabbed Shaw's hand and tugged her to follow. She came with no resistance. Fog condensed behind us, covering our retreat.

We circled around the outside of the clearing. The specter's howl finally cut off. The spirits did their best to replace it with screeches of rage and moans of regret.

"We need to distract the specter before it goes after Chao," Shaw said.

I let go of Shaw's hand and shifted into the wolf. The bone pines just in front of us slid to either side, giving us an opening to jump back into the clearing.

"I'll be right behind you," Shaw promised, but I was already launching forward. I didn't need the assurance. Shaw wasn't going to abandon me to fight this alone.

The specter was crouched, teeth bared, watching as the spirits convened on the bone witches and familiars. Chao had both hands raised and I saw two spirits falter. Their colors flickered, from red and blue to clear, then back again.

Shaw was right. The specter was smart. It had hung back to look for the biggest threat. Any second now, it'd use that terrifying ability. It'd teleport across the clearing and attack Chao before any of the other students could react.

I had to direct its attention onto me first. I snarled, as loudly and viciously as I could. The specter turned to face me. I'd lost the element of surprise, but there was no time to wonder if I'd made a mistake. The specter locked eyes with me, and then it vanished.

"Left!" Shaw called just as the specter reappeared at my back left leg.

I shifted into the horse, kicking out. The specter's teeth ripped the skin of my heels, but the force of my kick sent it flying. It would have hit a tree, but it vanished before impact.

I had only seconds to think. How was I going to catch the specter for Shaw if it could vanish into thin air at will?

But was it really vanishing? Not completely. Shaw had seen it in time to warn me. I wasn't sure if she was just sensing the specter's energy, or if it was fully visible to her, but it had to be enough to work with.

"Above you!" Shaw called.

I went squirrel. The specter landed on top of me—it must have leaped to try to catch me by the neck. Before I could be flattened, I twisted, shifted into the raccoon, and clawed at the specter's stomach. Only the first scratch cut skin before the specter flickered away again.

"Follow me," Shaw commanded, arms up.

I shifted back to the bone wolf, ready to run after her, only to realize what she meant. Shaw didn't move, but something else did.

A skeletal . . . thing attacked thin air several feet away from me. It looked like Shaw had called upon the bones scattered across the floor of the clearing, but there was no order to the monster the bones had become. A human's pelvis with a deer's back legs. Ribs that ranged in size from bear to raccoon. A moose's skull, antlers still attached. The arms were two different lengths, both ending in an assortment of claws and talons.

The specter flickered in and out of sight as it dodged the skeleton's attacks. I ran to help. I had a hard time tracking the specter's movements, but Shaw's skeleton helped. We drove the specter to the edge of the clearing. The specter bit through the skeleton's right leg, but the undead didn't falter from injury. I managed to bite a chunk off the specter's side before it vanished again.

Then the specter appeared *inside* the skeleton's rib cage and it burst apart.

Shaw cursed. I shook fragments of bone out of my fur.

"Me!" Shaw called, a touch panicked, just as the specter appeared in front of her.

*No.* I rushed forward. Shaw had pulled up a shield of bones, but the specter broke through them. She fell backward, arms up to defend herself. My heart was in my throat. I pushed my legs to go faster, but I knew I wouldn't get there in time.

Hooves kicked out, flashes of bone white and night black. The specter drew back, away from Shaw. It snarled at the creature, the horse, that had come between it and its prey.

"Cow?" Shaw gasped.

Cow squealed, a high-pitched challenge. She planted all four legs and lowered her head, putting herself between Shaw and the specter. I skidded to a stop just next to her, but Cow only flicked one ear in my direction. I shifted into human so I could help Shaw to her feet.

"Where did you—" Shaw began, still speaking to her mare. "I tied you outside the clearing! Where are the other horses?"

I should have thought of it before—should have wondered where the horses were that the group must have ridden in on. It was unclear if Cow had been the only one to break free of the picket line, or if the whole herd had panicked and run when the commotion began in the clearing. Perhaps when the specter had done its horrible howl.

It didn't really matter, because Cow hadn't fled. She'd rushed to the clearing instead, to her rider's defense. I'd never known a more loyal bone horse. Not even Tempest—

*Tempest.* He and what was left of his herd were in the Forest too. They were miles away, but that was nothing to a horse's gallop. If the Forest would work with me, I could use them.

*Will you bring them here? If you open a path, Tempest will come. He's been cooped up, he'll want to run. The herd will follow.*

The wind picked up. I hoped that meant the Forest agreed. It wouldn't take long for the herd to arrive, less if the Forest shortened their path like it had for me.

The specter turned as translucent as a ghost. Its feet came off the ground and it floated away from Cow. The bone horse's head jerked up as if startled.

"What—?" I started, taking my hands off Shaw to shift again.

As soon as my fingers left Shaw's skin, the specter vanished. I paused, as startled as Cow, then quickly grabbed Shaw's bare arm.

"Our right," Shaw said.

But she didn't need to. I could see it circling around Cow to try to get at me and Shaw.

"I can see it," I told her. "If we're touching."

There was no time to talk strategy. I crouched down, gesturing for Shaw to get on my back. She clumsily hitched a leg up to my waist, as if she knew what I was about to do. I shifted into the horse and Shaw righted herself. One hand tangled in my mane, and the other came out to pull more bones to us.

The specter darted forward. I waited as long as I dared, then reared up just as it went from ghost to solid. My front hoof clipped the specter's jaw and it faded translucent again. A horrible crawling sensation went through me as the specter's ghost passed through my body and out the other side.

I fell to all four legs, shifted my weight, and bucked. I couldn't see directly behind me, but I felt my back hoof hit something. It was too dangerous to linger over it. As soon as my back legs were on the ground, I lunged forward.

Shaw kept her balance, moving her weight with mine. Her thighs squeezed my sides, but I ignored it. Without a saddle, that was the only way she could stay on.

I could feel the subtle shift of Shaw's head and shoulders as she tracked the specter's movement. I pivoted to the side so that I could see it again. The specter made to leap at us, but before it could, the bone pines behind it moved.

Cow whinnied, hearing the pounding of hoofs. Tempest burst through the opening the Forest had made, his herd following behind. They didn't see the specter in its ghost form, barreling over where it stood. Tempest threw his head, neighing in surprise at the commotion going on. He turned the herd to the left, avoiding the mass of spirits and bone students on the other side of the clearing. Cow joined them, instinctively wanting safety in numbers. Struck by inspiration, I followed.

The herd formed a tight circle, slowing out of necessity as they realized they were now trapped in another clearing. I kept my eye on the specter. It was obviously confused, crouched low as it waited for the herd of bone horses to settle down. I watched it turn solid for a split second, then quickly fade again.

"It can't stay a ghost long," Shaw told me, seeing what I did. "If we time it perfectly—"

I knew she was right. We'd never get a better chance. I broke away from the herd just as we circled around the specter's left flank. Pinning both ears back, I hoped Shaw would understand. She let go of my mane, legs bunching.

I shifted. Shaw fell off my back. I didn't have time to look back to see if she'd landed on her feet. I reached for the specter with three-inch claws and dug them into its shoulders just as it went solid again.

The specter howled in pain. I expected it to vanish again. I was prepared for it. Shaw was just behind me, and together we could corner it.

Instead, the specter hesitated. It was as if there were some part of it, deep down, that recognized me. Or rather, recognized the bone badger I'd become. The part that was Gran, mourning her husband. The part that was Pops, seeing a reminder of who he used to be. Perhaps even Madam Dyer's part had been startled by a shift she hadn't seen me use before.

The pause didn't last long, but it was enough. Shaw scrambled forward and grabbed the specter's raised hackles. It had been half-way to ghost, but at Shaw's touch it solidified again. I bit into the specter's scruff and held on as hard as I could.

Caught, the specter snarled and snapped. It tried to pull away from me, to flip around and dislodge my grip, but badgers were stubborn and I held on.

Shaw kept one hand on the specter and used the other to brace herself as she threw her legs over its back, helping me pin it down.

Slowly, the specter stopped struggling. Like a wolf forced into submission, it slumped against the ground and pushed the back of its neck up into my teeth. I didn't dare let go, even though the wolf in my heart wanted to reward the submission with a lick to the ears.

It didn't matter because Shaw wasted no time. Once the specter was still enough, she got both hands on it. I just barely had the vantage to be able to see her dig her fingertips into the middle of its back. With obvious effort, Shaw pulled in both directions, like she was trying to tear the specter in two.

A huge blast of dark energy rose from the gap Shaw had made. Shaw and I were both thrown back. The herd spooked, taking off again. The Forest opened a path for them to funnel out of the clearing before they trampled us. I hit the ground in time to see three shadows rise out of the specter.

The body of the specter collapsed. Fur shed in clumps, skin melted away. Within seconds, all that was left was the skeleton of a bone wolf. My eyes lingered on the unnatural lumps in the skeleton, all that remained of the places where the exposed bone had once covered Gran's ribs and jaw.

The specter was dead, and my grandmother with it.

# Chapter 33

SHAW HELPED ME TO MY FEET AND I SWAYED AS THE PAIN of my wounds hit me all at once. Blood dripped down to the ground at our feet. I tried to wiggle the fingers of my left hand and winced as my entire arm protested. I'd been too focused on the fight to notice the wound, and now I was paying for it. I cradled my elbow and pulled my arm close to my chest like a makeshift sling.

"I need to help Chao with the rest of the spirits," Shaw said.

"Can I help?"

Shaw shook her head, then stopped halfway through the motion. "It'd be easier, with a familiar to anchor my magic to."

"You don't have to be bonded for that?"

"Normally, yes. But you're a wolf familiar. And . . ." Shaw hesitated for only a second, before forging on. "Our magic is highly compatible, even without a bond."

I wondered if I would have been able to fight the specter, were that not the case. Would Shaw's touch have worked like it had, without that unusual compatibility?

"Is it easier if I shift?" I asked. It wasn't the time to dwell on those thoughts. What was next would come after.

"The bone wolf, please," Shaw said.

I shifted, making sure to keep my weight off my front left leg. Shaw twisted her fingers in the fur of my scruff, then lifted her other hand in the direction of our classmates. Chao had already settled a good half of the spirits, but I could see the familiars struggling to corral the ones that remained.

I expected to feel something, anchoring Shaw's magic. But all I felt was the same warmth I always felt when Shaw touched me. I wanted to sink into it, to let myself rest, but we weren't done yet.

With Shaw helping, it only took another ten minutes before the last of the spirits' colors drained away. The ghosts that remained floated aimlessly, expressions confused as if they didn't remember what they'd been doing.

Almost as one, the familiars shifted back to humans and the witches broke the power-sharing ritual. All our classmates crowded around Shaw and me. Questions flew over my head, asking if we were okay, where the horses had come from, what had happened to the specter—

"Not now," Shaw said. "We need to complete the ritual first."

"How?" one of the bone familiars asked. "Madam Dyer is dead."

"It doesn't matter, that part is done," Shaw said. "The ghosts are already here. All we need to do now is speak with them. Convince them to move on."

"Ghosts have a hard time saying no to us," Chao added. "They can't lie in the presence of bone witches, and they'll be attracted to the magic that bone familiars carry. It will make them long for a peaceful rest, especially after all this chaos."

"Split up into pairs, one witch, one familiar," Shaw commanded. "I know you're tired, but this can't wait. Find a ghost and talk to them. Ask them why they lingered, let them tell you their story, and then encourage them to move on. If we all work together, we have a chance of finishing before midnight."

Our classmates looked as tired as I felt, but no one complained. They began to pair off. Charles looked from me to Shaw, then turned to find a different witch to work with.

I stayed as a wolf through several ghosts, listening as Shaw coaxed them to speak to her. Their tales were tragic, every one. The first had died at Multah. The second hadn't—his death had been a freak accident at home—but he begged the princess to make sure his children were okay. They'd been orphaned with his death and had no other family to care for them. When she agreed to reach out to his local jarl, he faded away without another word.

Not all the dead were so easy. There were angry shouts and whispers of betrayal. Hatred for the loved ones who, in the ghosts' minds, moved on too soon. It was harder to get those ones to speak their truths, to come to peace with the lives they had lived so they could move on.

After seven ghosts, we came across one I barely recognized. It was the girl Shantie had been trying to save at the market. She looked younger without the charred skin and melted flesh. Or maybe she was just projecting herself that way. Many ghosts did, appearing as the age they'd felt most comfortable while living.

I shifted to human for her story. I felt I owed it to her. I didn't know if I would have been able to save her. I couldn't go back now, couldn't try, like Shantie had, but at least I could listen. I could hold her story close and never forget it.

Another ghost drifted to us as the girl faded away. "It's not fair to hate her," he said, staring at the place where the girl had vanished.

"But I do. If she hadn't been there, we might have gotten out. Those men might not have noticed us."

I had a hard time drawing another breath. "Guanyu," I choked out. "I didn't realize you were here." I hadn't seen him among the ghosts earlier, but there were so many and I hadn't been looking for him.

Guanyu's ghost shook his head, sighing dramatically. "Life is cruel, isn't it, Rosy? You try to be a good person and you die for it."

Shaw wrapped an arm around my waist, and it was the only reason I didn't collapse where I stood. "I'm sorry. Guanyu, I'm so sorry I didn't save you." I knew I was panicking. My vision grew spotty. I couldn't breathe properly.

"Rosy, Rosy, that's enough." Guanyu drifted forward. Cold fingers, like misting rain, brushed over my arm. "You saved Shantie. That was all I wanted. She's the light of my life and they would have hunted her down. Familiars are one thing, but you know how those terrorists feel about witches."

I took several shaking breaths. Shaw's murmured assurances tickled my ears. "I'm here, calm down. It will be okay," she whispered.

"But—" I tried, once I was strong enough to speak again.

"Thank you," Guanyu interrupted. "You got her away. If you'd stayed to help me, we all would have died." He looked away for a second, frowning, then turned back to me. "Will you do me a favor?"

"Anything."

"Tell her to swim upstream. Exactly that, she'll know what I mean. Tell her that Guanyu says to swim upstream. That I love her, and I know it's hard, but if she knows what's good for her, she'll respect my dying wish. You tell her that for me, Rosy."

I swallowed hard. "I promise. Next time I see her, I'll give her your message."

Guanyu winked, grinning. He turned to Shaw. "And you. Will you grant me a favor too, Princess?"

"If it's within my power, it's yours," Shaw said immediately.

Guanyu's grin widened. "Then, avenge me."

Shaw's arm tightened painfully around my waist. "I promise you."

Guanyu's venomous grin softened into a real smile. "Thank you," he whispered as he faded away into nothing.

I twisted in Shaw's arms, pulling away enough that I could look her in the eyes. "Me too, Shaw. I'll help get justice for Guanyu. I have to help."

Shaw looked at me in silence. I waited as patiently as I could. Conversations happened all around us, our classmates and the other ghosts in their own little worlds.

"You feel guilty for what happened at Multah," Shaw said finally.

"I could have killed those men before they set Guanyu on fire. I could have shifted into the wolf and killed all three of them." I held up a hand before Shaw could speak. "No, it doesn't matter now. I'll live with that guilt for the rest of my life. What matters is what I do next. I spent six years being afraid of myself, of my wolf. Of the weapon I could become in the army's hands. But I don't care about that anymore. I won't be their weapon, but I will be yours."

"I never wanted a weapon," Shaw murmured. "I wanted a partner."

I let myself think about it. Imagine what that would mean,

being Shaw's partner. I could picture it all too easily. The companionship she offered, the subtle affection. The loyalty she gave to her entourage, combined with the protective righteousness that came out when those she cared about were threatened. I pictured more dances, like the ones we had at the equinox ball. The warmth of her touch was imprinted on my skin.

But I could picture more than that too. Jingyi's words, that day in the library. *You can lead us, all the familiars of this kingdom.* Charles's accusation, when I ran away from Witch Hall. *You don't even seem to realize what a blessing it is to be loved by someone like that. Someone with the weight of the kingdom on her shoulders.*

Shaw herself, the day she manipulated me into accepting her necklace with the promise of a fake courtship. *Do you truly believe you would be happy in some backwater village when you are powerful enough to be Familiar Queen?*

I had a responsibility to use my power, I understood that now. Charles had been right—it was cowardly of me to hide away when I was strong enough to make a real difference in this war. But he was wrong too. I did realize what it meant to be loved by Shaw. What it would mean, to let myself love her back.

What could a backwater ranch girl offer a kingdom?

"I can't be your queen, Shaw," I said. It hurt to watch those words land, to see the way Shaw's expression closed. That mask coming back inch by inch. I made myself continue. "I won't rule this kingdom with you. I can't give you that. But I will make sure you live to rule it. We don't need a bond to work together, to fight together. Tonight proved that. So"—I swallowed around the sudden lump in my throat—"let me be your weapon. Use me to win this war. And when we've won, because we *must* win, when the war is over, you'll gift me a ranch, like your grandmother did for mine.

I'll raise horses and you'll find a familiar who can rule beside you. And that will be our victory."

I couldn't bear to look at Shaw's face anymore, that smooth surface, seemingly unmoved by my ripples. I knew the truth behind it now. It hurt to know that I'd shattered that fragile trust. But I also knew she'd recover. No matter what Charles said, Shaw hadn't loved me. Not really. Not like Gran loved Pops. We'd only spent a few months together.

Shaw's heartbreak was made more by disappointment than real feelings, that was all.

I almost didn't pay attention to where my gaze had wandered, but tangled hair caught my eye. It wasn't red anymore, but the shape of those curls was unmistakable. Madam Dyer's ghost was talking with Chao and Jingyi, gesturing just like she always did when lecturing us in class.

If Madam Dyer's ghost was here, did that mean—? I spun in place, frantically looking over all the ghosts in the clearing.

"What is it?" Shaw asked. Her voice was a touch cold, but she asked anyway. She still trusted me in this, at least.

"My grandparents," I said. "Madam Dyer's ghost is over there. Did their ghosts get released when you killed the specter?"

"They must have. Look, there."

Shaw had seen them. Standing at the base of the massive pine that represented the heart of the Bone Forest. They were holding hands, watching Shaw and me calmly. Gran looked as young as Pops—perhaps thirty or so. Around the age when they'd had their children.

I rushed over to them and Shaw followed me.

"We were waiting for you to be ready for us," Pops said. "Princess." He inclined his head toward Shaw.

"General Holt," Shaw replied.

"Gran." I reached forward and Gran reached back. We couldn't clasp hands—her fingers weren't solid enough for that—but I could feel the cold press of her ghostly form.

"Don't grieve for me, girl," Gran said. "I'll miss you, if I'm able to miss anything when I fade, but I don't regret dying. I've been ready for six years now."

Pops put a hand on Gran's back, giving her a sad look. She leaned over to kiss him.

I pulled back, a touch embarrassed and equally happy I could see this. I would grieve for Gran, no matter what she said, but it helped to know she was content in her final moments.

Shaw cleared her throat. "If you're both ready, I'm sure Rosamund will be happy to take any final messages back to your family."

"Rosy knows what to tell our family, I'm not worried about that," Pops said. "It's you we have a message for. If you're ready for it. We'll wait as long as you need."

"You can't linger," Shaw said. "If your guilt consumes you—"

"Whatever guilt or regret I carry from my life is my burden to bear," Gran snapped.

Pops touched Gran's arm and she subsided. "We will do our duty. This is no easy thing to hear, and you've had a long night."

Shaw frowned, looking between them. "What is it? What message do you have for me?"

Pops lowered his voice. "Six years ago, I was murdered for the crime of knowledge. I'm sorry to tell you this, Princess, but the anti-magic protests in Vinland are no coincidence. This war was planned, deliberately, for years."

I started to understand, then, what Pops was dancing around.

He'd said the Witch King had ordered his death. If this was why—but I didn't know what the point would be. The Witch King had no reason to court war, especially not with Vinland. I suddenly needed to know. What possible reason could there have been to cause the kind of destruction war would ravage over his own land, his own people?

The Witch King was more than just the ruler of the Cursed Kingdom though. He was also Shaw's father. Her only family left.

"Shaw," I said, to make her look at me. "Maybe not tonight. Tomorrow, you can summon them again."

"No," Shaw replied. She turned back to Pops. "I know you can't lie to me, so you must believe what you're saying. If it's true, if someone sabotaged the relationship between the Cursed Kingdom and Vinland for their own gain, to spark this war, then I need to know."

"Shaw," I said, firmer. I was all too aware of the other witch-and-familiar pairs in the clearing. No one seemed to be paying us any attention right now, but that could change at any second. This kind of information was dangerous, Pops's murder proved that. We had to be careful.

"This is important, Rosamund. Don't you see? If we can prove the war was instigated maliciously, then we can take that evidence to Vinland. We can stop this war, before it truly begins. We can save so many lives."

I looked at Shaw, let my eyes catch on the way her cheeks glowed under the light of the half moon. Nobility looked so good on her. I felt a stirring of regret, that I couldn't be what she needed.

I didn't know the intricacies of inter-kingdom politics, but I trusted what Shaw said was right. There was a chance to stop the war, and it was our duty to see it through. To Guanyu and everyone who had died. To everyone who might yet die. To Yuyan and Einar and Aklemin, Oluk and Toketie and even Charles.

"Okay," I whispered. "I'm with you, Shaw. I told you that. I'll fight for you. Whether to win a war, or to stop one."

Shaw's mouth trembled, just for a second, before she got control of her expression again. I didn't have time to figure out what emotion she was hiding. She turned back to my grandparents, head high. Regal to the bone.

"Tell me everything," Shaw said.

Pops beckoned us to walk to the other side of the pine, so we wouldn't be easily overheard. I touched the tree and asked the Forest to help keep our conversation secret.

The bone pines began to rustle with a haunting song. A soft, grieving melody. Pine needles rubbed together, wind caressed bark, and, in the distance, I could hear a wild pack of bone wolves howling.

There was a deeper echo to the Forest's song. I listened to it, eyes closed, letting the woods speak to me, and through me.

This was Shaw's song. Verses of prophecy, told in a dozen different voices. The Witch Queen, on the eve of the final battle, crying out. The Familiar Queen's last words, as she held her baby close. The Witch King, staring into his wife's funeral pyre, telling his court of his newborn daughter's destiny.

Beneath it all, the melody was familiar. I'd heard it all my life, even before I first shifted into the wolf. Every time I ran through the Forest, raised my arm to hug the pines and sing with the wind. It was the Bone Forest's song for me, a lullaby to rock me to sleep, a hum to keep me company while I played.

*Give us strength*, I pleaded. *We'll need it, for what is to come.*

The pine needles shook, the branches creaked, the wind whistled.

The bone wolves howled a promise to the moon. First softly, and then with growing fervor, the Bone Forest sang its love for me and for Shaw. I let that song settle into my heart, as if the voice of the Forest could nestle with the animal voices I kept there.

When Pops began to tell his story, I was ready.

## TO BE CONTINUED

# Acknowledgments

There are so many people I need to acknowledge for the journey this book went on. So here are my profuse thanks to everyone who stuck with me:

To my agent, Mary C. Moore, who saw Rosy and Shaw's potential before anyone else.

To my editor, Holly West, who helped turn this book into the best version of itself.

To Rich Deas, for my beautiful cover, and to his team for designing the book of my dreams.

To the whole group at MacKids and Feiwel and Friends, for all your work behind the scenes. Especially to my copyeditor, Melanie, for putting up with all my silly made-up words and excessive number of characters.

To Cassie Schau, who sat through so many brainstorming sessions with me, and to Alan Bittenson, who always chimed in with the best suggestions.

To Arianne Lewin and Camille Kellogg, who both pushed me and gave me hope in turn.

To my CPs and readers, for all your collective, insightful comments across all seven major revisions this book went through:

Sam Chapman, Dyani Sabin, Sarah Mack, Alex Crepso, Marissa Macy, Kamilah Cole, Clare Edge, Tovah, Sage, and Dillon.

To Audris (and Tessera Editorial) for going over my manuscript with a fine-tooth comb pointing out microaggressions regarding race, ethnicity, immigration, gender, sexuality, and disability. Any remaining issues, however unintentional, are my fault to bear.

To my MFA advisor, David Anthony Durham, and all my mentors: Elizabeth Searle, James Patrick Kelly, Theodora Goss, and Nancy Holder, for your writing advice and your belief in my future writing career.

To UMass for the two classes I got to take in undergrad that directly inspired Witch Hall: Intro to Shamanism and Wild Edible Plants. Seriously, who knew I'd be looking over those class notes almost a decade later?

To my family, friends, teams, and coworkers, for all your love, support, and enthusiasm. With specific thanks to my grandmothers for fostering my own spirituality and my love of magic.

Finally, to the GeoFORCE Texas program, for those weeks, spread over years, I got to experience the flora, fauna, and geology of Oregon. And for the days spent on top of Mt. Hood, imagining a kingdom stretched out below me.

Thank you for reading this Feiwel & Friends book.
The friends who made

possible are:

Jean Feiwel, Publisher
Liz Szabla, VP, Associate Publisher
Rich Deas, Senior Creative Director
Holly West, Senior Editor
Anna Roberto, Senior Editor
Kat Brzozowski, Senior Editor
Dawn Ryan, Executive Managing Editor
Kim Waymer, Senior Production Manager
Emily Settle, Editor
Rachel Diebel, Editor
Foyinsi Adegbonmire, Associate Editor
Brittany Groves, Assistant Editor
Ilana Worrell, Senior Production Editor

Follow us on Facebook or visit us online at mackids.com.
Our books are friends for life.